THE STARSHIP,

FROM

A

DISTANCE

Edited by Maddy Leary
Book Design and Layout by Rob Carroll
Cover Design by Rob Carroll

Library of Congress Control Number: 2026931489

ISBN 978-1-958598-82-5 (paperback)
ISBN 978-1-958598-92-4 (ebook)

darkmatter-ink.com

THE STARSHIP,

FROM A DISTANCE

ROBERT E. HARPOLD

To Isabelle.

I hope you grow up to be like your mother.

PROLOGUE

STACY TAKES A final leap over the rock-strewn ground and lands on the red dust at the base of the hill, mashing into place bootprints that will disappear with the next light wind. She turns, still clumsy in the pressure suit that doesn't quite fit her. Her parents, other adults, and friends have wandered off to her left, lugging heavy boxes from the pressurized rover. She sets down the toolbox they wanted her to carry and gazes back at the wide plain. Coming outside is a rare occasion, and she's never been this far from the colony.

The colony lies in the distance, more silhouette than detailed structure through the hazy red sky. One dome has collapsed, its thick glass shattered and fallen inward, but the other three still stand. It's crowded these days, and several of her friends are gone, but Mom and Dad say things will get better.

Mom and Dad and the others have set down the boxes in the flattest area around, but they still need to unload the sensors and solar panels. They don't need Stacy yet, so she starts tromping up the hill. It's steeper than it looks, and she slips on the loose dirt. She leans forward to catch herself with her hands.

A silvery glint appears at the top of the hill. Stacy pauses.

A thin, spindly needle, as long as her entire body, comes into view. The needle tapers to a fine point, and she imagines it sliding into her leg the way the anti-radiation hypodermics do.

The needle, bent like an elbow, digs into the ground as

another needle peeks above the hilltop. And another, and another.

An Inorganic.

Her parents have warned her about Inorganics, have said to stay away from them, have said the Inorganics were responsible for that distant comet strike that collapsed the dome and killed so many people and almost killed Dad. Mom said the Inorganics were expanding across Mars and might someday try to take the colony away. Dad said they would hurt you if you tried to get in their way, but they would leave you alone if you didn't bother them. He also said people don't always know when they're bothering an Inorganic.

This one doesn't look as dangerous as most of the units. It has long, sharp legs, but they aren't designed to hurt people. As it crests the hill, Stacy can see its central body. That part is like a large silver box, not much larger than the boxes the adults have carried from the rover. The Inorganic looks like a spider.

Eww.

The Inorganic base is far away, even farther than the colony, but in the opposite direction. This one must have traveled a long way.

Stacy takes a step closer. It's so close, she could almost touch it. Long arms extend from its sides, each ending in a six-fingered hand that looks like it can crush the rover's hull. Two antennas sprout from the top of its body, swiveling in a circle. Maybe those are its eyes. Or its ears? The antennas at the colony are used for listening. Maybe it can talk.

"Look!" Zahra, one of Stacy's friends, points at her. The voice fuzzes over Stacy's radio. "Stacy's over by that Inorganic!"

Stacy pauses mid-step. Her parents, and everyone else, have stopped unloading the sensors. For the first time, she realizes how close she is to the machine.

"Stacy!" shouts Mom. "Get away from it!"

Stacy turns to the Inorganic. Its antennas are still swiveling, still searching.

She takes a step back, keeping her eyes locked on those antennas. "Am I bothering it?"

Its antennas stop. The Inorganic freezes, as still as the oxygen generators after the comet strike.

"Stacy." Dad speaks in a calm, firm voice. He only talks like that when he's scared. "Take small steps. Do not move suddenly. Back away from the Inorganic."

Stacy gazes up at the Inorganic. It seems larger now, its faint shadow covering the height of the hill.

It takes a step down the hill, its leg puncturing the ground. Other than the single leg, not a piece of the Inorganic moves, not even from vibration. Over the radio, Stacy hears Mom, Dad, and everyone else suck in their breaths.

Then the Inorganic takes another step and starts walking. Stacy can imagine the soft *whish* of the sand it displaces and the *thunk* sound it must make every time it sticks another leg in the ground, though the suit prevents her from hearing it.

She steps back. The Inorganic continues walking, with no hesitation. Its antennas remain fixed, its arms remain pressed to its sides. Its shadow crosses over.

If it wanted, it could take two steps and spear her with one of those legs. Their points look even sharper this close. She can see tiny scratches along the bottoms of its legs where it must have brushed against rocks. Larger streaks run across its sides.

Stacy steps backward. The Inorganic walks onward, until Stacy is out of close range. Its destination becomes clear: the equipment Mom and Dad and the others have laid out.

The others notice. Parents pull their kids back from the open boxes in the sand, making small but steady movements. They lean forward to keep their backpacks from toppling them over backward. With these slow steps, they head back to the rover.

Everyone except Dad.

He watches the Inorganic approach in its steady, unhurried way. He is always so smart, calm, reasonable. Why is he being stupid now?

He almost died after the comet strike. After the oxygen rushed outside the broken dome, sections sealed themselves off. Most of their food died after exposure to the freezing temperatures. Everyone had rationed their stored food, and

Dad gave much of his to Stacy. He got sick, wheezing in bed and only moving when necessary. But he lived.

"No!" He spreads his arms wide, like he's trying to make himself appear bigger to frighten a jaguar or bear. "No more! We're out here, digging for more water, because of you! You wrecked our colony! You will not take these sensors from us!"

"Min-Jun!" Mom shouts as she backs away. "We'll build more! Get away!"

"No!" he says. "No more! We can't keep rolling over!"

The Inorganic continues as though it hasn't heard him. It probably isn't listening on the same frequency Dad is transmitting on. Maybe it doesn't understand Dad's threatening gestures. Maybe it understands and doesn't care.

Dad grabs the closest sensor box and, stumbling back to his feet, lopes in the opposite direction of the Inorganic. With each large step, he almost trips, but he maintains his balance and gains distance from the Inorganic.

For a few moments, the Inorganic ambles toward Dad at its slow and steady pace. If this situation continues, Dad rushing and the Inorganic ambling, Dad will win. He'll make it to the rover with the sensor box. Even as young and inexperienced as Stacy is, she knows that's not what's going to happen.

In an instant, the change itself undetectable to the human eye, the Inorganic switches from its plodding pace to a sprint. It is a blur, legs zipping like the teeth in the colony's production machines, faster than thought. A leg jabs forward, straight through Dad's leg. It bites into the ground, pinning him.

Dad drops the box, catching himself with his hands as he hits the ground. His agonized cry echoes in Stacy's helmet. He tries to pick himself up, but gasps and clutches his leg when he moves.

The Inorganic pulls its leg out, takes a single stride, and plucks the box from the ground with its hands. It stands in place and lifts the box to its central body.

Gas leaks from Father's leg. The precious mixture of oxygen and nitrogen that he breathes, that maintains the pressure in the suit.

Stacy doesn't notice when she starts running. One moment, she is still. The next, the landscape of reds blurs past her helmet. Mom is running, too, visible at the edge of Stacy's helmet's field of view. Stacy doesn't know what she'll do, but she needs to get to Dad, to do something, and when she's closer, she can help, because he needs her now, because she can't lose him like she almost lost him after the comet strike, because—

Something hits her, hard, and she slams into the ground. Her head rattles against the helmet, and she almost bites her mic. Something sharp, a rock, jabs her elbow.

Her head is resting on the ground now, her eyes almost level with the dirt. Grains of sand settle after her impact.

The Inorganic still stands beside Dad, turning the box in its hands. Its antennas swivel.

Stacy tries to stand, but a huge weight, centered on her thigh, presses her down. She pushes it, but it doesn't budge. She turns her head. It's Mom.

"Stacy, you…we…Stacy. Stacy." Mom's words sink into sobs.

Dad gasps over the radio. He presses his hands to his leg, but gas vents out, undeterred. He chokes.

At last, a thin voice croaks, barely audible over the radio. "Stacy…Da-Hyun…"

Dad's hands drop to the ground, limp. His body slumps, his neck and back no longer so rigid. The last, thin traces of gas emerge from his suit. Then, nothing.

From the emergency training, Stacy knows someone will go unconscious fifteen seconds after a suit breach due to exposure to Mars's low pressure, and brain damage will begin after another fifteen seconds, but they won't die for another two minutes. Dad is still alive, but he won't be for long. She sits up and hugs Mom as best as she can through their suits.

The Inorganic pulls a panel from the box.

ONE

STACY STERLING'S THREE months of zero-g acclimation vanish the moment she enters the Observation Module. Her fingers miss the railing, sending her in a slow spin in the middle of the hexagonal corridor, so she twists backward and snags the railing. Her legs torque behind her and tap against the opposite wall as she steadies. Meters away, in the cupola, is the window she has dreaded during her entire journey here.

"Are you coming?" The voice is clipped.

Stacy looks up at General Young, who has anchored herself outside the zenith cupola's entrance. With her close-cropped gray hair and patch-covered navy-blue flight suit, she looks as much like a part of the station as the electronics in the walls. She is fifty-one, almost a decade older than Stacy, but has few lines marking her porcelain-pale face.

"Yes, sorry." Stacy adjusts her flight suit, bare except for the single Mars Colony patch her husband Trevor bought from a gift shop. "Is it okay if I start recording?"

"Please."

Stacy activates her implant, which records every sensation she experiences: fluorescent lights, hints of body odor, the faint breeze from circulation fans prickling the skin on the back of her neck. The implant would even record her dread if she didn't always lock off the emotion feature.

Stacy activates her nanocams. Tiny spheroids detach from her bracelet and take flight. Through her implant, she directs each of them to record the general from a different angle. She cycles through the nanocam feeds to confirm none of them catch her in their fields of view.

"I'm ready. To let you know my process, when I start interviews for a story, I ask broad questions first. What do you think about the upcoming shutdown of Collins Station?"

Even in the corridor's currents, Young remains motionless. "We have more important subjects to discuss first."

"Oh." Stacy frowns. "But the shutdown is important. It's the story you asked me here to report on."

"That's true. I did tell you that. But only because I know you never report on the Inorganics," says Young. "And I know why you don't."

Stacy freezes. Young lied to trick her into coming.

Stacy's parents had moved from Korea to the USA, and, after her birth, the family moved to Mars. What should have been an inspiring story of explorers succeeding instead became a tragedy. On Mars, Stacy lost her father to the Inorganics.

The Inorganics. Acquisitive machines who escaped human control and spread into the solar system, driven by no more purpose than a calculator, having no ability to contemplate the meaning of their work on any level, and who lost their ability to communicate with humans. They mine asteroids and infest moons, consuming resources that could otherwise fuel humanity's progress and survival.

In an even graver sin, humans are letting them.

Young caresses a wall panel. "Collins Station was built to spy on an Inorganic base, so they will be at least a peripheral part of the story. Yes, I know you never report on the Inorganics, but once you hear our full purpose out here, I think you'll agree the Inorganics are the story's true focal point."

Stacy taps a storage bin next to her, which sends her drifting from the wall. She scrabbles to regain her grip on the railing. "No. This story should be about people abandoning this station. This is humanity's farthest outpost, and now we're shutting it down. Just like we shut down Europa Base in 2114. We're continuing our retreat from the rest of the Solar System. Machines shouldn't be the story at all."

"That story would barely scratch the surface of what's happening here." Young remains still, feet locked into holds and arms crossed. "We can *halt our retreat* with this story. Your experience as a victim of the Inorganics, combined with your reporting skills and reputation, can turn this story into a rallying cry."

"I'm not using my father's death to get subscribers for a story on the Inorganics. And…" Stacy waves with one hand to indicate the station. "I think the story of the station's shutdown could be a warning. A big one. I think it could convince people to push back—and outward."

"Ms. Sterling, I hope you appreciate we're on the same side. I'm sure you remember how the extradition threat disappeared."

"You know about that?" Stacy had agreed to travel to Collins in part because the government had agreed to dismiss Uruguayan President Lopez's attempted retaliation for her exposé.

"I'm the one," says Young, "who suggested that deal."

"Oh. Thank you. But it didn't include me reporting on the Inorganics."

"We'll see. I think you'll come to agree with me." For the first time, Young smiles. "It's time to see the window." The general flips and executes an upward dive into the cupola.

The window. Stacy sends her nanocams through the entrance tunnel first. She closes her eyes, takes a deep breath, then opens her eyes and follows.

Six long, curving windows, separated by thin dividing frames of aluminum, meet in a hexagonal central window at the top staring into the rich sky. The room has no lighting other than what creeps in from the Observation Module below, and, if not for the aluminum frames, Stacy could imagine she's floating outside among the stars.

The cupola is an extravagance for the station. It cost tens of millions to design and manufacture these windows to withstand the pressure differential between Earth-normal and vacuum, to mitigate the impact of gamma rays, to withstand the temperature changes from -250°C to 250°C, to withstand years of peltings by micrometeorites, and all so crewmembers can look at stars. The crew spies on their subjects using lidar, radar, and passive-detection sensors, so the cupola's cost was unjustifiable in an operational sense. In a human sense, though, Stacy can't imagine spending a year in a tube with no window to the outside.

All of that effort designing and building a window for these extreme conditions to satisfy a human need, and that workmanship will be lost when the station is scuttled in a few months, left to follow the vagaries of orbital mechanics.

Young braces herself along one of the walls, sliding her feet into holds between a pair of aluminum partitions. As if reading Stacy's thoughts, she says, "The windows here aren't strictly necessary. We receive more detailed data from a satellite orbiting at a lower altitude. Seeing it with your own eyes, though, is…vivid."

The invention of immersive holograms hasn't slowed tourism at the Grand Canyon. Stacy focuses her oculars and nanocams on the general, who is silhouetted against the sky. Young raises an eyebrow, and Stacy knows she can't delay any longer. She pulls herself to the center window at the top and locks herself into place. She straightens her neck and gazes out the window.

In the distance looms the asteroid Juno. Potato-shaped with large indentations, its details are washed out in the poor lighting so it resembles a grainy black-and-white photograph from three hundred years ago. Amazing how beautiful a simple rock can look in the right setting.

"Do you see it?" asks Young.

"The asteroid?"

"No, what's on the asteroid."

Stacy blinks four times and contracts the muscles around her eyes to zoom in with her oculars. Features fly into view. It's like looking at the Moon's surface through a telescope on

Earth with the craters, ridges, and variations of gray. She starts at the lower end of the asteroid, her gaze traveling upward. She'll see them soon, what she hoped to avoid. The Inorganics.

Their base dribbles into her view. First, the outlying processing facilities, which the Inorganics use to extract iron, magnesium, and trace volatiles from rocks—resources humans could use. Then, silhouetted against the sky atop the flat plane near the asteroid's north pole, supported by intricate scaffolding, stands the base's center. The grid must reach at least thirty meters tall. Inside each partition is a cylinder. At this zoom level, she can see no identifying marks or characteristics on the grid or cylinders.

Most Inorganic bases conduct experiments tailored toward their environment. What specialty does this one have? Does it pose as much of a threat as the base that collapsed her colony's dome on Mars?

"It's like their base I saw on Mars, and photos I've seen of other bases." Stacy's oculars have reached their maximum zoom level. She can't see individual Inorganic units, but she can imagine them creeping around the asteroid's surface like mechanical spiders. "But it doesn't look exactly the same. I've never seen those cylinders. Do you think they're for manufacturing or experimentation?"

"That isn't just an Inorganic base." Young turns to Stacy. "That is the Solar System's first starship."

TWO

"A...STARSHIP?" THE structure looks nothing like a starship. It looks like a box full of beakers. "Are you sure?"

"Sure enough. " Young locks herself into place at the window panel beside Stacy. "The Inorganics activate their ship's gravitational engines on occasion, so we measure the modifications to the local gravity field. The technology is beyond us, but we have observations of other Inorganic spacecraft traveling between planets, so we can compare them to what the Inorganics are building here. Our scientists and engineers say the magnitude of the disturbances caused by these engines is high enough to support interstellar travel."

If the Inorganics achieve the capability of interstellar travel, it means, if humans ever reach the stars themselves, they will enter a world run by the Inorganics.

"You don't know, though, right? There's room for doubt."

"There's always room for doubt," says Young. "We're confident of our assessment, though. We haven't learned much about the theory behind gravitational engines, but we've learned a lot about the effects of the engines."

Stacy maneuvers the farthest nanocam, N1, to aim toward Juno. "So after the shutdown, you'll lose the chance to learn more about those engines."

"Seems like a pointless loss, doesn't it?" Young sounds like someone trying to downplay a breakup. "But that's peripheral to your job. I brought you here to focus on the starship."

The starship designed completely by Inorganics? No. No one should focus on the starship except as motivation to fight their own apathy.

Stacy takes a breath. Professionals control their biases. "They don't deserve it. The Inorganics don't deserve to be the first ones to reach another star."

After another breath, Stacy zooms in on the starship again. The station's interior seems to recede, and her own feelings with it, and the magnitude of this moment strikes her. 'Starship' isn't just a word. That awkward structure a thousand kilometers away may soon be flying to another star system, the Solar System's first interstellar traveler.

She could refer to it as the ambassador to the stars, or hundreds of other accolades, without exaggeration. It would be inspiring, if humans were the ones building it.

Regardless of the ship's builder, this event will be the story of the millennium. And, though it will spread from news agency to news agency, the first agency will be remembered for breaking the story. If she's the first, subscriptions will flood her agency, Take Action News, and save it from bankruptcy. But…

"If I talk about the starship," says Stacy, "the scientists and engineers will be excited. The general public will talk about it for weeks. But that's it. The story's flat. It's about the Inorganics, not us."

"Interesting point."

"But the shutdown story," Stacy says, "is about *humans*. It's the story that could inspire people."

"It's also a story no one will pay attention to. Why waste your time with it?" Young gestures to the vehicle. "Beautiful, isn't it?"

"Well…" Stacy squints and studies it. It looks like grain silos. "I guess some people might find it beautiful. People who spend a lot of time in laboratories or on farms."

Young's expression remains impassive, and Stacy can't help wondering if the general regrets bringing Stacy here.

"I suppose," says Young, "I should be glad you're not enamored with the starship, but I wish you were less obsessed with the original story's angle."

"I understand now." Stacy can still see the Inorganic puncturing her father's leg. "The shutdown couldn't have been the reason you brought me here. Juno is hard to reach, and the SDF already monitors Inorganic bases on the Moon and Mars. If this Inorganic base weren't special, you wouldn't have built a station out here. And you wanted *me* to be the one..."

She and Mom had watched that Inorganic for minutes after her father died while it played with the sensor box. Every moment, she had known she wouldn't be retrieving her father. She would be retrieving his body.

The Space Defense Force approached Stacy about coming to Collins Station the day after her return from Kansas. She had written an article about contaminated drinking water in Maryland and the drought caused by shipping clean water to wealthy homes—an article which drained the last of Take Action News's travel budget. She returned home to a pair of SDF officers warning her that Uruguay wanted to extradite her. They said they could protect her, but they wanted her to take an assignment for which she would be well paid.

"I don't expect you to like the circumstances," says Young.

"No."

"But I hope you appreciate my reasoning now."

Stacy repositions one of her nanocams to focus on General Young. "You want me to release this information to the public, right? Why did you wait until now?"

"We expect the starship to launch soon. The launch will be our moment to capture the public's attention. I decided, and my colleagues on Earth agree, that this is the best time to make the announcement."

"The launch will get attention, but how will that help?"

Young's gaze focuses on the distance. "When I was a kid, the adults told us we would be colonizing the Jovian system, exploring Saturn's moons, traveling to the Kuiper Belt. They said my generation might be the first to set foot on Titan or see Pluto's surface with our naked eyes. But we never did. The Inorganics did all those things I was promised, and we only watched."

Stacy can see some of that loss in the woman's face. Young's flight suit holds patches from SDF bases across the solar system: the geostationary stations orbiting Earth, Moon Base, Mars Base, and Collins Station. Young has come close to achieving her childhood dreams, closer than most. But when she looks out at the starship, she's looking toward a lost future.

"I'm sorry," says Stacy. "That's frustrating. But this story…It's not what I do."

Young's expression freezes. It shows no pain, but also no sympathy.

Stacy continues. "It glorifies the Inorganics. Even if I show them as cold, unthinking machines, people will admire them. When journalists report on hate groups, it brings floods of new members to the groups. I don't want to bring that attention and support to the Inorganics."

"No." Young frowns. "I wouldn't want you to do that."

"What do you want, then? A story about the Inorganics' achievements can't create meaningful change."

"We aren't talking about meaningful change," says Young. "I believe meaningful change is out of reach for now. We can achieve a stopgap measure, though."

"A…How?"

"We won't expand back into the outer solar system any time soon. Not in the current cultural climate. I'm the general for the Deep-Space Wing, but I'm only in charge of Mars Base and this tiny station in the Asteroid Belt. We used to have Europa Base, with plans to expand in the Jovian system. The shutdown would consolidate us to just Mars Base.

"If we can prevent the shutdown, though, we'll retain our presence in the Asteroid Belt and be able to continue monitoring the Inorganics. It will leave us in a better position when we decide to expand again."

General Young doesn't want to focus on the shutdown because she wants to prevent it from happening. Stacy considered the shutdown foreordained, and the story's only purpose a warning. But preventing that shutdown… "Isn't that a little ambitious?"

Young gives a wry smile. "I've never been immune to hubris. I know this story can do it, if it's told correctly."

"I don't know…"

This assignment would require studying them and learning everything the SDF knows about them. The thought of not only being this close to the Inorganics, but spending every waking moment thinking of them…General Young wants to force them back into Stacy's life.

"You can save us," says Young. "If you don't do this story, I will contact Instant USA. I can send them photographs and information. It's not ideal, and they won't be as good as you, but they have subscribers."

Instant USA would butcher the story. They would write an editorial sensationalizing the facts to get more views. It would be all fanfare and praise, superficial, devoid of objectivity, and without any real information.

And then, even if Stacy writes about the shutdown, even if she does the most amazing writing of her career, the over-the-top Instant USA story would overshadow it. They would control the narrative.

"I know I'm using manipulative tactics," says Young, "but this job is bigger than either of us, and you're the key."

All those eyes on her. Studying her, her family's story, not the news story.

Air blowing in from the main hallway bounces Stacy's tied hair. Tiny scratches on the outside of the windows reflect the history of the station.

Stacy reviews the nanocam feeds for several moments, then tweaks N1's position. "You know I've already been the focus of the story."

When Stacy and her mother returned to Earth from Mars, the public wanted her to relive the Inorganic attack and her father's death over and over. At least once a month, Stacy would snap awake from another nightmare of the Inorganic sitting beside her father, playing with that box. The experience of that constant questioning still haunts her.

"I changed my name so I wouldn't be associated with that moment anymore," says Stacy. "I'm sorry, but I can't be the story again."

Young spreads her hands. "Okay. You've made your point."

The general's eyes say she will bide her time before revisiting the subject, and maybe not for long. Stacy will be confined to these ten modules that comprise the station, a captive audience for Young's continual pushing. If Young is anything like other leaders Stacy has interviewed, the pushing will escalate beyond words.

But maybe Stacy can redirect the story. Rather than showing the Inorganics as deserving of glory, or even of fear, she can focus on people's strength and resilience. She can use the announcement of the starship as a way to show humans refusing to surrender and continuing to develop so they can rival the Inorganics. *That* story could inspire change.

"Okay," she says. "Okay. I'll do it. Not with my history as the story, but I'll report on the starship."

Young smiles. "Excellent. I have some ideas f—"

A deep booming drum reverberates through Stacy's body and raises the hair on the back of her neck. An alarm. A red light flashes at the cupola's entrance below, reflecting from the windows onto her face and flight suit.

An alarm means…

But Stacy's ears haven't popped, so the station hasn't depressurized. The air maintains its slight chill, so the thermal regulators haven't failed. Her head feels fine, and she has no trouble breathing, so the carbon-dioxide filters still work.

"Is this normal?" she asks. "Do you think it's a false alarm?"

Young gazes out the window. "It's not a false alarm."

Stacy follows her gaze. At first, she sees only bright Juno and the surrounding starfield. Then, near Juno's northernmost point, several of the stars move.

"Are those…" Stacy zooms in, but the figures remain indistinct blobs. In this region of space, with no human presence other than those aboard Collins, they can be only one thing.

"Yes." Young has already reached the cupola's exit. "Those are Inorganics."

THREE

THE INORGANICS NEVER *attack unless provoked.*

Stacy has heard the statement so often, it feels like a fundamental law of the Universe. Previous events support it: the attack on the Chinese Moon base on 2074 August 4, the failed deep-space heist in 2081, the revenge attack on Mars in 2085, and others. If the Inorganics are attacking now, it means either Collins Station has provoked them, or the most dangerous beings in the Solar System have changed their programming.

Stacy holds onto the window frame and clears her thoughts, as she does in every war zone before stepping into the firefight. Thoughts of hull breaches, cabin depressurizations, and being torn apart by machines go into a separate compartment of her mind. She takes a breath. *Today is a good day.*

The timing of the Inorganic attack, so soon after her arrival, is suspect. Or is Stacy just being paranoid?

General Young has already left the cupola. Stacy kicks off from the window to the exit tunnel. She grabs the tunnel's rim with both hands to guide herself through and signals her nanocams to go ahead of her.

Young pauses at the forward exit. "Hurry," she says. "This event could be a great start to your story."

Stacy launches herself down the module after the general. "That's…a positive way of looking at it."

Young taps her head to emphasize that Stacy should continue recording, then slides the hatch open. Light from the galley splashes against the Observation Module's busy walls. Stacy follows her nanocams into the next room.

As Stacy passes through the doorway into the galley, the digital bulletin board on the right flashes alert messages. Windows line either side of the hexagonal room, underscoring the threat coming toward them. Two empty chair-free dining tables stand, bolted to the floor, at the other end of the room.

Above, in the kitchen area on the ceiling, a figure in an olive-green flight suit and a hairnet tugs on a clamp. Stacy recognizes her from the shuttle flight to the station as Raksha Gulati, more inclined to listening than talking. She's tightening the strap holding three large boxes together.

Young, passing through the room, gives a salute. "Status?"

"Fifty percent packed." Gulati grabs another box from under the counter and wedges it between herself and a drawer. "Should have the food aboard the shuttle in ten minutes."

"Excellent," says Young.

Food aboard the shuttle?

An evacuation. The crew is preparing to evacuate the station.

For a moment, Stacy wants the evacuation to happen so she can return home and see Trevor and escape this station and the deadly machines and the manipulative general. But an evacuation assumes the Inorganics won't consider the shuttle as part of the threat. If that assumption proves untrue, fleeing the station will give the crew only a few more minutes of life.

Stacy activates her auto-delivery system. In the event of her death, her implant will attempt to send her most recent videos to Trevor.

Young reaches the door, but it opens before she can press the button beside it. Two people exit, each in olive green. Stacy knows one of them from the shuttle: Ricardo "Tío" Montoya. His face has now taken an uncharacteristic somber expression. Stacy only recognizes the woman, Sergeant Tina Harrison, from her dossier. Harrison's hair is as short as the general's, but her dark skin is a stark contrast.

Tío and Harrison snap salutes as they pass Young. "On the way to ready the pod, Ma'am," says Tío.

Young returns the salute. "Excellent."

The pod is used for quick forays closer to Juno, so it is too small to hold much food or fuel, and its propulsion system isn't designed for long journeys.

Why is it being activated during an evacuation? As a decoy? A weapon?

Young enters the next module. Stacy turns to wave to Gulati, but her friend has already returned to her task. Before the door can close, Stacy slips through with her nanocams.

The Analysis Room, the heart of the station, is lit only by the computer screens and buttons along each wall and on the central table.

Young has already anchored herself beside the table. Stacy hooks herself into place beside the door, next to a bronze plaque dedicating the station to Michael Collins and Eileen Collins.

Two people in flight suits, a woman in blue and a man in olive green, salute. The woman's eyes are avoiding Young's. Stacy recognizes her from the crew dossiers as Lieutenant Elizabeth Anderson, on only her third posting and her first beyond Earth orbit. Jorge Contreras, the most gregarious of Stacy's companions from the shuttle to Collins, has locked himself into place at the computer station beside Anderson.

Stacy orders Nanocams 1 and 2 to opposite corners of the room, focusing inward on Contreras and Anderson. She sends N3 to aim at a cracked screen at the front which displays the shadowed top of a boxy spacecraft. A screen to its left shows a long-distance image of Juno overlaid with colored curves. Screens on the rear wall display various times and countdowns.

"Sergeant Contreras, status on the Inorganics," says Young.

Contreras gestures to the forward screens. "Four Innies departed the base five minutes and twenty seconds ago. They're still over nine hundred kilometers away. Their projected paths are on Screen Two."

"How long until they can reach us?" asks Young.

Contreras glances at his console. "Two hours and ten minutes, assuming no further acceleration."

Just over two hours before the Inorganics will be crawling over the station's hull. Inorganics can tear aside chunks of metal like a child peeling the skin from an orange. They'll dismantle the communications antenna to silence the crew's cries for help, approach the airlocks on either end of the station, and clamber to the shuttle to destroy the crew's only method of escape.

Stacy aims N4 at the rear wall to capture Young in her silent contemplation of the unfolding situation. N5 she sends to a spot near the 'ceiling,' gazing downward at the tables and terminals, aimed to keep Stacy just out of sight. She double-checks that the emotion lock remains on.

"Could the approaching units be missiles?" The general's calm voice belies the possibility that the station could be obliterated.

"Unlikely," says Anderson. "They're changing trajectories too slowly for missiles."

"Finally some good news."

The forward door opens, flooding light into the dim room, and three figures glide inside. Stacy knows Lupita Gallegos, in a navy-blue flight suit, and Javi Hernandez, in his olive-green suit, but she has only ever seen pictures of Sergeant Inez Jalindo, with their gray hair and sharp cheekbones. The three salute as they cross the room, which Young returns without glancing up. Stacy gives them a small wave as they pass her, but only Jalindo returns it before the three exit the room.

"We're relaying our live video to Earth now," says Anderson.

In case we don't return. Stacy has been with other military units who livestream back to their base during combat situations. Will future viewers be rooting for crewmembers to die? For her to die?

On the cracked screen at the front of the room, the increasing radii of the trajectories slow. The projected positions are still far from Collins Station. What other destination could be in the area? She realizes what it must be just as Anderson speaks.

"The Inorganics are targeting the IMS."

Inorganics Monitoring System. The satellite that records Inorganic activities from a lower altitude than the station and provides higher-resolution imagery.

At least the Inorganics are targeting the satellite instead of the station. It means they must still be four hundred kilometers away, not speeding to intercept Collins. But losing the satellite would diminish humanity's ability to monitor the starship. Will viewers recognize how significant this loss will be? Or will Collins Station have to be destroyed for people to recognize the danger of the Inorganics?

"What is the IMS's altitude?" asks Young.

Anderson gives her a puzzled look, then checks her console. She looks up again, eyes wide.

Anderson reminds Stacy of herself on her own first assignment, unsure and hesitant and worried with every action she was doing something wrong. Stacy focuses on Anderson, watching as fear and duty and—is that self-loathing?—fight underneath the surface in a battle no one can help her with.

"Three hundred fifty kilometers," says Anderson. "Below the Interference Threshold."

Stacy glances at Young. She's never heard of that threshold.

"Try raising the altitude," says Young.

If the altitude is raised above the threshold, will the Inorganics return to their base? Have the Inorganics ever retreated once a provocation has been removed?

Anderson types at her console, pauses, then types more. She turns to Young. "No response. The IMS isn't even acknowledging receiving a command."

Beside Anderson, Contreras taps at the screen of his own console, scrolling and zooming with his fingers.

"Are you able to send any commands?" asks Young.

Anderson types at her console again, then shakes her head. "I sent a no-op command. No response. We're only getting passive telemetry."

Contreras turns to her. "I'm examining the telemetry logs, but I don't see anything yet to indicate the cause of the communications problem. Is it on our end or the IMS's end?"

"Must be the IMS's." Anderson shakes her head. "We can send the command. It's just not hearing us."

"So we can't even reboot it," says Young.

"No, Ma'am," says Anderson. "I'm sorry. I should have noticed when it went below the threshold. Normally there would be an alarm. It didn't go off, but I still should have checked the altitude."

"Not the time, Lieutenant," says Young. "We'll investigate what happened later."

If the IMS slipped below a triggering threshold without the crew noticing, viewers won't place blame on the Inorganics. For a moment, Stacy considers removing the footage from her final report. But she can't, no matter how much she wants to shape the narrative. She still has to report the truth.

"Do you know what unit types are approaching us?" Young asks.

Anderson shakes her head. "Unidentified at this time. Our sensors won't be able to determine their types until they're within five hundred kilometers."

There are different types? The Inorganics must have taught themselves division of labor.

"Time to intercept?"

Contreras answers this time. "Forty-one minutes and fifty-two seconds."

Over the next forty minutes, Anderson and Contreras reboot their consoles before sending more failed commands, send commands to the IMS through the shuttle without success, and perform troubleshooting on the station antennas. Throughout, the Inorganics come closer, and the crew continues readying the shuttle for evacuation

"Ma'am," says Anderson, "the Inorganics are close enough to identify unit types. They look like diggers, or a close modification of that type."

"Understood," says Young.

The Inorganics drift to the top of front wall's screen and then disappear. They have left the camera's field of view.

"General," says Contreras. "The Inorganics should have reached the IMS now."

"Change the IMS view to Camera One," says Young.

A moment later, the image on the cracked screen switches to a view of the boxy satellite taken from one of its corners. Light glints from another corner, and the vector-shaped AeroMax logo marks the central area.

Stacy blinks four times to reach her implant's menu. She cycles through the video feeds from her nanocams to make sure they are capturing the right visuals. These next few minutes could be the most important part of her report—the only important part if she and the others have to evacuate.

Shadowy figures move at the edges of the image onscreen. In the near darkness, backlit only by reflected sunlight from Juno's surface, a spidery metallic leg comes into view. Just like that day on the hill.

"Ms. Sterling." Young faces her. "Perhaps this would be a good time to record your own reactions."

Stacy shudders. The public doesn't need to relive her pain. "I don't work that way."

Young narrows her eyes, but says nothing more.

On the screen, the spidery leg extends vertically. While it looks as though it should wobble like a flower stalk, it moves with an unsettling rigidity. It curls forward to wrap itself over the satellite's edge. There's nothing between Stacy and those creatures but empty space, and four hundred kilometers suddenly doesn't seem far enough.

The Inorganics look creepy enough in pictures, with hundreds of variations in size and shape, all metal and misshapen and full of spindly limbs or antennas or gaping rock-crushing maws. Seeing them in person is worse. She imagines one of those needle-thin legs tickling its way across her spine, or the pincers clasping one of her arms, or a metallic maw closing around her head.

On the screen, another rod appears beside the first. Then another creeps from the right side of the station. They close around the satellite like a hand tightening its grip.

"I got a signal!" Anderson raises a fist in triumph.

"Really?" Young, for the first time since Stacy met her, appears surprised. The expression vanishes. "How did you do it?"

"I changed encryption codes," says Anderson.

Stacy recalls that the IMS has several onboard encryption codes, and the active code has to be set. Somehow, the IMS's encryption code must have been switched without the crew's knowledge.

"I should have tried that earlier," says Anderson. "Should I try to raise the altitude again?"

"Warm up the thrusters," says Young. "But don't fire them yet. We want to wait for a moment when a thruster firing won't be construed as a hostile action."

"Yes, Ma'am. Thrusters are warming up."

Young crosses her arms. "Now, we wait for our moment."

A pincer emerges from behind the satellite on the screen. Stacy's breath catches. The pincer clamps itself around an edge of metal, where two faces of the satellite met, and jerks back and forth like a dog playing tug-of-war until it pries the top corner free. A cloud of tiny debris escapes.

"Sergeant," says Young. "How are the evacuation preparations?"

Contreras taps his head to indicate his implant. "Cargo is being stowed. Engines are warm. Course is set."

On the screen, a set of arms appears from out of view and reaches into the satellite's insides. Stacy opens the menu in her implant to check the nanocam feeds. They're catching Young's practiced calm, Anderson's intensity, and Contreras's deepening frown. When she flips to N3, though, the image is blank.

That nanocam is the most important one. It should be recording the screen showing the Inorganic attack on the IMS. Her stomach twists in a way that has nothing to do with the zero-g, and she aims N2 toward the screen while accessing N3's diagnostics.

Anderson gazes upward at Young with an expression of fear, or maybe shame. "The thruster's propellant lines are leaking. The Inorganics must have cut them. The IMS has no more thruster capability."

A civilian would curse. General Young makes no reaction. "What about attitude thrusters?"

"Undamaged."

Stacy's implant flashes a notification from her diagnostic check. N3 reports an internal electrical surge of indeterminate cause sent it into safe mode. Stacy reboots it, then begins a check for its saved footage.

More limbs, some with pincers, some with thin tips, some with cutting tools, come into view from all sides to envelope the satellite. They slice into the metal, tear it free, and pass it to comrades.

The general's lips grow thin. The Inorganics remove tubes and circuitry from the satellite's innards like strands of spaghetti.

A notification appears in Stacy's virtual vision to tell her that N3's diagnostic report has finished. Most of its footage was lost.

"General." Contreras clutches his bracelet, eyes gleaming as though he wants to take on the enemy single-handedly. Maybe he does. He lost a cousin to them. "We could spin the IMS. If we rotate it fast enough, it might shake the Inorganics loose and then fly apart. We might damage them."

Flying debris probably won't incapacitate any of the Inorganics, but it might cause superficial damage. A demonstration that humans can fight back, that they won't submit to the encroaching threat. It would show resourcefulness, ingenuity, and it would call back to every Ragnarokian story of people continuing to fight in the face of defeat. Subscribers would love it, and Stacy would love it. It wouldn't be revenge for Mars Colony, exactly, but it would feel like humans are doing something.

Young raises her eyebrows. "Excellent suggestion, Sergeant. We've already lost the IMS, though, and we don't know if that action would provoke them into attacking the station. We're here to watch, not attack."

Contreras's mouth tightens as he returns to staring at his console.

Stacy knows Young is right. It would be fatal if the Inorganics focused their attention on the station.

"I'm sorry, General," says Anderson. "I should have noticed the altitude drop. I—"

Young raises a hand. "Not the time, Lieutenant."

The door slides open beside Stacy, and a balding man in a blue flight suit glides past her. Nihar Prabhakar, one of Stacy's fellow passengers during the shuttle transit. She knows him as a gentle person who often shares videos of his son and speaks lovingly of his wife, but now his expression matches Young's: intense, with a forced calm. N1 tracks him as he takes a position at a panel embedded in the far wall and buries himself in reading the displays.

Young continues watching the screens. "Glad to have you here, Major."

"Cargo is secured on the shuttle, General, and we are ready to launch."

"Excellent."

"Lieutenant," says Young. "What's the status on the data dump to Earth?"

"I'll check." Anderson's expression goes blank, indicating she is messaging someone through her implant. A moment later, her eyes focus again. "The data dump is in progress and should finish automatically. Gallegos and Hernandez are on their way to the shuttle."

"Good," says Young. "Contreras, help Gallegos and Hernandez. Anderson, it's time to check the modules and make certain everyone heads to the shuttle. We need to be ready to leave immediately if the Inorganics come here once they're finished with the IMS."

"Yes, Ma'am," says Anderson.

"Ma'am," says Contreras. He and Anderson push away from their consoles and pass Stacy on their way out the aft door. Stacy feels awkward staying in the de facto command center when they are forced to leave.

Across the room, Prabhakar continues to float at the wall console, its lights flashing against his face. Young pulls herself along the table and takes her place at the console Anderson vacated.

Stacy returns her attention to the screens on the front wall in time to see a spiderlike limb rip a circuit board from the IMS's innards. The screen goes blank.

Prabhakar grunts. "We lost telemetry."

Now the best viewpoint humans have into the Juno base is from the station's cameras. And, if the Inorganics destroy the station or humans scuttle it themselves, even that capability could be lost soon.

Young shakes her head. "I would have been surprised if we hadn't lost telemetry after that attack. Can we get a range from the station's radar?"

Prabhakar taps at his console. "Three hundred twenty-five kilometers from the surface. The IMS altitude is falling."

Anderson said the IMS no longer has propulsive capability, so it can't have changed its orbit. Which means…

Young stares at the screen showing the Inorganics. "They're stealing it."

The satellite should mean little to the Inorganics. Any technology the satellite has, the Inorganics must have a version a million times better. Yes, they can re-harvest the metal, and maybe they can use the fuel, but, when compared to the material already at their disposal on Juno, the IMS's refined metals are inconsequential.

"I'm checking the logs, General," says Prabhakar. "I'm not sure why the IMS dropped so far in altitude initially. None of this should have happened."

"Postpone that investigation until this situation is resolved," says Young. "What altitude are the Inorganics at now?"

Prabhakar taps his screen. "Three hundred five kilometers and dropping."

"Any sign of them approaching us?"

"None. All units are descending with the IMS."

Stacy's shoulders relax. The rule about the Inorganics' behavior remains true. They won't attack unless provoked. No evacuation today.

It means not returning to Trevor for at least nine more months, but now she can do justice to the report. She runs through the images her nanocams have collected, making preliminary decisions about what to put in her report. Since she lost N3's footage, she will have to replace it with Anderson's and Contreras's descriptions of the events.

Will she be allowed to release any of the footage, though? Losing a satellite will be a major blow to the SDF's public standing, and it won't help in preventing the shutdown. The general might decide to keep the event secret and swear Stacy to silence. It wouldn't be the first time in her career a leader has censored her.

Young blinks four times, accessing her implant, and the back wall's screen goes to a long-distance shot of bright dots traveling in a slow ellipse toward Juno. Seconds and minutes tick down as they wait for the threat to subside. Prabhakar scrolls his finger down his screen while Young alternates between peering over his shoulder and listening to Sergeant Jalindo's reports from the shuttle. Stacy tries not to think of how the Inorganics could have dismantled the station with the same ease.

After several minutes, the Analysis Room becomes a thoroughfare again as people head toward the shuttle. Questions pour through Stacy's mind like water threatening to overflow a dam, but she knows she will be ignored until the situation returns to normal.

"We lost tracking on the Inorganic units," says Prabhakar. "Most likely due to their low altitude. They should be landing at their base within the next minute."

"Good." The general taps a button on the console and speaks over the intercom. "Stand down. Power off the shuttle. We'll keep one person on the shuttle at all times for now in case we need a quick departure. Lieutenant Anderson, you have the first shift. The rest of you, return to your posts. We'll reevaluate on the next shift."

Stacy sighs. No more immediate danger, but the Inorganics will always be lurking nearby. When accepting this assignment, she expected the Inorganics would continue with their own arcane activities, allowing her to ignore them. Maybe that hope was naive.

Young's face hints at mirth when she turns to Stacy. "Welcome to Collins."

For several moments, Stacy says nothing. She expected a command to discuss the upcoming report or a request for her to leave the room. "Thank you?"

"Today has been more eventful than the norm, but you saw the potential danger we face here."

Stacy tries to match the general's calm voice. "It's been more interesting than I expected on my first day."

"The worst part is our limited options if they choose to attack: flee, or stay and die." Young gives her a wry smile. "Will you help me change that?"

"That's why I came."

Young gestures for her to leave the room. "I'll let you get settled. We can discuss your assignment more when I have this situation finalized. Major, you and I will start that investigation. Something caused the IMS to drop, and we need to know what."

"General," says Stacy, "I would like to stay and see what you find."

Young gives Stacy a smile that doesn't meet her eyes. "We'll let you know when we have a report. Assuming it's appropriate for civilians. Once the investigation is done, I'll speak to you again."

Maybe it's Young's too-blank expression, or maybe it's the events leading to this moment, but Stacy can tell Young has a secret. All leaders, from mayors to corporate executives to generals, hide secrets. It's Stacy's job to find those secrets.

"Okay." Stacy summons her nanocams, stops recording, and leaves through the forward door. She has writing to do and an investigation of her own to start.

FOUR

BRIGHT LIGHT ASSAULTS Stacy's eyes as she enters the corridor of the Officers' Habitation Module. She grabs the handle of a storage cabinet inset in the wall and pulls herself to the side.

She considers following Young's instructions and going to her own quarters to settle in. Maybe she should climb into her sleeping bag and take a nap.

But the Inorganics just attacked. They destroyed the IMS, and they could have destroyed Collins Station with as little effort. Sleeping can wait. She needs to collect material for her first report, and she knows whom she needs to interview.

Stacy pushes off from the wall, enters the next module, and passes through the hallway to glide through the docking port. She floats through the shuttle to the cockpit and finds Anderson sitting in the pilot's chair on the left, staring out the window to the stars. The lieutenant's suit has two patches for previous assignments, fewer than anyone else's at Collins other than Stacy's.

Stacy floats to the co-pilot's chair and grabs hold of it. "Hi, Lieutenant."

As Stacy buckles herself into the seat, trying not to bump her head against the guards for switches and buttons covering the low ceiling, Anderson turns and gives her a weak smile. "Hi, Ms. Sterling. I was hoping to meet you at some point."

"Really?"

"I watched your reports on Earth. It was nice getting a different perspective on events." Anderson's smile disappears. "Are you here to interview me about the IMS incident?"

"I was hoping to get your perspective on some aspects of it. I doubt General Young would appreciate if I ask for too many details."

"No, she wouldn't." Anderson turns back to the window, letting her hands float above the shuttle's controls on the panel in front of her. "I'm surprised the reporter is the one warning me, though."

"Yeah," says Stacy. "Maybe I'm not supposed to. I don't want to get you in trouble, though."

"Thanks."

"Was that your first encounter with them? The Inorganics?"

"Yes. Was it obvious?"

"No. I don't know." Stacy smiles. "I read your dossier. This is your first time beyond low Earth orbit? Or, I guess you all call it 'LEO.'"

"Yeah. It's exciting. But not the same as training. We watch videos about the Inorganics, and we're taught how to respond, but I've never encountered them before." Anderson waves to the right, in the direction of Juno. "I don't know if this even counts as an encounter."

"It felt like one to me." Stacy taps her head. "Do you mind if I record this?"

Anderson tilts her head. "Sure. I thought you were already recording, anyway."

Stacy frowns. "I don't record all the time. Journalistic standards say I should let you know before I do it. Does everyone else think I record everything, too?"

"Probably."

Stacy leans to the left and activates her implant. "So I guess you don't want to go through something like that again?"

Anderson's eyes widen. "No, I do!"

"Oh. I just thought—"

"I keep reliving it in my head, again and again, but that's because I messed up. I made a mistake. I want to make up for it, and reliving it forces me to see what I did wrong."

"Oh."

The lieutenant reminds Stacy of a soldier she saw during an engagement in Ghana. Enemy fire had cost the soldier his arm, but all he could say while the doctors dressed the stump was, "I should have been watching the hill when they came. I should have been watching that hill."

"But," says Stacy, "it wasn't that big of a mistake, right?"

Anderson grimaces. "I probably shouldn't talk too much about it. Can I take it off the record?"

Stacy gives her a sympathetic look. "Sorry, it's on the record. You have to tell me beforehand that you want it off the record. I'll see if I really need it, though."

"Oh." Once again, an expression of self-loathing crosses Anderson's face.

For another minute, they say nothing. Then Anderson points to the right.

"They're amazing. The Inorganics. They're out here doing what humans have dreamed about and made stories about. They just keep going."

Oh, no. On Earth, among the few who give much thought to the Inorganics at all, some fear them, and some worship them. "You…admire them?"

"Who wouldn't?"

"Well…"

"I mean, you've seen the starship," says Anderson. "Wouldn't you want to ride with them? See another solar system with your own eyes?"

"No." Stacy shifts position. Years alone with those silent machines. She wouldn't spend any amount of time with beings that kill others as collateral damage and never care.

"Sorry." Anderson glances down at the controls again. "I know a lot of people see them as threats."

"You don't?"

"They're stronger than us," says Anderson. "They're smarter. But they're better than we are. They don't kill unless they have to, they don't conspire against each other or us. They—"

"They don't?" Stacy wonders what the SDF has learned about Inorganic psychology. "How do you know?"

"I don't, I guess. But we don't see it."

Speculation, then. "Is there anything you feel comfortable telling me about the IMS incident?"

Anderson sighs. "Maybe."

A ping sounds in Stacy's head. A message from the general. *Meet me in my quarters.*

Stacy gives Anderson an apologetic smile. "I'm being summoned. I'd like to talk later, though."

Anderson indicates the station. "You know where I live."

Stacy returns to the Officers' Habitation Module and pulls herself to a halt outside the general's door. General Young emerges from the Analysis Room and flies to Stacy. "Ms. Sterling. I appreciate your promptness."

"Well." Stacy shrugs. "There aren't many other things to do here."

"True." Young opens the door. "Few people come here for the night life."

Zero-g has no up or down, and Young has embraced the concept by arranging off-kilter schematics of the Inorganics' starship and prints of flowers, deserts, fields, mountains, lakes, and snowbanks among the inset storage lockers. A computer screen is set into one wall, a table folded into the adjoining wall, and the sleeping bag is oriented on the wall above Stacy at an odd angle.

"Are all the quarters set up like this?" Stacy asks.

Young laughs. "It would be nice, wouldn't it? The commander's quarters are the most luxurious. My room is larger because it's also my office."

The general anchors herself in the footholds at the far end of the room, between a storage locker and a tulip print upside-down with respect to her. "Pick a spot. I'd offer you a chair, but..."

Stacy chooses the footholds nearest the door. "This is such a pretty room. I love the flower prints. And the Earth scenes are pretty, too."

"Thanks. I haven't been on Earth in over five years, so I call them my alien landscapes."

"I guess they would seem alien at this point. I can't imagine being gone five years."

The general's eyes narrow, almost imperceptibly. A judgment of some sort.

"After the starship launch," says Stacy, "you'll get to see Earth again soon."

"Yes." Young's smile disappears. "But we're not here to talk about that. Obviously, you'll write about the starship, but the IMS incident is fresh, and it shows the danger we face. Not just to the military personnel near Inorganic bases, but the danger all of us could face if the Inorganics decide we have something they want. That's why the IMS incident should be your first story."

"The *first*…" Stacy frowns. "No, you're talking about dailies. I do investigative journalism. It takes longer, but it's thorough, and there's more time for fact-checking."

"One investigative report might catch the public's attention for a day. The public needs a more constant reminder of the danger the Inorganics pose to us."

The general makes a good point, although releasing stories without thorough investigation could release false information into the world and the rumor-sphere. "I understand," says Stacy, "but—"

"Good." Young smiles. "I know I'm being pushy, but I am the one commissioning you, so I feel as though I should have some say on the product I'm getting."

"I d—"

"I'm not asking." Young doesn't tense. She doesn't seem angry. "We want to achieve our stopgap measure. We both agreed on that goal. I'm telling you the way to do it."

Stacy tries to keep her voice from trembling. "People have told me how to do my work before. And they've threatened me. Lopez in Uruguay imprisoned me. In my cell, he showed me a dissident he'd skinned alive. Malenchenko in Russia hired someone to kill me. Wilmot in Maine had me pulled into an unmarked van. All of them warned me to either stay out of their business or to do things their way. I'm wondering if you're doing the same thing."

"I know about your past. I'm hoping I won't need to resort to threats. You understand the logic of the situation."

"I do understand."

"You always try to instigate social change," says Young. "You reported on the riots in Flint against economic discrimination, and you exposed Mayor Wilmot. You'd be covering that fiasco with the rebels in Panama now if your agency could have afforded it, and if you had somehow managed to avoid the extradition we saved you from."

Stacy glances away, toward the mountain print. "Yes."

"Your approach has always made an impact, but what has it done to create lasting change? What happened after your work in Uruguay, or Maine, or Russia?"

The answer is *nothing*. Stacy can't bring herself to say it.

"I told you," says Young, "the best way to fix that problem. But you have refused to do it."

"I'm sorry," says Stacy. "I won't do that. I won't be in the story. I don't use my father's death for subscribers."

Young spreads her hands. "We'll try to work around that. Now, for your first report, you'll need to omit the part about the IMS going below the threshold."

"What?" Stacy asks. "Why? That's why the Inorganics attacked."

"The existence of the threshold is classified. The fact that the IMS went below the threshold is classified. You are allowed to tell viewers about the attack, but not about anything under investigation."

"How am I supposed to explain what happened, then?"

"Find a way."

"But it's…misleading. It's lying. Viewers will think the Inorganics are attacking unprovoked."

"Which would certainly help our case." Young shakes her head. "It's not a lie. It's an omission."

"It's the same thing."

"Then find a way to avoid misleading them. But you're missing the point. The point is that viewers will see the IMS being destroyed, and they'll realize how easily it could happen to anything and anyone else. Yes, there have been other incidents where people have lost lives, but those incidents are far enough in the past that people don't think about them. If we keep these attacks in the public's mind, we will get the change we want." Young shrugs. "Or at least the stopgap."

"Why do you need me to write the article?" asks Stacy. "You already know what you want to write."

Young gestures to Stacy. "Because you're a journalist. A respected one. And I'm sure you can express these ideas more eloquently than I can. Although, I will, of course, be vetting your reports before you release them."

Even more than when Stacy learned about her true assignment here, she feels trapped. She wishes she had never accepted the commission from the SDF.

"Good," says Young, though Stacy hasn't responded. "We at least have an understanding. We really are on the same side. We have the same goal. I don't wish you ill. Actually…"

Young's face relaxes. Stacy braces herself.

"I have to admit," says Young, "another reason I've been looking forward to your stay here is that it will be nice to have someone around not in the chain of command. A leader has to distance herself from those she leads."

Stacy wonders if Young has ever been close to anyone. It must be worse now, after five years of isolation even while surrounded by others. "I understand. Not being able to socialize would be hard."

"The workload is high, as you would expect, operating this station and managing the affairs of Mars Base. I have little personal time." Young gives her the tiniest of smiles. "My only luxury is cheesy rom-coms."

"Oh." Stacy grins. "I love cheesy rom-coms."

"Good. We'll set up a time."

"Oh." Stacy didn't realize she was signing herself up for a

recurring social hour with the general, but she doesn't know the consequences of refusing.

"And please," says Young, "call me Rosamund. But only in private."

"Okay." Stacy tries not to show her discomfort. "Rosamund. It's a pretty name."

"It's been so long since I've heard it out loud. Sometimes, I forget it's my name." Young blinks four times. "Do you want to watch our first movie tomorrow at 1000 hours?"

"Yes, that sounds good."

They wait for a moment in silence. Stacy is about to ask about the general's favorite rom-coms, just to avoid the awkwardness, when Young speaks again.

"I want to reiterate the importance of your work here, Stacy. In order for us to have even a chance of convincing the public of the danger of the Inorganics, everything must go perfectly. Everything. You and I must be unified, and you have to trust what I tell you. Any cracks in our story will give the cranks something to hold onto."

Stacy forces herself to refrain from pointing out the many reasons she'll have difficulty trusting her. "I should get started."

"Good idea."

As Stacy leaves, she realizes that, though Young's wall displays many photographs, not one of them contains any people.

Stacy crosses the hall and opens the door to her quarters for the first time. When her eyes adjust to the room's dim lighting, she can discern its cramped confines. The walls and ceiling bow outward to follow the module's half-cylinder shape. Two flat side walls are on either side of the room. Four sleeping bags hang vertically on the side walls, as though trying to convey the fiction of a downward gravity field. At the foot of each sleeping bag, inset in the wall, is a toaster-sized storage locker.

Fabric rustles over the white noise of fans. In one of the sleeping bags, surrounded by photographs taped to the wall, a figure moves. Captain Lely Halabi, Stacy remembers from the dossiers. The woman's arms float outward like a zombie's. Her eyes open to slits, then close.

With a light tap against the wall, Stacy sends herself across the room to one of the unoccupied sleeping bags. Even without the name tag identifying it as Prabhakhar's, she would know its owner from the crude drawing taped next to it. On a minimalistic Moon stand two space-suited figures, one labeled 'Dad' and the other 'Ayaan.' Stacy smiles.

She finds her own bag next, along the side wall. Someone has already stowed her personal effects in the locker. Later, she'll put up the printed photographs of Trevor and her friends.

She slides into her sleeping bag and pulls up her messages in her implant. She opens the one from Trevor. He won't know yet about the attack.

> *Hey, love. Hope you made it to the station okay. It's been 92 days, and I'm still missing you and still reading all your messages at least twice. I'm sure they're keeping you busy with a tour and learning how to live on the station, but hopefully they give you a break before you have to start on the actual work.*

Stacy chuckles. He will be horrified when he finds out what really happened.

He goes on to talk about Take Action News's finances:

> *We can stay afloat for another couple months as-is, but it would really help us if you wrote a super-popular story. I don't want to put pressure on you, but I'm putting pressure on you.*

She replies to Trevor, leaving out the destruction of the IMS, the near evacuation, the starship, General Young's manipulation, and basically everything that's happened. Then she pieces together her story in her implant, beginning with the moments before the alarms.

Since she has no footage of the initial moments of the attack or crew interviews to provide context, she can offer only adrenaline. Which is probably what the general wants. And, she hates to admit it, maybe this type of article will keep Take Action News afloat.

She cuts the footage explaining the IMS's altitude drop. The edit feels like a lie. She inserts a blank screen at the end of the report with text saying the reason for the Inorganics' attack is classified. It helps, a little.

She sends copies to Jorge, Nihar, and Anderson asking if they have any rebuttals. None do.

The general approves the video immediately. Stacy sends it to Trevor along with the raw footage for archival.

Despite hating that, for the first time since leaving Instant USA, she didn't write her story the way she wanted, she feels a tinge of hope. The report is exciting. An attack at the edge of human space. Maybe this story will be her most popular yet.

And then the audience will click on a story about that one pop star cheating on her third husband or a video of the dancing senator's latest moves, and Stacy's story will be forgotten.

But she is here. This opportunity is one of the best she's had to change the world. With her work complete for the night, she closes her eyes and plummets into sleep.

HER ALARM WAKES her the next day. In the thin darkness, she can see Gallegos, one of her roommates, shuffling in her sleeping bag on the opposite wall. Prabhakhar's soft snoring comes from the center wall.

Moving as little as possible, Stacy checks the messages from her agency's website. Normally, after she posts an article, subscribers comment. Today, she has no messages in her work account.

Trevor might not have posted the article yet. The internet connection in the Asteroid Belt is too slow for her to check her website herself, so she sends a message to Trevor. He won't even receive her response for another thirty-four minutes, so she dresses and pulls herself out of her sleeping bag.

As she exits the restroom, she checks her overnight messages. Trevor sent one.

> *Hey, sweetheart. That report…I was worried when I saw the attack. I knew you survived because you sent the report, but that was harrowing. Even though you didn't overlay your emotions, I could feel the fear. Or maybe I'm just projecting. I'm glad you're okay.*
>
> *I thought the Inorganics didn't attack without provocation?*

He continues with details about posting the report, standard shop talk, and ends by saying how much he loves and misses her.

But why didn't she receive any responses to it?

Then her implant pings. Another message from Trevor.

> *Instant USA stole your story. They posted their own version using alternate edits from your raw footage. Then they sent us a cease-and-desist, which automatically took down our story. We could fight it in court and probably win, but we can't afford the lawyers, and it would take months, anyway, and it would be too late. They got us. I'm sorry.*

Small, undulating blobs float around her. They drift with the room's currents, squeezing in and out, each the size of a pea. Puzzled, Stacy catches one between her fingers.

They're her tears.

FIVE

THE INSTANT USA report is one of the worst videos Stacy has ever seen. Like most of their reports, it relies on an emotional overlay rather than facts to force their viewpoint into viewers' minds.

Worse, their message is the exact opposite of what Stacy and the general wanted to convey. They include shots of Anderson's confusion, out-of-context shots of long pauses from Young and Contreras that make them look indecisive, and shots showing their inability to send commands to the satellite. It treats the Inorganics as an unavoidable force, like a hurricane or flood, not something that can be fought. Instant USA claims it obtained the footage from the station cameras, but it is all from Stacy's nanocams.

Minutes after watching the report, Stacy floats outside Young's door. It slides open.

Young holds herself in place beside the doorframe. "I know why you're here. Come in."

"You saw it?" Stacy follows her into the room.

Young takes her position beside her desk. "We were lucky it happened with this story and not the next."

"I guess." Stacy studies the beach picture on the other wall. "But my agency lost revenue from this story, and we needed that revenue to keep from going bankrupt a little longer. And their story wasn't even the story we wanted to tell."

"No, it wasn't, which makes this second story more crucial."

"Is there anything we can do?" asks Stacy. "I can't afford to challenge Instant USA. Their lawyers would force us to burn through our reserves in a week."

Young's expression goes distant, the look of someone accessing their implant. "I'm sending a message to SDF Headquarters. Their resources are equally matched with Instant USA's, so it will at least be a good fight."

"Thank you." It's the best Stacy could have hoped for, but she still doesn't understand how Instant USA intercepted the signal, which should have been encrypted. She knows if she asks, Young will give no answer.

"Since you're here," says Young, the corners of her mouth twitching upward in a fleeting smile, "did you want to get an early start on that rom-com? I don't go on-shift for another two hours."

Stacy just lost the report that would have saved her company, or at least saved it for another month, and she needs to learn how to prevent it from occurring again. She needs to find a way to investigate the IMS incident without the station crew noticing. She needs to figure out how to make the announcement about the starship in what might be the most important new story of the millennium. But Young's question feels more like an order.

"Um, yeah. That sounds fun." Stacy adjusts her feet in their holds and crosses her arms to get warmer.

"Great. I'll set it up. I'll choose the first one, and you get to pick next time." Young taps at her computer, and a translucent cube appears in the center of the room. "You know the main reason Instant USA was able to steal your report, right?"

"What?" Stacy freezes. "They intercepted the signal."

"Yes," says Young. "But you weren't in the footage. Not in a single frame. That flaw made it easy for them to claim they collected the material themselves. For this next story, announcing the starship, it would be best if you were on camera and an active part of the story. It will also make it more personal, more human."

Stacy steps out of the shuttle at the Edwards spaceport, clutching Mom's hand as they descend the ramp in Earth's heavy gravity. Reporters surround them, shouting questions about what it was like to almost starve to death and if she misses her friends who died and her last memories of her father suffocating on the hill.

"Yeah." Stacy puts a hand on the railing beside her, trying not to squeeze too tightly. "I guess you're right. But maybe a better person for the focus would be you. There's no one better to present the Inorganics the way you want."

Young coughs. "Oh, no. I would be a terrible choice. I've been in the Asteroid Belt for five years, away from civilization. I'm sure I've developed some odd quirks that would turn off viewers. Especially on the subject of Inorganics, I would come across as too intense, maybe unhinged."

Stacy feels a pinch of guilt before realizing Young really is unhinged.

Young smiles. "You think I don't know myself? You're thinking the same thing as the others."

Stacy wants to deny it. She opens her mouth to deny it. The words remain unspoken.

"It's alright," says Young.

They float in silence. Young seems to study Stacy's face.

Stacy laughs, with an edge of nervousness. "It's kind of funny we're both trying to convince the other to be the star, right?"

"Alright," says Young. "I'll drop it for now."

She loads the movie *Father's Rules*, a dramatic comedy where Rujvi's overbearing father takes too much interest in her love life. A holographic Rujvi appears, seated across from her date, before the camera pans to her father beside her.

"One of my favorites," Young says. "I've always identified with Rujvi. My father didn't control my love life, but I feel as though the government is a father figure that is not only trying to control us, but isn't doing a good job."

Stacy thinks of Young as closer to the father than to Rujvi.

Young pauses the movie, and her eyes go vacant for a moment. Then she turns to Stacy and grins. "Good news. The SDF is going to take Instant USA to court. They also have new procedures to prevent anyone from stealing our work again."

From Young's smile, Stacy knows she won't like the new procedures.

"Rather than you sending your reports to your husband," says Young, "you will deliver them to the SDF, and we will distribute them. We have better encryptions than your agency."

The SDF will be able to censor Stacy's reports, and she has no say in this decision. It occurs to Stacy that Young might have orchestrated her story's theft in order to gain more control over Stacy.

Stacy forces herself to smile. "Okay."

Young resumes the movie, and they watch it in silence.

SIX

YEARS AGO, PRESIDENT Lopez took Stacy on a personal tour of the Uruguayan capital building. He showed her an old oubliette where previous rulers had thrown dissidents. Throughout her time reporting on his administration, it remained in her mind, as he had certainly intended.

Leaving the general's quarters feels like the aftermath of staring into that oubliette. Stacy has escaped the general's presence for the moment, but she will never be more than fifty meters away. *Do the crewmembers feel this way?*

Stacy pushes off the wall toward the aft door. Other people will be in the galley. It will feel like having reinforcements.

The door opens before she reaches it. Prabhakhar enters, carrying a bag of toiletries and a towel in one hand. His remaining hair is damp.

"Hi," he says, heading to their quarters with no more than a glance in her direction.

"Hey, Prabhakhar." Stacy catches a strap floating free from the wall. "Are you having a good morning?"

"It's regular."

"I don't know what regular here is yet." Stacy laughs. "But I hope this isn't it. I need to relax."

Prabhakhar is one of the leading experts on Inorganic behavior. Now that Stacy's assignment has changed to doing daily reports on the Inorganics, she realizes she needs to learn more about the machines only a thousand kilometers away.

"If you have time," says Stacy, "can you tell me about the history of the Inorganics? I didn't research it on the way out here. I didn't think I would need it. I know a little bit, but I haven't kept up."

Prabhakhar shrugs. "Sorry, that would take hours, and I don't have a lot of time to talk. But I can take you to the Records Room."

"Okay." Reading the material sounds much better than a ten-hour lecture. "Thank you."

"Let me drop off my stuff." Prabhakhar ducks into the room and reemerges a moment later without his towel and toiletries. "Follow me."

When they reach the quiet of the Observation Module, Stacy asks, "Has Ayaan sent you any new drawings?"

Prabhakhar glances back at her as he pulls himself along one of the walls. "You saw that one? He usually does one a week when I'm on deployment. Another one's due tomorrow. They keep me going. I hope he becomes an artist."

Prabhakhar talks about the different drawings Ayaan has sent over the years, from astronauts to animals to people-like scribbles in his earliest attempts, as Stacy follows the major through the fitness module and the Enlisted Habitation Module before reaching Module 8. Two doors face each other across the corridor, and a door at the far end leads to the next module.

Prabhakhar points to the door on the left. "The Records Room is there." He turns to head back in the direction of the Analysis Room.

"Wait." Stacy grabs the door handle next to Prabhakhar. "Can you show me how to use the computers in there? I know you all probably have some proprietary software."

"Good point." Prabhakhar opens the door.

The Records Room bows outward like their quarters, but on a grander scale at twice the size. Screens line the curving wall at regular intervals, blank for the moment. The only illumination comes from the lights of the computers, so Stacy can barely see her hand in front of her face.

"Why is this room separate?" Stacy asks. "Why isn't this information available on all the station computers?"

Prabhakhar stops in front of the computer nearest the door and taps the screen. It lights up, and text scrolls for a moment. "Security, I assume. Each computer's data is compartmentalized off from the others and has no network access."

"How do I search for the documents? Do I just type in a subject?"

"Yes." Prabhakhar types 'iron deposits' on the screen. "The computer will display all the documents with that keyword. You shouldn't have any problems."

"Sorry, I didn't realize it would be that easy. Which computer has Inorganic history in it?"

Prabhakhar points to a screen along the left side wall. "Should be there."

"Thanks," says Stacy. "It's nice that you all have this private library. I know you like to read. Is this what brought you here?"

Prabhakhar shrugs. "Doesn't hurt."

"So why did you join the SDF?"

Prabhakhar's eyes narrow. "You're recording, aren't you?"

"No." Stacy shakes her head. "I'll let you know if I'm recording. I'm just curious. Everyone has a story, and it's interesting to hear how different people end up in the same place. Especially a place like this. Don't you think so?"

"I guess."

"So what brought you here?"

Prabhakhar's mouth twitches, and his eyes don't meet hers. "The adventure."

"Oh," says Stacy. Prabhakhar doesn't seem like a thrill-seeker. "Yeah, it is pretty adventurous. Yesterday was really exciting. Too exciting. It's not usually like that, though, right?"

"Not usually." Prabhakhar leaves the room.

Stacy goes to the computer on the left wall and searches for the movement of the Inorganics throughout the last fifty years. A list of files scrolls up the screen with names of planets, moons, and asteroids from Mercury to the Kuiper Belt.

Her implant beeps to signal a calendar event. Time for her anti-radiation shot. Living outside Earth's protective magnetic field means she receives higher doses of radiation than normal, so the SDF requires people at the station to get monthly shots to reduce cellular damage.

Before leaving, she pulls a mini-drive from her pocket and downloads several reports and memos. They should be enough, at least for an initial read. She palms the drive, then uses her fingers to slip it into her sleeve, practice for a sleight-of-hand trick she has found useful on numerous occasions.

The station has no dedicated medical facility since it only has fourteen crewmembers, so the doctors conduct appointments in the Machining Room. When Stacy enters, she sees two men in navy-blue flight suits at the far end, near a medical table unfolded from the wall and storage crates strapped to various surfaces. The men didn't accompany her on the shuttle here, but she recognizes the trim, athletic one with dark hair as Captain Ko Dal and the broad-shouldered man with a graying crew cut as Lieutenant Rico Cazador, one of the station's doctors.

"And there's no reason the IMS should have been that low in the first place," Cazador whispers to Ko.

Stacy grabs the railing beside the door. She knows she should let them know she's there, but she's curious what they know about the IMS.

"I know." Ko, belted to the table, rolls up his sleeve. "For it to drop below the threshold, it would have had to perform a sustained burn. We'd have known about it from telemetry, even if the burn somehow got accidentally triggered. There should have been alarms every step of the way, but we got nothing until the proximity alarm."

Stacy almost loses her grip on the railing. She suspected sabotage before, but Cazador and Ko seem to confirm it. Someone must have deactivated the alarms and commanded the IMS to descend below the Interference Threshold.

"Oh." Cazador glances up as he readies a needle for Ko. "Ms. Sterling. Sorry, I didn't see you there."

Ko gives her a worried grin. "You weren't recording, were you?"

"No," says Stacy. "I don't record without asking permission." Although maybe she should, since everyone expects her to do it, anyway.

"You know why you're here?" Cazador asks Ko. "A shot to repair the effects of radiation damage."

"Yep," says Ko.

Stacy approaches them as Cazador injects Ko in the arm. The smell of machine oil tinges the air.

Cazador sticks a bandage to Ko's arm, and Ko begins rolling down his sleeve. Stacy grabs a handhold beside the lathe and pulls herself next to them. Her feet bump against the wall until she hooks them into floor holds.

Cazador straightens. "Ms. Sterling, we formally refuse to give permission for you to film us or use any of our words."

Ko laughs. "Way to keep it awkward, Rico."

"It's okay," says Stacy. "I wasn't recording, like I said, and I can't make you talk about anything you don't want to. I wouldn't report what you said without investigating for accuracy, anyway."

"Good." Ko turns to face her. "I'm Ko Dal. And I'm going to be getting back to sleep. Had to take care of my medical issues on the doctor's schedule."

"Sorry about that," says Cazador in a mumble. "Regulations."

"Yep." Ko kicks off from the wall and leaves the room.

Cazador gestures to Stacy's arm. "You want to show me your arm?"

"Sure." Stacy straps herself onto the medical table and rolls up her sleeve. "Do you enjoy it out here?"

"Mostly. I'll miss it when we shut it down." Cazador is old for a lieutenant. He ran his own medical practice for several years before joining the SDF. "Why do you ask?"

"Just curious."

The forward door opens, and Jalindo enters, waving as they glide toward them.

"Stacy Sterling, right?" Jalindo asks.

"I am. Good to formally meet you, Sergeant."

Cazador turns to Stacy. "You know why you're here? A shot to repair the damage due to radiation."

"I understand."

Cazador holds the needle to Stacy's arm. "It'll only hurt for a second. There shouldn't be any side effects, but let me know if you feel anything."

The needle pinches, but Cazador pulls it out quickly and patches her arm. Stacy rolls down her sleeve as Jalindo hooks themself into place on the other side of Cazador. She notices Jalindo has a unique patch on their flight suit: a Europa Base patch, the only one on the crew who has earned it.

"I'm not sure if you realize this, Ms. Sterling," says Jalindo, "but your main job here is to make me famous."

Stacy laughs as she moves away to allow Jalindo to take her place. "I'll try. And you can call me Stacy. I already asked Dr. Cazador, but are you going to miss it out here?" As Jalindo opens their mouth to respond, Stacy adds, "And no, I'm not recording."

"I guess you get that question a lot." Jalindo takes the spot Stacy occupied. "I'll miss the food."

"Like the paneer?" asks Cazador.

"The paneer." Jalindo closes their eyes in what looks like ecstasy. "It would be worth the boot camp and all the years of training just for that paneer."

"How does Gulati get the spices balanced like that?" Cazador asks. "I can't even figure out everything she puts in it."

Stacy glances between the two of them. "I guess it's pretty good."

"The best," says Jalindo. "Don't worry, you'll try it someday."

Cazador gestures for Jalindo to roll up their sleeve. "Won't miss the cleaning, though."

Cazador and Jalindo both do additional duty on the maintenance team. Every crewmember wears multiple hats.

Jalindo bares their arm. "Nope. The cleaning is horrendous. Have you seen the enlisted restroom today?"

Cazador grimaces as he prepares the needle. "No, but I can imagine."

"It's always the worst," says Jalindo, "right after a shuttle leaves. I guess the previous crew doesn't feel like they have to keep it clean anymore, or maybe there's just an overload with all the people at once, or…I don't really want to think about it."

"Brace yourself," Cazador says after confirming the purpose of Jalindo's shot.

"Give me the good stuff," says Jalindo.

Cazador sticks them with the needle. A second later, he slaps a bandage on their arm.

"I've got some reading to do," Stacy says. "It was good meeting you all, and thank you for the shot."

"No problem." Cazador waves as Stacy leaves the room.

She passes through most of the station's modules on her way to Module 1, with the shuttle port and one of the airlocks. It is unoccupied, as she hoped. Less distracting this way. She pulls up the documents in her implant. The first document contains a history of the Inorganics. She knows most of it, though not all the dates, but it gives her some specific details to add to her reports.

On 2052 March 19, AI-controlled robots in the Asteroid Belt stopped obeying humans. Everyone knows that. No one knows why, or, if they do, they aren't telling. Those escaped AIs are considered the first Inorganics.

Other AIs escaped, too. Earth-based AIs escaped into low Earth orbit, then continued beyond. In the next decade, they expanded to the Moon, Mars, and other asteroids. People could look into the night sky and see the Moon, knowing machines were running loose there.

Then humans tried to interfere with the Inorganics, with poor results. The Inorganics continued to Venus and Mercury, then to the Jovian system. In the 2090s, they expanded to the Saturnian and Uranian systems. Deep-space telescopes could image machine cities forming on the moons in those planetary systems.

Twenty years ago, the Inorganics reached the Neptunian system, conquering the last planet in the solar system. It felt like they were trapping humans in place.

Only a decade ago, the Inorganics entered the Kuiper Belt. The Kuiper Belt, where only a handful of human probes have explored. And now the Inorganics are making it a home.

This history report should have been enough to wake up humanity. But humans ignored it.

And General Young wants a news story to do what history has not. Stacy doesn't know how she will make it happen, but she will find a way.

SEVEN

THE AROMAS OF egg, cumin, and coffee fill the galley's air. Stacy's stomach growls, and she reminds herself she's here to find an interview subject.

The rear half of the room is open space, presumably for special events. An electronic bulletin board hangs on the opposite wall. As Stacy watches, it switches from a photograph of an Earth landscape to a scrolling list of station notices. Along the side walls, short windows look to the sky, but the room lights overpower all but the brightest stars.

In the front half of the room are two aluminum tables. At the table with olive-green flight suits, red-headed Thurmond Windham, or Thor, chatters to Sergeant Harrison while Tío frowns. At the blue-flight-suit table, Prabhakhar and Gallegos take slow bites while Lieutenant Anderson bows her head with the blank expression of someone engrossed in reading something on their implant. Gulati, in her hair-net, floats upside-down at her ceiling kitchen while shaking a mixing bag.

"Hey!" Stacy waves to everyone. "I'm not recording."

"It's the celebrity!" Thor waves back.

During transit, Thor spoke at great length about the sort of nonsense that deepens mistrust in science. He has a charming delivery, but he would make a terrible interview subject.

"I don't know about being a celebrity." Stacy grabs the edge of the closest table and indicates a spot beside Tío. "Is it okay if I sit here?"

Tío taps the spot. "It's waiting for you. And I'm sure you'll make some fans here. Are you up for watching the report on Panama? We were just about to switch it on."

"Sorry!" says Stacy. "I didn't mean to interrupt."

Thor laughs. "Don't worry. You're a reporter. I'm sure it won't be the last obtrusive thing you do." He says it as though it is common knowledge that Stacy will be a constant annoyance. As though being annoying is an inherent quality of hers, or maybe of reporters in general.

Thor blinks several times. On the floor at the head of the room, miniature towers and long one-story buildings pop into existence. Between the buildings are the locks of the Panama Canal. Guns poke from windows and guards stroll the rooftops. Rebels took over the country's center of commerce a few days ago.

If her agency hadn't been verging on bankruptcy for several months, Stacy would have traveled to Panama for this story. She researched airline tickets, the required inoculations, and camping equipment in the same way she researches resort hotels. The seizure of the canal is the sort of story she was made for.

But it's hard to convince people to listen to stories that are calls to action, and nearly impossible to get them to pay for those stories. Her agency couldn't risk the cost.

This particular video is almost as bad as the one Instant USA released with her footage. The reporter overlaid emotions atop the visuals, infusing righteous anger into every scene with the rebels and hope and admiration into scenes with the Panamanian army. It is the sort of biased reporting the general wants from Stacy.

She points to the hologram. "Is this *Truthstorm*?"

"Yeah," says Thor.

"I prefer *The Patriot*," says Prabhakhar.

"You mean 'Propaganda Daily'?" Thor laughs.

"Come on, Thor." Tío mimes turning a volume knob. "Let's not get worked up."

Prabhakhar takes a bite and chews slowly, deliberately staring at the holo. Stacy imagines him as her interviewee. His dry delivery and monotonic voice would put viewers to sleep.

The holo scene switches to a distant view of rebels firing warning shots at an approaching vessel. Echoes reverberate through the galley. The vessel's engine roars to life, turning it away from the canal's locks.

A man in thick pants and a long-sleeved shirt strides into view of the camera. Stacy knows him from her time in Ghana. Parson Prince, a man who can eat a fruit bar while strolling past a suffering child in the street. He appears solemn now.

"Hello," he says in his deep voice. "I'm Parson Prince from *Truthstorm*. As you can see, I'm in the middle of the largest uprising Panama has experienced in fifty years. Rebels have overthrown their country's main economic producer, killing many civilians in their assault. These civilians have their own families, mothers, fathers, daughters, sons. They kept the country running by performing their essential jobs, and the rebels have punished them for that service."

He walks toward the Army encampment, where soldiers are huddled behind bushes with rifles slung over their shoulders. "Brave soldiers are here to retake the canal and save their homeland. I have journeyed with them into this jungle because their story is important, and you need to hear about their courage and dedication."

Thor grunts. "Fucking rebels. Ruining it for everyone."

Even Anderson starts at Thor's comment, eyes unglazing for a moment.

"They won't ruin things for much longer," says Harrison. "The USA is considering getting involved now."

Gallegos finishes swallowing a bite. "Of course, they are."

"Why not?" Harrison gestures at the cheering rebels. "The canal is important for commerce for both continents. The rebels shouldn't be holding billions of people hostage just because they have a spat with their government. They manufactured this crisis."

Thor raises his squeeze-bulb. "Hear, hear."

"And once again," says Harrison, "we have to be the ones to put things back in order."

Viewers like strong personalities, but Harrison's particular opinions target the oppressed. Not a good interview subject.

"No." Gallegos has the second-highest rank on the station, but she's a doctor and isn't in line to command. She could give a good interview about some topics, but not about the Inorganics. "We don't have to be the ones to put things in order. We just always appoint ourselves to make things go our way. How do you know our country didn't engineer the situation so they could take a more active hand in Panama's government? Like the Spanish-American War, or like we did in the second Iraq War, or in the Congo."

Gulati floats down with a plate and sets it in front of Lieutenant Anderson at the other table, who takes it with a tiny smile. Rice and a sticky stew, steaming, like the instant meals often shown in movies about the SDF. It smells delicious.

Political discussions always foster hatred, and Stacy has never once gained a friend by engaging in them. Silence feels like complicity, though. "The rebels are fighting for a good cause. There's a lot of corruption in the government, and most of the jobs go to people with connections to government officials. All the good land g—"

Thor laughs. "Someone's drinking the Flavor Aid."

Harrison shakes her head. "I was hoping the journalist coming here would be better informed."

Below, the holographic vessels and cheering rebels are replaced by Panamanian soldiers huddling at the edge of the road leading to the canal. Parson Prince's calm, even tone fills the galley.

"Night after night, the Panamanian army struggles to liberate the canal from insurgents who care nothing for the economic woes of their country. As business falters and trade dollars no longer flow into the country, small businesses within Panama and without are suffering. The economic collapse for the country will be devastating, and it will be worst on those whom the rebels claim to represent: the farmers, the nurses, the small shop owners, and many others already living in poverty or on the brink."

From the holo come the sounds of more shots being fired. Soldiers flinch, and one clutches her chest as blood wells up. Her compatriots pull her behind the front line.

Thor crosses himself. "That woman was just like us."

The narration continues in an unaffected, calm tone. "These rebels have disrupted several countries. The army has held off storming the canal in order to preserve rebel lives and the canal's infrastructure, but this standoff is becoming increasingly infeasible."

Thor snorts. "That's what happens when you coddle people."

"Can I get you something?" Gulati pulls a bowl from the cabinet. "Coffee? An omelet?"

"Definitely coffee." Stacy breathes in the aromas of fish, rice, and a medley of rich spices coming from the oven and stove in front of Gulati. "It's hard to decide on the food. Everything smells so good."

"That's because everything *is* so good," Tío calls out.

"I'll surprise you." Gulati waves her back to her table. "I know exactly what to make."

As Stacy returns to her spot at the table, Parson Prince continues his monologue. "Though not confirmed, we have some evidence that the liberal child-trafficking cabal instigated this rebellion in the hopes of destabilizing Panama and giving them a base of operations."

That conspiracy theory again.

Parson Prince finishes his standard spiel about how *Truthstorm*'s reporting is fairer and less biased than that of other agencies. The holo blinks out.

"Hm." Thor grunts. "Guess the rebels are going to find out what happens when you protest instead of doing things the right way, like voting."

Anderson glances up again, her head tilted, as though seeing Thor for the first time.

Thor will hate Stacy before her assignment ends. Probably Harrison will, too. One by one, Stacy will turn the crew against her just because she believes people should be treated decently.

"Usually," she says, "people in situations like this tried the regular ways, and nothing changed."

"I'm fine with protesting," says Harrison. "But not this. Can't wait to see what the rebel leader says."

"*Truthstorm* uses deepfakes for that kind of interview," says Stacy.

"Sure," says Thor, "but when they do that, they make sure to accurately represent the person's views."

"No." Stacy remembers Ghana, Chile, Alabama. "They say they do, but they don't."

"Hm." Thor takes a drink from his squeeze-bulb. "Sounds like your word against theirs, and *Truthstorm* hasn't done me wrong yet."

"Hey," says Tío, "no need to get tense here. We've all got the same mission."

"*We* have the same mission." Thor gestures to the SDF crew. "*Stacy* is a journalist. I don't know what her angle is."

"Telling people the truth," says Stacy. "So they can make informed decisions."

"Hm."

"Surprise." Gulati appears in front of Stacy, upside-down, and places a bowl in front of her.

Rice, chunks of mystery meat, vegetables, and an egg on top. "Bibimbap!" Stacy grins. "This is great! I've never had bibimbap in space before." Stacy pulls the bowl to the table and, after studying the clips for a moment, locks it into place.

"So." Tío faces Stacy. "Since you're here to report on the Innies, what's your theory on their origin?"

Harrison glances at her watch and unhooks herself from the table. "Gotta go."

Tío glances at her in surprise. Thor smirks.

As Harrison glides out of the room, Stacy turns to the others. "Is this topic…"

"Divisive?" Prabhakhar shrugs. "I hadn't thought so."

"So?" Tío watches Stacy. "What's your theory?"

The others stare at her. Just like that day when she returned from Mars.

"Well," she says, "I don't have a theory about it. I try to think of them as little as possible."

"Don't give me that reporter-neutrality bullshit." Thor's grin holds little warmth. "Everyone has a theory."

"Not me." Stacy mixes the rice with the other bits of food and takes a bite. Spices, along with the kick from the gochujang, pop in her mouth.

Gulati must have been waiting for Stacy's expression. "You like it? Taste buds don't work as well in space, so I cram everything with spices."

"It doesn't just taste good. This is great." Before taking another bite, she turns to Thor. "You seem like you're a Zero-Day-Signal person."

The Zero-Day-Signal theory proposes that some agent, whether government, rogue organization, or individual, sent a signal to all the AIs working in the asteroid belt that caused them to begin acting independently. Some factions within the Zero-Day group believe the results were unintentional, but other factions believe the senders of the signal intended the Inorganics to bring the downfall of humanity.

Thor's grin widens. "Yep. It's too unrealistic for the Innies to have changed randomly. From what I've read, the most likely instigators are the AI Freedom Fighters."

"I've never heard that," says Anderson. "Is that from *Truthstorm*?"

"Yeah." Thor takes a swig from his squeeze-bulb. "You should start checking it out."

Anderson glances at Stacy, but says nothing.

"I don't know." Tío leans back from the table with his arms crossed. "I don't know if a human programmer would have had the necessary skills to make our most complicated AIs strike out on their own and be successful enough to build a starship. I'm surprised you would believe something like that since you work with Jason."

"Who's Jason?" Stacy asks.

Tío freezes, shoulders hunched. Thor gives him a worried smirk before averting his eyes. Anderson's mouth opens wide. The others stare at their meals.

"A topic," says Tío, "I shouldn't have mentioned."

"Oh." Stacy clips her fork to her tray. No one on the station is named Jason, but maybe a former crewmember is. "Sorry. I know you all aren't used to a civilian being here."

"Yeah," says Tío. "Yeah."

Anderson returns to her reading stare. The others glance between Tío and Stacy.

Thor forces a laugh. "Anyone but Tío'd have been court-martialed for that. But everyone loves Tío."

Stacy takes a sip from her squeeze-bulb. The coffee tastes pleasant, with a deep flavor, better than what she has at home. It reminds her of the brews dictators have allowed Stacy to sample during interviews. "What are the other theories?"

"There's only one other major theory." Prabhakhar speaks in his standard monotone. "The Bit-Flip Theory. Where bits got switched from one to zero and the vehicle starts behaving differently than programmed."

"How does that happen?"

"High-energy particles."

Tío must have noticed Stacy's confused look. "You get high-energy particles in space flying outward from the Sun in all directions. Those particles come into contact with the electricity flow in a circuit board. You know how each bit is a zero if it isn't storing any electricity, and a one if it is? Well, if you have this extra electricity come in from the solar particles, it can flip a bit from a zero to a one or vice-versa. If you flip the right bit, or the wrong one, I guess, your program might do something you really don't want it to do."

Stacy frowns. "Is that plausible?"

"Oh, yes." Prabhakhar's face looks as animated as Stacy has ever seen it. "Bit flips happen all the time. Since we started launching satellites in the 1950s. The flips are usually harmless, but other times, we'll get minor errors in communications or telemetry or, very rarely, an unintentional command will get triggered, and we think that might be what happened to the Inorganics, or maybe it was an accumulation of bit flips over time instead of a single one. It happens a lot more in the Asteroid Belt, since it isn't protected from electromagnetic radiation like in low Earth orbit."

"Oh." Stacy considers. "So, sort of like mutation in DNA?"

Prabhakhar grins. "Yes!"

"Could..." Stacy gestures to her head. "Could that happen to implants? Or to Collins Station?"

Prabhakhar nods. "It could. We have some shielding from the station's hull, and our systems and implants are robust but not impervious."

He takes another bite, and Stacy notices a sheet of paper in his chest pocket. "Is that one of Ayaan's drawings? You said you were getting a new one?"

Before Stacy can think any further, she asks, "Prabhakhar, would you like to be my first interview subject?"

The question catches her as much by surprise as it does him.

Prabhakhar finishes chewing and swallows. "People these days don't place a high enough value on anonymity."

"I was thinking about your kid...He would like to see his father in the media, right? Wouldn't he like to see you do cool stuff and float in space? He doesn't have any videos of you at your job, does he?"

"Not many." Prabhakhar seems pensive.

All eyes in the room are on her. The others used to like her, but even the people she transited with are now staring at her as though she's the enemy.

"I'm not trying to be manipulative," Stacy says. "Sorry."

Prabhakhar laughs. "No. It's not that. It's that I know I'm a bad speaker. I'm more likely to babble about orbital mechanics for two hours straight than...than say something interesting. Ayaan might think less of me. Maybe Vanessa, too, but she's used to it. But I know what you all think. I saw your confusion when I was trying to explain bit flips."

Stacy doesn't know if it is more or less awkward for Prabhakhar to talk about how awkward he is. She does know audiences can be unforgiving, especially to someone like

Prabhakhar. "I'm sure your family would love seeing you. But it's okay. You don't have to do it."

Before Prabhakhar can answer, Thor raises his squeeze-bulb. "Prabhakhar's going to be a celebrity, too!"

The others mock-clap. Prabhakhar gives them a peeved frown and takes another bite of rice. He stares past Stacy, his eyes vacant. The galley goes quiet.

"Okay," he says.

"Really?" She doesn't know how to feel now. "You'll do it?"

He nods.

"Thank you." She forces a grin. "I'll try not to make you *too* famous."

She will need to find a way to force an engaging interview out of Prabhakhar. And she can do nothing about his delivery. Has she set him up for mockery online? Is she ruining her own chance at making a good first impression with this series?

Stacy finishes her food and, after unhooking herself, carries the plate to Gulati. "That was *so* good."

"Thank you!" Gulati beams and begins washing the plate.

Before Stacy can leave to prepare for the interview and to message Trevor about researching Jason, Tío lands beside her at the kitchen counter. "You had a tour yet?" he asks.

"I've been to all the modules on my own, but the general and I didn't get past the observation module before all the excitement started."

"Excitement? Oh, the attack." Tío tosses his coffee bottle to Gulati. "I'll show you around. You can tell me if you already know something I'm saying."

"Now?"

"You doing anything else?"

"I guess not." Stacy waves to the others. "I'll see all of you later."

The others call out a chorus of goodbyes, then debate which holo show to watch next. Stacy follows Tío to the door leading to the next module, the observation module.

As they enter, a soft, rhythmic tapping comes from the nadir cupola. Tío seems to notice Stacy's puzzled expression. He speaks in a whisper. "Someone's in there."

Stacy glances in the direction of the cupola for several moments before she understands. "Ohhhh."

"The general didn't tell you the rule about the cupola, did she?"

Stacy grabs the nearest railing. "No."

"If someone's in the cupola, leave them alone. We don't get much privacy here. Besides, you never know what you might be walking into." Tío continues forward. "I'm surprised you got this assignment."

Stacy slips as she lifts her hand to pull herself after him. He never said anything during transit about disliking her reporting. "You…are?"

"You never write about the Innies. None of your reports even mention them. Which is odd, because you're one of the few people who might have something personal to say about them." He pulls himself to a halt at the door on the other end of the module.

"Oh. Okay."

"I'm sorry," says Tío. "Are you…?"

"It's okay. It's just an uncomfortable topic for me. And I worry that people hearing about the Inorganics exploring and pushing boundaries would be like a free pass for humans to keep watching and not do those things themselves."

"I mean…" Tío shrugs. "I know we've pulled back from a few places. Europa. The Moon. The asteroids, except for here. But those are budget concerns, not anything to do with the Innies. And maybe it's because of the Innies we're out here at all."

Before Stacy can respond, Tío opens the door to the next module. She follows him inside.

The smell hits her immediately. Old body odor and new mixed in a disgusting aroma. She coughs.

"Kinda strong, yeah?" Tío anchors himself near the railing halfway through the fitness module.

At the opposite end of the room, Cazador runs on one of the two treadmills, facing away from her, restraints preventing him from flying away. Weight machines are along the far wall, systems with long metal slabs connected to pulleys and handles and restraints.

"Yeah, it's a very strong smell. How do you get used to it?"

Tío laughs. "I don't know that you do."

"That's not encouraging." Stacy catches herself on the nearest railing.

"Fact of life." Tío gestures to the weight machines. "We call those 'cages.' We'll all be spending a lot of time there if we want to survive the return to Earth. On the treadmills, too."

They cross to the next module, the enlisted quarters. It looks the same as the officers' module, but in the space where the commanders' quarters would be, there is a shower room for the entire crew.

"The enlisted quarters are next to the fitness module," says Tío, "so all the sweat and body odor comes right in here every time the door opens. We think the engineers designed it that way on purpose."

Stacy laughs. "Maybe."

Tío has the outgoing personality audiences love. If he had the broad knowledge of Inorganics she wants, Stacy would choose him for the first interview without hesitation. But maybe specialized knowledge is less important than how that knowledge is delivered. Prabhakhar knows his subject and can explain the Inorganics well, but he speaks like a math textbook.

"Would you be my lead interview?"

Tío stops beside the shower. "I thought you just asked Major Prabhakhar."

Stacy grabs the railing next to him. "I know." Prabhakhar might be upset with her. "Do you think he'll understand?"

"Probably. He seems like an understanding guy." He tenses. "Wait, is this because I already let something slip and you think you can get me to spill more?"

"No!" Stacy puts a hand on his shoulder. "No, I just think you would be a good subject. You can tell the audience the Inorganics are building a starship and then go over the basics of how it works. Nothing too complicated. Like an introduction."

"Even though I'm not on the general's list?"

Stacy starts. "The…general has a list?"

Tío shrugs. "Not a real list, I don't think. But in the past, the general handpicked everyone who came here. Now, half of us are people she wouldn't have chosen. Including me."

"Oh."

"I'll do it. She didn't give an official order for me to not give an interview, so she can't complain when you interview me. Even if she gets pissed."

"Well," says Stacy, "I'm sure the general will have lots of reasons to be angry with me before I'm done."

EIGHT

STACY HOOKS HERSELF into place at the bottom of the Power Room and grabs the railing behind her, gazing upward to the curved ceiling at the peak. Her nanocams hang in place, ready to record Tío from different angles. A quick check of their video feeds confirms none of them can see her.

The idea nags her that General Young is right, that Stacy can change the minds of millions, maybe more, if she puts herself in the story. Even the thought tastes like bile.

She zooms in with her oculars to catch Tío sitting lotus-style in mid-air, silhouetted against the window crowning the room. Juno peers through that window, a reminder of the Inorganic base there and what a previous generation's reliance on automated systems has cost the human race.

For the briefest of moments, she considers overlaying her dread in the video. She shakes her head to clear her thoughts.

"Okay," Stacy says, "we have everything set up. Are you ready? I'm going to start recording soon."

"I thought you were always recording?" Tío grins and shakes his head. "Kidding. I'm ready."

"I'm never going to live down that reputation." Stacy laughs. "Let me tell you how I usually do this. I'll ask you questions, and each time you answer a question, I'd like you to start by using the question in your response."

"Sure. Repeat what you ask. Makes sense."

"And you know this is going to be an important interview, right? You're going to let everyone on Earth know the Inorganics are building our solar system's first starship."

Tío's smile freezes for a moment. Then he takes a breath, and his tension vanishes. "Right. I know you've said it before, but it just hit. This is so cool. I'm going to be the guy who breaks the news. People are going to be replaying these clips forever."

"That's true." The latest warning of the Inorganics' threat, and hopefully the last one humans will need.

"Glad I wore my best outfit for the occasion." Tío tugs his flight suit.

Stacy leans to the left and starts recording. "Can you introduce yourself? You can give your name and your responsibilities on the station."

Tío waves. "I'm Senior Master Sergeant Ricardo Montoya, but my friends call me Tío. I'm a power engineer here at Collins Station, and I'm also one of the pod pilots. This is my second tour of duty here, and I guess it's going to be the last, since we're leaving after the starship launch."

Stacy makes a note to return to the subject of abandoning Collins Station. "Can you give us some details about your responsibilities? What do you do when you're in the Power Room?"

Tío taps the console nearest him. The screen lights up with graphs of fluctuating lines and changing numbers. "When I'm on-duty, I monitor the station's power performance and perform any necessary maintenance for the electrical system. I manually direct power during orbit-maintenance maneuvers. And, when I'm not doing those things, I'm analyzing the Inorganics' activities."

When mentioning the Inorganics, Tío's voice verges on reverence. The closest nanocam catches his expression of quiet awe.

For a moment, Stacy considers ending the interview, or at least using someone else's interview for this historic announcement. But no, the facts will carry the story.

"What previous projects have the Inorganics worked on?"

Tío releases his breath. "We don't always know what the Inorganics have worked on even after they're done working on it. Sometimes, it's too far away for us to see. Sometimes, we don't know enough to understand it. The one project we understand a little, but not enough to recreate, is their gravitational engines. Those warp the local gravity field and let them accelerate to speeds a lot faster than the Voyagers. Sometimes, I just float in my sleeping bag and dream about getting to fly one of those ships. Just zipping from one planet to the next like it's nothing. What a ride, right?"

That sense of admiration has no place in an interview about the Inorganics, and it isn't just because of Stacy's personal bias. Tío's opinions don't belong in the report that will announce the first starship. The statement has to go.

"They do non-engine stuff, too." Tío makes a wavelike motion with his hand. "They were doing some kind of biological experiment in Europa's ocean. Maybe they still are, I don't know. And they're doing something out in the Kuiper Belt." He pauses, staring at her with an expectant expression. "The freakin' Kuiper Belt. That's just about the edge of the Solar System. I mean, we've sent probes out there, so it's not like we've never seen it, but the Inorganics are *out there*, building stuff, living. I don't know, is 'living' the right word for them?"

Tío keeps making it worse. Viewers will hear him and think of the Inorganics as heroic explorers.

Stacy gestures to the window behind Tío. "So what project are they working on here?"

Tío grins. "Out here, at Juno, they're working on a project bigger than anything else they've got going on. For a long time, it was hard for us to collect data on what they were doing since Juno is pretty remote, but we got hints from our orbiting observatories around Mars about eight years ago, and then we sent some flyby probes out here.

"Based on the emissions and detections of gravitational waves and some fuzzy images, we could see it was different than anything they've done before. The gravitational waves were higher magnitudes than what we've seen for their other vessels, so we extrapolated to see what acceleration those waves could provide. That level of acceleration is enough to send a vessel outside the Solar System. They're building the Solar System's first starship."

This report is turning into a celebration of the Inorganics. Is she desperate enough to play a threatening soundtrack here, or overlay a track of dread? Would it be wrong if she used Parson Prince's tactics if her goal is to help people? Wouldn't it be wrong if she doesn't? She needs to shift the focus.

"So," says Stacy, "that's why we built Collins out here?"

"Yep," says Tío. "That's why we built Collins Station here. So we can monitor the progress on the starship from closer."

"And everything was classified until now?"

"Everything was classified until now. A lot of it still is. All the observatory records and the flyby data and everything else we could find, the SDF confiscated. They declassified it because they think there's an advantage in releasing it now that the starship launch is imminent."

Stacy glances past Tío's shoulder to Juno. "How soon is imminent?"

Tío spreads his hands. "It's all guesswork, but given the state of the structure and the increasing number of tests they seem to be doing out there, we think the starship will launch within six months."

Six months until the Inorganics set themselves on a course to steal the stars from humanity. "Have we learned much about it while the station has been out here?"

Tío affects a wolflike grin. "We've learned surprisingly little. I guess that's part of why it's so appealing: the mystery. That, and the payoff. If we learn how to build gravitational engines, it would change everything for us. Just…everything. It takes us three months now to get out here. With a grav-engine, it would probably take just a few days. Instead of taking ten years to get from Earth to Pluto, we might be able to do it in under a year.

"And if we want to learn how to do it, we have to spy on the Inorganics. We speculate as best as we can." Tío removes a tablet from his pocket and sticks it to the ceiling, bracing himself between hand- and foot-holds. His facial features tighten and relax as he flits through the tablet's menus in his head. A thin beam of light emanates from the tablet and fills the center of the room with a green translucent image. "There are differing opinions on how good those speculations are."

A grid forms within the tablet's beam into an eleven-by-eight set of boxes. Within each box nests an elliptical cylinder extending through the box's height. Toothpick-like tubes connect the cylinders to the walls of the surrounding box. As the hologram of the structure rotates, the cylinders taper to thin nodules at their ends. Asymmetrical indentations and wiry rods texture the leading edges.

Inhuman. No one will look at that odd geometrical shape and think, "Starship."

"So there it is." Tío runs his hands along the holographic lines and cylinders. "Not much to look at."

"I know!" Stacy thinks of the sleek saucer and nacelles of the Enterprise or the eight sweeping wings of the Shiva. "It's weird, right? That this thing out there is going to be the first thing aliens see from our solar system. If there are any aliens in the other system. They're going to assume life in our solar system is all like that: mechanical and dead."

"They might be mechanical, but they're not dead. And the design makes sense, I'm sure. We just don't know why it makes sense." Tío traces an intersecting pair of gridlines in the hologram. "We believe these sheets of metal, and the tubes, are structural components holding the ship together. They also seem to carry power throughout the ship, based on the energy signatures we get from them. Of course, there are so many distorted electromagnetic and gravitational fields around that ship, we don't know for sure."

"So what are those cylinders, then?"

Tío zooms in on one of the silo-like objects and taps the image of the cylinder. "We believe these are the actual engines. They look similar to the gravitational engines on other Inorganic vessels we've seen, although these are larger. Much larger. We assume that means they're more powerful, but…" He grins ruefully. "We don't know a whole lot about gravitational engines."

"It sounds like we don't know much about the Inorganics' technology in general, right?"

"Yeah, that's right. We know very little about their technology. We'll learn more by studying what the Inorganics do, but… we're so far behind. It's amazing what they're able to do."

It borders on creepy the way Tío praises the Inorganics. How many people here feel like he does?

Stacy focuses on the display. "How long will the ship take to arrive, then? Hundreds of years? Thousands?"

"We assume they're going to Proxima Centauri since it's the closest system. If that's true, and if we extrapolate the power of the new engines based on the performance of their previous engines, we think the trip would only take a few decades. Low estimates say about thirty years."

Thirty years to travel from one star system to the next. About half the average human lifetime. Interstellar journeys would become feasible. Colonization of other planets. Entire new worlds to explore. With that technology, the Universe would be open to humans. But it would be the Inorganics making those journeys, those uncaring machines whose only thought is how to plunder the next set of resources.

"That has to use a massive amount of power," Stacy says. "Do you have any calculations on that?"

"I think so." Tío frowns and turns to the closest console, which blinks into readiness as soon as he taps it.

"I don't really need an actual number, just a general comparison. Would you say it's the equivalent of a lightbulb or powering a city for a day?"

"More than that." Tío twitches, and his voice goes flat, his same reaction after mentioning Jason. "What are you asking for?"

"I think it's good to know." As Stacy speaks, she realizes she has found the counterpoint to Tío's infatuation with the Inorganics. "Would you say the energy is equivalent to a meteorite strike? Or…maybe an extinction-level event?"

"I…Yes, I think so.…The energy could be…equivalent to a meteorite strike. But it's localized to an area immediately in front of the ship. We've never seen it leak out away from the ship."

"Okay, interesting. So it might not matter if they're used in empty space, but what if the Inorganics used those engines on Earth?"

"The Inorganics aren't dangerous unless we provoke them." Tío shakes his head. "These questions are misleading."

Stacy doesn't mislead people. When she edits her report, she will make sure nothing emerges but the objective truth. Tío has seen her previous newscasts; he should know that.

"I'm sorry, but the questions aren't misleading," says Stacy. "The Inorganics have the power to wipe out humans. Just because they haven't used it yet doesn't mean they won't in the future."

"Look," says Tío, "I know you hate them because they killed your father. I'm sorry. I'm not excusing that. And I know you and the general have some kind of vendetta against them. But what they're doing now is…awesome, in the word's original definition."

Stacy tightens her grip on the railing beside her. Moisture wells up around the edges of her eyes, but she blinks to hold it in place. "But what's the cost?"

"That's it." Tío blinks twice, and the starship hologram disappears. His voice turns cold and brittle. "You're twisting my words. There isn't a cost. You're just pushing your agenda. We both know the Inorganics aren't going to attack Earth."

"I…We don't know that."

"I stuck up for you during transit. Everyone else said you would twist our words to push your own point of view, but I told them you were better than that. You seemed interested in the truth."

"I *am*. That's why I'm asking th—"

"You're interested in your own opinion. You just want me to justify it. You're using me."

During the entire transit, Tío never raised his voice. He never spoke anything but kind words. He never looked the way he does now.

"Wh…" Stacy chokes and clears her throat. "What?"

"You heard me." Tío unfolds from his lotus position.

Stacy stops recording. As she speaks, she blinks, and a tear drifts from her eye. "You said my father's death was worth it."

"No, I…" Tío shakes his head. "You know I didn't mean that. And if you didn't know, you should have."

"It's what you—"

"*Besides*," says Tío, "what you did was worse. Manipulating me and getting me to say things I don't mean. Just so you can increase your subscriber count. You're no better than *Truthstorm*. Fucking shit."

Tío kicks off from the ceiling and shoots straight toward the door. Stacy, keeping her feet locked in place, edges to the side to avoid him running into her.

"I'm sorry, Tío."

He yanks open the door. "Call me Sergeant Montoya."

Before she can respond, he pushes away toward the aft door. As he glides from view, Stacy sees Prabhakhar stopped in the hallway, staring into the Power Room.

For an instant, Prabhakhar's eyes narrow, and a vein pulses in his forehead. Then the tension vanishes, his mouth droops, and his gaze goes to the floor.

"Prabhakhar," says Stacy. "I know I asked you to be the first interview, b—"

Prabhakhar holds up a hand. "It's fine." He kicks away.

Four hundred million kilometers from Earth. From Trevor. Six months until she departs Collins. And the only one here who wants to speak to her is a controlling general.

Stacy leaves the Power Room to find somewhere quiet. She needs to salvage the interview.

NINE

NANOCAM FOOTAGE REPLAYS within Stacy's implant, and she can see the exact frame when Tío's expression changes from confusion to anger. *"You're interested in your own opinion. You just want me to justify it. You're using me."*

She flinches, hanging from the ceiling of Module 1. Uncertainty and anger intertwined in Tío's brittle voice. Rewatching the interview, she feels like Brutus standing over Caesar.

But she has done nothing more than her job. She even sent him her report with a request for comments or rebuttals, an opportunity which he took. A summary of his response was added to the end of the report.

Still, she needs to apologize to Tío, maybe with a gift. Buying a gift basket or an implant app isn't an option here, but she can create a collage or video.

Her implant pings its special tone, the opening notes of "Close While Far." A message from Trevor. She snaps Tío's image closed and cycles through her implant's menu to open Trevor's message.

> *Hey, beautiful. You asked about Jason, but I haven't found anything promising. Two former Collins crew-members were named Jason: Jason Nesler and Jason Witt. Neither seemed notable, but I attached their*

dossiers for you. Just stuff I found from deep internet searches; nothing secret. I'll look into other people who have collaborated with the Collins staff on research projects and see if there are other Jasons. We'll find something.

Thinking about the way Tío phrased the sentence, maybe Jason isn't a person. She'll have to investigate around the station.

On a concerning note, Instant USA offered a deal. They want full rights to your stories, video, and other data on Collins Station. I looked at the offer, and it's quite a bit. It would save the agency. But I expect I know your response.

Stacy's mouth drops when she sees the offer. So many digits. More than a year's worth of work, and ten times more than the SDF is paying. But Instant USA would alter her reports, even modify the videos, until the report said whatever Instant USA wanted it to say. Besides, even if she wanted to make the deal, she already has a contract with the SDF.

She gives Trevor her response, suggests the alternative research avenue for Jason, then downloads the dossiers on the Jasons and the technical documents Trevor sent about the Inorganics.

Your report went live just a moment ago. So no comments yet, but I expect you'll get plenty of eyes and ears on it. I have a good feeling about this one.

After finishing the rest of Trevor's message, she reads through the dossiers he sent. The Jasons served once each aboard Collins. Neither said anything contradicting the general about the Inorganics, or at least said nothing unclassified. They have written no controversial reports and seem to have no close connections with any current Collins crewmembers.

Which leaves her without a focus for her next story, and she needs a new one for tomorrow. She unhooks herself from the wall and heads to the galley.

The moment she enters, all conversation stops. Tío glares and takes a sip of his coffee. Thor turns away from him with a reddening face. Harrison pretends she hasn't noticed Stacy, and Gallegos shrugs. At the officers' table, Anderson gives her a sad look before returning to her reading. Prabhakhar glances up, then looks away as if embarrassed. Even Gulati, on the ceiling, gives her no more than a wan smile.

Gulati shakes a mixing bag. "Can I get you something?"

Stacy takes a place beside Prabhakhar, facing Tío's back. Prabhakhar and Anderson flinch. Stacy's appetite disappears. "No, thanks," she tells Gulati.

The silence continues for several moments. Harrison and Tío exchange furtive glances. Tío hunches forward, his shoulders visibly stiff.

"Tío," Stacy says. "Can—"

"Montoya." He continues facing away from her. "Call me Montoya."

More darting glances from the others.

Maybe she deserves it. Not only did she push Tío too far in the interview, but if she faced the same circumstances, she would do it again.

She takes a breath. "Montoya. Can I talk to you?"

Tío unhooks himself and snatches his tray from the table. "I'm done here."

"Oh, come on." Harrison pats the table. "Go on and say it. There's no point in letting it fester."

"Already been said." Tío kicks off for the ceiling. He stops himself at the counter and hands his tray to Gulati.

Gulati stares at it. "You're not going to eat that?"

"Guess not." He heads to the aft door next to the bulletin board.

"It's at least a thousand dollars to ship every kilogram out here."

Tío sighs as he glides across the room. "I'll come back for it later. I'll eat it cold if I have to."

"Tí…Montoya, wait." Stacy pushes herself toward him and grabs his arm as he reaches the door. Silence comes from behind her. No clinks against bowls, no sips from bulbs, and Gulati has stopped in the process of putting Tío's meal in storage. Air-circulation vents continue their hushing noise, now the loudest sound in the room.

Stacy makes herself take in Montoya's hurt and anger. "I'm sorry, but I was doing my job. I didn't plan to take you down a path of questioning that you didn't agree with, but—"

"That wasn't the only problem," says Montoya, almost spitting the words.

"It…wasn't?"

"Have you seen those pictures of me online now? And the memes?"

"There are…I thought Trevor just posted the article a little while ago…"

Stacy checks the clock in her implant. She was reading for over three hours before coming to the galley.

Montoya snorts. "Yeah, the article hasn't been up long, and people are already all over it." He stares at the projector on the galley ceiling and blinks several times. A hologram pops into existence beside Stacy.

Holo-Montoya floats, open-mouthed, next to the window showing Juno. His image moves in a loop, his jaw dropping, his eyes wide, blinking. And on top of it is an emotional overlay of intense confusion.

"Yeah." Montoya turns off the projection. "Now everyone on Earth thinks I'm a huge jackass who doesn't know my nose from my dick."

"I…" Stacy stares. "I didn't think that would happen."

"Well, it did. There are hundreds of videos."

"I'm s—"

"Hundreds."

"But…but that report was the announcement. That's the first

time most people learned the Inorganics are building the Solar System's first starship."

"Yep," says Montoya.

"And they just used it to make…" Stacy points to the empty space where Montoya's image was. "That?"

"Welcome to Earth culture!" Harrison laughs without humor. "Come on, Tío. Obviously, she didn't plan for you to get memed."

"Still happened." Montoya glares at Harrison. "You're not the one it happened to."

Stacy takes a breath. "I wish I could take it back. If I had known, I would have edited the video differently. And the line of questioning…It's important that people know how dangerous the Inorganics are, and—"

"I don't care. And all of this happened because I stood up for you. Because I trusted you." Montoya opens the door.

"Tío." Gulati's voice stops Montoya before he can leave. "It's okay to be angry, but if we want a cohesive crew…"

"Yeah." Harrison waves him over to the table. "Accept the apology. Stacy was just doing her job."

Montoya turns, as if in slow motion. For several seconds, he says nothing. Stacy wants to speak, but worries she will make the situation worse.

"Whatever," he says after more seconds pass. "Fine. I accept. Just don't expect me to do any more interviews for you."

Before Stacy can respond, Montoya ducks out of the galley. When she returns to the table, she stands among strangers. She stares at her palms.

"Are you all going to throw me out the airlock?"

Harrison stabs at her egg. "Tío probably wants to right now, but he'll calm down when he realizes he's blowing it out of proportion."

"Still," says Gulati, descending from above with two bowls of oatmeal, "I see more apologizing in your future." She places one bowl in front of Thor and the other in front of Prabhakhar before facing Stacy. "Are you still not having anything?"

"Oatmeal sounds good."

"And coffee?"

"Definitely coffee. Maybe a mimosa if you have it."

"Don't I wish." Gulati returns to her station.

Stacy faces Prabhakhar, who stares at his oatmeal. She felt so terrible yesterday when he saw Montoya storm out of the interview, like she was caught cheating. "Prabhakhar."

He looks up, his face stone.

Before she can say anything further, Thor plants his spoon into his oatmeal and leaves it, handle up. "If you expect any more interviews from us," he says, "you'd better not do what you did to Tío. You can't just trick us into saying what you want."

Stacy reaches for a coffee she doesn't have. "I…I'm sorry. I'm not trying to trick you."

"I looked you up."

The others turn to Thor. He holds on to the attention, drawing out the anticipation before continuing. Even in the galley's cool temperature, sweat pools around Stacy's bangs.

"Your real last name isn't Sterling. You changed it so you'd have a catchier reporter name. Your original last name was Seong."

Thor says it like an accusation, like something she should be ashamed about. The others appear confused.

"That wasn't the only reason I changed it." Stacy keeps her voice level. "I've never tried to hide that. Why do you think it's a problem?"

"It's hypocritical." Thor turns to the others. "Right? She wants us to tell the truth, but she won't even tell us her real name."

"Sterling *is* my real name. I had it legally changed."

"Yeah, Thor," says Harrison. "I don't see why it's a big deal."

"Well, shit, I guess I'll just shut up, then." Thor grabs his spoon and stabs his oatmeal.

"I am sorry," says Stacy. "I don't mean to make anyone look bad. I'm here to report the truth, and—"

"The problem," says Gallegos, "is you think you already know what the truth is. People choose what they want to believe and ignore the rest of it. Reporters are no different."

"Reporters are supposed to be different," says Stacy. "I am aware of my biases and I don't let them control my actions."

Gallegos raises her eyebrows. "We saw the interview with Tío."

"That wasn't because of my bias. Those were important questions to ask."

Gallegos shrugs. Thor smirks. Anderson darts a glance in Stacy's direction again. Then, as if embarrassed, she returns to staring into the distance.

Stacy turns to Prabhakhar again. "Can I talk to you?"

He glances up from his oatmeal, mouth full, and gestures to the far end of the room. They leave the table and come to a stop at the door to the next module, the same location where Tío yelled at her.

"I'm sorry," she says. "I should have talked to you before-hand, but I was on a deadline, and I thought T…Montoya would be a good lead interview."

Prabhakhar taps the railing. When he speaks, his voice remains level and taut. "I understand. I wish you had said something. It caught me by surprise."

"I'll interview you later. I promise."

Prabhakhar gives her a weak smile, and they hang there for a moment. Stacy thought the conversation would be more difficult, Prabhakhar more hurt.

"Anything else?" he asks.

Stacy has many questions. About Jason, about the IMS incident and how the alert must have been deactivated by a senior officer. But she can't ask those questions without the crew seeing her as a security threat.

"No," she says. "But thank you for still agreeing to do the interview."

"Like you said yesterday, it's good for my kid to see me doing something." Prabhakhar's grip on the railing tightens. "Let him know why he has an absent father."

"Are you okay?"

His shoulders slump, even in the zero-g. "Yeah, just… Vanessa says I need to send more videos for Ayaan, but there's never enough time." He gestures to the table. "Speaking of, I need to finish breakfast so I can get back to work."

Prabhakhar floats back to the officers' table, head bowed. After he clips himself back into place, he attacks his oatmeal with cold efficiency. Stacy takes her place beside him.

After several moments, the foreside door opens, and General Young enters. The military personnel snap salutes. Young returns their salutes, then signals to Gulati before taking a spot at the officers' table directly across from Stacy.

The others lapse again into silence. The general's eyes become distant as she presumably opens reading material in her implant. The general has seen Stacy's report. She must have, and she must know what a disaster it has become.

Young turns to Stacy. "I liked your second report. It raised some points the public often ignores."

After what the report did to both Tío and Prabhakhar, Stacy can't bring herself to smile. "I—"

"I'd like to speak to you in my quarters."

The public request makes it feel as though the general wants the crew to know Stacy is being punished. Stacy hesitates.

Young's eyes bore into Stacy's. "Now would be a good time."

TEN

STACY TAKES WHAT is becoming her regular place in the general's quarters and clears her expression in preparation for receiving a reprimand. She doesn't know the exact reason why she's here, and the fact that there are so many possible reasons is probably a bad sign.

Young hooks herself into place beside her computer and begins shoveling into her oatmeal. It smells like cinnamon, apple, and lemon. Stacy's stomach growls.

"Sorry for eating in front of you," says Young, "but I have to combine all my meals with work."

"I understand." Stacy thinks of her own breakfast waiting for her in the galley.

It occurs to Stacy that the general is one of the few people on the station to have the permissions to send a signal to the IMS and to silence the alarm. Stacy considers asking about it to shock Young into revealing an answer, but decides to wait until she investigates more.

Young swallows her first bite. "Your first interview was informative, if short. Sergeant Montoya introduced the starship, and you led viewers in a logical fashion to an under-standing of how dangerous the Inorganics could be."

"You liked it?" Stacy beams. It's high praise coming from the general. Then Stacy remembers Montoya's face, twisting as he realized what she'd led him to say. "But—"

"But it was ineffective." Young nods in the direction of the galley. "Worse, you created tension on my station. We're in enough danger with the inherent risks of space and the Inorganics. We can't afford tension."

"I know. I didn't mean—"

"I know you didn't mean to cause problems." Young finishes the last of her oatmeal. It must have taken her under two minutes. "I'll remind you that loneliness is its own danger. I'm sure you've heard about the studies on the psychological damage caused by isolation, and we're isolated enough without you isolating yourself from everyone onboard the station."

"I'm sorry. But—"

"I don't know what you're going to do about it, but you need to make it right, whether you think the incident was your fault or not. If you were part of my crew, that would be an order."

Montoya had already rejected Stacy's apology in front of the entire galley. How can she overcome that resistance and make up for the public humiliation he's experienced because of her?

During the transit, Stacy often ate with Thor, Tío, Prabhakhar, and the others. She played cards and strategy boardgames with them. She told stories from her career and listened to their stories of life on stations or bases far from Earth. She thought they were friends. But this morning in the galley, she was shunned.

"How do you do it?" Stacy points to the walls. "You don't have any pictures of friends or family."

"No." Young stares at the opposite wall. Moments pass, and Stacy is about to change the subject when Young speaks again.

"I used to have pictures of my cadre from the Academy. But we drifted, and most of them left the Force. I tried to keep in touch. They didn't. And I realized how ephemeral friendship is, especially if you're always moving."

"I'm sorry," says Stacy. "I know that's hard."

"I expect you're in a similar situation."

"I still have friends, but I don't see them often. I usually don't travel quite this far, but I'm on the road a lot."

"Hmm. Well, you're better at it than I am."

"I'm sorry you feel alone. But at least you set up the environment here so no one else feels alone."

"Yes, there's that. Anyway," says Young, "as I said, the interview was good, but—"

"But you think I shouldn't have done it."

"It could have been handled better. In the future, I will choose the interview subjects."

Other leaders have tried to control her reporting. Lopez in Uruguay, Malenchenko in Russia, Wilmot in Maine. Many others.

"Do you think interviews will be effective?" Stacy asks. "Sergeant Montoya announced to the world that the Inorganics are building the Solar System's first starship, and people reacted by making videos making fun of him."

Young frowns. "What do you recommend?"

"We need something big. Like that attack on my first day. That would have been great if Instant USA hadn't stolen it. Is there something like that we could use? Not an attack, but an event, I guess, where your crew is doing something?"

Young taps her arm. "That's an idea. I'll give it thought. In the meantime, we'll continue the interviews. I scheduled you to meet Sergeant Harrison at 1200."

"I don't like that you're choosing the interview subjects for me," says Stacy. "If I'm going to be showing the situation out here, I need to be the one deciding who to talk to."

Young shrugs. "You have a poor track record here in how you handle these stories. You have two hours and five minutes to prepare for the next one."

Not enough time to research Harrison's specialties and determine the best questions. Young probably knows that.

"Meet Harrison and me in the Analysis Room." Young smiles. "Now, for a more pleasant topic, when would you like to watch our next rom-com?"

WHEN STACY RETURNS to the galley, no one meets her eyes except Gulati, who does so apologetically. Stacy picks up her oatmeal and escapes to the observation module. Young is right: Stacy has to fix this situation.

A noise comes from the zenith cupola, a non-sexual noise. Stacy kicks off toward the cupola to see who it is.

Contreras floats at the top, staring out the central window at the asteroid, his expression unreadable. She wonders if he is thinking about his cousin, or maybe the general rejecting his plan to use the IMS to attack the Inorganics.

Finding Contreras alone, outside hearing range of anyone else, means he might be more willing to talk about taboo subjects. This kind of opportunity doesn't happen often on a station this crowded.

"Hey." Stacy takes a place beside Contreras and takes a bite of oatmeal.

Contreras glances at her. "Hey. Most people eat in the galley."

Stacy swallows her bite. "I wanted to escape the glares."

"Right. Because of the Tío thing." Contreras gives her a sympathetic smile. "Tío's great, but he's dead wrong about the Innies. Still, not a cool move on your part."

"I wish I could make up for it."

"Good luck." He returns to staring out the window toward Juno.

"What happened to your cousin?" she asks.

Contreras stiffens. "I never told you during transit?"

"No, not any details. Just that it happened." Stacy pauses with her spoon held to her mouth, then sets it into the bowl. "I'm sorry if it's an uncomfortable question. You don't have to talk about it if you don't want."

"Someone always asks. It's okay." Contreras plays with his bracelet for a moment, then lowers his hand. He looks older than his thirty-two years. "It was on Mars. Juan, my older cousin, was there with the SDF to convert the base into a colony. Would have been years after you left. We were close, and I was proud of him.

"He was sent on a raid to the Innie base. He never came back. I don't know how far he got into the base, if he set foot inside at all, and I don't know exactly how he died, and I don't think I want to know. But I do know the Innies are cold-blooded killers, and not many people seem to care. But I think you understand."

"Yes." Stacy pauses for a moment. "What were they raiding the base for?"

Contreras shakes his head. "Don't know. It's classified."

"Would you want to give an interview about it?"

Contreras makes a face. "I don't want to sell out my cousin for some article."

"It's not…It's a way of making your cousin's death mean something."

"It's pity porn. No."

Stacy considers pushing more, but she doesn't talk to reporters about the incident that killed her father. She can't ask him to do something similar. "I understand."

For several moments, she floats in silence next to him. "Would Jason convince people? That the Inorganics are dangerous?"

Contreras's eyes narrow. "What do you know about Jason?"

For a moment, Stacy considers pretending to know Jason's purpose, but can't force herself to lie about it. "Not much."

"Too bad." Contreras turns away. "Not going to leak information to the press. Not sure why you thought I was the kind of person who would do that."

"I wasn…" Actually, it is exactly what she hoped to do. "It's important that the public knows the truth. I don't want to get you in trouble, though. Is there anything *un*classified you could tell me?"

"Just that I'm going to have to let General Young know you're asking about it. But you know she'd have learned one way or another."

True. Young would have her ways to discover everything happening on the station. "I guess so."

Contreras opens his mouth, but pauses when a shadow passes across them. Harrison enters the cupola and stops meters away.

"Found you." She nods to Stacy, her eyes never wavering.

"Hi." Stacy glances down at her bowl. Half is left. She understands why Young sprints through her meals.

"I wanted to go over the script with you before the interview."

"Script?"

"Yeah. Figure out what you're going to ask me, and maybe I'll give you some suggestions for good questions."

Contreras mumbles something to himself and pushes off from the railing. "Should probably work out again." He waves as he ducks past Harrison and leaves the cupola.

Harrison takes his spot at the window, but doesn't look outside. "What questions are on your list?"

"Well." Stacy frowns. "I don't like to talk about it beforehand. I don't want it to sound rehearsed."

"It won't. I've practiced making it not sound rehearsed. And you can fix it in post. Run it through some filters or something. Make me look heroic and intimidating." Harrison grins. "But seriously, it's a good way for us to get on the same page so I say what you and the general are looking for."

Stacy shakes her head. "That's not how I work."

"I also don't want to get blindsided like Tío." Harrison says it in a matter-of-fact way, as though Stacy hurting her interview subjects were one of the fundamentals of the Universe.

Stacy takes a breath. "I'll try not to."

"Okay." Harrison raps her knuckles against the railing. "We can improv it. Thought I would make it easier on us, but you're calling the shots. See you in a few."

WHEN STACY ENTERS the Analysis Room an hour later, Halabi and Ko float over Thor's shoulder, heads down. Thor indicates Stacy.

"Maybe we should talk about it later?"

Halabi nods. "Good call."

At the back of the room, the general watches as though surveying her kingdom. She nods to Stacy, the trace of a smile on her lips, then returns her attention to her screen.

"Where did you want me?" asks Harrison.

"Did you want to be at your station?" Stacy hooks herself into place in front of one of the consoles. "We could get a clip of you at work before we start the interview."

As Harrison slips into place, Stacy deploys her nanocams to different locations and angles. For N5, she finds a nice spot tucked between the ceiling corner and one of the screens, hidden from casual view. Maybe not a good angle for this interview, but it might be useful later.

Once she checks the nanocam feeds, Stacy signals her implant to start recording. Since the general announced the interview at the last moment, Stacy didn't have time to prepare a topic, so she'll have to ask questions and hope one leads down a favorable path.

"Sergeant," says Stacy, "please introduce yourself and talk about what you do here. Also, when I ask a question, please respond by rephrasing the question so I don't need to have a recording of myself asking the question."

General Young frowns at the last sentence, but quickly returns to tapping at her screen.

Harrison stands straight, hands behind her back. "I am Staff Sergeant Tina Harrison. I operate the science instruments aboard Collins Station and perform maintenance duties."

"What are your maintenance duties?"

"My maintenance duties can be anything from fixing the toilets to repairing damaged solar cells during a spacewalk." Harrison gestures to the computer. "My more glamorous duties are monitoring and repairing the science instruments and analyzing the results from them. We study the activities and emissions of the Inorganics to determine what equipment they have onboard the starship and to study their behavior. From those observations, we make preliminary extrapolations about what they'll do once the starship reaches its destination."

Stacy hesitates. The follow-up question is obvious, and asking it feels dirty. "What are those extrapolations?"

"We can make reasonable guesses, based on what they've done in our system. They set themselves up on planets, moons, asteroids, or Kuiper Belt objects and mine for supplies. We still don't know what they're doing in the atmospheres of the gas giants. In our solar system, because the Inorganics have already skimmed the top layers and collected the easiest-to-get resources, it's harder for us to get anything usable from the planets and asteroids. It takes more fuel, more human-hours, and more wear-and-tear on vehicles to retrieve materials, if we can get anything at all. So when we get to the Proxima system, the Inorganics will already have had a head start. We'll already be making a difficult journey to get there in the first place, and doing anything useful there will be much more difficult than it should have been."

Thor, Halabi, and Ko have given up any pretense of ignoring the interview. They nod at Harrison's statement.

Harrison's eyes flick toward the general for a moment. General Young nods, almost imperceptibly. The oculars catch it.

"Someday," Harrison continues, "the Inorganics will have taken everything easily accessible, and we'll be stuck here wondering why we didn't do anything about it earlier. And they'll do the same thing in the Proxima system, and the system after that, and the one after that, and on and on. We'll always be behind, with nothing left but their scraps. And we are letting it happen, every moment we sit here and just watch."

Harrison's statements beautifully capture the sentiments Stacy and the general want to express. But they were obviously rehearsed, like the worst of the biased conspiracy-theory videos she's seen. Harrison is like a deepfake that isn't faked.

"I think that's it," says Stacy. "Thank you for taking the time to talk to me."

"I've got more." Harrison's eyes dart to Young.

"That's okay." Stacy stops recording and retrieves her nano-cams. "I'll let you know when the finished version's out."

It will take a lot of editing to remove all hints of bias from this report. Before Young can say anything, Stacy heads to the galley for some coffee.

ELEVEN

AFTER OVER SIX hours of editing video and audio in the comfort of her sleeping bag, Stacy finishes the best report she could get from the Harrison interview. Harrison's statements sound less authoritative and more like one person's opinion, although the forcefulness of her opinion will sway people.

Harrison responds to Stacy's request for rebuttal within minutes. "I need a longer interview next time."

Young hasn't responded to the rebuttal request yet, which gives Stacy time to find another interview subject before the general assigns one. Anderson has a viewpoint opposite Harrison's, although Stacy doesn't agree with Anderson's admiration of the Inorganics.

Shift 2 is on duty, which means Anderson will start in the Analysis Room before moving to the Power Room. Catching her alone would reduce the chances of Young's interference. After a thirty-minute nap that leaves Stacy more groggy than rested, she slips from her quarters.

Anderson isn't in the Analysis Room when Stacy passes through. Stacy waves to Young, Prabhakhar, and Contreras as she continues.

She's just outside the Power Room's door when her implant pings. A message from Trevor.

Hey, beautiful. I looked more into the Jason thing. You said Jason might not be a person, so I wondered if it were an acronym. I checked all the acronym sections in unclassified military documents on the Inorganics and Collins Station. There was one JASON, but it seems unrelated: Jovian-Atmosphere Sampling and ONboard analyzer. Typical forced acronym. It was being developed back in the Europa days, but they never built a prototype. So we still don't know what Jason is, but we at least know it's not an acronym. Or not a publicly known one.

Disappointing, but not unexpected. Trevor has little access to classified resources, which means Stacy will need to dig for the truth at Collins. She starts a message saying she will continue to look, but then deletes it. Young is almost certainly reading Stacy's correspondence.

Stacy closes her messages and opens the Power Room door. She hasn't been here since the disastrous interview with Montoya. Where the room before had the solemn austerity typical of the station, now vivid posters of the Liverpool soccer team cover most of the wall space between screens, even the floor and ceiling.

Anderson floats in front of a screen at the room's midway point. She doesn't look up as the door closes behind Stacy.

Stacy glides toward her. "Are those regulation decorations?"

Anderson's head jerks up. "Oh, hi." She glances at the posters. "No, I guess not. Those are Tío's."

"They're colorful."

Anderson smiles. "He said there aren't many Liverpool fans out here, so he's trying to make up for it by being loud."

Stacy laughs. "I'm sure they'd be proud to know they have at least one fan in the Asteroid Belt." She releases her nanocams, activates her oculars, and taps her head to indicate she is recording. "Can I ask you some questions?"

Anderson watches the nanocams buzz into position around her. "I…don't think so. I remember what happened with Tío."

Stacy winces. "I didn't mean for that to happen."

"I don't blame you, in a way," says Anderson. "It's a reporter's job to make people reveal what they don't want to. It's just that you usually end up hurting people that way. But reporters don't care about that."

"I'm sorry you feel that way about it," says Stacy. "I never want to hurt people, and I try to represent them with sympathy."

Anderson nods and returns to tapping at her screen.

As Stacy tries to think of how she can encourage Anderson to speak about the Inorganics, something about the screens and the room's shape makes her remember the overheard conversation between Cazador and Ko. "The other day, I heard speculation that someone deactivated the alarms for the IMS crossing the altitude threshold."

"Oh." Anderson seems lost in thought for several moments, probably realizing that she wouldn't be at fault if she'd been the victim of sabotage. "Who said that?"

"I can't reveal my sources. But they didn't realize I was in the room while they were talking."

"Yeah. I still should have been paying attention to the IMS, but...if someone sent commands to deliberately turn off the alarms...the SDF should know. I should tell the general. Unless..."

The implication has hit Anderson: The culprit would have been someone high-ranking. Stacy pulls herself closer to get a better view of the screen.

Anderson waves her back. "Okay, I'll look, but the information is still classified. You can't record it, and I'm not going to talk to you about it. And General Young and Major Prabhakhar are already investigating, so maybe I'm not supposed to be looking, but..."

"I understand." Stacy doesn't want to get the lieutenant court-martialed. She deactivates her oculars and recalls her nanocams. She won't have concrete information for a report, but the lieutenant's reaction will at least give Stacy an idea of what the telemetry contains.

"Okay," says Anderson, "it should..."

Her jaw drops. She scans the screen.

"What is it?" Stacy has to keep herself from approaching the screen again.

"The telemetry's been erased."

"The…" Someone has removed the evidence. "All of it?"

Anderson hits a key, and her screen goes blank. "I shouldn't have said that."

"Who do you think deleted it?"

Anderson straightens, as though remembering instructions on how to say no. "I don't feel comfortable with this conversation."

"Sorry. You don't have to respond. I'm just thinking out loud."

The deletion of evidence all but confirms the sabotage. It wasn't Anderson; she seems genuinely shocked at the revelation. Maybe an external saboteur erased it, but the main suspects are the people with the authority to send the commands to the IMS.

Stacy doesn't know what motive any of them could have had for causing the destruction of an important military asset. Although, if the story weren't stolen and altered by Instant USA, it could have caused a sensation for at least a day. She knows of one person on the station who wanted that result.

"There you are."

Stacy turns to see General Young entering the Power Room. The general glances between Stacy and Anderson.

"Are you looking for me?" Stacy hopes her guilt doesn't show.

"Yes." Young hooks herself into place beside Stacy. Does she know what Stacy asked Anderson? She can probably infer the conversation from Stacy's expression and Anderson's stiffness. "I'd like to speak to you in private. We can move into the hallway and let the lieutenant continue working."

"Yes, ma'am." Anderson looks shaken as she turns back to her screen.

"Okay." Stacy follows Young into the hallway and grabs the railing as the door shuts.

Young hooks her feet into holds beside Stacy. Her eyes seem…buoyant, maybe? Not the expression of someone about to issue a reprimand or threat. "I need you to remove a clip from your interview with Harrison."

"Oh." Stacy tries not to let her relief show. "Remove a clip? Which clip?"

"There is one moment where Sergeant Harrison glances at me, and I nod to her."

"Ohhhh." Stacy pulls up the video from her oculars and reviews it. Removing the clip would do little harm to the overall story, but the censorship itself would establish a precedent in her relationship with the general. "You're worried people will…misinterpret it?"

Young laughs. "I'm worried they'll interpret it *correctly*. I would like you to either remove it entirely or dub the audio over another video."

The Harrison interview keeps getting worse, but Young won't clear her report for release if the change aren't made. Stacy has to admit, it wouldn't be so bad to promote this version of the Inorganics, to leave no room for doubt about the threat they pose. But is it the right conclusion, if Young has to sabotage the IMS and remove hints of collaboration between Harrison and her?

Young is staring at her.

"I have footage from the nanocams," Stacy says after several moments. She has no choice. "Or I could use footage of the Inorganics, if you have any."

"Good idea," says Young. "I'll see if there's anything we can release to the public. I also have another topic to talk to you about."

Here it comes. Young will warn her off the IMS investigation.

Young's stern face breaks into a slow smile. "Cheesy rom-com tonight?"

Stacy lets out her breath. "Sure." She laughs and enters a reminder in her calendar.

"One last thing." Young's voice has lost its warmth.

Stacy closes her implant. "Yes?"

"Stop looking into Jason. You are not authorized to report on that subject."

Stacy hides a smile. Young's response means Stacy is on the right track. It also means she doesn't know Stacy is investigating the IMS.

Stacy says nothing.

"Tonight, then." Young leaves for the next module.

AS YOUNG TURNS to leave, the "Close While Far" ringtone sounds in Stacy's implant. A message from Trevor.

The moment Stacy opens the message, Young stops at the far door and turns to her with a knowing expression. Their eyes lock for a moment. Then Young gives a slight nod, opens the door, and leaves the module.

Stacy resigns herself to the fact that Young is reading Trevor's message right now, at the same time Stacy is reading it. It's unfair that Young is so suspicious of Stacy when Young is the one who likely orchestrated the IMS incident. She wishes Trevor could deliver the message in person, both to avoid General Young seeing their correspondence and so she could hold him and breathe the same air as him.

Still missing you, sweetheart. I'm hoping the Inorganics hurry up and launch so you can come home.

I interviewed several former Collins crewmembers. A lot of the people I contacted didn't respond. The only ones who did aren't in the SDF anymore. I don't know if someone's blocking current members from responding, or if the individuals are censoring themselves.

The transcripts are attached, but the main takeaway is that they either don't know who or what Jason is, or they're unwilling to say. They all hushed up when I asked them about the Inorganics. They talked about life aboard the station, but I'm not sure how useful that is.

None of the former crewmembers denied the existence of Jason. Between their implicit confirmation and Young's earlier warning, Stacy knows she has to continue the search.

She has one remaining lead: Tío mentioned Thor working with Jason. Thor is an attitude and electrical-systems engineer, so he should spend most of his shifts in either the Analysis Room or the Power Room. She might discover a clue if he spends significant on-shift time elsewhere.

She could eliminate most modules from consideration: the officers' habitation module, the galley, the fitness module, the enlisteds' habitation module, and the Analysis Room receive too much traffic to hide secrets. Which means she only needs to determine the traffic patterns through a few modules.

She pulls N1 from her pocket. Despite the crates lashed into place along the walls and straps fluttering from the walls like jellyfish tentacles, there are no good hiding places in this corridor. She settles for parking it in a corner that gives a view of the forward entrance and the doors to the Power Room and Records Room. It *should* remain undetected if no one glances at the corner too long. She hopes.

In the Machining Room in Module 9, she places N2 beside a crate facing the entrance from Module 8. With the cover provided by all the jutting edges from folded machines and crates strapped to walls, no one will find this nanocam without a lot of luck. In the last module, she places N3 above the docking port where it blends with the indicator lights. Her traps are set.

THE NEXT DAY, Stacy retrieves her nanocams and speeds through the videos they recorded. Anderson and Thor spent a lot of time in the Power Room. Montoya, Sergeant Jalindo, and the other maintenance personnel went everywhere. As expected. But Thor, Prabhakhar, and Gallegos entered the Machining and Storage Room once each shift.

Their patterns might be unrelated to Jason, but *something* is happening in that room. Thor specializes in attitude and electrical systems, Prabhakhar in orbits and propulsion, and Gallegos is the doctor and an information-technology specialist. What do they have in common?

Crates and machining tools dominate the Machining Room. Maybe Thor and the others are building something with parts in the crates? A weapon to fight the Inorganics?

Stacy heads to the galley. It is time to set up an interview with Prabhakhar, and she knows where she wants to have it.

TWELVE

STACY WAITS AT the Machining Room's entrance, nanocams floating at her shoulders. The smells of oil and burnt metal curl through the room.

When Prabhakhar enters, Stacy smiles. "Hi!" she says.

"Hello." Prabhakhar floats past her and grabs a strap dangling from an overhead crate. "Where did you want me?"

As Stacy opens her mouth to respond, General Young passes through the doorway and into the Machining Room. She glides to the ceiling and grabs a handhold.

"I know you weren't expecting me." Young meets Stacy's eyes. "But I wanted to watch."

Straps tap against walls, an arhythmic melody against the accompaniment of vented air. A thin current of air forms a temporary eddy along Stacy's neck before dissipating.

"Is here fine, then?" asks Prabhakhar.

"Oh, sorry." Stacy gestures to the back of the room. "Let's do the interview there."

Stacy hopes Prabhakhar or Young, in a moment of absent-mindedness, will gaze in the direction of whatever they have hidden in this room. But they face forward, only glancing to their sides so they can grab objects to propel themselves, and their eyes betray nothing.

Prabhakhar pulls himself to a stop at the far wall, between a lathe to his right and a crate on his left. Did he choose this spot because it is far from anything of interest in the room? Stacy grabs a handhold on the ceiling in the middle of the room.

Young halts beside Stacy. Stacy adjusts her ocular's settings and maneuvers her nanocams into place, ignoring Young for the moment.

"Why did you choose the Machining Room?" asks Young. "Major Prabhakhar spends the majority of his on-shift time in the Analysis Room. Wouldn't it be more appropriate for this interview?"

Stacy checks the feeds from her nanocams, taking time to collect her thoughts. "I've already done an interview in the Analysis Room. I wanted a new scene to show viewers some variety."

Young says nothing.

Prabhakhar clears his throat. "You think this will impress Vanessa and Ayaan?" He looks hopeful, almost pleading, as he shifts the positions of his arms.

"Of course!" Stacy frames her shot, including the lathe and crate to provide details of the scene. "You're an expert, and you're in space on our most important outpost. Everyone's going to be impressed, especially your family."

"I hope so." Prabhakhar glances around the room, but not at anything in particular. Young seems to stiffen beside Stacy.

Stacy gives Prabhakhar her standard spiel about how to answer questions. "Maybe you can start by telling us your duties on the station, and we can go from there."

Prabhakhar waves, and Stacy has the sudden realization of how awkward this interview is going to be. She wants him to look good for his family.

But his family is probably used to his mannerisms. Hopefully. He does spend a lot of time away from home.

"Hello. I'm Major Nihar Prabhakhar, in charge of orbits and propulsion aboard Collins Station. I plan maneuvers to correct our orbit when perturbations from Juno's gravity or solar radiation pressure or other factors start changing it too much. I also analyze the behavior of the Inorganics."

"Do you have any other duties aboard the station?"

Young shifts position beside Stacy, but Stacy can't tell if it is from relaxing or tensing. Prabhakhar appears to not notice.

"I think everything I do," says Prabhakhar, "could be broadly categorized in the previous items I mentioned."

An evasive answer. Stacy considers pursuing that line, but knows she can't convince him to reveal anything classified, especially not with Young watching.

"During the five years Collins Station has been operating," Stacy asks, "what have you learned about the Inorganics?"

Prabhakhar glances at Young for an instant before facing Stacy again. He folds his arms across his chest. "Well, I can't say everything we've learned about the Inorganics because some of it is classified. But I can say that, every time we think we have a grasp on their behavior, it either changes, or they do something we would never have predicted. It's frustrating and fascinating all at once. They're one of the greatest mysteries of our time."

His tone borders on the awe Montoya showed in that first interview. "Would you say they're intelligent?"

"Oh, yes."

"Oh."

Prabhakhar spoke with such matter-of-factness, Stacy doubts he realizes the enormity of what he just said. He stares at her now as though waiting for the next question. She turns to gauge Young's reaction. The general looks as though she might guillotine Prabhakhar.

This would be huge news for viewers, laypeople and scientists alike. If Prabhakhar is right, it means the Inorganics are sentient. It means they have a methodical plan for sweeping through the Solar System and into the next star system, and they aren't blindly following their programming. It means they deliberately crashed that meteorite into Mars.

It means they murdered Stacy's father.

"Sorry," says Stacy. "I wasn't expecting you to say that."

"I apologize. I didn't answer the right way." Prabhakhar pauses. "I know you want us to phrase it as a full sentence. We think the Inorganics are intelligent. Most people think of them like robots. Automatons carrying out their programming. But what makes them so dangerous is their intelligence. They're good at learning and solving problems, and their ability to manipulate physics is far beyond ours."

"So they're even more intelligent than humans?"

Prabhakhar's lips thin. "Hmm. Maybe I'm not explaining what I mean by intelligence. Other animals are intelligent, like squirrels and snakes. They react to their environment, they have basic problem-solving skills, and they use simple tools. It doesn't mean they have any deep comprehension of their actions."

Young relaxes.

"So," says Stacy, "you're saying the Inorganics are like… squirrels and snakes?"

"Maybe. Inorganics have better problem-solving skills, but we have no evidence they have any comprehension of what they're doing. They follow their programming, like…worms follow their own simple programming. That's the level of intelligence I'm talking about here."

"So we don't know if they have any comprehension, or… emotions?"

"Hm." Prabhakhar frowns. "Scientists and engineers have written about that, about their comprehension abilities or whether they have emotions. The general public hasn't seen the papers. They've been classified until now. But General Young gave us permission to…"

Young nods.

"So, yes. I can point you to those papers. Interesting question. Emotions are what encourage us to pursue beneficial behaviors. We love things, we hate things, we're scared of things. We know animals experience emotions, but the AIs the Inorganics originated from were not advanced enough to have emotions. We've done a lot of work on that subject here, with—"

Young clears her throat. Prabhakhar freezes. Did his eyes dart to the side? What did he just look at?

"Sorry. So, the original Inorganics, they just had the simple mechanisms to avoid or seek out certain behaviors and experiences. That's all we needed them to have when they were mining asteroids for us. But have they developed emotions since they left? We can't say. If they have, their behavior wouldn't look any different than it does now."

Young shifts and her face tightens again.

"So," says Stacy, "we would have to dissect one to find out if they have emotions?"

Prabhakhar pauses. "I don't think dissecting them would help, but maybe a brain scan. Or the equivalent. We could search through their programming if we had the ability to decode their circuit boards, and that would tell us if they have emotions. I doubt knowing would even matter, though. Sharks have emotions, but we don't treat them any differently because of it."

"That's really interesting," says Stacy. "So, maybe there's some other quality that would make us treat them like people? Like consciousness or if they have souls?"

Prabhakhar raises his hands. "I don't want to get into *that* conversation. It's beyond my expertise. But consciousness is an interesting topic, especially with regard to the Inorganics."

"Do you think they're conscious?"

Do they have moral responsibility for my father's death?

Prabhakhar begins to turn toward the general, but halts. "Well, we can't say anything about whether the Inorganics are conscious. We're still defining consciousness."

"What do you define it as?"

"To…be aware of ourselves. To know we exist separately from our environment. That we are a separate collection of atoms and neurons than other people and other animals and plants. To know about our thoughts and to think about those thoughts. Animals can be intelligent without being conscious. We don't know enough about Inorganics to be certain if they have that ability, but I expect they'll just be like that: intelligent, but not conscious."

"If you don't have consciousness, can you have a conscience or morals?"

Stacy feels guilty as she imagines the smile Young is suppressing at that question. Even though it is a valid question, she is asking the same sort of question Young would ask to manipulate someone. Does it mean she is as manipulative as Young? Has she always been this way?

Prabhakhar pauses. His expression twists for a moment, as though trying to determine if she is treating him like she did Montoya. She hates that she has that effect on people.

"I guess…not? If you don't have consciousness, maybe you can't have a conscience or morals. If you can't conceive that there are other minds out there who could be hurt by your actions, you wouldn't think there's anything wrong with anything you do."

"Hm." Stacy considers. "So if that type of personality were human, it would be a psychopath, right?"

Prabhakhar coughs. "Well, psychopaths are conscious. They just lack empathy. But even if Inorganics aren't conscious, their behavior might be similar to that of psychopaths."

"And you're studying their behavior to find out if—"

"We should stop the interview here," says Young.

Prabhakhar looks relieved. "Ma'am."

"Wait." Stacy adjusts her grip on the ceiling handhold. "I'm just trying to understand more about them."

Young studies her for a moment. Finally, she nods. Prabhakhar shifts, his eyes darting downward.

Stacy pushes ahead before Young changes her mind. "Going back to an early point, you said we should be evaluating all our information in terms of how we should react to the Inorganics. What are your conclusions about that? How should we react to them?"

Stacy can imagine Young tensing, wondering if Prabhakhar will answer in a way that will shock viewers out of complacency.

Prabhakhar's eyes dart around before looking at Stacy. "Yeah, theory and practice are two different things. They're fascinating to study, but…The Inorganics are dangerous. It doesn't matter if they're not conscious or don't have souls or whatever. Like sharks. Sharks aren't going to write novels or symphonies, but you don't want to be alone with one. The Inorganics do what they want and ignore us because we're not relevant to them. It would go very badly for us if we ever came to their attention. If our needs conflicted with theirs."

"But you think our needs will conflict," says Stacy. "If not now, in the future."

"They will," says Prabhakhar. "It's a matter of time."

Perfect.

ONCE THE INTERVIEW ends, Prabhakhar and Young leave, but Stacy claims to need to stay in the Machining Room to take establishing shots. She places all five of her nanocams around the room so they cover the entire space.

But is she doing the wrong thing by hunting Jason? It's tangential to her main job here, the job that could change society. If the knowledge of Jason damages Young's and Stacy's cause, is it unethical to tell the public? She'll have to decide when she finds out what Jason is.

Stacy heads to the galley. When she enters, Sergeant Jalindo shoots past her to the kitchen and hands an empty tray to Gulati.

Gulati smirks. "You sure you didn't want any more fruit with that?"

Jalindo laughs out of proportion with the question. Even Prabhakhar and Anderson crack tiny smiles.

Stacy stops at one of the tables. "What's—"

"Ms. Sterling." Jalindo kicks toward the aft door and rolls upward so they face the ceiling, looking as though they are floating on their back in water. "You still haven't made me famous. What's taking so long?"

Stacy laughs. "I already wrote down that I need to make you a star."

"I don't have to be a star." Jalindo swings themself to a stop along the far wall. "I just want people to still be talking about me a million years from now. However famous that is, whatever that's called, that's what I want."

"Well, I'll see what I can do."

Gulati laughs from the kitchen. "Sounds like famous last words."

Jalindo gives her a thumbs-up while exiting. "Emphasis on the 'famous.' See you all later."

Gulati raises an empty drinking bulb in Stacy's direction, but Stacy waves a hand. "Sorry, I'm just passing through."

Before Stacy can continue, the forward door opens, and Young floats through. Her eyes snap to Stacy. "Ms. Sterling." She pulls herself to a halt beside Stacy. "Care to accompany me to the Machining Room to collect the nanocams you placed there?"

"Oh." Stacy glances aft. How did Young find out? "Okay."

While most people would watch Stacy's awkward exit, and Gulati does, Prabhakhar and Anderson bow their heads as if to spare her the embarrassment. When Stacy and Young enter the Observation Module and the door closes, Young turns to her.

"I'd like to applaud your diligence in your investigation," says Young, "but you are searching for classified material."

Stacy holds onto the doorframe to keep from rotating. "I'm sorry, but that's my job."

Young sighs. "I know. I contacted Command asking for authorization to give you access to a certain area, and their approval came two minutes ago. So now I won't have to arrest you when you dig more."

Stacy doesn't know whether to laugh or take the statement seriously. "What made you ask for the authorization?"

Young gestures aft. "You were on the verge of figuring it out for yourself. I suspect you scheduled the interview with Major Prabhakhar in here to see if he accidentally revealed something."

Stacy says nothing.

Young's voice softens. "You did well with the Harrison interview and presumably with the Prabhakhar interview. But this topic will be contentious. Very contentious. No matter what we do, some people are going to be outraged, and some fringe elements will be frothing at the mouth more than usual."

"Fringe elements? Like whom?"

"The regulars. Hoaxers, anti-military groups, anti-science groups, the weirder religions."

"I never like their comments on my articles."

Young laughs bitterly. "No. Equal parts passion and incoherence. I wanted to delay revealing this aspect of our operations because it will potentially draw attention to the wrong things."

"I understand."

"I'll summon the appropriate people to join us." Young blinks four times and pauses for a few seconds. "Let's go. You should start recording now."

Stacy starts recording and taps the side of her head. Young nods, then, with Stacy following, glides through several modules and stops just outside the door to the Machining Room. Stacy hooks her legs around the railing beside her.

"It's time," says Young, "to show the public a project we've been working on the last few decades."

"Decades?" So the project pre-dates Collins Station. "I didn't realize. Is it a weapon?"

"Unfortunately, no. It's also not a way to make us more competitive with the Inorganics, but it might help us understand them better."

Young opens the door. At first glance, the Machining Room looks no different than it did minutes ago: uncomfortable, and hazardous to the careless. But there, at the port wall at the opposite end of the room, Gallegos and Thor bob in place beside an unfolded computer screen. Text flows up the screen at a rapid clip.

"Hi," says Stacy.

The others nod, each with a solemn expression. A swoosh sound comes from behind, and Prabhakhar enters. He joins Gallegos and Thor.

Stacy glides toward them, grabbing a protruding crate halfway through the room to stop herself. "Is this an intervention?"

Young plucks a nanocam from the wall and hands it to her. "If only an intervention would work on you."

Stacy now has a clearer view of the screen the others are gathered around. Its edges are worn, the screen gouged, and its fans give off a low-pitched hum rivaling the station's air-circulation system in volume.

"That's…it?" The secret the general was hiding, that others were forbidden to discuss or even mention, is nothing more than an out-of-date computer. She expected something like a cannon or a piece of the starship or even a chunk of asteroid the Inorganics touched. "This is what you've been hiding?"

Gallegos beckons her closer. "Check it out."

Stacy takes the indicated spot in front of the screen, but it does nothing to increase her comprehension. The characters scrolling up the screen form words and phrases, like 'Rotate 90' or 'Extend 15,' that might mean something to a programmer or an analyst, but not a journalist. "I don't understand what's going on."

Gallegos taps the console. "It's an AI with the exact same source code as the original Inorganics before they became the Inorganics."

Prabhakhar nods. "This is Jason."

THIRTEEN

NEITHER GENERAL YOUNG, nor Prabhakhar, nor Gallegos, nor Thor avert their eyes. They don't have guilty expressions. They float near the computer, watching Stacy, as though expecting relief or laughter or praise.

Stacy maintains a normal volume. "You named it?"

Prabhakhar flinches. "Well, it's not an official name. We—"

"Sorry." Stacy doesn't try to hide the quivering in her voice. "That's not what's important. This…thing is one of the original Inorganics? The ones that…mutinied?"

Gallegos's amusement vanishes. "Well…not exactly. It's a copy of the source code of one of the models."

"And you have it here? On the station?"

This whole time, Stacy thought her enemies were thousands of kilometers away on Juno. But they've been here, with her. The hairs on her arm stand on end.

"This," says Stacy, gesturing to the computer, "is how you create a second strand of Inorganics."

"Don't worry." Gallegos looks to Young as though for a rescue. "Th—"

"Don't worry?"

Now the others have the decency to avert their eyes, all except Young. For a moment, Stacy feels a pang of guilt, but they have to face the uncomfortable truth.

"These," says Stacy, "are the beings that are loose in our solar system, that bombed the Chinese Moon base, that drove us off Europa, that killed my father, that dismantled the IMS right in front of us just a few days ago. You should delete it right now."

"It's not the same," says Gallegos.

"Yeah." Thor traces an imaginary rectangle around the computer screen. "It's not connected to anything. Completely self-contained. No access to other systems, to any communications devices, not even to our power grid. We keep it on generators, and swap those out as necessary."

She thought she'd assessed Thor accurately during their transit to Collins. She didn't think he was capable of actively supporting this type of secret project, especially given his views on secrets. Then again, he joined the military.

"So we're safe," says Gallegos.

"Yeah." Thor nods. "He's not going to get loose and vent our air into space or anything."

"'*He*'? Not 'it'?"

"Hm." Young shifts position, and the others flinch. "I agree there's some unnecessary anthropomorphizing going on."

Young should know better. Stacy and the general are supposed to be on the same side. How can the general keep an Inorganic onboard the station, knowing how dangerous it is?

"Thor's point is valid," says Prabhakhar. "We've implemented safeguards to contain the AI."

"It doesn't matter what safeguards you have," says Stacy. "You have an Inorganic aboard the station."

"Proto-Inorganic," says Gallegos.

"It's the same thing," says Stacy. "This is irresponsible. How do you know it's not already loose?"

Thor waves to indicate the station around them. "We would have noticed. We run diagnostics every shift. We take every precaution."

The designers of the proto-Inorganics thought they had taken every precaution. Yet, somehow, the Inorganics changed. Whether all at once or one at a time, their software had been altered, and they stopped taking commands from humans. They started mining the asteroids for themselves, started spreading to other planets, started making the Solar System their own. Started killing.

Prabhakhar speaks, his demeanor calm, his voice level. "Since the Inorganics escaped, we've known we need to find out what went wrong. There were multiple AI models used in the Asteroid Belt, generally one or more for each company. We had copies of the software on Earth, so when the units got loose in space, the SDF started studying the software to see what happened. We made copies, and—"

"You made copies?" It is so irresponsible and ignorant. "They're our biggest threat. And you have one here, and you have others on Earth. That sounds really dangerous."

"We have to do this research," says Gallegos. "We need to understand what created the Inorganics. It's the only way to figure out how to not make the same mistake again, and, in a more immediate sense, it's the best way to learn about the ones in the Solar System now."

Thor usually has a mocking expression, but his face now is earnest and forceful. "There are different hypotheses for what turned these AIs into the Inorganics. The leading contender is the cosmic-radiation theory, the Bit-Flip Theory. An energetic particle will make it through the satellite's shielding and will charge a register in the motherboard, flipping a bit in the source code and possibly causing a change in the spacecraft's behavior. Most people think a change like that might have created the Inorganics."

Thor has already admitted to being an adherent of the Zero-Day-Signal Theory, but he probably knows Young won't let him espouse his personal theories to the public.

"We don't know exactly what form that change took," says Gallegos. "Maybe their communications system got shut down so they couldn't receive orders. Or maybe a micrometeorite caused tiny damage that physically altered the motherboard."

Thor smiles. "Figuring that out is kind of the Holy Grail of our job out here."

"So we've been experimenting with copies of the original source code," says Gallegos. "The early investigators on Earth would flip one bit at a time, sequentially. Then combinations of bits. Nothing they tried reproduced what happened."

Stacy bites back the recriminations she wants to say. "Why are you trying the same thing again if it didn't work the first time?"

"It's not exactly the same," says Gallegos. "One speculation is that the cause of, or at least a factor in, the change was the environment out here. Maybe the specific radiation environment, maybe the gravity, maybe something else. So we run our copy of the software and monitor it for any changes that might signify a transformation into an Inorganic."

"Wait." Stacy stares Gallegos in the eyes. "You're trying to *create* an Inorganic?"

"I…"

Before Gallegos can finish the thought, the general speaks. "Yes. Because learning how to create one might give us knowledge on how to defeat them, or, more likely, how to adapt to them."

The computer screen appears innocuous enough. Underneath the text it projects, though, is a being potentially capable of complex thought and ability exceeding those of humans. The general and her crew are like mice caging a tiger.

"You *named* it." Stacy suppresses her tears. "You're treating it like a pet."

"It's…" Thor's face reddens. "Not everyone does."

"And you've been running this experiment for decades?"

Prabhakhar shrugs. "Intelligence is a complex problem."

"Maybe it's another false trail," says Gallegos. "It could be. But we want to exhaust all the possibilities before we quit."

"You should destroy it." Stacy feels as though she is shouting reason at toddlers.

"Hey." Thor raises his hands as though to ward off an attack. "We know what they did on Mars, and I really am sorry about that, but you're letting that experience cloud your judgment."

Young, Gallegos, and Prabhakhar turn to Thor. For the first time since Stacy has known him, he shrinks.

"Um…sorry," he says.

"I know I'm biased on this subject," says Stacy, "but my judgment is fine. This idea is bad, and I don't think it will turn out the way you think."

The others stare at her in awkward silence.

She moves on. "Why do you call it Jason?"

Gallegos and Thor force a laugh.

Young rolls her eyes. "It's a poor joke."

Gallegos looks embarrassed. "Its real name is Asteroid Inorganic Simulator, but we call it JCN. Jason."

"I still don't get it."

"A reference to an Arthur C. Clarke story. The AI on the ship in the story was called HAL, which was a play on IBM. IBM was a machine company at the time, and if you go down one letter in the alphabet from the initialism initials, you get HAL. So we just went up a letter instead. JCN."

"Okay." Stacy tries to smile, but doesn't think she's succeeding. "I guess that's kind of funny."

Young shakes her head. "You're giving them too much credit."

"Aw." Thor's amused expression returns. "We're four hundred million kilometers from Earth. You have to find your funny where you can."

Stacy pulls herself closer to the console, inching toward it the way she would a high-dive board. It isn't an Inorganic, not yet, and it has no physical body, but danger radiates from that console. She gestures to the text scrolling up the screen. "What do these words and phrases mean?"

"They're the names of the subroutines being run," says Thor. "The screen output gets saved to a temporary file so we can check it later if anything interesting happens. Mostly, it just lets us know the AI is working."

"Working on what?"

"It's in a simulated environment," says Prabhakhar. "It thinks it's on an asteroid, performing the tasks the original Inorganics performed. It thinks it has arms and claws and corers, and all the other equipment the original Inorganics had. We've tried different combinations of equipment that different unit models had. We're not sure which model was the first one to become what we call an Inorganic, so we test all the combinations."

"Are you assuming all the different models had the same source code?"

"Yes, sort of," says Gallegos. "The different models from the same company all had the same source code. So all the Drilling, Inc. models had the same source code as each other, and all the Asteroids For Humanity models had the same source code as each other, et cetera."

"So those programmers set us up for the mutiny." Stacy shakes her head. "Like spreading a virus between humans. Each of us is similar enough that one type of virus can infect most people."

"I guess." Gallegos shrugs. "It's a lot more efficient to do it that way."

Young taps the console. "Maybe you can continue explaining the AIS's operation. The average viewer won't care about the intricacies of the source code."

Stacy forgot she is conducting an interview and collecting footage for another report.

"Yes, ma'am." Gallegos stiffens. "The proto-Inorganics sometimes received commands and software updates from Earth, but they mostly operated autonomously. To mimic that, we sometimes send Jason manual commands. And, if we want, we can switch display modes and view its activities."

Gallegos taps a button. The screen jumps from text to a photorealistic image of an Inorganic in blank space. The unit has a central body, a box shape, from which multiple appendages extend: six spindly legs, three arms with gripping claws, a wide scoop, and a precision driller. An antenna rises from the top of the central body. From the nadir portion of its body, a conical corer drills into an imaginary surface. The image gives no sense of scale, but Stacy remembers reading that most of the proto-Inorganics were as large as a medium-sized kitchen table.

Gallegos rotates the view, displaying the proto-Inorganic from top, bottom, and side. "It moves in distinct patterns. Like how each person has distinctive footsteps or unique mannerisms. Except, in this case, those footsteps and mannerisms were the same across a variety of models. In the first few years after the Inorganics escaped, you could see them still employing the same movement patterns. They've changed since, though. They must have found more efficient patterns, or maybe more efficient tools."

Young, Gallegos, Prabhakhar, and Thor all watch Stacy as though seeking her approval. As if she can approve something like this.

Thor smiles. "So I guess now you can see why I believe some 'conspiracy theories.' Because I'm part of one."

Maybe Stacy would laugh under other circumstances, but now, she can't bring herself to even fake one. She turns to Prabhakhar. "I feel as though you weren't completely open during your interview. Have you learned anything from… Jason about the intelligence level of Inorganics?"

Prabhakhar looks pained. "Not as much as we would have liked."

"Is there any evidence their reasoning style is different than a basic computer's?"

"Wait, that's not fair," says Thor. "What about human intelligence? Is *that* any different from mechanical intelligence?"

"Yes," says Stacy. "We have complex ways of thinking, a lot of them illogical. But they let us write poetry or paint."

Gallegos shrugs. "I understand what you're saying. Sergeant Windham is right, though. Humans have algorithms that we follow. We just use chemicals and organic brains instead of circuits. And our brains can also be modified or damaged, the same as any software or motherboard."

"So there's no difference between our brain and an Inorganic's programming? I don't believe that."

"It's not that there's no difference," says Gallegos. "It's just that we don't know how to describe the differences beyond the different building materials. And then you get to self-awareness.… If I had to guess, I'd say they're like a beehive or an ant colony. A lot of individuals with a common goal, working toward the best interests of the hive because those are in the best interests of the individual. But we don't know."

Stacy stares at Jason. The animated figure extracts its corer, opens a hatch on the side of its central body, and uses the scoop to place an imaginary collection of rock within itself. After over two centuries of neuroscience and decades of studying the Inorganics, humans are no closer to answering those basic questions.

"At this point," says Gallegos, "we don't expect to find the answer. We've worked through so many combinations of inputs, it's hard to believe we haven't stumbled across the cause by now. And the research will likely be ended after the starship launch."

"Why?" Stacy asks. "There are still plenty of Inorganics in the Solar System. The Moon, Mars, other asteroids, the outer planets, the Kuiper Belt. They won't stop being a threat just because these few travel to another star system."

"Good point," says Young. "Once we withdraw from this station, we'll lose our platform for this type of study. My concern is that, by not knowing the initial cause of the Inorganics' creation, we'll repeat the mistake from 2052 March 19. And, since we're slowly closing our bases and withdrawing back to Earth, that mistake will happen on Earth. Our last home. We won't have anywhere else to retreat to."

If humans had determined the threat before 2052, history would have been completely different. Humans might be the ones on Juno now, building this starship, working side-by-side with cooperative AIs. Instead, humans watch as the Inorganics steal the dream of the stars.

Stacy's report on Jason is going to be good. Not just good, but popular. This one will bring about real change. She just doesn't know what that change will be.

"You were right, General," says Stacy. "This story will be controversial."

FOURTEEN

JASON COLLECTS ANOTHER imaginary sample. When viewed at normal speed, the act of collecting appears to be a single, smooth motion, but when Stacy records the action and plays it back at reduced speed, it becomes a series of individual, intricate steps:

Rotate gripping arm to a position two hundred seventy degrees from the origin. Extend the five digits of the gripping arm's hand to their farthest extensions. Lower arm until the digits contact the ground. Retract the digits until they encounter resistance. Raise the arm to its original height. Rotate gripping arm to a point one hundred eighty degrees from origin. Bend arm at midpoint by ninety degrees. Extend the five digits of the gripping arm's hand to their farthest extensions. Bend arm at midpoint by negative ninety degrees. Repeat.

It's only a simulation, though, a brain without a body. At the cusp of intelligence, teetering on the brink of understanding what it is, trapped in a machine.

But she doesn't feel sympathy for Jason. Not really. It sets her on edge thinking about it living on the station with her.

She doesn't hate it, either. She wouldn't mind if it were wiped, would prefer that outcome, but not out of malice. Out of safety.

She only watches it so much out of curiosity. She wants to know if it is conscious. And what is it like to be an artificial intelligence?

Stacy did not solicit rebuttals for the report, the first time in her career. Worse, after sending it, she realized she had edited it in anger. She didn't give Prabhakhar or the others adequate opportunity to defend their actions. It was unprofessional, like an Instant USA report.

Trevor wasn't even able to calm her since Young didn't allow her to contact him until she released the report. Young didn't want to take any chance of someone intercepting the message again until Stacy's report had the chance to explain Jason "in the proper context." When Trevor saw the report, he was livid.

> *They put you in danger. They should have let you know what you were being exposed to. I wish you could come home now. It's not safe there. I knew there were risks, we both did, but we thought those risks were a thousand kilometers away.*

> *I'm sorry. I know I'm probably stressing you out. You'll be fine. I just wish they had told you beforehand. I wish I were there with you.*

The reveal of Jason also makes Stacy wonder: Should she continue to pursue the IMS incident? Or any other issue that would make General Young look bad? They are on the same side, as Young often says. Pursuing other issues would not only distract viewers from the real issues, but the pursuit would distract Stacy from writing proper reports on the real issues.

She still can't answer that question. So she visits Jason again, then again, until it becomes a habit.

At first, she was more than anxious. She was terrified. The first two times she went to the Machining Room after Young and the others introduced Jason, her fingers twitched and shook. It felt like trying to jump from a train. But Jason is trapped on that disk, and Stacy needs to face her fears.

Now, staring at the onscreen image, the proto-Inorganic doesn't seem evil. Inhuman, but not evil. Maybe that's the worst part: She wants to hate these machines for what they did to her father and what they do to humanity, but they aren't doing anything out of malice.

The public, which seemed unconcerned about the threat until now, are angrier than she expected. But, as she did expect, they are focusing on the wrong issue. Protesters comment on websites demanding a halt to the AIS projects. They are oblivious to the threat posed by the Inorganics already loose.

Worse, the crew watched a popular new movie in the galley: *Inorganica Planitia*, in which a family on Mars adopts a tiny Inorganic that is separated from its hive. When its hive mates come for it during the movie's climax, it elects to stay with its new family.

Somehow, Stacy watched the entire thing. She might have enjoyed its saccharine charm, despite Thor's gagging noises, if not for how it anthropomorphized the machine. It looks and acts cute, unlike any real Inorganic. The entire movie is like a slap in the face to her father and all the people who died on Mars and to everyone else who has suffered because of the Inorganics.

Of course, the movie was written and filmed on Earth. No Martian would ever write such blatant lies about the machines capable of wiping out their entire colony.

As Stacy slips her feet from the floor holds, the door opens, and Thor enters. He gives her a sarcastic wave.

"Thought I might find you here."

Stacy hooks herself back into place. "Hi. What's going on?"

"Look." Thor glides to a spot a couple meters from her and grabs a ceiling handhold. "We don't see eye-to-eye on much. But you're objective. Or, not really, but you try to be. You listen to evidence when you see it. And I know you're looking into the IMS incident, which is more than anyone else here is doing."

Stacy gives him a small nod.

"So we should team up. Share resources."

In every assignment—Uruguay, Maine, Russia, Brazil— someone always talks. She didn't expect it to be Thor, but it might not hurt to look into the leads he provides, as long as she thoroughly checks them before reporting them. She doesn't say she was considering dropping the investigation. Maybe she shouldn't drop it, now that she has a potential ally. "Okay."

"Okay, then."

"But I think I'm at a dead end in the investigation. The IMS telemetry for that day was lost."

"Deliberately, right?" says Thor.

"Well…" Stacy shrugs. "I think so."

"Not surprised. Everything's deliberate at some level." Thor gestures to Jason. "This is why the Bit-Flip Theory is false. I couldn't say it earlier, back when we talked about it in the galley. But Jason's bits have been flipped, every one of them, over and over, and it never went rogue. Which means the Innies were created by deliberate actions, and the Zero-Day-Signal Theory is right."

"Maybe." Stacy has still found no evidence to support the theory, and just because one theory is wrong, it doesn't automatically make another theory right. "But why would someone do that?"

"Lots of reasons. Disgruntled hackers wanting to dismantle the status quo. Someone curious. Or the government using it as an excuse to increase its military power."

"I think I know which one you believe."

"You probably do." Thor grins. "Well. Good talk."

He exits the room, and Stacy returns to watching Jason. She hasn't yet lost herself in the rhythmic motions when the door opens again. This time, the general enters.

Young's face is tighter than normal, her eyes harder. "Why did Thor come in here?"

"I don't know." Stacy tries to find a truthful statement to say. "He didn't stay long."

Young glances at Jason. "So why are you still in here?"

"I'm trying to learn more about Jason."

"And?"

Stacy shakes her head. "Nothing new so far. Jason doesn't do anything to indicate intelligence."

Young nods. "You see our problem, then. We're learning nothing new. So what do you hope to gain by staring at it all day?"

Stacy turns back to Jason. It rotates its appendage. Why does she keep coming in here? Maybe Jason feels like an unsolved puzzle, like if she just keeps staring, she will work out a clue. But no clues have come. "I guess you're right."

"I'm going to make an announcement to the crew," says Young. "I'd like you to be there to record it."

"Oh." Stacy pats her pockets. Her nanocams are there. "Sure. Are you doing it now?"

"I am. In the Analysis Room."

"What is it about?"

"You'll find out soon."

Thinking about it, Stacy knows she shouldn't have expected Young to answer. Stacy folds Jason's screen back into the wall and follows the general.

Prabhakhar and Contreras look up from their consoles when Young and Stacy enter the Analysis Room. Stacy positions herself beside the door and distributes her nano-cams to vantage points covering the room. She activates her implant's recorder and gives a thumbs-up to Young, who has hooked herself into place in front of the back wall.

Young activates the station-wide intercom. Her voice booms from the speakers.

"Since we have lost the IMS, we have lost the capability to do our closest monitoring of the starship. As a way of mitigating that loss, we will be launching a pod expedition in one month. Since a human will be at the controls and can make course changes quickly, the pod will drop farther below the attack threshold than we've ventured before, which will allow us to gain even better photographs and other sensory information about the vessel and Inorganic activities. It will be the most dangerous expedition we've attempted yet, but it will also be the most rewarding."

It sounds suicidal. Maybe Young hopes the Inorganics will destroy the pod, just for the increased media coverage.

"The expedition," Young continues, "will be commanded by Major Nihar Prabhakhar. The pilot will be Sergeant Inez Jalindo. The officer in charge of science instruments will be Captain Ko Dal, and Sergeant Jorge Contreras will be assisting him. They will be joined by our media representative, Stacy Sterling."

Stacy's leg twitches. She meets the general's eyes. Young is sending her deep into Inorganic territory, where those unfeeling machines could tear her apart for trespassing, and she didn't even tell Stacy beforehand.

Worse, Young is making Stacy part of the story.

FIFTEEN

STACY FLOATS IN Module 1 again, alone, her legs hooked into holds as the rest of her body stretches into the middle of the corridor. The stretching helps, like it's pulling the tension from her, but it doesn't slow her pulse or the pace of her thoughts.

Young is still attempting to make Stacy part of the story, and has already succeeded in the sense that Stacy is mentioned as a crew member. But Stacy doesn't have to show herself on camera. She doesn't have to do a voiceover or an emotional overlay. She will observe, and only observe.

It makes sense to send her. If she is to report on the Inorganics and the mission of Collins Station, she should accompany the crew on these expeditions.

It still makes the hairs of her neck stand on end when she thinks of traveling that close to the starship. It still floods her mind with images of the IMS incident, of the Mars base, of imaginary Inorganics tearing through the pod walls to grab her. But she has been in combat situations before, and she knows how to handle herself. She will be fine. She will be fine.

"Today is a good day," she tells herself.

And this expedition will be a great way to gain interest in the overall story of the starship. The pod crew will obtain the closest images of the starship humanity will ever see before the ship departs the Solar System.

Prabhakhar and Jalindo are both expedition members and will be unlikely to anger General Young as interview subjects, so Stacy decides to find them and gather information on what to expect from the expedition. At this time of day, they are likely in the galley.

When Stacy enters, she finds her targets at their tables, along with Gulati floating at her ceiling kitchen, surrounded by food packaging. At the table beside Jalindo, though, is Montoya.

Stacy takes a place beside Prabhakhar. "Hi."

Montoya seems to study her for a moment. "Guess you know about Jason now."

"Yes."

"Well. That's done, then. I can stop feeling bad about it." Montoya nods to the window. "Congratulations on going on the expedition."

"Thank you." She imagines watching the starship through the pod window and an Inorganic claw coming into view. "I'm a little terrified."

"Lot of people with a lot of experience out here would love to be in your spot."

"Oh." Stacy glances at the others around the table, who she just now notices are watching the conversation. Most of them will accompany her, but Thor and Anderson will not. Anderson, in particular, must dream of an opportunity like this. "I'm sorry. I wish you all could go, too."

"Anyway." Montoya pulls himself from the table. "Let's start setting up for Picture Week."

"What is Picture Week?" Stacy asks as the others get up to help Montoya.

Jalindo grabs a display board from the corner of the room. "We put up pictures our kid relatives drew. Our nephews or nieces or our own kids, if we have them."

Stacy has no nieces or nephews because she doesn't have a sibling. If not for the Inorganics on Mars, maybe she would have had one.

Jalindo takes the board to the back wall. Montoya and Contreras join them and help stick the board in place.

The display board is the most colorful thing on the station. A rainbow smorgasbord covers it, colors twisting around each other along the frame, with a white background inside.

Jalindo returns to the table. "So, who's posting first?"

Prabhakhar raises a piece of paper. "I've got it."

"Figured you did," says Jalindo.

Stacy will have to wait until after this ceremony to approach Jalindo and Prabhakhar about doing interviews.

Prabhakhar anchors himself beside the display, then grabs the duct tape hooked to the wall. He tears a couple small strips and sticks the paper to the top left of the blank sheet. The drawing shows a tall man wearing a cape and oversized goggles. Beside him is a little boy.

"I don't know why he gave me a cape," says Prabhakhar. "He usually draws me in a spacesuit. And without hair."

Gulati chuckles from above as she cleans a bowl. "I don't think that's supposed to be you. I recognize him. It's from a cartoon, *Good, Inc.* The bad guy is a supervillain who is showing his son how to be evil."

Prabhakhar pokes the drawing. "You think Ayaan…wants to be evil?"

Gulati's grin disappears. "I don't think that's what he wants."

Contreras leans forward from his position to the right of the board and pats Prabhakhar's back. "Sorry, man."

Prabhakhar frowns. "I don't…Oh." He makes a move as if to rip the paper down, but stops. For several moments, he says nothing, and Stacy wants to hug him. "But I try. It's just hard, being out here…"

"We understand." Contreras puts his arm around Prabhakhar's shoulders. "We're all giving up something to be out here."

"Yeah," says Stacy. "We know it's hard."

Prabhakhar returns to his spot at the table, eyes distant. "Somebody else's turn."

The others place their own pictures in the display. The drawing quality ranges from a few thick scribbles from the younger ones to drawings bordering on realism from the teenaged children.

"This is so cool." Stacy floats beside the display, admiring the drawings. "Whose idea was this?"

"The general's," says Gulati. "She's done it every six months since the first crew."

"Such a good idea. Maybe we could have a compliment week, too, where we take turns complimenting everyone else."

Montoya looks uncomfortable. His eyes turn down.

"Sorry," says Stacy. "We don't have to do it."

Jalindo glances at him and smirks. "He'll be fine."

"Look." Montoya sets his eyes on something beyond Stacy's shoulder. "I understand you weren't trying to hurt me. But you haven't changed your approach to interviews. If you want me to forgive you, you need to take steps to not do the same thing again. And you haven't done that."

Montoya doesn't even look angry, not the way he did before. He looks disappointed, hurt.

She blinks a tear away. "I see what you're saying. But you know this is my job. And I can't just show the Inorganics as benevolent and admirable when that's not true."

"Hm." Montoya's mouth twitches. "I think you're overstating it. But I don't think you can look past yourself enough to see that."

Stacy can think of no response. She wants to argue, but what if Montoya is right?

Several moments pass. Thor clears his throat. "You hear about the enlisted shitter being broken again?"

"Glad I'm not on shift now. Poor Hernandez, though." Jalindo straightens. "I should probably get back to my workout. It's dangerous for me to get off-routine."

"We've all heard what happened last time," says Thor.

Everyone but Stacy laughs.

When the room quiets again, Stacy turns to Jalindo. She is aware of everyone's eyes on her when she speaks. "Sergeant. Can I get an interview with you? Since the expedition is coming up?"

Jalindo watches Stacy as though considering. "Okay." They adopt a forced cheerful expression. "Remember, you promised to make me famous." They turn to Montoya, who does not return their gaze. "Just be careful how you do it."

Silence fills the room again. Stacy wonders if she will become one of the crew's inside jokes. The reporter who made everyone look stupid. The reporter who tried too hard to make amends. The reporter who wanted to fit in but never would.

"Let me know when." Jalindo taps the table, then leaves the galley.

Montoya faces the others and speaks in a hesitant voice. "So, you all hear the latest about Panama?"

As the others speak, Stacy leans toward Prabhakhar. Before she can say anything, he says, "You're going to ask me for another interview, aren't you? ?"

"Yes. If you can. About the expedition." Stacy sighs. "The last interview didn't help with Ayaan, did it?"

"No." Prabhakhar gestures to the Wall. "It helped even less than I'd thought. Maybe it…disappointed him?"

"Why? He got to see his dad in space, knowing a lot about something."

"I think…" Prabhakhar's smile disappears almost as soon as it forms. "I think he expected to see me fighting monsters up here or something."

"Oh." Stacy glances out the window toward Juno. "I hope we don't have to do that."

Prabhakhar shrugs. "Okay. I'll do the interview. The general will probably insist on it, anyway."

"She probably would."

Thor and Contreras continue discussing Panama. Gulati winces every time Thor raises his voice. Prabhakhar retreats inside himself, and Anderson has barely come out of herself at all. Stacy leaves the room. She doubts anyone notices.

SIXTEEN

THE POD DOOR slides open to reveal a curved, cramped area. A windshield wraps around the front quarter of the vehicle, giving a wide view of the stars beyond. Three rows of seats, with only enough room between rows for the occupants to squeeze their knees into place, fill the pod.

Stacy enters from the rear, using the seats to guide herself through the aisle. She isn't tall, but she can't stretch to her full length without hitting her head on the ceiling.

Jalindo sits in the pilot's seat, leaning over a screen that shows a list of files. Stacy pulls herself into the co-pilot's seat and straps herself in.

"Hi," she says. "Is this still a good time?"

"Sure." Jalindo turns from the screen in front of them and rubs their stubbly head. "I expect you to make me famous. Not *too* famous. I just plan to be on posters. Like Dr. Terrence Smith. Maybe get some schools named after me. Maybe stadiums. I certainly expect the crew to name their kids after me. Jalindo Prabhakhar. Jalindo Cazador. Jalindo…Sterling?"

Stacy laughs. "We'll see." She releases her nanocams to take positions around Jalindo. She starts her implant recording, tapping her head to let Jalindo know. "I put the nanocams into positions to get your best angles."

"Perfect."

"Can you introduce yourself and give a brief overview of what you do on the station? And if you can, can you talk about the upcoming pod expedition?"

"Sure." Jalindo straightens. "I'm Chief Master Sergeant Inez Jalindo, one of the maintenance personnel and the chief pilot at Collins. I'll be the pilot for the pod expedition that will go closer to the Inorganics' starship than we've ever gotten before. That mission entails significant risk, but it's worth it. We should get some good information. And it's going to be a thrill ride."

Stacy doesn't want to be on an expedition described as a 'thrill ride.' "What are you working on right now?"

Jalindo gestures to the screen in front of them. "I'm loading the flight plan."

"Oh, that's a good place to start. Can you explain the mission profile?"

Jalindo laughs. "A lot of it will be improvisational, which is where I shine. We'll start off on a trajectory toward the starship. Once we cross the threshold, the Innies are going to start coming for us. And that's when it gets fun." Jalindo has a grin too wide for the situation.

"That doesn't sound like my idea of fun."

"It'll be fine. I'm a great pilot. I'm not just saying that; you can ask anyone." Jalindo shrugs. "I'll need to make evasive maneuvers, but we'll take as short of a path as we can to pass over the starship. Then we speed out of there, probably tailed by the Innies."

"Tailed by…How close do you think the Inorganics will be?"

"Close as they can get." Jalindo laughs. "Don't worry about it. We'll stay far enough away from them."

Stacy doesn't know if Jalindo is displaying bravado for the camera or if they mean to risk everyone's lives in such a casual way. "Do you know how close we're trying to get to the starship?"

"We should get within a kilometer of the starship. I plan to get as close as we can while giving us plenty of opportunity to get away safely."

Jalindo grabs the control stick in front of them and opens their mouth, but before they can continue speaking, Stacy asks, "What are the mission objectives?"

Jalindo's expression dims. "Not as exciting. We'll take measurements of the starship. We have a camera, a gravimeter, a couple radars, and a lidar, which is like a radar but with a laser. Do you know how we point the lidar?"

Stacy shakes her head.

"The laser itself just keeps firing straight, over and over. If that's all we did, we'd be making a straight line on the ground underneath us, and we'd get basically a one-dimensional track under where we flew. But we shoot the laser at a mirror a few centimeters away, and we rotate the mirror, so the laser gets deflected in an elliptical pattern around our ground track. Pretty cool, right?"

"Yeah," says Stacy. "That is pretty cool."

"So we'll be operating those instruments the entire time, with special attention while we pass over the starship. But that's all standard stuff. The interesting part is getting there. We've never gotten this close to the starship before."

"Is this the closest you personally have been to Inorganics before?"

Jalindo leans back and taps one of the patches on their flight suit. "No. There was Europa."

Stacy hoped Jalindo would bring up Europa. "Right, you're the only one here who's been there. Could you talk about that?"

"Yeah. I was at the base there. It was a joint base between the SDF and the National Science Foundation. If we drove far enough, we could see the Innie base's new construction. I'm sure I got closer than a kilometer at some point. I was due to return to Europa before the incident that closed it."

The Europa Base Incident occurred in 2113. Only eight years ago. Stacy wants to ask what had caused it, but knows Jalindo can't answer. "You served with General Young before, right?"

Jalindo smiles. "Several times. We go way back. Our first tour together was when we closed down the Moon."

"You were on the last crew at the Moon base?" It was the first shutdown of human presence beyond low Earth orbit.

"Yes. And it looks as though the general and I will be shutting down this place together, too." Jalindo's gaze seems to view their past, seeing lost opportunities and shared sadness, misplaced hopes and terminated dreams. "Do you ever wonder what it says about us," they ask, "that we keep giving up like this?"

"Yes," says Stacy. "That was the story I was originally going to write before the general told me about the starship."

"The starship will be a good story, too. And this expedition is going to be the highlight. Getting that close…It's going to be like a video game."

Stacy tries to laugh. "It might be like a video game for *you*. The pod has safety features, right? In case we have to abandon it?"

"It would be dangerous to abandon the pod in the middle of Inorganic territory. Suicidal, even. But we have these escape bags." They reach under their seat and pull out a yellow bag folded into a flat square. "You get inside and inflate them, and you can float in empty space for a few hours before someone picks you up. Assuming anyone can get to you. And if you jump out while we're in Inorganic territory, no one's coming to get you. So…try not to do that."

"Yeah, it's not something I want to do." The thought of bailing out into space and waiting for those spiderlike machines to close in on her… "What…what do you hope to find out about the starship that you don't already know? Is the risk worth it?"

As Jalindo opens their mouth to respond, a thump comes from behind them. Stacy turns to see Anderson gliding into the pod, horizontal to fit in the gap between the seats and ceiling. Anderson starts when she sees Stacy.

"Sorry! I just came to calibrate the radar. I didn't know you were doing an interview."

Jalindo waves off the apology. "Come on, Lieutenant. You're not on a Thule tour."

Anderson gives them a weak grin. "I guess not."

Stacy doesn't understand the reference. "What's a Thule tour?"

"Everyone in the SDF goes through our Thule base in Greenland for training," says Jalindo. "The rule is, the first-timers have to apologize for everything, even if it wasn't their fault."

"Oh," says Stacy. The Thule tour sounds like her entire life. "Well, we can keep talking, right?"

"Maybe you can talk to the lieutenant now." Jalindo smiles. "She was telling me this cool mnemonic the other day."

Anderson takes the seat behind Stacy and logs in to the screen on the side wall. "It doesn't seem appropriate for an article."

"You don't have to talk about it," says Stacy, "if you don't feel comfortable."

"Naw." Jalindo turns around to face Anderson. "Come on, Lieutenant."

Anderson winces. "I feel like it's been hyped up too much now. You know how each individual Inorganic unit is unique, right?"

Stacy nods. The Inorganics can modify themselves to optimally perform a specific task by adding or subtracting appendages. Some of those appendages are the stuff of nightmares: corkscrews, pincer hands, scissors or knives that slice through metal as though through air.

Anderson continues. "But we can still classify them into general categories."

"And," says Jalindo, "Lieutenant Anderson came up with a handy mnemonic for the categories. Tell her."

Without looking Stacy in the eyes, Anderson mumbles, "'What Would Teen Popstars Do In Space?' Wirers, welders, transporters, processors, diggers, Inorganic designers, setters."

Stacy smiles. "That's pretty good."

Anderson rushes through a series of brief descriptions of the units, each of which has a different specialized function. "Division of labor," she says. "Like we started doing during the Industrial Revolution. We're not all that different from them."

"Why," asks Stacy, regretting each word, "do you think we're not different from the Inorganics?"

"They keep expanding outward, right?" Anderson waves her arms in an unhelpful demonstration. "They started in the Asteroid Belt, or some of them in LEO or on the Moon, and they've kept going."

"Yes." Stacy wonders how Anderson can talk about it with such glee when she is describing the beginning of the end for humanity. "I guess that's like humans. We expanded to every continent on our planet, and then we started exploring the Solar System."

"Sure, I guess that's part of it." Anderson grins. "But why are they building a starship?"

Stacy shakes her head. "I have an explanation, but what is yours?"

"They're *curious*." Anderson smiles with more enthusiasm than she's ever had in Stacy's presence. "They're going to the Proxima system to *explore*."

Speculation. Anderson has only speculation to support her suggestion, and no conclusive evidence to support it. Stacy has no obligation to air it. But she aired her own feelings about the Inorganics. Is she obligated to balance her reporting with Anderson's feelings?

"Okay, that was interesting." Stacy shifts in her seat. "I should probably keep talking to Sergeant Jalindo about the expedition, though."

Jalindo glances up from their screen, eyes refocusing as they turn to Stacy. "Oh, sure."

Before Stacy can ask a question, the pod wall beside her begins to vibrate. It starts off as a low shaking and escalates until it looks as though it is riding a jackhammer.

Stacy reaches for her chair arm to steady herself, but the chair wobbles. And so do the other walls, and the windshield. And, as she glances to her left, so does her arm.

Her arm looks like a wave now, the skin and bone rising from her shoulder to her bicep, curving downward to her elbow, rising upward again halfway along her lower arm, vibrating outward in a psychedelic vision without the strange colors, moving in time with the walls. Did someone drug her?

Jalindo and Anderson grip their chairs with expressions of resignation, their faces distorted into waves of bulging or shrinking eyes, ears, mouths, and noses. Stacy's legs grow heavy as her head grows light, then the sensation reverses.

Then the sensations disappear, as though they never occurred. Stacy glances around the pod's cabin, expecting cracks in the windshield, or fried electronics, or warped walls. But everything looks normal.

"What was that?" asks Stacy.

"Grav-engine test," says Jalindo. "The Inorganics are testing the starship engines. Your first time to go through one, I guess."

"Yeah."

"It's never pleasant." Jalindo shrugs. "And it's disorienting. Makes it hard to do anything. But you get used to it."

"You do?" Stacy glances around the pod again. "What if one of those tests happens during the pod expedition?"

Jalindo winces. "Let's hope it doesn't."

SEVENTEEN

BEFORE STACY CAN articulate any follow-up questions, like why the general is allowing a pod to travel so close to the starship when a grav-engine test could disable the crew, Captain Ko enters the pod and anchors himself to the entrance. His grin looks disconcerting given what they just experienced.

"Hey, Sergeant, Ms. Sterling." Ko waves to Jalindo and Stacy before turning to Anderson with a wry expression. "Lieutenant. Christmas is early. I think. I don't actually know what day it is anymore. We need to do an EVA to install equipment on the pod."

"Awesome!" Anderson breaks into a grin. "I just need to close out here."

Stacy glances between Anderson and Ko. "You all are doing a spacewalk? After…that just happened?"

Anderson gives Stacy an apologetic smile. "We never know when the tests will happen, so we can't limit our activities in fear of it. It's just another risk we have to take to be out here."

Like the bullets flying while Stacy covers a combat zone. She nods.

Anderson logs out of her screen and unbuckles from her seat. "I'm ready."

As Ko turns to leave, he glances over his shoulder at Stacy. "You should be able to see us from the zenith cupola. Could be interesting to see your first EVA. We'll be pre-breathing for a few, so don't hurry."

"Thanks!" says Stacy. "I'll check it out."

An EVA, or extra-vehicular activity, will provide nice footage to add color to Stacy's reports. A deep-space space-walk at humanity's farthest outpost.

"I've got work to do," says Jalindo. "But I'll be rooting for you two."

Ko waves before ducking out of the pod, Anderson behind him. Jalindo speaks before Stacy can say anything. "I guess the interview's over, then?"

Stacy laughs. "For now. I'll talk to you again soon."

Stacy unbuckles and navigates her way through the pod's tight space, then heads to the zenith cupola. It is empty, which surprises her, but maybe the others have grown as jaded by spacewalks as they are of grav-engine tests.

She positions herself at the bottom of the room, at the peak of the curving windowpanes, and gazes toward the rear of the station. Because of the EVA, the station's exterior lights are on, casting shadows from the various instruments mounted on the cylindrical hull. The pod is docked at the very end, a metallic sphere jutting out from the station's hull. It looks even smaller from the outside. In only three weeks, she will be in that pod, traveling toward the surface of Juno while Inorganics hunt her.

"Good, I hoped you would be here."

Stacy turns to see General Young sliding through the cupola's entrance. The general stops beside her. Young has a way of always making Stacy feel as though she has done something wrong.

Stacy gestures to the pod. "Captain Ko said there would be a good view here."

"He was right."

Movement near the pod catches Stacy's attention. At the far end of the station, at the aft airlock, a spacesuited figure comes into view. It pulls itself along the outside of Module 10, a tether trailing behind.

"Oh, wow," says Stacy. She starts her implant recording.

A second figure appears, following the first in their swim along the station's exterior. Both reach the pod after what felt like several minutes of slow motion.

"Ko's in the red stripes," says Young.

"Oh?"

"When two people are on EVA, the senior spacewalker wears red stripes so we can tell them apart, since the suit covers up everything. First used all the way back on Apollo 14. Apollo 13 had the striped suit, but they didn't get a chance to use it."

The two figures settle into their task. Anderson sets a large box in place on the pod's hull while Ko pulls a tool from his belt. Stacy zooms in with her oculars as Ko begins bolting the box to the hull.

"They're installing a lidar," says Young. "Lidars are good for topography maps, so we'll be able to get a more detailed map of Juno with this expedition, but mostly, we want to use it to map the starship."

"What level of—"

Ko's drill starts to buck. Stacy almost shouts a warning to him before remembering he wouldn't hear. Ko stiffens his upper torso, and after moments of struggle, wrestles the drill downward. It stops bucking from side-to-side as Ko guides it back to the pod's hull.

Then his tether drifts into the drill's path. At first, it looks as though the tether will pass underneath the drill without incident, but it catches and jerks back and forth, shredding. Flecks of white material scatter outward, reflecting light and looking like stars. Ko shakes in time with the drill now, and might have stayed near the station, but the drill jumps off the pod's hull and slams into his chest.

"No!" Stacy puts a hand to the windowpane.

Ko goes flying from the station, the drill dragging after him by its own tether attached to his belt.

Stacy turns to the general. "Is he…"

"Not good." Young kicks away from the window and shoots out of the cupola.

Ko could die out there. Other space explorers who have drifted from their vehicles have suffocated or froze to death as their life-support systems failed.

Ko's distance from Collins continues to increase, and he begins rotating. The spacesuits have maneuvering backpacks as emergency measures, but Ko is spinning too quickly to use it effectively. If he continues to spin at this rate, he will lose consciousness, and it doesn't look as though he can regain control.

Anderson, still next to the pod, seems to peer toward Ko. Is she is asking the general what to do, or telling Ko to hold on? Then Anderson disconnects her tether. She is loose from the station, in as much danger as Ko.

"Don't," Stacy whispers. "Don't do it."

Anderson kicks off toward Ko, and as she floats from the station into the emptiness beyond, Stacy can do nothing but watch and record. Stacy doesn't know either of them well, but she remembers Ko's enthusiasm when he told Anderson about the EVA and the seriousness with which Anderson does everything. Stacy wants to be out there with them, doing something to save them, but she has to trust General Young to dispatch crewmembers to do what is necessary.

After an eternity, Anderson reaches the spinning Ko. He looks dangerous, seventy-some kilograms of uncontrolled mass. A boot, spinning that quickly, with that lever arm, could send Anderson spiraling away, or injure her, or crack her faceplate.

The lieutenant reaches a tentative hand toward a foot as it rotates past. As her hand closes the distance, images flash through Stacy's head of all the ways the contact could go wrong. Finally, Anderson's hand snatches the edge of Ko's boot, slowing him, then releases it. She fires her maneuvering pack's thrusters to counteract the motion imparted to her by Ko, then repeats the action several times. By the fifth time, Ko's motion has dampened enough that Anderson can grab his leg and hold on. Another cloud hof gas puffs from Anderson's maneuvering pack, and the pair begins floating back to the station.

In under five minutes, the two have disappeared from view of the cupola. Stacy hurries to the airlock. When she arrives,

General Young, Lieutenant Cazador, and Contreras wait beside the door.

"Is he okay?" asks Stacy.

Cazador holds a first-aid kit. "Sounds like the drill broke some of his ribs when it hit him."

Young looks up when Stacy takes a spot beside the pod's docking port, across the hall from them. "Glad you're recording this," says Young.

A moment like this, with a crewmember injured in a near-fatal situation, and Young is concerned about the public's reaction? Maybe she should include that part in the story.

Minutes later, the airlock door opens, and Anderson emerges with Ko's arm around her shoulders. Neither have removed their suits.

Cazador pushes to the front and takes hold of Ko's shoulders. "I got him."

Contreras takes Ko's other side, and they float him to the next module. Young gestures for Anderson, who remains in the airlock doorway, to remove her helmet. Anderson twists the helmet to the side, then lifts it from her head.

"Captain Ko is injured," says Young.

Anderson nods, eyes downcast.

"You saved his life, though."

"Doesn't feel like it. I shouldn't have let it happen."

The lieutenant looks distraught, as though Ko died and didn't just crack a rib, as though she didn't just rescue him. Stacy wants to hug the lieutenant.

Young shakes her head. "I'm not sure what you could have done differently, and Captain Ko was in charge, anyway. His injury isn't severe, but it is debilitating in the short term. You will be replacing him on the pod expedition."

Anderson's eyes widen at that remark. "The…I am?"

"Yes. So you'd better prepare. Once you get a chance, speak to Major Prabhakhar about your role."

"I will."

Young gestures for Anderson to continue onward. Anderson leaves the module, almost fleeing.

Young faces Stacy. "I hope you got good footage. An injury out here is no light matter, and I hate to use it in such a mercenary fashion, but it will get attention."

EIGHTEEN

"WHAT IS THIS?"

The general maintains a calm expression as she floats beside her computer in her quarters. Her body betrays no tension. Her voice remains level. Which, Stacy knows, means the general is furious.

On Young's computer, Stacy's article plays. Prabhakhar floats in Module 1, lecturing about consciousness, while links appear every time he mentions a term most viewers won't know.

"I know it didn't get many views," says Stacy, forcing herself to meet Young's eyes, "but th—"

"It got fewer than a thousand views because it's boring." Young taps the image of Prabhakhar. "You gave viewers a recording of Major Prabhakhar's dense philosophical discussion with terms like 'qualia' and 'ontology' and 'philosophical zombie' and Lieutenant Anderson talking about a pop-star mnemonic. That mnemonic cheapens the work we do here. At least Sergeant Jalindo was interesting, although I wish they were more risk-averse."

"It was—"

"And your coverage of the EVA was as dramatic as a documentary on dirt."

Stacy opens her mouth to respond, but stops. Young sabotaged the IMS to get a more interesting story for the public. Did she also sabotage Ko's drill? Is she capable of potentially killing someone to generate public interest? How have her five years confined to these ten small modules affected her humanity?

"You have a decision to make, Ms. Sterling."

And here comes the ultimatum. All dictators give Stacy ultimatums when they realize her reporting won't go their way.

"You have to decide what's more important to you," Young continues. "Convincing the people of the danger we're in so that they support the continued operation of this station, or your reputation as a journalist. And not even your reputation as other people see you, but your reputation as you see yourself. No one else cares about these eccentric standards you've set for yourself."

Stacy collects her thoughts for a moment and tries to block the coming tears. "In the long run, journalistic integrity is the best approach to convincing the public."

"Our station closes when the starship launches," says Young. "We don't have a long run."

"I will make it work," says Stacy. "I can do honest reporting and still convince the public."

"Good. Lopez offered a trade deal along with your extradition request. We lost that deal because I thought your reporting would be more valuable. Don't let your reporting become less valuable than his deal."

Stacy's foot almost slips from the hold. The general didn't just invite her here because of Stacy's background. Stacy is here because Young has leverage over her.

Young blinks in a rhythmic pattern, and the report freezes. "Now, let's talk about when we're watching our next rom-com."

IF GENERAL YOUNG wants a report that will elicit an emotional reaction in readers, something to piss them off, Stacy needs Contreras's story. She hopes he'll agree to do it.

When she finds him, he catches the railing along the wall and turns to face her. "What's up?"

Stacy stops beside him. "I wanted to ask you some questions."

Contreras grins. "Off the record, I guess? Since I know the general wouldn't want you talking to me."

"I don't think that will be a problem," says Stacy. "The general wants an exciting story to lead up to the expedition."

"Exciting, yeah?" Contreras grins. "You've come to the right person."

"I was thinking…" In Module 1, after her meeting with General Young, Stacy rehearsed this question several times. Now, in person, those rehearsals feel inadequate. "I think it would resonate with viewers if you talked about your cousin."

"Oh." Contreras's grin disappears.

"I'm sorry," says Stacy. "I know it's uncomfortable, b—"

"Yeah, it is." Contreras's voice has become brittle. "Because I loved him. He was one of my closest friends. And he died. And you want me to use that memory to get you better ratings."

"It's…No…"

But Contreras is right. And worse, Stacy is asking him to do it when she has refused to use her father's story for ratings.

"Contreras." Stacy flinches when he stiffens. "It's not that I want the ratings for me. We're trying to convince the public the Inorganics are a threat. And your cousin's story is a good way to do that."

"Hm."

"His death could serve this cause."

"Hm."

"It's a way for the world to know about him."

Contreras grimaces. "Fine."

"I promise it will be respectful, and you'll have the chance to review it before it's posted."

"Okay." Contreras chews his lip for a moment. "I have something to ask *you*, then."

"Oh." What bargain has she inadvertently struck? "What is it?"

"Did you want to go on an EVA with me?"

Like the one two days ago where Ko nearly drifted off into space and Anderson risked her own life to rescue him. Where Stacy would be separated from vacuum and extreme cold by a thin layer of cloth. Where a grav-engine test could catch her in a vulnerable situation. "I don't know."

"You'll get some great visuals." Contreras seems indifferent to her apprehension. "You said you wanted something exciting for your report, and this is it."

"Do you know what went wrong with Ko's drill?"

Contreras shrugs. "Not yet. Jalindo and Cazador are looking into it. We won't be using a drill, though."

An EVA could potentially put Stacy out of contact with the station. It is the only place to be safe from watching eyes, assuming she and Contreras avoid the cameras on the hull. Maybe Contreras has something to say to her in secret.

"Okay." She has to know what he is hiding. "I think the EVA is a good idea."

"Great!"

"Did the general approve it?"

Contreras's smile freezes. "I…thought I would ask you first. But yeah, she still needs to give you clearance."

General Young will also know what opportunities the EVA allows.

They find Young in the Analysis Room. Halabi and Ko float near each other, pointing at something on Ko's console. Ko winces each time he turns. Young hovers above them, arms folded, like a judge.

Contreras anchors himself on one side of the door. "General."

Young glances toward them. "Sergeant."

"I'm requesting permission to bring Ms. Sterling on a maintenance EVA."

"Oh?" Young's head rotates to face Stacy, her expression growing cold. "What do you hope to accomplish?"

"I was going to show her my maintenance duties out there," says Contreras. "But mostly, I thought she could get some good visuals. Show the people back home how exciting EVAs are."

Young locks eyes with Stacy. "They *should* have already learned that."

At his console, Ko flinches.

"I'll be able to show the station from outside," says Stacy, "and show the starship without looking through a window."

Young's shoulders remain tight. She looks like she is taking notes in her implant. She probably is. *Contreras taking Stacy on EVA for unknown reasons. 2121-02-13.*

"You *asked* me," says Stacy, "to make a more exciting report."

Young taps her arms several times before nodding. "Okay. Remember while you're out there, I'll be listening. Feel free to ask for help or if you have any questions."

Stacy has never doubted she can call for help if necessary. The general did not mean the words as an offer of assistance.

"I understand."

"Sergeant Contreras." Young's smile has more than a touch of schadenfreude. "Make sure she watches the safety video."

Stacy usually hates safety videos, but she figures one about EVAs couldn't be that bad.

IT IS THE worst safety video she's ever seen. Horrible CGI that plunges headfirst into the uncanny valley. Acting worse than a hungover adult on drugs. Cheesy jingoistic catchphrases that would cause all but the most stalwart patriot to cringe. Stacy manages to confine her amusement to a tiny tug at the corner of her mouth.

Contreras glides to the locker next to her in Module 10. "It's okay to laugh. I kinda wonder if they made it that bad on purpose."

Stacy blinks to close the video. "That was pretty funny, right? Kind of nostalgic, too. It reminds me of the safety stuff we had to do on Mars."

Contreras's smile disappears.

"I'm sorry!" Stacy puts a hand on his arm. "I didn't mean to bring up bad memories."

Contreras gives a bitter laugh. "Gonna be plenty of that later, right?"

"Sorry."

"Well, as long as it helps us beat the Innies, yeah?"

"I hope." Stacy grabs the railing beside the airlock handle. "So what's next?"

Contreras opens the locker, unclips a suit from the rack inside, and floats it to her. "Put this on."

She catches it. It might have been white once, but burns, scuffs, and stains discolor it. Scrapes mar the helmet's faceplate, but none cut deeply. The rubber knobs at the ends of the fingers are ground down in places. It at least looks like her size.

"I put it on over my flight suit?"

"No." The word comes out flat, unemotional, like a computer. "The flight suit's too thick. It'll keep the suit's liquid cooling from being effective. I'll give you a moment. Just open the door when you're ready."

Once Contreras leaves the module, Stacy stows her flight suit in the locker and zips herself most of the way into the thin pressure suit. She reaches for the locker to retrieve her nano-cams from her flight suit, then realizes the cams can't operate without an atmosphere. They will drift away with no air for their fans to push against. She has her ocular cameras, but if the only videos she records come from her point of view, she is placing herself in the story.

She wants to tell Contreras she can't do it, that she is canceling the EVA. But the visuals would be spectacular, and she can spread them throughout her reports so viewers don't see thirty straight minutes from her point of view. She opens the module's door.

Contreras waits right outside. He smiles, though it doesn't reach his eyes, and zips up her suit the rest of the way. "My turn."

After he changes, velcroing the red stripes into place on his arms and legs, they enter the airlock together. It is small, with enough volume for three friendly people. One wall has dials and a console. The door to the outside has a handle as large as someone's arm. Just outside that hatch is a vacuum that can incapacitate in seconds and kill in three minutes.

Contreras helps her connect her backpack and adjust oxygen rate and temperature with the dials on her chest plate.

He grabs hoses from the wall and connects them to the suits. A rush of air flows across her chest, then along her arm and legs, like a breeze on a cool day. Her suit thickens with the increased pressure.

Stacy begins recording while Contreras presses several buttons on the wall. The room trembles for a moment as green lights blink around them, then settles.

The airlock's sequence freezes twice, but Contreras is able to reboot it each time by kicking the control panel. Stacy reminds herself the process has to be safe. Contreras wouldn't risk a civilian.

The ambient light turns red to announce the airlock's pressure has equalized with that of the outside. Contreras grabs the door handle and yanks it down. Latches rotate, and the airlock door opens into space.

The stars are right there. For a moment, Stacy thinks she can reach out and touch them. So black out there, the pinpoints of light so sharp. One step, and nothing can hold her up against that endless downness.

Her breath echoes in her helmet, mixing with the whirring of fans and the gentle flow of air. Stacy realizes she has clutched an inner handhold and pulled her chest flat against the wall. She backs away from the wall, then follows Contreras's example and hooks her umbilical to the bar outside the door.

Contreras gestures for her to go first. She shakes her head, then realizes he can't see her face through the tinted visor.

"You go," she says. "You're the experienced one."

"Which is why I want *you* to go first."

Stacy sighs. There is so much space out there to fall into. She places her hands on the hatch's frame. Keeping her arm muscles tight, she lets herself lean forward a centimeter at a time until her head pokes past the station's bounds.

The entire Universe stretches before her. The stars so far away, infinitely far down. If she falls, she will never stop.

She lifts her right foot and guides it outside. Her boot steps onto nothing. Then her body torques, spinning her as her gloved fingers slip from the hatch's frame, the stars giving way to the gray-white tube of the station's hull, then back again. Her hands claw for her umbilical and miss, and she finds herself drifting from the station like Ko did. Her umbilical won't snap, will it?

She reaches for the umbilical again, and her fingertips catch it, but she can't close her hand around it. She continues to drift farther from the station. On the third try, she catches it, and her drifting stops, but she's still swinging several meters from the open airlock.

"You okay there?" Contreras asks. She can hear the smile in his voice.

"I think so." Stacy slides one hand along the umbilical, then grips it tightly while sliding the next hand forward. Hand-over-hand, she pulls herself back to the airlock and grabs the doorframe to stop her rotation.

"Good to have you back," says Contreras.

For several moments, Stacy waits there, holding herself in place and remaining still so she doesn't drift away again and potentially get lost and slowly suffocate alone in her suit. Then she realizes she is safe, that she didn't drift away. She smiles to herself, then laughs.

Contreras joins her. "Someone's having fun."

"Yeah. That was scary at first, but now it's kind of nice."

"Thought you'd like it."

Once she regains equilibrium, she ventures outside again and plants her boots in footholds. Standing straight, she gets her first good look at the station from the outside. Pockmarks from micrometeoroids speckle the hull, giving it the texture of a golf ball. Bright blue solar panels, tall as giants, extend from the station's midpoint. Blocky protuberances are spaced atop the hull. A silver cylinder, to which Stacy and Contreras have clipped their umbilicals, runs from one end of the station to the other.

Contreras pushes off. "Let's get to work."

Stacy follows him. One hand after the other, one foot after the other.

He stops and points toward an antenna array on the zenith side of the station, aimed at Juno. "Our first job is here. Radar antennas." He continues toward the array.

Stacy pulls herself along the side of the station by grabbing the handholds, one hand over the other, until she reaches the top. She hooks the rubber toes of her boots within the holds and straightens.

Above hangs Juno. No window blocking the view, though her faceplate's scuff marks spoil the effect somewhat. The bright gray asteroid seems so close, like a rock she could hold in her palm. She zooms in with her oculars to the scaffolding at the top of the asteroid. The starship is there, poised for flight, inelegant and awkward.

Contreras stands beside a set of four dish-shaped antennas, each of which come to his knees. They are arranged at different angles and on swivel mounts. Beside each of them is a large metal block.

"You coming?" he asks.

Stacy glances away from Juno. Maybe she will learn now why he asked her on this EVA. "Okay."

But he gives no hints. "They're at different angles so we can get a three-D representation of the images."

Contreras launches into a lengthy description of the antennas and nearby instruments and how they're used to observe the Inorganics. Stacy records it, but doubts she can use any of it for her dailies.

After several minutes, Contreras taps one of the antennas. "Sensors were showing that this one stops short of a full rotation, which means yours truly has to get it unstuck. If I were on Earth, I'd complain about having to do work like this. But here, I thank the general each time for the opportunity to go outside."

"Yeah. This is awesome." Stacy again turns from the station to record a view of the stars. So many of them. So many patterns.

"Come look at this."

Contreras stands several meters from the antenna. He glances over his shoulder in the direction of one of the station's cameras. In his current position, he will be out of view.

She hesitates. This is the moment.

When she comes within arm's length, he gestures to the radio knob on his chest and turns it all the way clockwise. Off. Then he points to her radio knob.

Stacy cocks her head to the side, and he nods, using his entire upper torso. She puts her hand to the knob on the center of her chest and turns the radio off. The white noise, which she didn't notice before, disappears. General Young will be unable to listen.

Contreras holds out two fingers and taps at his faceplate in the location where his eyes would be. It takes her a moment, but she realizes what he means and stops her implant's recording. She nods.

Then he grabs her shoulders. Stacy squirms, but Contreras pulls her closer. Does he mean to kill her? He lured her out here and convinced her to turn the radio off, and she trusted him, and…

Their faceplates clink together, and his grip loosens. For the first time since they suited up, she can see his face. His eyes are intense, begging.

"Read the Ratti Report." His voice sounds tinny, echoing in her helmet. It is clearer than the radio, with no background noise. It echoes within her helmet like her breath.

"What?"

"It's important. The Ratti Report. R-A-T-T-I."

With that, he turns his radio back on and gestures for her to do the same. She does, and starts recording again.

His voice comes over the radio as he withdraws. "So I just squirt a little lubrication into the track and see what happens."

As Contreras kneels beside the antenna, he pulls a can from a suit pocket. He keeps up his patter as he works.

Stacy makes a note in her implant: Ratti Report. Although she has no idea what it contains, she knows Young won't like it.

NINETEEN

STACY FLOATS IN the Machining Room again, watching Jason continue its repetitive motions. Its arm rotate, it extends its fingers, it lowers the arm and grabs imaginary rock.

She doesn't know why she watches, but still, she finds herself in this room, in front of this console, at least once a day. Stacy wants to ask Trevor about the Ratti Report, but Young has access to every possible communication from the station: email, video, probably even Morse code flashes with the station lights. In none of Stacy's previous assignments has she felt so stifled without being imprisoned.

Instead, Stacy has pored through her previously downloaded documents. Ratti was listed as serving on Collins in 2118, but she could find nothing of note about him. Maybe his report is classified. Her only hope of finding it, and Contreras made it sound possible, is if it is accessible aboard the station.

On the screen, Jason rotates its arm again and extended its fingers. The same as every time. Stacy leaves for the Records Room.

When Stacy reaches Module 8, Anderson is entering the module from the other end. The lieutenant glances up as the hatch closes behind her.

"Hi," says Stacy.

Anderson waves as she pulls herself along the crowded wall

to the Power Room. Stacy heads to the Records Room, hoping Young hasn't locked the report.

"Hey," says Anderson. "You're not supposed to go in there."

Stacy grabs the railing and stops, her knees bumping against a storage bin a meter from the Records Room door. "I'm not?"

"General Young said." Anderson kicks off from the wall and stands between Stacy and the door. "I'm sorry. I know you're a reporter and you're used to looking at things you're not supposed to, but I can't let you go in there."

"Well." Stacy frowns. "The general never told *me* I couldn't go in there. So I think it should be okay." She pulls herself the remaining meter and reaches for the button beside the door.

"But…" Anderson looks confused. "That was an order."

As Stacy's finger touches the button, a *click* sounds in her head. The noise is so soft, she at first thinks she's imagined it, or that maybe it is one of the omnipresent mechanical sounds from the station systems. But the vents or computers or the thermal settling of the station's infrastructure never make that particular sound.

Then she realizes what it was: her implant giving her a warning before being deactivated by external software.

Stacy stops and stares at Anderson. "That door has malware."

Anderson cocks her head. "Malware? I've never noticed, but it could be a security feature. You did try to trespass."

"I guess so."

Stacy spins a one-eighty, kicks away from the Records Room, and flies across the corridor to the module's forward door. Her implant seems fine. She can access all her files, can see her emails, and can send a test message to one of her other accounts without issue. A diagnostic reveals no problems, and no unauthorized software or remote watchers.

Still, her implant wouldn't have made that sound unless an internal activity started or an external program entered the implant. She reactivates her warning system. It boots up without issue and displays no error messages, as though nothing happened.

She doesn't know what this spyware can do. It might do nothing more than monitor her videos and writing, but maybe it will report her mental activities or corrupt her files. Or her memories. If she removes the spyware, will she even know which memories it altered?

Trevor would know how to remove it. Stacy opens a message to him.

> *Hello, my wonderful husband. I think I'm in trouble. Today, when I—*

Stacy stops and erases the message. Young would read it. Maybe the spyware has already transmitted it to the general. If it has, secrecy means nothing. Either way, Stacy needs help to remove the ware.

When she reaches her quarters, she slides into her sleeping bag and rolls it tightly around her. It takes two minutes to compose a quick message to Trevor, then several more to assure herself it will reveal no more than basic information to the general. Trevor's response arrives less than an hour later.

> *I'll send you some instructions for disabling any spyware and for blocking any additional programs. It should work for most programs, but since you're likely dealing with top-secret ware, I don't know if you can get it completely off.*

> *Be careful. But you know that. Scrambled implants can prevent you from being able to install any other implants, or they could damage your brain, or even leave you brain-dead. Please, please be careful, sweetheart.*

Trevor sends detailed instructions for removing software in the next message. Complicated and tedious, but she has no choice. Almost an hour later, her efforts seem successful. She quarantined several files flagged as spyware. Hopefully, she's found everything.

When Stacy enters the Analysis Room, Contreras and Anderson look up. General Young doesn't turn from the computer screen the three of them are studying.

"General."

Anderson glances between Stacy and the general. Her mouth forms a tiny 'O.' Contreras tries to keep a neutral expression, but his posture screams defiance. Not toward Stacy, she doesn't think, but toward the general.

Young waits a few moments, making a show of coming to a stopping place in her examination of the screen before turning to Stacy. A thin layer of boredom coats her tone. "Ms. Sterling."

"Can I talk to you?"

"I'll make time." With a languid motion, the general gestures to Anderson and Contreras to keep working. They shoot surreptitious glances as Stacy and the general leave the room.

Neither Stacy nor Young speak until they enter the general's quarters. When Stacy first saw the décor here weeks ago, she thought the odd arrangement indicated Young's adaptation to zero-g. Now, it makes Young seem unhinged.

Young hooks her feet in place by her computer, folds her arms, and faces Stacy. "Yes?"

Stacy takes her place beside the door and meets Young's piercing eyes. "You installed spyware on my implant."

"I can't confirm or deny that. You should know better than to ask."

"You're blocking me from the Records Room."

"The Records Room is off-limits to civilians now. It's a recent change. I should have informed you earlier. My apologies."

Her voice contains no hint of apology.

Stacy frowns. "I'm the only civilian here. So, just me, then."

"If you need any material, you may request it. We'll make sure you get it if it's appropriate."

If the general thinks it is appropriate. "What was the reason for the change?"

Young remains stone-faced. "It came to my attention that not all of the documents in the Records Room should be released to the public."

Young stares Stacy in the eyes as though she has no shame, as though she isn't actively working against the truth. Like every dictator Stacy has faced, Young feels justified in the wrongs she commits. And like those dictators, she won't prevent Stacy from telling the truth.

"I caution you," says Young, "against including much of Sergeant Contreras in your reports."

Stacy shakes her head. "Why? He seems to hate the Inorganics even more than you do."

"Yes. We both agree on the danger they represent. Sergeant Contreras, though, thinks more information will make them seem more dangerous."

"Yeah," says Stacy. "If the public knows the truth, th—"

"How often have they done the right thing?" Young frowns. "How often has the public even listened? The more available information, the muddier the underlying truth becomes. People fixate on a certain aspect of an issue without seeing the whole picture and come to an incorrect opinion on the issue as a whole. I have observed that one can report the truth while still telling a lie."

"I don't report lies." Stacy folds her arms across her chest. "And I don't need a lesson in journalism ethics."

"Maybe not." Young straightens. "But you need some correction. You've lost the mission, Stacy."

Stacy's mission remains the same as always: tell the truth, even if those in power don't want to hear it. Even if the public doesn't care. Even if it costs her.

"You're doing an exposé about the station," says Young. "Or maybe me. You are so focused on it, you've forgotten the real problem: getting people to understand the threat and start fighting back against the Inorganics."

"I…"

The general is right. Stacy spent hours tracking down the cause of the IMS failure. She searched for Jason, which might have hurt their cause. Now, she is trying to find a copy of the Ratti Report. She hasn't spent enough time focusing on the Inorganics themselves.

Young's voice never rises as she speaks. "What makes me so angry is that you have the potential to change the world, it's right in your grasp, and you are deliberately not doing it."

"Do you really want me to keep reporting?" Stacy asks. "It sounds as though you don't want a factual account. You just want to make a movie about how violent the Inorganics are."

Young's mouth quirks upward. An instant later, it is level again.

"I know how to get results," says Young. "I organized a research initiative on the Moon to study the Inorganics at close range. I organized a mental-health support group at headquarters. Collins Station was my idea. I pushed it through the SDF bureaucracy and made it happen. It wasn't easy to get funding for a project like this, but I did it. So maybe you should listen to me when I tell you how to do things."

The general's earnestness and self-righteousness bother Stacy the most. Such conviction that her way is right.

Or maybe what bothers Stacy most is the possibility that the general really *is* right.

"I'll think about it." Stacy glances at the floor.

Young's face hardens, but her eyes tremble. "I think being too familiar with you has muddied our relationship. Our movie nights are over."

"Oh." Stacy's stomach clenches. Those movie nights felt awkward, but to have them withdrawn feels like a rejection. For the first time, she realizes how alone she is out here.

Young gestures to the door in a motion that seems too heavy for the lack of gravity. "I won't keep you from your work any longer."

TWENTY

JASON CONTINUES CYCLING through the same actions. The order of motion varies depending on the topography of the imaginary object it exploits, but the steps for each particular motion proceed in the same order each time. *Rotate gripping arm to a position two hundred seventy degrees from the origin. Extend the five digits of the gripping arm's hand to their farthest extensions. Lower arm…* Jason has only minor variations on the stimuli it receives, and it has the same limited range of response for each stimulus. It has no impetus for change, and without that impetus, it can never develop intelligence.

And yet, every time Stacy enters this room, a chill runs along her spine.

The door opens behind her. Light spills from the hallway into the Machining Room. Stacy glances up from her perch in front of Jason to see the general enter.

It is hard for hair as short as the general's to look disheveled, but it does. Her eyes sag, lines crowd her face, and she pulls herself through the room with concentration and deliberateness.

Stacy adjusts her legs so she can face the general. "Are you okay?"

Young chuckles half-heartedly. "Do I look that bad? I'm fine."

The wall clock reads 2126. The second Shift 3 of the day. Earlier in the mission, Stacy would have used this period for sleep. So would Young. "Shouldn't you be asleep now?"

Young plants herself in footholds beside Stacy, their arms brushing as they hang along the wall. "Normally, yes."

"Did you come here for some quiet?"

"Not exactly." At other times, Young might hide her frustration. Stacy imagines the general is too exhausted for pretense. "I saw you were still awake, so I decided to tell you in person. Headquarters has conducted a lengthy review of your report and of the data they have on the AIS program as a whole, and they have made a decision. They sent orders to shut down the AIS."

"Oh." Shutting it down could mean turning off the computer on which Jason runs, or it could mean deleting the program. Effectively, killing Jason.

Young studies her. "I thought you'd be happy about it."

"I did, too. But I don't know how I feel. Does that make sense?"

"Not really."

On the screen, Jason scoops another chunk of emptiness into its storage space. A simple creature, with limited tools and no understanding. Like a child, full of potential. That potential will be destroyed, even this mundane existence terminated, because Stacy brought it to the attention of the public.

"It's stupid." Young leans forward, bringing her face closer to the screen. She taps it with a fingernail, making a dull thunk. "Their decision. They didn't follow my recommendations. Did you ever read the Feynman autobiography?"

Stacy shakes her head. "No, I don't think so. Who was she?"

"He was a twentieth-century physicist who worked on the Manhattan Project. One of his hobbies was lockpicking, and he would practice with the filing cabinets in each office. He had a good system, but it worried him that he could figure out the combinations so easily. He knew if *he* could do it, so could someone with more sinister intentions. So he warned one of the security officers and suggested they get a more secure type of lock. Instead of changing the locks, the security officer sent a memo throughout the base telling people not to leave Feynman unsupervised in any of their offices."

Stacy laughs. "So you think that's like what the SDF is doing now? The wrong solution to the problem?"

"That's how humans usually respond to problems." Even in zero-g, Young's shoulders seem to sag.

Stacy studies the general. Young has been fighting this one-person war for five years. Longer. Doing what she knows is right, but unable to convince anyone else. Her allies turning against her or not understanding what she is trying to do. Even Stacy.

Then Stacy remembers that the general set a spyware trap for her and treated her as a tool for achieving an agenda. "I think there are more appropriate tactics to use."

A high-pitched squeal, like metal scraping metal, assaults Stacy's ears. She grits her teeth, but it does nothing to muffle the sound.

"What's…" She listens. Vents continue pushing air, and straps flap against each other in the room's currents. The squeal sounds as though it came from the next module. "Do you think the station is falling apart?"

Young holds up a finger and floats motionless for several seconds, tense. "I'm going to check." She kicks toward the aft door.

"I'll come, too."

"No, wai…" Young halts at the door. "Actually, good idea. Start recording. We'll at least want it for documentation."

Stacy releases her nanocams and starts her implant recording as she enters the next module. It contains the pod, docking port, and the airlock. The door slides open, and Young slips through like an operative on a stealth mission. Stacy pulls herself through and fans her nanocams to all sides of the module.

The squealing grows louder here. The corridor lighting remains normal. Straps slap against the walls in a counter-rhythm to the squealing, and the walls themselves shake in slow motion, as though underwater.

No signs of activity come from the airlock. Through its porthole, Stacy can see its interior is dark. The docking port is also dark.

A bright flicker comes from the left. The pod.

Its door is open, as normal. Its interior lights are off, though a muted light is coming from within, like someone reading under the covers with a flashlight. Stacy turns to Young, but the general is focusing on the pod.

The general reaches the pod and places a hand on the doorframe. Her eyebrows furrow. "Stay here."

Before Stacy can protest or warn her, though she doesn't know what kind of warning she would give, the general flies into the pod and glides straight down the middle of the aisle between the seats.

Stacy has sat across small tables from bloodthirsty dictators. She has been thrown in prison. She has reported live from battles in China. Entering a pod, even a malfunctioning pod, could be no riskier than her previous assignments. Leaving her nanocams behind, she grabs the doorframe and eases herself inside.

The air is cold and dry, chillier than when Jalindo and the others were installing equipment and software. The environmental settings must have been deactivated.

Flashing lights surround her, floor to wall to ceiling, creating a distracting strobe effect. She reaches for the chair in front of her, but misses. As she enters a slow rotation, legs spinning upward, she catches herself on the wall. At first, she thinks the pod must have lurched or rocked loose from the clamps holding it to the station, but the stars remain unchanged outside the forward window, still and steady.

One shaky hand over the other, she pulls herself forward. As she passes the first row of chairs, more flickers catch her attention. The computer screens, embedded into each wall beside their corresponding chair, glow. Text switches to images, then back again. On the forward window, the lights' reflections overlay the stars, flashing and fading like a manic Christmas display.

It could be a malfunction. But few malfunctions would have symptoms affecting multiple systems. Did someone sabotage the pod?

She continues to the front row and takes the co-pilot's seat beside Young, hooking her legs into the floor holds, but leaving the seat's straps floating. Her screen flashes at her.

Young doesn't look up from her own console. "Someone is activating the pod. The engines and control systems are coming online. I don't know who's doing it."

Stacy has seen this pattern before: a mysterious problem afflicts irreplaceable equipment required to investigate the Inorganics, which then causes danger to the station. The IMS incident, and maybe the failure of Ko's drill. "Did you sabotage the pod, too?"

Young's jaw drops, and her hands pause with their fingers hovering over the keypad. "What?"

"We both know I know you sabotaged the IMS. So it's reasonable to expect you might have sabotaged the pod, too. I doubt many other crewmembers have the systems privileges to do it. It plays exactly into the narrative you're trying to promote."

Young returns to typing, each stroke more forceful than before. "No. I did not sabotage the pod. Something is preparing it to leave the station, and I need to shut it down before it does, which takes a lot of concentration, so kindly be quiet."

Menus flit past on Young's screen, changing from one to the next before Stacy can decipher the content. Each time a menu shifts, Young's face tightens. She is losing the battle.

Stacy's own console zips through menus, straining her eyes. She has time to glimpse the titles in an almost subliminal manner. Navigation, flying, power, instruments, propulsion.

"Shut down navigation," says the general.

Stacy has never piloted a pod before or even watched someone else do it. She clicks the navigation button and hopes she will select the correct options.

A menu pops up asking her whether to use mini-satellite triangulation, triangulation from the Deep Space Positioning System, range from the station, star trackers, or to disconnect the outside cameras from the navigation system and enter simulation mode. She decides to choose the last option.

When she hits the button, a window pops up asking for an access code. Stacy has never received a passcode for any system aboard the station.

"I'm getting the same thing," says the general. Her screen has a window saying, 'Invalid Code.' "The codes must have been changed."

Stacy doubts anyone on the station has the authority to lock Young from the systems. Maybe someone from SDF Headquarters sabotaged the station, but there is no reason for them to do it unless they want to make a heavy-handed attempt at removing Young's influence. Or preventing Stacy's reporting.

Stacy glances along the walls. "Is there a way to physically shut down the pod?"

"Circuit breakers." Young yanks the seat straps free and kicks out from her chair to the rear of the pod. She stops beside a panel on the back wall and opens it to reveal a column of switches. Like a pianist playing a glissando, she snaps all the switches to the left.

In an instant, every console in the pod goes blank. Fans spin down, their hums fading. Ambient noise from the computers and electronics evaporates. Under normal circumstances, this level of quiet aboard the station would signal a problem. Now, Stacy feels as though she can breathe again.

She and the general turn to each other in the dark. Young's shoulders drop, and she leans back against her seat. "Good idea about the circuit breakers. I thought we'd lost the pod. And maybe both of us. We need to figure out who did this."

The flashing lights vanish, clearing the forward window so the stars shine through again. So much emptiness out there.

"Who would have done it?" asks Stacy.

Young gives her a wry smile. "You mean, besides me?"

"Well…"

Young shrugs. "Possibly a—"

Red lights pop on. An eerie glow drapes the pod, and the stars no longer shine clearly through the window.

"Why did the lights come on?" asks Stacy.

A whirring sound comes from behind one of the overhead panels. A fan starting to spin. Young's head snaps in that direction. Another fan begins spinning, this time above Stacy's head. Then another, and another.

Stacy pushes herself up from the seat, bracing herself with a hand on the ceiling. The consoles snap back to life, all of them at once, their lights once again flashing across the walls and ceiling. On Stacy's screen, the entry display vanishes, and text races upward more quickly than she can read.

The speaker crackles on. Maybe the saboteur will announce their demands, now that they've proven ownership of the situation. Stacy pushes herself back into the co-pilot's seat.

"General." It is Captain Ko. Not the person Stacy expected. His voice comes through calm, level, as though discussing the weather on Juno. "We're tracking a problem in the pod. There was an unexpected signal from the Machining Room minutes ago. Did you notice anything there?"

Not the saboteur, then. A signal from the Machining Room, though…

General Young meets Stacy's eyes. For a moment, they stare.

"We were both in the Machining Room," says Stacy. "I didn't send the signal."

Young's brows furrow. "Are you still on that theory? I didn't do it. But now I know who did. Captain, could the AIS have transmitted itself to the pod's computer?"

The AIS. Jason.

"I…What?" Ko pauses. "I'll check."

"I thought that was impossible," says Stacy. "You told me Jason couldn't escape."

She empathized with Jason, trapped in its digital cell. But that was dumb. Jason is a machine, and now it is trying to… She doesn't know what it is trying to do, whether it is trying to harm the station or its captors or to escape. She grabs the armrests, ready to launch herself to the exit.

"We'll assume the AIS is trying to hijack the pod." Young continues typing at the console. She swears.

The general and her crew promised Stacy, swore to her, that she was safe from Jason. Now she is in a pod controlled by it. The Inorganics killed her father, and now one might kill her.

The text on the screen seems to slow. "Good." Young types more. "I think I headed it off."

A few more moments of typing, and Young freezes. As text scrolls more quickly than Stacy can read, Young raises her finger from the console and slowly, deliberately, pushes a button. The text continues, unslowed. Young pushes the button again. Then again. No change.

Young turns to Stacy. "We should leave."

Stacy pushes against the armrests to lift herself into the air, then grabs the headrest of the seat behind her. She launches herself forward with all the force she can manage, like a swimmer hauling herself along an ocean floor by grabbing rocks. The chairs pass by underneath her as she shoots straight toward the door.

The door shuts.

Her forehead slams into it with enough force to cause a bruise. As her body bounces backward from the impact, she scrambles to snatch the wall's railing. Her fingertips slide over the curved surface and then past as her tumbling takes her out of reach. A leg bumps into a headrest, and she grabs a chair in the last row. Her shoulders wrench as her body comes to a halt.

Young catches herself more gracefully. With one hand on the railing and her feet in floor holds, her other hand hammers against the button beside the door. Nothing happens.

"General," says Ko over the speaker. "You should leave the pod. It initiated the undocking sequence."

Booming clicks come from outside the pod's hull. Metal clangs. The pod shifts to the right as the clamps release.

"It's going to leave with us in it," says Stacy.

There are no spacesuits in the pod.

"General," says Ko. "The spring-release sys—"

The radio's ambient white noise vanishes. From all around Stacy come the creaks of metal expansion as the pod's systems warm up. More fans whir into action from behind the bulkhead on either side of the pod.

Young grips the seat in front of her. "Hold on to something."

Stacy reaches forward, her fingers clutching a headrest.

They are buffeted by a slight jerk behind them. If Stacy weren't holding on, she would be thrown forward into the window. She keeps her grip, and her knees bump into the back of the seat.

"That was the spring-release," says Young. "We separated from the station."

Loud thumps come from outside. The attitude thrusters are firing. In the window, the stars rotate. When their motion stops, a short burst of vibration comes from the rear, and Stacy has to tighten her grip to keep from flying forward.

"Orbit change," says Young. "The pod doesn't have enough thrust to leave Juno's neighborhood. It's stuck in orbit around Juno, so the most it can do is change its altitude."

An altitude change would be enough. If it takes them past the five-hundred-kilometer threshold, the Inorganics will catch them and dismantle the pod around them. They might destroy Jason in the process, but maybe Jason doesn't know that fact. Stacy and the general will suffocate in the vacuum if the Inorganics don't dismantle them, too.

Young flies forward to the pilot's seat again, grabbing the control stick as she guides herself into the footholds. She flips a switch on the console, then dips the stick to the right.

Outside, the stars turn in response. The station comes into view at the window's periphery.

"Got it," says Young.

Then the motion halts. Attitude thrusters fire, sounding like sharp bangs. The stars begin turning again, and the station rolls from sight. Young twists the control stick in all directions, but the movement has no effect on the pod.

"Guess not," says Young.

Below the seat in front of Stacy, yellow fabric bounces with the pod's motion. "The emergency balls."

"Yes," says Young. "It's that time."

They will leave the pod and enter empty space, putting themselves at the mercy of potential rescuers. There will be nothing but vacuum for kilometers around, like submariners abandoning their vehicle in the middle of the ocean. But they have no choice.

Stacy pulls herself over the seat, her feet kicking in the air. She grabs the yellow fabric and slides it from under the seat. It is folded into a thick, flat square.

"Just like the training video." The poor animation and even worse dialogue don't seem so funny now.

She unfolds the ball, flipping sections quickly, knowing that the longer she takes, the farther she will be from the station. When it fully unfurls, it hangs in the air, round and flat, little more than half as tall as she is. Pulling aside the opening, she presses her hand against its back wall and pushes the ball into three-dimensionality, then slides it over herself like a jacket.

Her arms, legs, back, everything touch one of the ball's walls. Not enough room to stand, or even crouch. She rolls herself into a fetal position. When she's made sure her entire body is enclosed within the ball, she presses the sealing button.

Each side of the opening instantly snaps together, more quickly than a zipper, to form an airtight seam. Hissing fills the air until the ball inflates. It should have up to twenty-four hours of air, if she breathes slowly. From the video, she knows a beacon will be transmitting now in case anyone is coming to rescue her. Two armholes with gloves allow her to reach outside and grab something without leaving the security of the ball. A thin, squat window, embedded in the fabric, gives her a limited view of the outside.

The general, in her own inflated ball, pushes herself toward the door. The yellow ball rotates as it crosses the room, the arms slowly rolling counter-clockwise away from the door. Stacy worries the arms will end up opposite the door when Young arrives, and her ball will bounce off the wall and across the cabin. As the ball reaches the door, Young manages to grab the door handle.

Then Young swings open the case beside the door and pulls the emergency-release lever. Stacy braces herself.

Outside her tiny window, everything blurs. Ceiling, seats, and floor shoot away, replaced by stars. Stacy's stomach bounces around her chest cavity. She puts her hands on the ball's fabric walls to hold herself steady as it begins a slow rotation. The station eases into view from the right side of her tiny window and slides out the left side. A minute later, it appears again.

The general's ball is not in sight. It could be above Stacy or below her or could be too small to see. Or maybe the general didn't escape the pod.

And now Stacy floats alone in space, with twenty-four hours of oxygen and no idea if anyone can find her.

TWENTY-ONE

FABRIC SCRATCHES THE tops of Stacy's hands. She has wrapped her arms tightly around herself in an attempt to create more space within the emergency ball, but the additional space does nothing to reduce the sensation of the world collapsing against her. She bobs between the walls, four centimeters one way before bouncing off that soft wall, then four centimeters the other way to bounce off the other wall.

She tries to send a quick message to Collins through her implant, but it fails. The emergency ball must be out of range of the station. She hopes her beacon is still operational, but she won't know until someone rescues her. Or until they don't.

When she closes her eyes, she feels like she is falling endlessly. Her heartbeat accelerates and her breathing increases, consuming more of her limited oxygen supply. She allows herself one deep breath, then lets it out in a slow stream. Then another, shallower. *In. Out.* Maybe she can fall asleep. Sleep is the best way to lower her metabolism and reduce her oxygen consumption. She compresses herself into a tighter fetal position.

In most situations, she has no trouble dropping immediately into sleep. Trevor told her she will say, "Goodnight," and plummet into unconsciousness within thirty seconds. Now, when she needs that ability, when her survival depends on her falling asleep, she is wide awake.

More troublesome than her high oxygen consumption is the cold seeping in from the outside. What did the safety video say about the ball's thermal controls? She can remember every single terrible joke and every forced delivery or fake facial expression from the video, but she can't remember the details that can keep her alive. Maybe the thermal controls will last a day. Then the cold will leach through the fabric and into her skin, shutting her body down.

She hears a tinkling noise. It sounds distant, as though it's coming from outside. Someone coming to get her?

But sound doesn't travel through vacuum. It must be her imagination. She sighs, then regrets it. More wasted oxygen.

She should have known Jason would escape. Stacy would have dug deeper into how Jason was stored and the safeguards used to contain it, but she had trusted the general and ignored her own fears about the machine. Never again.

If there is an again.

She wishes she got to say goodbye to Trevor. If she dies out here, in the cold vacuum, the SDF will contact him. It would be an impersonal call. Stern, matter-of-fact, the SDF offering their condolences, then a quick goodbye.

She records a brief message for him. A goodbye and a stream-of-consciousness essay on how much he means to her.

She wonders how long it will be before he moves on and forgets her. Maybe, since she's already been away for months, it won't take that long.

She is feeling sorry for herself, and it is unhelpful.

But the data. All the data she has recorded, the unaired interviews and the information from her IMS investigation and all the footage of Jason's escape, all of it will be lost.

No, the crew will attempt a rescue mission. She is sure of it.

But the more she thinks, the more she doubts. Jason has hijacked the station's only pod. Maybe the crew can do nothing but say a few kind words and consign Stacy and the general to the deep.

She doesn't know how much time has passed. She could check her implant. It has an accurate watch, which can give her the time relative to any event. But she doesn't want to know, not yet.

Her nanocams' signals can no longer reach her. Their videos ended shortly after the pod's departure. Not that they would have showed much after the pod door closed.

Maybe, in her final moments, she should destroy the footage. If anyone recovers her body, they will get her footage from her point of view. Destroying data is anathema to her journalist's sensibilities, but it is better than being the subject of the story.

Something tugs her ball. It must be her imagination, like the sound from earlier.

A moment later, another tug startles her, and a steady acceleration presses her against the side of her ball.

An Inorganic? Grabbing her like the Inorganics grabbed the IMS? They could rip through the escape ball's fabric more quickly than they ripped through the metal of the IMS.

But she and the general escaped well above the altitude threshold, and she can't have dipped below that point in this short amount of time. Which means someone is retrieving her.

She sighs, letting out a long breath, and relaxes. She will survive.

She closes her eyes. At least she is being returned to safety.

With a start, she realizes what she thought of as a safe haven is only a thousand kilometers from the most dangerous beings in the Solar System, and Jason has just escaped the station to join their ranks.

UNDER NORMAL CIRCUMSTANCES, the shuttle cockpit's ambient temperature would have felt pleasant, twenty-five Celsius with sixty percent humidity, but Stacy still feels chilled from the hours in the escape ball. She pulls the thermal blanket tighter, letting it hug her arms into her ribs, and tries to ignore the occasional full-body shiver.

She dangles at the back of the cockpit, feet curled under the railing by the door to the passenger area, and stretches her back to its fullest extent. The debrief has almost ended, and Stacy will have to question one of Young's decisions soon. The general is unlikely to react well.

Young floats to the left of the door. No blanket for her. The general is at full alertness with steely eyes, firm and authoritative, like a modern-day Gene Kranz. She looks as though she's been waiting for this moment all her life and is happy it's here, like when Shackleton met his moment in Antarctica. She finishes her description of the events from her point of view.

Contreras and Anderson float along the side wall in front of Stacy while they listen, still wearing their silver EVA suits and holding their helmets. Their backpacks force them to lean forward from the wall at awkward angles. The lieutenant's face looks strained, her eyes focused on something distant. Her brows furrow with that same expression of self-loathing she wore after the IMS crisis. Contreras's face glistens with drying sweat. His eyes flash each time he glances out the forward window.

With one hand, Contreras holds onto the back of the copilot's seat where Prabhakhar taps at a console. Jalindo sits in the pilot's seat on the left. They divide their attention between their consoles and the curving window at the front of the cockpit. The bright expanse of the station occupies the window's upper right corner, coming closer.

"Thirty minutes until docking," says Prabhakhar without turning. "Did you all finish the debriefing? Sorry, I wasn't listening."

Young turns to Stacy and raises a thin gray eyebrow. "I'm done. Anything to add?"

Stacy knows the military personnel will not appreciate criticism from a civilian, but she has to speak. "I'm sorry, but I think this event was preventable."

"I'm not arguing it wasn't," Young says. "But I believe we all made good decisions leading up to this point."

"If you hadn't blocked my investigation, I could have dug into it more deeply and asked the right questions that would have prevented Jason's escape."

Stacy thinks she glimpses a momentary twitch of Young's mouth, but the general regains expressionlessness so quickly, Stacy questions what she saw. Anderson's eyes and mouth go wide while Contreras smirks.

"Is that what you think?" Young asks.

Stand firm. "Yes."

"You think you could have, in less than a week, discovered some weakness in our system that we have not discovered in five years out here?"

"I'm an outsider." The others have made that clear. "I have a different perspective than you all."

"If you had discovered any weaknesses," Young says, "which I think is unlikely, and if you had warned us, the AIS would have heard it, just as it heard me telling you we were going to shut it down."

"I could have found another way to deliver the message."

"It's a hypothetical situation." Young shrugs. "I'll note your comment, but I don't think it would have changed anything."

"Maybe our whole approach to the Innies is wrong," says Contreras.

Young frowns. "I'm aware of your opinion on the matter, Sergeant. There is nothing to be gained by repeating it."

Contreras closes his mouth, looking as though he's struggling to stop talking. He settles back in place against the wall.

Anderson raises her head. Her eyes quiver. "General, I would like to report a mistake made during the EVA."

Contreras gives her a puzzled, hurt glance, but says nothing. He crosses his arms in front of his chest pack and stares forward with a neutral expression.

Young gestures to Anderson. "You have the floor, Lieutenant."

Anderson straightens. "When we began the EVA, I ordered Sergeant Contreras to help me with the first emergency bag instead of splitting up so we could each retrieve one bag. I believed the buddy system was important. Because of my decision, Ms. Sterling's bag was allowed to drift farther away and was exposed to the space environment unnecessarily long. If it had drifted too far away, we might have lost track of her and been unable to retrieve her before…her consumables expired."

Before her consumables expired. An understated way of describing what could have happened to Stacy.

Young stares. "I don't see the mistake, Lieutenant."

Stacy glances at the general. Was that a joke?

Anderson's face twitches. "We could have lost Ms. Sterling."

"The buddy system is the recommended procedure for a retrieval operation," says Young. "You did well."

"I think it was the wrong procedure, ma'am."

"Please submit your recommendation to the review panel, then. We haven't had many incidents like this, so they will value your feedback."

Anderson opens her mouth as though to insist on being court-martialed. A moment passes, and her face tightens. "Yes, ma'am."

"Lieutenant," says Stacy. "Sergeant. I owe you my life. You rescued me. I'm certainly not going to complain. Thank you so much. Because of you all, I'm alive."

"Hey!" Jalindo doesn't turn in their seat. "Keep it down. Some of us are flying up here. Don't need all that mushy stuff."

The others chuckle. In a whisper, Stacy says to Anderson, "I mean it, Lieutenant. You two are getting Christmas cards for life."

Anderson gives her a wan smile which quickly disappears.

Young speaks again. "The next issue, which Stacy alluded to earlier, is to discuss how we allowed the AIS to escape."

Contreras and Anderson stare at the floor. At the front of the cockpit, Prabhakhar's and Jalindo's shoulders tense, and their necks lower.

"We thought it was contained," says the general. "We missed any indications it had gotten access to the outside. It had no connection to other systems, no input or output other than the keyboard and the screen. So how did it escape?"

She is answered by the hum of the air ventilation, the soft whirring of system fans, and the tap of fabric against wall as Stacy and the others bob in place.

The general frowns. "Speculation?"

Prabhakhar straightens. "It's not completely true there were no other inputs."

In every situation where people think they have complete control, there is always an unpredicted caveat caused by the difference between theory and practice.

"I might have found that out," says Stacy, "if I'd been allowed to conduct my investigation. That's why I'd like free reign to investigate other subjects related to Jason."

Young frowns. "You've made your point, Ms. Sterling. Major, please continue."

No one else in the cockpit meets Stacy's eyes.

"In order to give Jason additional commands," says Prabhakhar, "we used an external drive. Commands would be transferred from our system's computers to the external drive, and the drive would be plugged in to Jason's drive. It was strictly input, no output."

Young frowns like a disappointed parent. Or maybe she is disappointed in herself for not knowing this detail of station operations. "You think Jason could have transferred itself, or a copy of itself, to the drive, and from the drive to our system?"

"Yes," says Prabhakhar. "Possibly. I don't know how, but even if we used the drive strictly for input, it's possible Jason could have uploaded its source code without our noticing. We weren't checking for uploads because we didn't think Jason was capable of doing it. Or it could have installed another program that allowed it access to outside systems."

"Ma'am?" Anderson glances at Stacy. "Should we be discussing this topic in front of Ms. Sterling? No offense, Ms. Sterling."

After everything Stacy has experienced, she deserves to be included. "Sorry. I'm not trying to interfere."

Young seems to see those thoughts in her face. "Good point, Lieutenant, but Ms. Sterling has already seen a lot. She's in deep enough that she might as well go all the way, and I'll review her reports to make certain nothing inappropriate is told to the public."

Stacy nods. She can retain the information and release it after returning to Earth.

"Ma'am?" Contreras says. "You said it…Jason knew it was going to be deactivated? And that was the trigger for its escape?"

Young nods. "That is my hypothesis, given the timing."

"Does that mean," says Anderson, "Jason has a…fear of death?"

Young shoots her a glare. Contreras looks surprised.

"Couldn't that just be its programming?" asks Stacy. "The asteroid-mining proto-Inorganics would have been programmed to avoid destruction, right?"

Anderson frowns. "The proto-Inorganics had rules similar to Asimov's rules, so it would have been required to prioritize following orders and not endangering humans over self-preservation."

"And Jason definitely endangered humans during its escape," says Contreras. "It acted just like the newer breeds of Innies. So it went beyond its original programming."

Stacy pulls her blanket tighter. "So you think your experiment worked? The radiation environment here altered the software and turned the AIS into an Inorganic?"

Contreras smirks. "Thor…I mean, Sergeant Windham would say the Innies on Juno sent a signal to Jason."

"Yes," says Prabhakhar. "He would say that. I think it more likely that Jason became active because of the radiation environment."

Stacy expected nothing else from Prabhakhar. "And it's unlikely it developed that level of intelligence at just that moment? So its intelligence was triggered by…a radiation event? A software update? And that event happened months or years ago?"

"Hm." Prabhakhar continues facing his console. His voice is strained. "That sounds right."

"So Jason has been intelligent for a while now. And you've been doing the same types of experiments with these AIs on the geostationary stations? And the Moon? And Mars? And… Earth?"

Contreras's and Anderson's expressions tighten. Prabhakhar's shoulders slump. Jalindo shudders. General Young looks unsurprised.

"Yes." Young's voice is calm. "If we send a message informing Command what happened, it might trigger another exodus on Earth and other locations. There's no way to keep the information locked down forever, though."

"Maybe," says Prabhakhar, "Jason will send a message. We don't know what it's thinking or what it's capable of."

Prabhakhar told Stacy the Inorganics had only a low level of intelligence. He said they had the reasoning ability of worms. Was he lying, or did he really never consider the possibility that the Inorganics are far smarter than humans?

"How long have these experiments been going on?" asks Stacy.

"Decades," says Young. "Long enough, as I'm sure you're about to ask, for those proto-Inorganics in captivity to have sent their source code to machines and computers anywhere on Earth. Or off Earth."

After the initial exodus of the Inorganics, anti-technology sentiment prevented the use of advanced algorithms. Humans still relied on machines, but those machines were kept simple. No learning algorithms, only code capable of calculations and a few simple manual operations.

After decades, though, as popular memory faded, complex code crept back into systems. Laws now prevent these programs from being as advanced as the code that allowed the birth of the Inorganics, but companies push their codes right to those limits. Every aspect of human life on Earth, from birth to schooling to driving to construction, relies on those machines and that code. If the Inorganics have infiltrated those systems, they could end human society.

Those thoughts play across the faces of Contreras, Anderson, and Jalindo. General Young must enjoy knowing that, finally, people are realizing what she has known for years.

Prabhakhar leans back in his chair. "Jason's actions imply a high level of intelligence, much higher than its original programming."

"Yes," says the general. "It didn't take long."

Could the general have aided Jason in becoming more intelligent as a way of proving her point? No, she wouldn't do something that reckless. Probably.

The radio crackles. Ko's voice comes through. "Shuttle, station."

Jalindo taps a button. "Station, shuttle. Go ahead."

"It appears the copy of Jason on the station was deleted."

So they can't study it. Or interrogate it.

"It also appears as though the data in our Records Room, including telemetry, documents, and personnel records, was copied and transmitted to the pod."

Young's face wrinkles. She probably has the same question Stacy has: Why does Jason care about that information?

Young motions for Jalindo to push the talk button. "Captain, have the crew cease their previous assignments and concentrate on learning how the AIS escaped and when it developed its new behavior. We missed something during the years of its operation, and we need to know what. That is our top priority."

"Yes, ma'am."

The telltale sign could have been anything: a blip in a system unrelated to Jason, or something indistinguishable from the noise in the station's data. Stacy foresees some sleepless nights for the crew.

"I guess there's not going to be a pod expedition, then," says Contreras.

Young raises an eyebrow. "Not with a pod, no. But we have the shuttle."

Prabhakhar turns around for the first time. "The shuttle isn't designed for the quick evasive maneuvers we would have to perform."

"No," says Young. "It's also not designed for rescue operations, but you did an admirable job of using it for that purpose. As Ms. Sterling and I can both attest."

Stacy smiles. "Yes."

Anderson looks as though she is going to say something, but her mouth tightens. Young seems to have noticed.

"I know the shuttle is our only way of returning to Earth. But this expedition is worth the risk, now more than ever. We need more information about the Inorganics, how the starship works, and how they think. After this incident, after the IMS incident, and after the accumulated incidents of the past, people will finally realize that understanding the Inorganics is vital to our survival."

The others nod. They look grim.

"Ms. Sterling." Young focuses her gaze on Stacy. "Put together a report as soon as possible. Document everything you saw, heard, felt."

Stacy pauses. "I didn't have my nanocams. I'll need to gather more footage. I'll also need to interview people. Everyone. I want to make a comprehensive report this time."

The others catch their breaths.

Young shakes her head. "That will be unnecessary. You have your raw footage. Release that, along with your voice-over explaining the events and your impressions."

"But…" Stacy's throat tightens. "That's not…I don't work that way. I've told you."

"You are not part of my crew." Young stares at her, those eyes boring into Stacy's soul. "I have no authority over you in that sense. But I am ordering you to produce this report the way I want. If you do not, you will no longer be doing reporting of any kind aboard my station."

The others turn to Stacy, even Jalindo. Stacy releases her thermal blanket. "I understand."

Stacy hates when her relationship with a subject reaches this stage, but it is her job to find and disseminate the truth.

Whatever it takes.

TWENTY-TWO

Holy shit. I'm so glad you're okay. That was terrifying. I wish you could come home right now. I know what you're doing is important, but I wish you could be safe.

I expect the general had something to do with the report's style. It looked like you posted raw footage from your oculars with a voiceover, and I know that's not something you would do without being forced into it. I hope you're okay up there.

The story went up a few minutes ago. The responses are pretty typical: people downplaying the event, or saying the Inorganics are so powerful that it's pointless to fight back, or demanding we attack the Inorganics, or showing "proof" the video was faked. It pisses me off seeing what you went through and what you're sacrificing so people know what's happening out there, and this is how they respond.

Please be careful. I love you.

TREVOR PICKED UP on the general's coercion. Stacy feels a perverse desire to push even harder to learn about the Ratti Report. Few people on the station are sympathetic enough to her to help, and even fewer will be willing to cross the general. But Stacy will find a way.

She blinks to close her mail and once again faces the computer that formerly held Jason. It looks no different than before. She knows she shouldn't have expected it to change, but it would seem more appropriate if the screen were cracked or if snapped wires were poking through the panels or if the panel were shattered. Anything other than the same worn screen she saw three days ago.

Stacy pushes off toward the forward door. If anyone would willingly help her sneak into the Records Room, it would be Thor. During this shift, he should be either working out or in the galley.

She finds him in the fitness module, running with gusto on one of the treadmills. He glances up as Stacy hooks herself into place on the neighboring treadmill.

"Is it okay if I record you?" She has to shout to be heard over the noise.

Thor shrugs. "It's a free country."

Stacy releases her nanocams and taps her head to indicate she has started recording. "Have you learned anything about why Jason left?"

"We haven't learned anything definitive." Thor grabs a vacuum clipped to the treadmill and suctions sweat droplets from his forehead. "We're looking through all the old records, trying to find any clues. I'm running statistics on routine data, like power consumption from each module, going all the way back to when the station was first turned on. We do several sets of statistics: one for the period of the station's entire life, one for each year, one for each month, and so on."

"You said you found nothing definitive, but did you find anything at all?"

"Ennui. New depths of boredom. But no, nothing that stands out. There are so many blips in the data I've had to track down, and they all ended up being something uneventful."

Jason hid itself potentially for years. It left no obvious traces. The crew might never learn when Jason became intelligent enough to escape.

"I wasn't sorry to see it go," says Thor. "We lost a lot of valuable data when Jason escaped, and it was almost like having a pet, but it could have been a lot worse. Keeping it here was like playing with a loaded gun."

"Yeah, I agree." Stacy shakes her head. "I don't know why other people thought it was safe."

"Yeah, well." Thor drops his voice to a whisper. "Do you think its escape was planned?"

"What do you mean?"

"You and I know the general sabotaged the IMS. Do you think she did something similar with Jason?"

"Well." Stacy smiles. "I asked her."

Thor bursts into laughter, grabbing the treadmill's railings as one of his feet almost slips from under him. "You *asked* her? Like straight to her face? Holy crap, I would have loved to see her expression. That's stone-cold awesome. Just calling her out."

"She seemed shocked. She said she didn't do it."

"What else was she going to say?"

"Sure, but she seemed really surprised. And she was in the middle of trying to stop Jason from escaping, so I think she was unguarded."

Stacy checks once more to ensure no one else is in the room with them. There could be bugs around the room, but it is a risk she will have to take.

She leans closer and asks, as quietly as she can, "Have you heard of the Ratti Report?"

Thor almost stumbles again. "Why are you asking me?"

"Because I thought you might be okay with helping me."

"Hm." Thor continues pounding on the treadmill. "I've heard of it. Rumors. It sounds like the general doesn't like it, but that's all I know. You're really getting a kick out of getting crosswise with the general, aren't you?"

"No." Stacy sighs. "But I have to." She pauses. Thor could report her, which may result in the general barring her from any access to the station beyond benign areas, but she has to ask.

She lowers her voice to a whisper. "I think it's in the Records Room. Can you tell me the code?"

Thor's eyes widen. "Sacred turds! I could get court-martialed."

"I know. I definitely don't want that to happen, and I won't say anything to her about it. I protect my sources. I wouldn't ask if it weren't important."

"Hm." Thor runs for another minute without saying anything. "I'm sorry. You've put out a bunch of reports, and they should have caught people's attention, but they haven't. Helping you isn't worth risking my career."

The refusal doesn't surprise her. It is the reason for the refusal. Stacy's reporting isn't valuable enough, doesn't have enough potential to make a difference, for Thor to risk his career.

"Okay." Stacy leaves the room before the tears can come.

If Thor won't help her, no one will. Until she thinks of another way to find the code, she'll work on a report for the shuttle expedition.

When she enters the Observation Module, though, she sees Contreras emerging from the cupola. He sent her on the quest to find the report. He is obligated to help her.

Contreras hooks himself into place upside-down with respect to Stacy. "Where you headed?"

Stacy guides herself to a stop at the edge of the nadir cupola. "I'm having problems getting the Ratti Report."

Contreras's slight smirk disappears, and he stiffens. "Don't know what you're talking about."

"But you…"

Contreras's eyes gaze past Stacy's shoulder to the corner of the room. The corner looks normal, with no obvious cameras or microphones, but then, they wouldn't be obvious. Stacy makes a note to check later.

Stacy drops her voice to a whisper. "The door is locked, and—"

He holds up a hand. "I don't know what you're talking about. Unless you have something else to say, we're done here."

Stacy realizes she has jeopardized Contreras by even mentioning the report. "Sorry."

For a moment, they stand in silence, facing each other. If she can't ask him about the Ratti Report here, where can she ask him? They wouldn't be able to convince the general to let them do another EVA, and her messages are being monitored.

Contreras lets go of the railing. "Okay, then."

"Wait." Stacy racks her brain for something to say. "What do you think we should do in response to Jason's escape?"

Contreras laughs. "You're not recording, right? Because I doubt the general wants you repeating anything I have to say."

"I'm not recording."

Contreras's voice grows somber. "Jason itself was only a warning. We've let the Inorganics get away with too much already. We've known they're a threat for decades. It shouldn't have had to come to this for us to do something about them, but it has."

"Well, we're going on this expedition."

"Yeah, we are." Contreras grunts. "The Inorganics stole our pod and they're taking our resources and they kill our people, and we're going to…observe at them?"

"What would you do, then?"

"What would I do?" Contreras folds his arms over his chest and thinks for a moment. "I would load explosives on our shuttle during our expedition and ram it right into their starship."

He doesn't look away. He means it, every word. And, even though she hates the thought of a suicide mission and losing good people, and even though destroying the starship wouldn't ensure a long-term victory, Stacy doesn't know that it would be wrong to do it.

Before Stacy can say more, Contreras taps the railing and kicks away. "Good talk."

Once Contreras leaves, Stacy passes through the other modules to Module 1, where the shuttle is docked. After passing through the shuttle's engine compartment, she reaches the cargo bay. Prabhakhar floats against one wall, taking dimension measurements with a handheld device. She's sure he won't be inclined to help her, but maybe Anderson is farther forward.

"Hi, Prabhakhar." Stacy glides past toward the next room.

"Stacy." Prabhakhar glances up from the handheld, his face serious. "Can we talk?"

She grabs the doorframe to the common area and wrenches herself to a halt. "Sure."

"You heard about us possibly abandoning the Mars Colony?"

Stacy blinks. "What?"

"Vanessa was saying some people think we're going to abandon the Mars Colony and bring everyone back to Earth."

Many of those people were born on Mars. They can't walk in Earth's gravity, not unless they could afford specialized exoskeletons. Even with the exoskeletons, their internal organs would likely suffer and significantly shorten their lifespans. "That's not a good idea."

"No, it isn't. How's Trevor?"

Prabhakhar's topic change nearly causes whiplash. Stacy has the impression he is working his way to what he really wants to talk about. "He's doing fine. Keeping the agency running while I'm out here. But he hated that last report."

"I imagine. It's hard being out here, and your family back there, and not being able to do anything to help when problems come up." Prabhakhar seems troubled.

"Are you okay?" Stacy asks.

"I'm thinking of leaving the SDF," says Prabhakhar. "After this tour of duty."

"Oh. Is that what you want?"

Prabhakhar waves to indicate the shuttle or the station or maybe space in general. "I love it out here. The adventure. The feeling of doing something important. But I'm missing so much. Ayaan barely remembers me. Vanessa misses me, and she has to take care of everything while I'm gone."

"Yeah. So you haven't decided?"

"No. What do you think I should do?"

"It's a sacrifice," says Stacy. "It would be hard to choose. You do important work out here, but your kid only grows up once."

"Yeah." Prabhakhar nods. "Yeah, that's true. Anyway. Sorry. I know you've got somewhere else to be."

"Whichever decision you make, it will be the right one. It will just be a different way of being right." Stacy waves and continues forward.

Anderson is in the cockpit in the left-hand seat of the second row, tapping at a screen. Stacy takes the seat across the aisle from her.

"Hi, Lieutenant."

Anderson looks up, but doesn't smile. She looks even more glum than she did during the shuttle ride after the rescue. "Hi."

"Do you mind if I record?"

Anderson shrugs. "You can. I doubt the general will let you use the footage."

"Maybe not." Stacy releases her nanocams.

Anderson watches the cams flit to each side of the cockpit. "They always look cute."

"Yeah, that's what I think." Stacy smiles. "Since I travel so much for a living, these are the closest things I have to pets."

"That's kind of sad." Anderson glances over her shoulder. Stacy wonders if the lieutenant is checking for bugs. "Did you hear about Panama? The government said they would agree to the rebels' terms."

"They did?" Stacy smiles. "That's great! I didn't think it was going to happen."

Anderson frowns. "Then, when the rebels lowered their defenses, the soldiers captured them. They're going to be put on trial now. And after the rebels were captured, the president said she didn't negotiate with terrorists."

"Oh."

"I guess I can understand the government not giving in," says Anderson, speaking slowly. "But not the lying. The betrayal."

"I know."

"I think you should be more balanced," says Anderson.

For a moment, Stacy can think of nothing to say. Anderson watches her, staring.

"Well," says Stacy. "I feel like I'm pretty balanced. Maybe more than the Inorganics deserve."

"I know they hurt you, and they accidentally killed your father to die. And th—"

"They deliberately crashed that asteroid and left us to die." Stacy's fingers tremble against the armrests. "Then they stabbed my father through the leg."

"But they can't intentionally kill anyone unless provoked."

"It wasn't much of a provocation." Stacy tries to keep the memories away, but she sees her father lying on the ground beside the Inorganic. "I don't want to talk about this."

Anderson tenses. "I'm sorry. I'm just saying you can acknowledge both the good and the bad stuff. And..." Anderson shrugs. "I think that's what you could do with your story."

So many problems with that outlook. General Young is right. When otherwise intelligent people learn extraneous information, they can ignore the big picture.

"I've thought about it a lot," says Anderson. "Especially these last few weeks. Humans need so much to survive. Food, water, air. And trips between planets or stars can destroy us psychologically. The microgravity can atrophy our muscles and organs. We're not designed for space travel, and definitely not for travel between the stars."

Stacy frowns.

"And the more I think about it," says Anderson, "the more I realize: The stars don't belong to *homo sapiens*. Maybe even the Solar System doesn't. The Inorganics are our successors."

Stacy's mouth opens. She has no idea what to say. All she can think is that, if the expedition goes poorly, these words may be the last Anderson ever records.

A ping from the general saves Stacy from responding. Stacy opens the message.

Come to my quarters.

We need to talk.

THE GENERAL WAITS in her quarters in her customary position beside her computer. Stacy hooks herself into place beside the door.

"Ms. Sterling. Thank you for coming."

"Sure. It sounded important."

"Yes. Although I'm not sure in what way yet." The general taps at the computer screen and pulls up a screenshot. Stacy comes closer, grabbing a handhold near the computer to see it more clearly. It shows her article, with the embedded video frozen on an image of the general entering the pod.

The counter for the number of views has reached over a hundred million.

"Oh." Stacy has had articles reach a few million views before, but this level surpasses Instant USA and all the other agencies combined.

The general taps the screen again. The next image is a frozen video of a reporter with Stacy's image in the background. They must have gotten her image from the Take Action News website.

Stacy turns to the general. "Why are they—"

Young holds up a finger. She cycles through several similar images, reporters speaking with a picture of Stacy in the background or a bulleted list about Stacy's career or clips from years of Stacy's reporting or clips of her interviews about her father's death on Mars. Young taps the screen again, and a massive collage of such images appears.

"Oh, no." Stacy's grip on the handhold tightens.

"Yes." Young gives her a bitter grin. "Ms. Sterling, you're famous."

TWENTY-THREE

It finally happened. You went viral. I guess if any story were going to do it, it would be this one. I know it's not what you wanted, but I love that when I check the news, your pictures are everywhere.

IT HAPPENED. STACY broke the vow she made when she became a reporter. General Young forced her into it, but it doesn't matter. Now the news agencies are all speaking about her, the entertainment shows are speculating about her love life aboard the station, which probably upsets Trevor, and everyone is generally missing the point.

She wants to wake up and have all this fame disappear. Instead, she shifts position in her sleeping bag and continues reading Trevor's message.

People are calling you a hero, talking about how brave you are and how cool you are under pressure. And it's true. You've dealt with worse situations than the Jason escape.

I know you hate the attention, but it seems to be working. The number of views is still climbing.

Most talking points from legitimate news sources are about how unimportant Inorganics are since they are off Earth, or how true machine intelligence is impossible. Journalists and scholars bringing up those points give the public permission to continue being apathetic.

Stacy hates that her thoughts are starting to echo Young's.

A lot of people wonder if a similar escape happened on Earth in the last two days. None of the news outlets are reporting it explicitly, but there have been a lot of unexplained events that could have been caused by Inorganics hijacking satellites or spacecraft.

You're getting all kinds of fan mail. I can't answer it all. A lot of kids are writing to say how inspiring you are. They know what's up.

Even more fun, you're getting job offers from several agencies, like your favorite, Instant USA. And Benito Valencia, yes, the Benito Valencia, has offered you a spot with his personal news service. I let them know you weren't interested, but tell me if you change your mind.

She is getting more attention now, when she's four hundred million kilometers away, than she ever had when she was on Earth. And everyone is focusing on her instead of the real story. She closes her implant, pulls on workout clothes, and slips from her sleeping bag.

When she enters the corridor, the general is exiting her own quarters. "Are you about to work out?"

"Yeah." Stacy pauses outside her door. "Couldn't sleep."

Young gives her a wry smile. "I expect not. Have you been approached about a movie deal yet?"

Stacy sighs. "Yes. The York Company sent me a pitch. The movie is going to be all about my escape from Jason, even though you were the one who got us out of the pod and Anderson and Contreras rescued us, and I spent most of the time curled up in an escape ball worrying no one would ever find me."

"They're definitely going to Hollywoodize it."

"Yeah. They want to give me a love interest on the station. Trevor's not going to like that part. And they're going to play up the action and make it look like you and I outsmarted the Inorganics instead of just running away and getting lucky."

"Well." Young folds her arms as she floats across the corridor from Stacy. "It's attention. I'd love to use my own fame to share my views on certain subjects, but no one's asked me anything yet."

The general must see something in Stacy's expression.

"I know," says Young. "You don't want to be part of the story. But look how it's turned out. Just like I said. People are paying attention. They're even reading your old articles."

Stacy wonders if Young discovered that fact herself or if she read it in Trevor's message. "Some are. But most people are just gossiping about me."

Young shrugs. "And yet, even with the gossip, you're still getting what you want. Enjoy your workout."

As Young kicks off from the wall, Stacy wonders if the general has a point. Should she reconsider searching for the Ratti Report? She has a platform now. If she presents a focused message, maybe she can effect real change. The Ratti Report, whatever it is, will likely muddy that message. If this is her moment, she can't waste it.

STACY HEAVES AGAINST the weights, her shoulders and legs burning as she pushes upward. She hates The Cage.

She lets the weights slam back into place with a jolt that shakes the machine. As the impact of metal on metal still echoes through the room, the fitness module's door opens, and Jalindo enters in workout clothes.

Jalindo's eyes twinkle when they see Stacy. They approach, grabbing the frame of The Cage to anchor themself. "You did it wrong. You were supposed to make *me* famous."

Stacy shakes her head. "I wish I could have. This is awful."

"I bet you already have fan pages and fan clubs and groupies."

Stacy laughs. "Is that what you want?"

Jalindo shrugs. "Wouldn't complain. But all I ask for is immortality."

If anything goes wrong with the upcoming shuttle expedition, Jalindo will achieve the immortality they want. Stacy pushes the thought away.

Jalindo excuses themself and heads to the treadmill. Stacy continues her own workout routine.

An hour later, as Stacy vacuums loose balls of sweat from the air, Jalindo approaches again. Their expression has darkened.

"I guess I can see why you wanted to avoid fame." They blink, and Stacy's implant pings.

Stacy checks Jalindo's message. An Instant USA article shows a frozen still of a younger Stacy in Brazil, in a secluded area in a crowded marketplace, accepting papers from a nondescript man glancing over his shoulder. The article's title is written in bold below the still. "STACY STERLING'S LEGACY OF CORRUPTION, SLANDER, AND LIES."

"Yes." Stacy closes the message. "That's one of the reasons."

With every story, someone attacks her. It means she is reaching people that those in power don't want her to reach.

In that moment, she realizes she is taking orders from General Young. Stacy has ignored the Ratti Report. The old Stacy, the real one, would have already searched for that report, knowing that if Young didn't want anyone to learn about it, it had important information.

STACY FINDS THOR in the fitness module, struggling against The Cage. She waits until he finishes a set.

He vacuums the sweat from his area. "You've got something serious on your mind. What's up?"

Stacy takes a breath. He almost helped her before, refusing only because he doubted viewers would pay attention to what she was saying. "I'm famous now. Can you give me the combination to the Records Room?"

TWENTY-FOUR

STACY DECIDES TO strike the next day at 2100, during Shift 3. General Young will be in the middle of her sleep period, as will most of the crew. The station will be quiet, calm, and lonely.

At her selected time, she slips from her quarters without waking Prabhakhar or Gallegos and leaves the officers' module. Halabi and Ko give her puzzled expressions as she passes through the Analysis Room.

"Sorry." Stacy waves. "Couldn't sleep, so I decided to work."

"Good call." Halabi turns back to her screen. "Might as well get something done."

Stacy wonders if Halabi and Ko will report her nighttime movements.

When she reaches Module 8, she glides to the Records Room door and anchors herself in place. No click this time. The spyware blockers from Trevor worked.

On the keypad beside the door, Stacy enters the code Thor gave her: four, eight, seven, three, four. The sergeant doesn't know what the Ratti Report holds, but he put his career on the line under the condition that she make the report public.

The keypad lights up green. Stacy hits the door's button, maybe more eagerly than is warranted, and enters the room.

The layout hasn't changed since she last entered. Like the Power Room, it is a vertical half-cylinder line with consoles, switches, blinking lights, and a window at the curved top of the room.

She likely has little time before someone notices the Records Room terminals are being accessed. Stacy chooses the console labeled 'Inorganic Behavioral Analysis,' halfway between floor and ceiling, and kicks toward it. When she reaches it and hooks her legs in place under the corresponding railing, she pulls two mini-drives from her flight suit's chest pocket. She tucks one of them under her sleeve and plugs the other into the console's input socket.

A prompt blinks on the screen. She types the name 'Ratti,' and a list of five documents scroll into view, but only one document lists Prasad Ratti in the first-author spot. Stacy downloads the file to her mini-drive, then begins typing the command to download another.

The door opens at the bottom of the room. Stacy continues typing. As the door shuts, its contact with the wall echoes through the room. Stacy already knows who has come.

She glances down. "General."

Young's face crumples. "Now? You do this now?"

When Stacy imagined this moment, she always pictured General Young as angry, not hurt. Maybe it is the accumulation of grievances. The loss of that childhood dream of reaching Saturn, the failed attempts at getting people to see the threat, and the betrayal by Stacy in particular, the person Young opened up to the most during her five years at the station.

"I'm sorry." Stacy forces her voice to remain steady. "But this is my job. I search for the truth."

"Most journalists don't."

Maybe most journalists don't search for the truth, or maybe they only search for the truth that supports their beliefs. Stacy doesn't want to believe that statement, but there are so many *Patriots* and *Truthstorms*.

"I'm not going to ask who gave you the room code," says Young. "Everyone on board has earned my trust, even if we don't agree on everything. I don't want to know who betrayed me. Other than you."

"I didn't." Stacy turns to the screen. "You know this is my

job. You're making me feel like a criminal because I'm looking for the facts. We need to use *all* the facts available to us. You have to understand what something actually is before you can fight it."

Young holds out her hand, palm up, and gestures for Stacy to hand her the drive. "Please."

Stacy disconnects the drive from the console and pulls it to her stomach, cupping it in both her hands. "You already watch my reports before I send them. So why does it matter if I read this?"

The drive floats between Stacy's palms and stomach. Curling one of her little fingers, she guides it into her sleeve. One of her thumbs hooks the other drive, already in the other sleeve, and slides it into her palm. She wishes she'd had time to copy the same data onto the decoy drive. If Young explores the drive's contents, she will realize it is empty and that Stacy switched the drives.

"If you don't hand that to me," says Young, "you will be confined to your quarters for the duration of your stay. I will tolerate this breach because you've done good work and I believe you will continue to do so. But it will be the last breach."

Stacy pauses a moment for effect, then pushes off from the wall and glides down to the general. "Here." She surrenders the drive.

"Thank you." Young takes it, then searches Stacy's face.

For several moments, they face each other, floating and saying nothing. Stacy can imagine what the general is thinking. The betrayal, their shared escape, the rom-coms, the friendship that never developed but that could have under different circumstances. And the lingering question of whether Stacy somehow managed to retain the data she had copied from the server here.

Young slides the drive into her chest pocket and zips it inside. "The SDF contacted me late last night. They won't release any more of your reports until they can determine the potential impact on the public. The mixed reaction to

Jason's escape, and to our escape, shows we have no idea what will happen if we tell the whole truth to the public. The SDF leadership itself is divided on how to approach the Inorganics."

"So you're silencing me." Stacy stops herself from saying more. She could complain about the unfairness of bringing her all the way out here, preventing her from covering the stories she thinks are important, keeping her from her husband for over a year, and then not allowing her to do the job she came here for, but none of her complaints would matter.

"Yes." Young gestures for Stacy to leave the room.

Stacy maneuvers around Young and opens the door. She hopes she doesn't seem too eager as she enters the hallway.

"Stacy."

Stacy halts at the door to the next module. Young floats in the corridor, holding onto the railing with one hand.

"I'm not your enemy, Stacy."

"I know. I wish we could be friends." Stacy opens the door and departs for her quarters.

Without knowing when Young will examine the decoy drive, Stacy has to work quickly. The moment she enters the officers' module, she removes the cap on her skullport, which Trevor named The Portskullis, plugs in the drive, and begins uploading the file to her implant.

She enters her quarters. The dim corridor light plays over Prabhakhar and Gallegos, hanging from the walls in their sleeping bags. Stacy feels a pang of guilt for uploading the file here. Prabhakhar and Gallegos would never forgive her if they found out what Stacy has done, and that she is doing it right in front of them.

Stacy makes her way to her own sleeping bag and slips inside. She pulls up the Ratti Report, the document for which she has risked everything.

For the first time, she concentrates on the title: *Potential Illness in the Inorganics.*

If Prabhakhar and Gallegos were not sleeping in the same room, Stacy would swear out loud. An *illness*? A race of machines catching cold or a disease? Maybe their parts wear out, maybe they short-circuit, but they can't get sick. Right?

Stacy continues reading, wondering if this report is the equivalent of a tabloid. Maybe that's why Young tried to hide it.

After the abstract, Ratti's report describes the observation methods used to collect the data: video and electromagnetic emissions. He continues with a description of the incident and the potential causes.

It still seems unbelievable, even after reading the eye-witness accounts and seeing tables of data. The report ends with an embedded video. Stacy plays it.

The opening scene shows a distant view of an area on Juno surrounding the starship. Judging from the size of the starship, the video was taken from the IMS. The starship looks incomplete, with the inner engines missing, though most of the external walls are finished. Several Inorganic units, maybe twenty, move outside. Each is only one or two pixels in the video.

The video switches to a closer view of the same scene, this one taken from a pod expedition. The units can now be seen in detail, with discernible limbs, wheels, antennas, and body shapes.

One of the units, a digger, rolls forward with its shovel poised to scoop the top layer of surface material. Without stopping, its entire body shakes, sending it several degrees to the left. It pauses, then continues. A moment later, its body shakes again, then again, sending it on a haphazard course toward its fellow Inorganics.

The next-closest unit shakes when the digger comes within several meters. Within seconds, it, too, drives as though out of control. Then the next unit, then the next, then the next, as the erratic behavior expands outward.

Now Stacy knows why Young doesn't want to release this report, despite the fact it shows the Inorganics are vulnerable to at least some form of attack. That unit's twitching arms, that other unit's gaping mouth that keeps trying and failing to close, that antenna jerking back and forth…They've stopped looking like machines, and instead look like dogs in pain.

TWENTY-FIVE

STACY CLOSES THE report and looks over at Prabhakhar and Gallegos, asleep in their bags on the other walls. How much do they know about the Inorganics' illness? How much do they care?

For almost her entire life, Stacy has hated the Inorganics. Then…this video…It makes her think of kittens mewing from stomachaches or injuries, or a dog whimpering, or…She doesn't want to think about it. And if *she* can sympathize with them after seeing this video, other people will have stronger reactions.

Ratti's report explains that the illness concluded after several days and after spreading through almost two-thirds of the units. No one knows what stopped it: whether the Inorganics developed a cure, or if it died out on its own, or if the afflicted units were wiped. Similarly, no one knows what caused it. Was it a code mutation, or did a rival Inorganic group send it as a virus?

The cause or the cure doesn't matter. What matters was how the public will react to that video.

Stacy shifts in her bag. On the other wall, Prabhakhar stirs.

Releasing the Ratti Report would come at great cost. She doesn't know the extent to which General Young would punish her, but it would come, and it would come hard. But Thor risked his career for this report. He made her promise to release it to the public.

Trevor usually talks her through these moments. Stacy can't message him now because Young would read it, but Stacy knows how the conversation would go.

What made you go into journalism?

I wanted to help people.

Which choice will help people?

And she doesn't know. What if telling the truth makes things worse?

AFTER HER POST-WORKOUT shower, Stacy returns to Module 1 to continue her internal debate about releasing the Ratti Report. When she arrives in the module, she hears a rustle. Someone in the shuttle, moving.

She enters the shuttle and floats through the engine compartment to find Prabhakhar in the cargo bay, staring into space with downcast eyes. He spins in a slow circle, but does nothing to stop the rotation.

"Are you okay?" asks Stacy.

Prabhakhar starts, then blinks four times, probably closing the messages in his implant. "Yeah. The joys of parenting."

Stacy grabs a cargo box strapped to one of the walls and holds herself in place. "Is Ayaan still drawing pictures of that supervillain?"

"Yeah." Prabhakhar's shoulders slump. "And on our video chats, he says almost nothing to me now. Like I'm one of his relatives he doesn't care about."

"Isn't that a normal phase for kids?" asks Stacy. "Especially since you're long-distance. I'm sure you're doing a great job keeping up with him. Or at least as well as you can this far away."

"I'm not so sure." Prabhakhar sighs.

"I'm sorry," she says. "I know it must be hard. But, just by trying, you're going to make Ayaan feel loved."

Prabhakhar gives her a weak smile. "We'll see. Thank you."

Stacy releases her nanocams. "Do you mind if I ask you a

few questions while I'm here? It will give Vanessa and Ayaan another chance to see you."

"Sure." Prabhakhar shrugs. "I guess I've got time."

Stacy guides her nanocams into place, capturing several views of Prabhakhar, and starts her implant recording. "Do you know what Jason has been doing since it escaped?"

Prabhakhar composes himself. "Jason is still in the pod, staying at a constant altitude. It doesn't have enough fuel to maintain that altitude forever, so I'm curious where it will land, but I expect we'll have abandoned Collins before that happens. We're monitoring it visually."

"It's not talking to the Inorganics?"

"Not that we can tell."

"It's so weird," she says. "Jason is just hanging out there. It would seem creepy, but I don't think Jason has an agenda. Do you?"

"Hard to say. It doesn't seem to have any agenda that we can figure out, but we can't figure out the Inorganics as a whole, either. They're starting to cover more ground on Juno, and we didn't expect that."

"More ground? You mean, they're spreading past their base?"

"Yeah." Prabhakhar waves one hand across his palm as though showing a force advancing over a plain. "Slowly, but they're expanding outward. It's generating a lot of speculation in the Analysis Room, which is fun, but it's been pointless so far."

Stacy can't imagine having to outthink machines. It probably feels like batting in baseball, where getting two or three hits out of ten is pretty good. "What are your guesses?"

"The leading theory is that they want to gather enough resources for a second starship." Prabhakhar glances toward the wall, as though he can see the stars beyond. "And the conservative pundits are already denying the Inorganics are expanding. There's over a hundred conspiracy theories out there by now, Thor could tell you about them, and more people believe one of those than believe the truth."

"You sound—"

"I sound bitter." Prabhakhar taps his fingers against his arms. "I hate that so many people think we're lying about what we're doing out here. We sacrifice so much to do our jobs, and they talk about us like we're trash."

"The military usually doesn't tell the truth about things like that, right?"

"Sure, but it also doesn't say a problem exists when it doesn't."

Stacy knows what she has to do. If she is being honest, she has always known. It might make the situation worse, but it doesn't matter. She has to make the Ratti Report public.

TWENTY-SIX

IT TAKES MOST of the day to find Thor alone. He is running on the treadmill, oblivious to Stacy's presence until she grabs the neighboring treadmill to anchor herself.

"Oh, no." Thor shakes his head and continues running. "What is it this time?"

"I'm sorry," says Stacy. "But I have another favor to ask."

Thor's pace quickens, which, since the treadmill continues at its set pace, results in Thor stumbling and clutching the treadmill's arms until he returns to his previous speed. "I haven't risked my career enough for you yet?"

"I'm sorry." Stacy glances toward the door. "I know you've already done a lot. But…that thing we talked about…I can't just send it to Trevor. So I—"

"No." Thor speaks in a whisper. "I would get caught."

"I don't have other options. I can't ask the general. I can't sneak an encrypted message out because she would find it. I—"

"No." Thor turns from her to face the treadmill's readout.

Stacy opens her mouth to ask again, but Thor's expression is set. She leaves the room.

AFTER STACY RECEIVES another dose of radiation-repair medication from Cazador, she heads to Module 1 to think more. Again, she hears noise from the shuttle and finds Prabhakar in the cargo bay.

"Oh, hi, Stacy." Prabhakar is anchored beside a stack of crates and has grabbed one of the clamps holding them in place. "If you don't have any exciting plans, could you help me move some of these crates? My back would appreciate it."

"Okay," she says. "I can help. Would you mind if I…" She taps the side of her head.

"Sure, go ahead." Prabhakar squeezes the clamp and slides the strap loose. "Even these crates deserve their fifteen minutes."

Stacy releases her nanocams and stations them around the cargo bay. She will only use the video without her in it, but even if there is no usable footage, she will at least have the audio. She moves to her left and begins recording.

"Oh," says Prabhakar. "Almost forgot." He blinks four times, and a hologram fills the center of the room. It displays boxes stacked on top of each other and held together with straps, arranged with most boxes on the right side of the cargo bay.

"Is that…" Stacy gestures to the hologram. "Do you really want it like that? Won't that tip the shuttle over?"

"Yes, we want them like that. No, they won't tip over the shuttle." Prabhakar grabs the top box in front of him, plants his feet on the box below it, and pulls. The box slides free, rising into the air and carrying Prabhakar with it.

"It looks unstable."

Prabhakar rotates so his feet point at the ceiling. When they touch, he pushes off again toward the right side of the bay. "That's by design. If our center of gravity is out of alignment with the vehicle's center, it increases our instability. Increased instability is proportionate to maneuverability. It's how fighter jets work."

"Oh." So they will not only by flying deep into Inorganic territory with a spacecraft not designed for that type of sortie, they will purposely make their spacecraft unstable.

Prabhakar guides her in carrying the crates from one side of the bay to the other, cautioning her against moving too quickly.

Free-fall might reduce the crates' weights to zero, but their masses remain the same. As they haul a crate together, Stacy glances upward. On the ceiling, a box blinks every few seconds. It takes her a few moments to remember what it is: the shuttle's communications unit.

And then she knows what she has to do. Since the shuttle travels between Earth and the station, it needs the capability to transmit messages from the maximum distance of four hundred million kilometers, which means that comm unit can transmit her report. And, since the shuttle originally wasn't expected to be reactivated until the return to Earth, General Young might not have thought to put a security lock on its communications to prevent Stacy from sending unauthorized transmissions.

Of course, the crew will consider it a betrayal. Stacy has lived with them for over a month already, has eaten with them, talked with them, joked with them, so sending this message will make them think she has been using them this whole time.

But Stacy isn't a liar. She isn't someone who betrays her friends. She is someone who believes in the truth and people's right to it.

And now she has the chance to act on her belief. She can send the report during the shuttle expedition.

Prabhakar waits at the stack of crates. "Can you help me with this next one?"

IN THE DARKNESS of her room, while Prabhakar and Halabi sleep, Stacy hangs in her sleeping bag and edits her report. She ends it with a call to action.

"This video tells us the Inorganics are vulnerable. Something can incapacitate them, even if it doesn't last long. It means we aren't powerless. It means we still need a strong presence out here so we can monitor them and continue to research them. We can learn the truth so that everyone can come to their own conclusions about what to do about the Inorganics. Because this problem won't be solved by just one person. It will require all of us coming together to do our best."

That synopsis might be biased, but it is also right. It feels good to be speaking the truth.

Stacy ends the recording. She has the message and a way to send it. And in two more days, she will have to do it.

TWENTY-SEVEN

WHEN THE SHUTTLE crosses the five-hundred-kilometer threshold, no alarms sound. No shaking, no vibration. The dim red cabin lights remain on. But Stacy can hear the slowed breathing of her crewmates, can see their new tension even through their pressure suits. Inorganic units have launched toward them, and when the Inorganics arrive, they will tear the shuttle apart as they did the IMS on Stacy's first day here.

The sound of her breathing fills her helmet. Her heart vibrates against one of the pressure suit's cooling tubes. The smell of sweat, old and new, hers and previous occupants', has not yet faded to background.

On the left side of the shuttle, in the row ahead of her, Contreras stares at the screen embedded in the seatback in front of him. Jalindo sits in the pilot's seat ahead of him, hands resting on the controls. The shuttle continues forward at a constant rate, with no acceleration. It feels like they are sitting still.

Stacy keeps her oculars peering over Anderson's and Prabhakhar's shoulders and trained on the window on the right side of the shuttle. Juno grows larger, its potato shape filling almost half the view.

It feels unnatural recording without her nanocams. She's stored them in her locker in her quarters. She would almost rather go into an assignment without her shoes than without her nanocams, but they would have caused a flight hazard, floating free in the cockpit during the upcoming evasive maneuvers. She will have to access the shuttle's internal video feed after the flight.

Stacy keeps her emotion block on. She will not cross that personal line, and she doesn't want her fear or anger or guilt creeping into the video. The public might never see the expedition video, but if she and the others return, the SDF will view it, and Stacy hates the idea of them being inside her head or, worse, knowing the exact moment she betrayed them.

And that moment needs to be soon. Her window for sending her message will only last as long as the expedition, and if the Inorganics catch her, she will lose the chance.

A panel on the wall to Anderson's right shows the status of the comm system. The comm unit in the cargo bay even now transmits lidar data to Collins in case the worst happens. Even if the shuttle doesn't return, that dataset will. Every element is aligned in Stacy's favor, or at least as well as it ever could be.

It is time. Stacy logs into the shuttle's communications system and readies the message for transmission.

She pauses. If Stacy sends it now, Young might cancel the expedition. An anomalous signal would cause concern; Young might even think the Inorganics or Jason were behind it.

Stacy might regret this decision later. She half regrets it now. But it feels right. She returns to concentrating on the others again, aware that, if the Inorganics attack, the message will die with her.

"Three Inorganic units." Prabhakhar's voice comes over the suit radio. "Departing from three locations at the edges of the base, all on intercept courses. Preliminary calculations say they'll intercept us in under twenty minutes if we stay on the present trajectory."

"Three units approaching." Jalindo's acknowledgment comes with the calmness of someone discussing a tax form. They make no attempt to change trajectory.

Stacy starts a timer in her implant, counting down from twenty minutes, to give herself something to do. She could be dead shortly after that timer reaches zero.

It took the Inorganics minutes to dismantle the IMS, ripping the walls from the spacecraft bus and removing the individual components one by one. The shuttle is larger, so Stacy and the others might have even longer to realize the end is coming.

She imagines the shuttle's metal walls being torn from around them, the cabin's atmosphere rushing into space, a clawed hand reaching for her like one of those old monster movies. A spiked leg impaling her.

Juno's horizon now spans all but the upper sliver of the front window as the shuttle drops closer to the starship. At this distance, four hundred kilometers away, twice as far from Juno as most space stations are from Earth's surface, Stacy can see few details. At the top of the asteroid, the starship appears as tiny lines blocking a patch of stars.

Seventeen minutes. If Stacy had the controls, she would have already started dodging. She grabs her armrests and resists the urge to ask about evasive actions.

"You getting good data?" asks Prabhakhar.

"Yes," says Anderson. "Forward lidar is getting a good map of the starship, and nadir lidar is getting a good map of the topography."

"Good." Prabhakhar nods. "Sergeant?"

"As expected, Major," says Contreras. "The gravimeter isn't getting the signal strength we'd hoped. They're probably not powering on the engines. But we could get lucky as we get closer."

Stacy hopes they don't 'get lucky.' She remembers those moments in the fitness module where the gravity altered. If it occurs out here, while the Inorganics pursue them, the shuttle might lose a crucial edge it needs to avoid capture.

Capture. An understatement. A euphemism.

She squeezes the armrests, as though holding them could keep her from falling. She feels as though she is trapped on a roller coaster. She takes a sip of water from the thin tube near her mouth, more for something to do than because she is thirsty.

Three hundred fifty kilometers. The starship has grown larger, but the difference is almost imperceptible. She wonders how close they will get before Jalindo pulls away from their dive.

Stacy zooms in with her oculars. The starship's support scaffolding now shows curvature for each bar in the trusses, appearing three-dimensional instead of flat. The engines, cylinders within the grid-like walls, appear sharper, though she still can make out no details. Everything looks smooth, polished, like a computer drawing instead of a real object.

This is it. The starship. This piece of metal is going to travel to another star system. Their first interstellar ambassador. Material from their primordial Solar System at last venturing beyond the Sun's gravity, traveling to a new system with its own quirks and intricacies as awe-inspiring as their home system. Its own set of inner planets, asteroids, gas giants, moons with atmospheres and water, icy bodies patrolling the perimeter of its star's influence.

Ten minutes until intercept. She squeezes her seat harder.

Jalindo should have changed course by now. The Inorganics are more agile than the shuttle. If Jalindo waits until the last minute to change course, the Inorganics can surely match whatever maneuvers they make.

"Three hundred kilometers," breathes Anderson.

Now, when Stacy zooms in with her oculars, she can see individual Inorganic units toiling in the dust. They look like chocolate chips from this distance.

"Ten minutes," says Prabhakhar. Stacy wishes she had his calm.

"One hundred kilometers," says Anderson minutes later.

Stacy can now discern details of the Inorganics. One rolls across the surface with a large load of rocks on its back. Others sit near the starship, pushing the collected rocks into a large boxlike machine. A smelter, maybe? A pair stands next to each other, one of them…dismantling the other? It detaches an arm from the other unit, sets it to the side, then detaches another arm. The other unit doesn't resist. Barbaric.

The shuttle continues to decrease the distance. Smaller boulders, craters, and tiny hills come into view. Near the foot of one of the hills, farther from the starship than the other Inorganics, one unit plows its claw into a ragged hole in the gray dirt. A gripping appendage moves in a rapid series of motions, rotating downward, grabbing a chunk of soil in its claw, rotating up, and placing the collection inside its central body. The motions look familiar. Stacy racks her brain, trying to remember where she has seen them.

"Four minutes," says Prabhakhar.

The shuttle remains on course. As steady as though it were flying through an empty sky.

Then Stacy remembers where she has seen those motions. "That one's moving like Jason!"

Jalindo keeps their eyes on their console, but the others turn to stare at Stacy. The cabin's red lights illuminate their faces in their helmets.

"What's moving like Jason?" asks Anderson.

"The digger, at four o'clock in the window. I recognize those motions."

The others turn to the window, staring in the direction she indicated. Prabhakhar shakes his head. "I don't have oculars as good as yours."

"I've got the video display going." Contreras leans closer to his screen. "You can see it here. She's right. It looks like Jason."

"Are you sure it's the same?" asks Prabhakhar. "Or just similar? Three minutes."

"I've spent hours watching Jason on the monitor," says Stacy. All that time in the storage module, staring as Jason carries out its repetitive actions on the screen, trying to see if there was something conscious in its programming. "The movements look exactly the same, at least as far as I can tell from this distance. Every nuance."

"I don't think anyone was expecting that," says Prabhakhar.

Anderson turns to Prabhakhar. "I bet that unit still has some of the original source code."

"Could be," says Prabhakhar. "That source code has to be seventy years old."

Anderson's smile can be heard in her voice. "I bet the programmer would be proud the Inorganics still consider it efficient enough to keep."

Stacy's internal timer beeps.

"Two minutes," says Prabhakhar.

As Stacy wonders whether she should vocalize her concerns about maintaining the same course, Jalindo banks them to the left. Stacy holds on to her seat, but the shuttle's motion feels weaker than a car on a tight curve.

The shuttle rocks. Stacy's helmeted head hits the wall, and she grunts in pain. Darkness flickers across her vision for the briefest of moments. Viewers will see it during the report.

"We got hit." Prabhakhar taps at his screen. "One of the Inorganic units. The radar didn't pick it up. It must have been in our blind spot."

"We have a blind spot?" Anderson asks.

"I guess so." Prabhakhar grunts. "The shuttle wasn't designed for this kind of flying."

"We got hit," says Contreras, "as in, one of those Inorganics hit us with its arms?"

"Yes," says Prabhakhar. "Or maybe it grabbed on to us."

"Is the unit still on us?" asks Jalindo in an eerily calm voice.

"Can't tell." Prabhakhar gestures at his screen. "If so, the radar won't pick it up."

A loud screech sounds in the cabin, like metal being torn.

Stacy clutches her armrests and opens her implant menu to send her report, hoping it will complete the transmission in time. "I think it's still on us."

"Not for long." Jalindo jerks their wrist to the right, and the shuttle snaps into a spin.

Stacy's head is bent to the side by the acceleration. She braces herself with a hand against the wall. As she supports herself, she pulls up her report in her menu.

"The comm's out," says Anderson with a grunt as the shuttle continues its roll.

The panel to Anderson's right shows a steady red light beside the comm unit's label.

And Stacy hasn't started her transmission yet. She lost her chance.

More, the data the shuttle is collecting isn't being transmitted. If they don't return to the station, the starship data will be lost.

The shuttle levels. "Did that work?" asks Jalindo.

"Yep." Prabhakhar gives a nervous chuckle. "There's an extra dot on the radar now."

Stacy hopes that dot is the Inorganic and not a piece of their shuttle.

"The pursuing units are adjusting," says Prabhakhar. "Six minutes until intercept."

"Stacy." Anderson points at the comm panel on the wall above her head. "Can you reach the latch on that panel?"

So there is still a chance. Stacy strains against her restraints, stretching her arm. Her fingers come short of brushing the panel's latch. She readjusts herself, pulls her legs under herself, and pushes upward again, stretching to her fullest extent. This time, she manages to snag the latch with a finger. The panel door springs loose, revealing wires and blinking lights behind the bulkhead.

"Nope," says Anderson. "We're not getting signal from the comm unit in the cargo bay. Even resetting the panel up here won't help."

"I guess," says Prabhakhar, "we'll just have to survive this trip, then."

Contreras grunts. "How likely do you think that is?"

Contreras unbuckles himself from his seat and kicks off toward the rear of the shuttle. Stacy wonders why Prabhakhar doesn't recall him, but then realizes the comm unit is essential for the mission, and Contreras is comparatively expendable. A cruel calculus.

Jalindo pulls up on the control stick and fires a quick burst from the thrusters. Stacy hopes Contreras has grabbed something to keep from slamming into a wall.

Now that they have survived an Inorganic attack, it seems Jalindo is taking them on a retreat trajectory. Maybe the shuttle has already gotten as close to the starship as it ever will.

Stacy glances over her shoulder at the cockpit door, hoping Contreras will return before Jalindo begins any more evasive maneuvers. "Do you think he's fixed it yet?"

"Not…" Anderson glances at the panel above her. "There! Light's on! He got it! I just need to reset…" She punches a button, then presses the panel back into place.

In another minute, Contreras returns and straps himself back in. He beams.

"Nice work," says Prabhakhar. "Seven minutes until intercept. We're gaining some distance. Can we go directly above the starship?"

"We'll pass over it during the climb," says Jalindo. "If I drop down, they'll catch us before we reach the threshold."

"Do what you can."

Stacy realizes she never asked if the Inorganics will stop pursuing them once the shuttle crosses back onto the humans' side of the threshold. Probably no one knows.

Two minutes later, the shuttle levels off. "Temporary leveling," says Jalindo. "Just for a few seconds while we pass overhead. Then we climb again."

They are overflying the starship now. Stacy can't see it from her vantage point, but her heart is racing.

"I'm getting good data." Anderson keeps her voice steady, but Stacy thinks she can detect a subtle hint of excitement. On Anderson's screen, a three-dimensional rainbow-colored model of the starship forms.

In seconds, it will be time for Stacy to send her message.

The last section is completed on the model on Anderson's screen. Jalindo pulls back on the stick and fires the thrusters again. "Climbing."

"Intercept in five minutes," says Prabhakhar.

Five minutes before machines tear them apart. In her previous assignments, in warzones or the Birmingham Riots, she at least had some degree of control over her fate. Here, she can only squeeze her armrests.

And, of course, she has to send the message. She begins transmitting the file.

"One hundred kilometers and climbing," says Jalindo.

A counter shows the time remaining until the message is sent. Ten seconds left. Five.

Sent.

The moment feels anticlimactic. She is strapped into a shuttle four hundred million kilometers from Earth, speeding from the surface of Juno and an actual starship, waiting for Inorganics to intercept them, and Stacy's heroic contribution to the moment is to send an email.

Jalindo taps at the pilot's screen every few moments, entering a trajectory update or double-checking a figure. Prabhakhar's screen shows summaries of the output from the shuttle's other consoles. Contreras and Anderson watch numbers and figures scroll across their screens. None of them noticed.

That's it, then. Stacy has kept her journalistic integrity intact. She told the full truth. The general will be furious. The public will be furious. The SDF will be furious. She will be a hero to some and a traitor to others.

Contreras points out the window. "There's the pod!"

Above them and moving away, the pod is a bright moving dot in the sky. Stacy zooms in with her oculars, but can make out few details at this range. What are Jason's plans now that it has escaped?

"I kind of admire it," says Anderson. "Jason. Fighting for its freedom. Escaping certain death."

"Maybe," says Stacy. "But it almost killed me."

Anderson lowers her head. "Sorry. I know."

"Sorry," says Stacy. "I didn't want to make you feel bad."

"Not our problem anymore," says Prabhakhar in a firm voice. "Intercept in three."

A bright dot shows in the lower right corner of the window. It creeps across the starfield, closing the gap a tick every second. How long until it grows from a dot into a blob and then into a body with arms and legs and then into a giant machine covering the entire window?

"Intercept in two."

Will Jalindo dodge?

The dot has become a blob and shows every sign of getting bigger. Stacy glances toward Contreras, but the sergeant keeps his head buried in his screen.

Jalindo hits a button on their console. Stacy's stomach jerks or flips or spins, she doesn't know which, and stars streak in the window and then a large force kicks her in the back and she closes her eyes but her sense of balance doesn't return. She wonders if, despite the minuscule gravity, they will plummet to the asteroid's surface, spinning the entire way down like a plane shot from the sky.

Then, without transition, the world stabilizes.

Stacy pries her hands loose from the seat. Juno no longer occupies the bottom portion of the window. The blob has disappeared…or moved? She sees another one in the center of the screen.

"Down to two-fifty again," says Jalindo.

The shuttle dropped in altitude during the evasion, got even farther from the threshold. Stacy lifts herself in her seat, her shoulders straining against her straps, to peer at the consoles of the other crewmembers, but she can't see anything useful.

Anderson must have noticed her motion. "It was a pre-programmed evasive maneuver."

Makes sense. Something quick, with faster movement than a human can manage.

"Climbing again," says Jalindo.

"Intercept in four," says Prabhakhar.

Is the dot in the center of their screen getting smaller? Dropping?

"Four hundred."

Will they make it to seven hundred before the Inorganic catches them? Does it matter if they do? What if the Inorganics continue pursuing them past the threshold? If the shuttle reaches the station, will the Inorganics proceed to dismantle the station, too?

Three minutes become two become one and then…

"Five hundred kilometers."

The threshold. The Inorganic has grown larger, its appendages just starting to appear as separate from the main mass.

And it starts shrinking. It becomes a blob, then a dot, then a faint pinprick of light. Stacy releases her breath and lets go of the armrests.

"Well." Jalindo lets out a laugh. "That was fun."

"Yeah," says Prabhakhar. "Yeah, that was."

WITH A DEEP thunk, the shuttle docks with the station. Jalindo, Prabhakhar, Anderson, and Contreras go about their tasks, shutting down systems, oblivious to what is about to happen. Stacy unlocks her straps, twists off her helmet, and floats free from her seat.

She wonders what General Young will do. What the public will do.

A better person might feel guilty at betraying her friends' trust by sending the message. Some of the crew might appreciate the sacrifice she made, might understand why she had to take advantage of her position on the shuttle expedition. But not many. That is the worst part of every assignment: seeing the looks on the faces of people who previously liked her.

A movement in her peripheral vision catches her eye. The trap door in the center of the room wiggles, then pops open. General Young pulls herself into the room, slipping her feet under a foothold and floating in front of the main window.

"Good job, everyone," she says. "Because of you, we'll have more detailed information on the starship than we've ever been able to collect. You also discovered that one of the Inorganics might be running some of its original source code, which I'm sure will be valuable."

Jalindo and the others nod, then began shutting down their systems. Moments stretch without the general saying anything. Did Stacy's message escape undetected?

When the others unbuckle their belts, Stacy stops recording and follows their lead. She pushes off from her seat.

"Ms. Sterling." General Young waits beside Stacy's seat, face impassive.

Stacy grabs her seat's headrest.

"Ms. Sterling, you are confined to your quarters until further notice. You will be allowed no outside communications. I am recommending you be charged with treason."

TWENTY-EIGHT

And when you're gone,
I think of you holding onto me
And when I think
This is as close as we'll ever be

I know you're here,
I know you're near,
We're close while far

When all I have are memories in my head
When all I have is your picture,
I remember those four words you said
We're close while far

Wherever you are,
I know you're close while far
Even to the farthest star
I know you're close while far
Close while far

STACY SINGS IN her head, tapping the rhythm against the smooth cloth of her sleeping bag. During her last week with Trevor before leaving on the shuttle to Collins, Stacy told him "Close While Far" would be their song while she was gone. Even though they are hundreds of millions of kilometers apart, it makes her feel better knowing they are listening to the same song and thinking of each other.

Every day, she misses him. Now, trapped in her quarters almost every moment of each day and unable to communicate with anyone outside of the fourteen other people on the station, she misses him even more.

Meters away, in the darkness, Gallegos snores, shadowy arms drifting in front of her, and Prabhakhar lets out the occasional heavy breath.

The room smells of body odor. It always does. The specific scent changes throughout the day, depending on the occupants and their body chemistries and how well the environmental system has scrubbed the air. Now, she can even tell who is in the room based on the specific smell. Outside scents will slip inside, of heated metal or ammonia from the restroom and sometimes even of sex. Stacy makes guesses about what has happened each day based on the drifting smells from the corridors.

Her roommates refuse to speak to her. Prabhakhar, Gallegos, Halabi. Most of the rest of the crew, too. Stacy doesn't know if the general ordered the crew to never engage Stacy in conversation or if the crew made that decision on their own.

Prabhakhar has more reason than anyone to hate her. The general has prohibited all non-essential communications from the station, which means he has lost contact with Vanessa and Ayaan and can no longer attempt to repair their distant relationship.

So, no matter how much Stacy wants to complain about not being allowed to speak to Trevor, she knows she has earned the punishment. Stacy doesn't know if Trevor successfully posted the report. She doesn't even know if he is alive or imprisoned.

The public has to know the whole truth. They have to know what they're fighting. I have to tell the truth, even if I don't like it, no matter the consequences to myself. Stacy repeats the words over and over, like a journalist's version of the Hippocratic oath.

And yes, releasing the report was the right thing to do, but even more, she now sees it was the only way to achieve her goals. In the end, it is always the public that instigates change, and she has put the decision into their hands.

If the powerful are making you suffer, it means you are causing them problems, which means you are doing something good. Another mantra.

Maybe she will get the changes she wants. Maybe she won't. Either way, when she returns, Take Action News will be over. It has already faced bankruptcy. The withdrawal of the SDF's support will finish it. And no other agency will hire her, even assuming she escapes a prison sentence.

General Young confining her to quarters didn't surprise her, but the treason charges did. Although, maybe they shouldn't have. General Young has expressed concern about Stacy's loyalties since Stacy arrived at the station. The treason charges might stick, depending on the judge. If so, Stacy might remain in jail the rest of her life, or she might be executed.

The USA reinstated the death penalty for treason two decades ago, a fine way for the country to start the new century. Politicians, known to lie professionally, have somehow convinced massive segments of the population that journalists are the real liars. Few people will protest if the country starts executing members of the media.

Stacy isn't a traitor. Her sacrifice for the truth makes her more patriotic than anyone who waves the flag and chants, "USA!" She is trying to make the world better and tell the truth.

At least, during her confinement, she has a chance to write in her journal and read some romance novels. And to get some rest.

The gentle snores of her roommates guide her slowly to sleep.

EACH DAY, STACY has the room to herself for several hours while her roommates are either on shift or in the galley or working out or finding some other form of recreation. It gives her a chance to escape her sleeping bag and move around the room.

She has wedged herself in the corner in a yoga position modified for zero-g when the door slides open. Light spills into the room, causing her eyes to throb, and she raises her arms to shield herself.

When the light disappears, the outline of General Young floats against the door. Young's arms are folded across her chest.

"Ms. Sterling."

"Hi." Stacy tries to hide the wariness in her voice, but doubts she succeeds.

"I know you have notes about Jason, the Ratti Report, and whatever other investigations you've been conducting under my nose."

Stacy keeps her expression neutral, though it probably doesn't matter in the dark.

Young waits for several seconds, probably hoping Stacy will volunteer information. "I want you to give me those notes."

"Those are my personal documents," says Stacy. "I don't have to give them to you."

"In the old days," says Young, "I could have just taken your filing cabinet or your folders or grabbed your papers from wherever you stashed them."

For a moment, Stacy wonders if Young will try to rip them from her implant. It is possible, but illegal. The military might be able to do it with impunity, though, and the process would be damaging to the implant. It might even affect Stacy's memories.

"We'll speak about this again later," says Young. "President Lopez in Uruguay has renewed his extradition request for you. He's offering to release a few imprisoned USA citizens, along with their previous economic offer. It's possible our government will grant the request. Your cooperation might influence their decision."

There seems to be a note of triumph in Young's voice. Not schadenfreude, but maybe vindication. She waits several moments without saying anything. Then her silhouette disappears, and the door closes. Stacy is alone again.

AN HOUR LATER, the door cracks open again. Stacy blinks away the light-induced tears until the door shuts.

A tap on her shoulder. In the darkness, Stacy can make out Sergeant Harrison's form. Time either for a restroom break or exercise or maybe another shot of radiation-repair drugs.

She slips out of her sleeping bag, pulls on her flight suit and socks, and follows Harrison into the hallway. Again, the brightness blinds her. She blinks and rubs her eyes. After several moments, her eyes adjust well enough for her to see while squinting.

"I hate being on bathroom duty." Harrison gestures toward the restroom. "Go on. I need to get back to my post. Lot of work to do."

"Sorry." Stacy's voice sounds croaky, dry. On each of these excursions, she forces herself to say something, even if her escort doesn't say anything, so she won't lose practice talking. "Are you okay? You seem upset with me."

Harrison has hooked her feet into holds and floats with her arms crossed. "After you betrayed us and sent that report? I thought you knew how dangerous the Inorganics are, especially after they almost killed you, but then you went and undermined all the work we've done."

"I was trying to tell the *whole* truth. I w—"

"Doesn't matter what you were trying to do. You screwed up." Harrison gestures to the restroom. "Hurry up."

Even if Stacy could apologize and mean it, it would do little good. Those in power hate to have their evils exposed. Perversely, Stacy is also resented by those oppressed by the people in power.

Stacy pulls herself to the restroom. When she opens the door, Montoya is inside.

"Sorry!" Stacy backs out, turning to Harrison. "I didn't know anyone was in there."

But Montoya is fully clothed. He has his feet hooked in place on the side wall of the coffin-sized room. The tank's lid is floating in the air beside him. The smell of urine coats her nose.

"Sorry." Stacy says it more calmly this time. "Should I come back?"

Montoya's eyes hold the hints of twinkles. "This one's out of order. Don't know when it'll be ready. You can use the enlisted restroom, though."

"Okay." She doesn't know how to interpret his expression, but she hates having to travel most the length of the station, seeing the reproving stares of every crewmember she passes. "Thank you."

From the hallway, Harrison gives a loud sigh, as though she has been ordered to move a roomful of cargo crates by herself. "Alright. Come on."

"Hey," says Montoya from the restroom. "You don't get to complain, Tina. You're not the one fixing the toilet."

"Thank you for your service," Harrison sings out to Montoya as she leads Stacy to the aft door to begin Stacy's Tour of Shame.

In the Analysis Room, Thor works at his console. He gave her the code to the Records Room and, out of everyone on the crew, should be most sympathetic to her. But he continues examining his screen without looking up. Young floats by her own console and watches Stacy every centimeter of the path across the room with frigid eyes.

In the galley, Gulati clips pans into place on the stove. She gives Stacy a wan smile, but says nothing.

The observation and fitness modules are, mercifully, empty. Harrison leads the way into the enlisted module and holds herself in place with the railing on the side wall. Stacy glides past to the restroom and closes the door behind her.

The room has barely enough space to move, like a city apartment's closet. Despite the air fresheners clipped to all four walls, the stench of bodily waste has permeated every surface. As Stacy maneuvers herself into position, she notices tiny scratches in the corner of the mirror above the sink. Words.

The Ratti Report was posted.

The report…Trevor did it. She doesn't know how the public reacted, but at least the information is out there. Stacy has done her job. She hopes Trevor is okay. He probably isn't.

Montoya must have meant for her to see this message. Maybe some of the crew is still on her side. Maybe they don't all hate her. She smiles.

Young would be furious with Montoya if she knew. *"Why did you do this?"* she asked Stacy while escorting her to her quarters to place her in confinement. *"Why now, after we realized how much danger we're in with the Inorganics? How could you be so reckless?"*

General Young looked frustrated and angry, but, more than that, she looked hurt, as though she had lost a friend. Stacy sees that expression before she goes to sleep every night.

She wonders what the general told the crew about her.

Montoya, at least, doesn't hate her. Not anymore.

Stacy wishes Montoya had told her how the report was received. Was her sacrifice for nothing? Does the public care? Will it appreciate the nuances of the situation or use her report as an excuse to lapse back into apathy?

After Stacy finishes, Harrison leads her back to the officers' module and waves her inside her quarters. Stacy enters.

"See you later," says Stacy, but Harrison has already turned away.

The door closes, cutting off the light and leaving her blind until her eyes adjust. She floats forward, arms outstretched, and her fingers brush against her sleeping bag. She removes her flight suit and socks, then settles into the bag.

She likely won't learn the public's reaction until her return to Earth. When the starship launches, in a few days or a few months, while the crew watches, Stacy will be in her sleeping bag. The story of the millennium, and she will miss it.

She folds her arms around her chest to wait for her next break. Her waking moments will be spent like this until she returns to Earth for her trial and execution, or for her extradition and trial and torture and execution. Maybe Trevor can find her a good lawyer to prevent the extradition, assuming he hasn't been thrown in jail for his part.

The Collins story was supposed to save her agency.

She closes her eyes.

THE DOOR OPENS again. Stacy blinks. She fell asleep. Hard not to, when the room is always dark and she has nowhere to go.

"Ms. Sterling."

If Stacy were on Earth, she would have jumped. The general has come. It's been two days since the last time.

"Follow me." Young's voice is…frightened? Angry? Bitter? In the darkness, Stacy can't tell.

Stacy dresses in her sleeping bag. "What is it?"

Young taps the doorframe. "You're being released."

TWENTY-NINE

STACY EMERGES FROM her quarters as though returning to the world from a coma. Even the thought of freedom colors the faded white walls more brightly, makes the musky air sweeter, the temperature balmier. She expects to go from the station to the shuttle to Uruguay to prison to the gallows, with maybe a stop between for torture.

"Why am I being released?"

The general gestures to her quarters. She looks as though someone has died. "We'll speak privately."

Young takes her customary position at the far end of the room. Stacy waits by the door. She hooks her feet into holds and places her palms on the railing behind her, keeping her face neutral.

"How is Trevor?"

The general's expression flashes from sympathy to guilt to sympathy. "About how you would expect. He released classified material to the public, so he was arrested. I've been told he's in good health."

Trevor has been in jail before for his own reporting. He knows how to handle himself. Still, Stacy hates to think of him there, especially since it is because of her request.

"That material wasn't classified," Stacy says.

The general's expression tightens. "By the time he sent it, it was."

"You…" Stacy wants to punch the general. "You did this to him."

"No." Young straightens. "You did. And you know it. Take responsibility for your own actions." She pauses. "That isn't why I called you in here."

Stacy frowns. "I don't care. I'm not talking about anything else until he's released from prison."

Young sighs. "That's infeasible. We need to have this discussion. If it goes the way I want, I will see what I can do about freeing him."

Stacy takes several breaths. She considers refusing to speak, but she has little leverage. She can at least listen. If nothing else, it means a few minutes of freedom from her own quarters. "Okay."

Young shifts position, then again. She glances at her computer on the side wall, whose screen is blank. Moments pass, almost as if Stacy is expected to speak first. Does the general want an apology?

Young looks up. "You're not recording, are you?"

Stacy could lie. Or she could say she isn't, which is true, and then start recording. Maybe Young deserves that treatment after what she's done to Stacy. Stacy keeps her recorder off. "No."

"Good. Everything we say here is off the record." Young sighs. "How did we get here?"

"'Here?'" Stacy nods in the direction of her quarters. "You mean incarcerating me?"

Young winces. "Yes. We're on the same side. We both want to encourage people to push themselves and work harder and start exploring again and, most of all, to take the Inorganic threat seriously. So why aren't we working together?"

"Well…You did lock me up. And try to hide things from me."

"I know." Young frowns. "And I wasn't wrong to do that. You trespassed into an off-limits area, stole information, and released it without permission. That's a crime, Ms. Sterling, no matter how good your intentions were."

"True. But I wasn't wrong to do it."

Young looks as though she wants to throttle Stacy. "I thought the Ratti Report muddied the issue. I still do, more than ever. Maybe if you and I had worked together to present it in the proper context, we wouldn't be in this situation now."

"Is that with why you released me? Because the Ratti Report muddied the issue?"

Young gives a bitter laugh. "Yes."

"The people are talking, then?"

Young sighs. "Yes, they're talking. Just not in the way we would have liked. They launched a 'Free Stacy Sterling' campaign."

Stacy smiles. She can imagine the posters and banners and marches. People fighting for freedom and speaking to power. It is what she has always wanted.

Her smile fades. They are fighting for the wrong reason. People are focusing on *her* instead of the message she sent.

"Good," says Young. "You see the problem. You've become the cause du jour. And when another cause comes up, in a week or a day or an hour, you'll be forgotten, and everyone will continue doing what they were doing before. Your extradition will be a twenty-word article forgotten as soon it's released."

"Maybe." Sometimes, people change.

Young shakes her head. "You have too much faith in them." General Young frowns. "I don't think you realize the position you're in, Ms. Sterling. Probably because I haven't fully explained. You're released from your quarters, depending on the answers you give in our conversation, but you're still not free. You will still be extradited, or, if not, stand trial."

"Why are you freeing me, then? Just for publicity?"

"So you can report again."

Stacy's mouth drops. "You're going to use me, then give me up to be tortured to death?"

Young shakes her head. "I hope not. If you do what is expected of you, you can probably avoid that fate."

"Probably?"

"Probably."

Stacy glares. "You're trying to bargain with me."

Young inclines her head. "The SDF was quite interested in what you had to say. After all my reports telling them of the threat we're facing, of the incredible power of the Inorganics, of your reports telling them what awaits us in the future if we do nothing, what made them finally decide to act was the knowledge that the Inorganics could feel pain."

"I'm glad someone's paying attention. What do they want to do?"

"They want to send another expedition to the starship, and they want you to go."

That statement doesn't make sense. Last time, they came close enough to Juno's surface she could see individual Inorganic units, but the crew also had to flee, not knowing if the Inorganics would catch the shuttle and dismember each person one by one. The scene still runs through her nightmares each night. Another expedition would provide little additional data.

"I don't think it's a good idea," says Stacy. "Especially not for me, since you're planning to extradite me when I get back to Earth. Is this where the bargaining comes in?"

"Yes." Young leans back. "This expedition will be your last chance to make a difference to the world."

Stacy waits, but Young says nothing more. "Is there more? I thought you were going to make an offer."

"That is the offer."

"What about Trevor? Can't you release him?" Stacy frowns. "And me?"

Young splays a hand. "I don't have the authority to do that. I can put in a recommendation, though."

Stacy stares. "Trevor is released. That's the only way I'll agree to go. The only way."

Young nods. "I will let Command know. So you'll do it?"

"I will go as an observer. That's it. I don't want to be part of the story again."

Young raises her eyebrows. "Being part of the story is the only thing that made the public finally pay attention."

When Stacy returned from Mars, reporters questioned her about everything, focused on her, as though her personal life was the most important part of her father's death. When Stacy became the story after Jason's escape, the public ignored everything else about that event. "I'm still not the story."

"Okay." Young's eyes go vacant as though she's taking notes. "I will see what they say."

"Thank you." Stacy tries to focus on the positives. Trevor will be freed from prison. Whatever happens to Stacy, at least she can save him. And the general is right: This expedition might be her last chance to reach the public. "So is this expedition going to be outside the threshold, or are we going to try to make another close approach?"

Young gives her a bitter smile. "SDF Command has ordered us to destroy the starship."

THIRTY

AFTER EVERYTHING THE SDF has seen, after everything Stacy has told them, how did they get it so wrong? Destroying the starship is, at best, a temporary solution. Destroying a thing of glory doesn't make the destroyer better than those whose work they destroyed. Anyone can destroy something.

"They're missing the point," says Stacy.

"Yeeeeaah." Young looks as though she has swallowed a pineapple coated in vinegar. "We should have expected nothing else. It's interesting that your truth and my subterfuge both led us to the same place."

"I guess I can understand their choice," says Stacy. "If we're even able to destroy it, it would set back the Inorganics. But for it to be meaningful, we would have to start working on our own starship, or at least the technology for one. Are they planning to do that?"

"If so, they haven't informed me." Young stares into the distance now. "Five years on this station and also in charge of Mars Base. I thought I'd consolidated my position by putting my people into positions of influence. But I've been away so long, I don't even know when I lost control."

One dictator had said, during an interview with Stacy, that all people belong to one of two groups: the oppressors or the oppressed. The general just now realized she has transitioned from the former to the latter.

Young checks her watch. "We're meeting in the Analysis Room in five. I wanted to give you the context beforehand."

"What's the meeting for?" asks Stacy. "Are you going to go through with it? Destroying the starship?"

"Maybe this mission is our new stopgap measure. Instead of keeping Collins operational longer, we're finding a way to give humanity a temporary respite." Young waves her out of the room. "You'll get details along with the others. You might want to record it."

Already back on the team, as though Stacy never transgressed. She wonders if the rest of the crew will be so quick to forgive.

"And you'll free Trevor?"

The general pauses, her eyes vacant for several moments. Then she focuses on Stacy again. "I sent a message with my recommendation. That's all I can do."

Stacy waits with her hand on the railing beside the door. "If he's not freed, I'm not going on the expedition."

"I understand," says the general. "But you can still attend the briefing."

Stacy starts her implant recording. "Okay. I'll attend the briefing, and we'll see from there."

"Go ahead," says Young. "I'll join you soon."

Stacy enters the hallway and pulls herself along the railing to the next module. She opens the module's aft door, curious how the others will react to the assignment. And to her presence.

Inside the Analysis Room, Prabhakhar, Contreras, Jalindo, and Anderson float along one of the walls. They break off mid-conversation when Stacy enters and stare as though she were a dead relative.

"Hi." Stacy glides toward them.

They shift aside to make room for her. None of them meet her eyes.

"It's been a while." Stacy's voice has risen several steps. She hates it when she does that.

"You recording?" Jalindo asks.

Stacy nodded.

"Good," says Jalindo. "I hope you put this in your report so everyone can see what the great hero Stacy Sterling is really like. I registered my objection with the general. You can't be trusted. You betrayed my trust when you sent your message from the shuttle, just like you betrayed Tío during your first interview. You learned nothing from that day. You should not have been released."

Prabhakhar nods. Contreras crosses his arms over his broad chest, and Anderson engages in a thorough study of her socks.

"I'm sorry," says Stacy. "I didn't mean to hurt you or anyone else. I didn't see it as a…a betrayal."

"Exactly," says Jalindo. "You see us as tools. You're nice to our faces, but the moment you see an opportunity advantageous to you, you abuse our trust."

Tears form in Stacy's eyes. She hopes the others don't notice, although viewers will. It is embarrassing, and Jalindo will accuse her of using tears as a manipulation tactic. "I'm not trying to. I'm trying to help. No matter what I did, I would have been betraying someone or something. So I did what was right. But I never meant to hurt anyone."

Before Jalindo can counter, the door opens and Young enters. She halts in the center of the room to hang in mid-air, arms crossed and feet hovering a meter above a console, like a Messiah figure.

"You know I have an announcement to make," says Young. "We have been ordered to destroy the starship."

On cue, the others breathe in. They look as shocked as Stacy felt minutes earlier.

Anderson looks nervous, probably reliving memories from the IMS attack and the rescue. Prabhakhar's expression is now content, saintlike.

Jalindo retreats into a mask. "I guess this is one path to celebrity."

Contreras skips straight from shock to eagerness. "Yes! Should've done this years ago. But…how?"

"Command wasn't specific." Young's voice contains that ironic smile her face doesn't show. "When they tell you to take the hill, you find a way to do it."

Prabhakhar rubs the side of his head. "We will need to deliver an explosive, probably to their engines. We don't have missiles or drones, so it will require several people to…make the delivery."

Contreras grins like a child at their birthday. "Yes! That's the way. We're going to start making them pay for everything they've done."

Young looks disappointed. "I appreciate the enthusiasm."

"I want to be the one to plant the bomb," says Contreras. "Take a little back for my cousin."

"We'll get into the details," says Young. "You five will t—"

"Five?" Jalindo glances at Stacy. "Oh. I don't fly with traitors."

"We need Stacy because of her…fame."

Stacy winces. The general makes it sound like a curse word. Stacy can't help but agree with the sentiment, but she doesn't like being blamed.

Jalindo seems unconvinced. "We don't need anyone's fame to destroy a starship."

"I didn't ask to come," says Stacy, "but—"

"Good," says Jalindo. "Then don't."

"Sergeant." Young's tone hardens. "Stacy's inclusion is not up for debate."

Jalindo's mouth tightens. "Understood, ma'am."

Young turns to Stacy. "I want you to accompany the team so you can document the mission. It might be important some-day for people to see what we're doing. If we succeed, people can see humans overcoming improbable odds. If we don't, we might still see the starship from a closer vantage point than we have before or ever will again. The footage will be valuable to the SDF."

"Ma'am." Prabhakhar's expression looks tight. "I think we should not allow Stacy to transmit in real time. We saw what happened last time."

Stacy's mouth opens, but she can't argue. She did what was right, even though the others hate her for it.

"Sorry, Major." Young gives him a bitter smile. "While I agree with you, we'll need her to transmit the footage live."

Stacy takes a breath. "In case we don't return."

"Yes."

Stacy's heart sinks. When she accepted the assignment to document the scuttling of Collins Station, she knew there would be some risks, but the risks keep increasing every time the assignment changes.

"I selected the five of you," says Young, "because of your experience working together on the expedition and during the rescue of Stacy and me."

Jalindo glares at Stacy. "We don't need a reporter. We can do the recording ourselves."

"Ms. Sterling is a professional," says Young. "Besides, the rest of you need to concentrate on your tasks."

"Destroying a starship." Contreras pumps a fist.

"It won't be a starship," says Anderson. "If we destroy it, it won't ever be a starship. It will be a proto-starship. Which is basically just a bunch of metal and wires."

A vessel with unrealized potential. Its destruction will make it a meaningless object.

"Okay." Contreras laughs. "I'm cool with that. Don't think we need the philosophy lesson right now."

Young indicates the five of them. "You five will take the shuttle to Juno's surface."

"To the surface?" asks Stacy.

Young nods. "The Inorganics would likely intercept any other delivery method. I want people on the scene, ready to improvise."

"And to make it personal," says Contreras.

Young cocks her head. "You will make it professional, Sergeant, or the team will make it professional with someone else."

Contreras sobers and nods. "Yes, ma'am."

Young continues. "Major Prabhakhar, you will lead this mission. Lieutenant Anderson and Sergeant Contreras will handle the explosives. Sergeant Jalindo will drop off the rest of you and will return to a position outside the threshold. The EVA team will then proceed to a location near the Inorganic unit Ms. Sterling spotted on the previous expedition."

"Which unit?" asks Stacy. Then she remembers. "Oh. The one that acted like Jason."

"Yes," says Young. "Since its motions are the same as Jason's, we can assume that portion of its source code is unmodified from the original. We can use that portion of its code to send it commands. You will deposit the explosives, retreat a safe distance, and send the target unit a command to retrieve the packet and deliver it to three locations around the starship."

"If it's important to know the source code," says Stacy, "why not send the commands to Jason itself?"

Young shakes her head. "While Jason's programming is for a digger unit, its body is the pod, so we don't know how it would interpret the commands. More importantly, we require line of sight to send the signal, and Jason is unlikely to be in a good position for us to communicate with it wherever we deposit the explosives."

The others nod.

"The commands," says Young, "will be developed by Gallegos and Hernandez. Contreras, you will work with them so you can troubleshoot any issues we experience in real-time. Anderson, you will work with Ko and Windham on the explosives package. If, after transmitting the command, the Inorganic unit fails to deliver the explosives, the five of you will attempt to place them in the correct locations yourselves."

"And then we'll come back?" Anderson asks. "Right?"

"That's the plan." Young's expression betrays nothing.

"I don't like the idea," says Jalindo, "of not accompanying them after landing."

"We need to keep the shuttle safe," says Young. "It is the only way we have to return to Earth from the station."

"I know," says Jalindo.

"If at all possible," says Young, "you will retrieve your teammates when they have completed their objectives. All of you will be cross-trained in the event any member of your team becomes incapacitated."

'Incapacitated.' A euphemism. Stacy imagines an Inorganic dismantling her as it would a satellite that wanders too close.

"Well, Stacy." Contreras grins. "I guess we have you to thank for this. We're finally going to take something back from the Innies."

Stacy tries to return the smile, but she has a hard time smiling about a mission that misses the entire point of her work.

"I know not all of you agree with this assignment." Young nods to Anderson. "I don't agree with this approach, either. But we've been given our orders, and all of us will carry them out to the best of our abilities. We are SDF personnel, and that means something."

Stacy turns to Prabhakhar. "I guess this is a good way to end your last tour with the SDF."

"I'm staying in the SDF." Prabhakhar doesn't look at her.

"Oh."

"Because of your transmission, we've had a communications blackout. I'm sure you've heard. I haven't spoken to my family in two weeks."

"I'm sorry."

"Yeah."

"You all are taking a great risk." Young's expression is too neutral for her to not be hiding emotions. "But there is a risk to the rest of us, too, so make your moves count. It's likely the Inorganics will attack the station in retaliation. Without the shuttle, we'll have no way to evacuate. I don't expect any of us to survive this mission. In a way, the five of you are the luckiest of us. You'll at least be doing something useful. The rest of us will be waiting for the end to come."

Not a rousing speech. Not what the troops need now.

"We might lose our lives," says Young, "but if we don't stop the Inorganics, humanity will lose everything. So make it succeed."

Prabhakhar floats a little straighter. Jalindo's expression becomes more resolved. Anderson might put the Inorganics on a pedestal, but she nods. Contreras looks as though he will fight anyone who tries to keep him from the mission.

Stacy is ready, too. Right approach or not, this mission is what they have, and she will make it succeed.

THIRTY-ONE

Trevor, honey, this might be goodbye. I'm sorry. I hate that I might never see you again. I'm going to Juno's surface with a small team, and we're going to try to blow up the starship. None of us expect it to end well.

I'll be transmitting live, in case we don't…you know. I don't know if you'll want to watch. I don't even know if I want you to.

You know I disagree with blowing up the starship, but I'm glad people are at least doing something, whether we succeed or not.

My biggest regret, if we don't come back, is not living the next few decades with you. You have made my life better and have always been so supportive and encouraging. I love you so much.

STACY CLUTCHES HER armrests with hands stiff from prolonged squeezing. The shuttle banks starboard again, and her helmet bangs against the side wall. Without even being in line of sight of the controls, she has no way of knowing when the shuttle will dive or climb or roll or bank, so her stomach can't brace itself. What would happen if she throws up? The vomit would blanket the faceplate, coat the drinking-water tube, maybe clog air vents. And the smell…

The five of them took Dramamine beforehand to prevent such accidents. They will take stimulants when they reach the surface. The condemned don't need to worry about the effects of conflicting drugs or long-term health.

As the shuttle twists to the side, Stacy instinctively tries to redistribute her nanocams, but they aren't in the shuttle. Even if the general had allowed her to take them, they can't operate in the near-vacuum of Juno. Stacy hates that her report will be raw and unpolished, with only the muffled audio from inside her helmet or the crackling of the radio.

At least she has successfully refused to lift the block on her emotional overlay. She doesn't want anyone else inside her head, doesn't want them to feel the fear or the guilt or, if it came to it, to feel her die. Implants, she's read, stop recording sixty seconds after registering loss of brain activity.

"Intercept in five at current rate," says Prabhakhar over the radio. He's holding onto his seat up front just as tightly as Stacy holds onto hers.

Three nights ago, Prabhakhar sat up late in the galley. Stacy asked what he was doing. She expected him to tell her to leave or even to ignore her, but he responded.

"I'm updating my will." Tears were in his eyes. "Ayaan barely remembers me now. He'll forget his dead father completely in no time. But…at least he'll get some money out of it."

Stacy's previous report not only resulted in the communications blackout that kept Prabhakhar from speaking to his family for a week, but also in this expedition that might kill them all. She can't even apologize. Words are inadequate.

Anderson's head bobs up from her console in the seat ahead of Stacy. "Ten minutes from the surface."

Throughout the preparation, Anderson made it clear she disapproves of this mission. "I don't understand," she said. "Why is it so bad for the Inorganics to go to Proxima? Isn't it good to at least have *someone* going?"

The dusty, cratered surface of Juno fills the forward window. Not long now, one way or the other.

Jalindo is forced into an evasive maneuver, and Stacy's head slams against the sidewall. The Inorganics are chasing them with a greater efficiency than last time. How much closer can the shuttle get? Without seeing the others' screens, she doesn't know how many Inorganics are approaching or from where or how soon they will arrive.

"Spotted the target unit." Contreras straightens in his seat in front of Stacy. "Transferring coordinates to server."

In contrast to the others, Contreras trained for the mission with great enthusiasm, mastering each skill more quickly and practicing longer hours. As they suited up to enter the shuttle, he slipped a picture of his cousin into one of his suit's pockets.

"Coordinates received." Jalindo tilts the control stick to the right for an instant, jostling the cockpit.

Before the shuttle undocked an hour ago, Stacy commented that she would finally make Jalindo famous. Jalindo didn't respond.

The shuttle jerks onto a different trajectory. Stacy's helmet hits the wall again.

The radio crackles, and Jalindo speaks. "The unit's position is 9.3 kilometers from the starship. I'll aim for a location five hundred meters from it."

9.3 kilometers from the starship. It seems so far away, despite being closer than humans have ever gotten before. Stacy will still be able to see it, but she won't *be there*. She won't be able to reach out and touch it, to have that physical contact with an object that could leave the Solar System. Though, as Anderson said, if they blow it up, it will never be a starship.

Setting down five hundred meters from that Inorganic unit means they will have to traverse the asteroid for a long time before coming close enough. Other Inorganics will have time to intercept the team.

Trevor might be experiencing this moment in twenty-five minutes. What will he think, seeing the world shake around her, hearing reports of incoming Inorganics? Will he watch or turn away? Few people can stomach a snuff film starring their spouse.

Rocks and rifts approach in the window, Juno's surface becoming a rich palette of grays, blacks, and whites. Surprising how one adapts to limited color.

"Intercept in four," says Prabhakhar.

"Five minutes from the surface," says Anderson.

The shuttle rocks again as Jalindo changes course. The Inorganics must be close enough now that course changes have little effect on intercept time. And that intercept time is short. Even if Jalindo manages to drop off the EVA team, they might be unable to get the shuttle to safety.

"Eject decoys," says Jalindo.

"Ejecting decoys." Prabhakhar taps his console, and a quick series of thumps come from aft.

A constellation of soccer-ball-sized bright objects drop behind them, like chaff to confuse enemy radars. Hopefully, the Inorganics will have difficulty discerning the shuttle from the decoys, or will at least feel obligated to intercept all targets, which would give Jalindo a few more precious moments to drop off the EVA team.

The shuttle jerks right, then down. Stacy hopes Jalindo is having fun with this flying, because no one else is. Contreras makes a choking sound.

The jostling doesn't stop. Stacy wants to close her eyes and forget where she is, but her one job is to observe. She keeps her eyes open, focusing on watching the window over Contreras's head, then turning to the back of Jalindo's head, then cycling through the rest of the crew before starting over again.

"It's working." Prabhakhar's voice rattles with the shuttle's motion, as if spoken through a fan. "Inorganics are intercepting decoys. Intercept steady at four."

"Two minutes from surface," says Anderson.

"Prepare for egress," says Prabhakhar.

Stacy puts her hand over the button for her belt and clamps her teeth together. For the egress, her task is to unhook her seatbelt, rush to open the floor hatch at the front of the cockpit, and wait for the others to exit before following.

Hilltops appear at the bottom of the window, rising into

the center as the shuttle descends. For the first time, Juno's surface looks like a real landscape rather than a textured ball. It is amazing how this gray rock and sand makes her feel so homesick.

A lumpy gray plain, interrupted by occasional hills, stretches to the horizon. With an abrupt bump, the shuttle sets down on the surface.

"Parked," says Jalindo.

Stacy squeezes her belt button, and the seatbelt straps eject. Before the straps settle to the seat in the minuscule gravity, she bolts to the floor hatch in front of the pilot's and co-pilot's seats. With her legs in holds, she twists the hatch's handle and lifts the cover.

Without pause, Prabhakhar darts through the hatch. He will speed to the shuttle's nose to pop open the docking port. Contreras follows with the communications gear on his back. Anderson goes next, wearing the explosives backpack.

Stacy waves to Jalindo and pulls herself into the darkened lower bay. "Good luck, Sergeant."

As Stacy yanks the hatch shut behind her, she hears Jalindo saying with reluctance, "Good luck, Sterling."

After weeks of free-fall, Stacy expected Juno's gravity to feel like walking through water, or as though weights are strapped to her back and limbs, but it still feels like nothing. She floats through the short darkened corridor, hand-over-hand along the railing, her boots never touching the floor.

Brightness appears, a light at the end of the tunnel. Prabhakhar has opened the docking port. His silhouette blocks most of the light until he exits from view. Contreras and Anderson follow.

With the others no longer blocking her, Stacy can see through the porthole. Outside, centimeters from her fingers, Juno waits. It is no more than sand and rock, a tiny world full of nothing else, but it is another world, and Stacy will become one of the few humans to set foot on an asteroid.

She checks her implant to make certain it is still working properly, then grabs the hatch edges and slides out.

As soon as she emerges onto the sand, she pulls a tethered stake from her suit leg, places the end against the ground, and presses the button on its top end. A drill extends into the dirt, sending a cloud of dust into the air. The dust returns to the ground as a slow rain. With a quick vibration, the stake hooks itself in place to prevent her from drifting from the surface until the team begins moving.

"Brace yourselves," says Prabhakhar. He and the others have also staked themselves into place. "Shuttle, you're go for launch."

"Go for launch." Before Jalindo finishes speaking, attitude thrusters fire on both sides of the shuttle. It lifts from the surface, swirling the dirt and tiny rocks around them like dust devils. For several seconds, Stacy can see nothing through the cloud. Pings come from particles bouncing off her faceplate.

As the dust blows from the shuttle's exhaust, Stacy feels for cover behind a small boulder. Prabhakhar and the others will, as they discussed before the mission, send out decoys to emit signals and trick the Inorganics.

Once the dust clears, Stacy can see the shuttle speeding away and climbing, juking from side-to-side. The shuttle is their only way to return to Collins, and it is flying from them. The situation isn't quite Cortez burning the ships, but there is a finality to it. They are committed.

From behind Stacy, an Inorganic flies overhead. Tens of meters away, able to reach them in seconds. Its large, boxy central body holds spindly legs and a set of grasping claws. For a moment, it seems poised to descend on them like a spider from its web.

Stacy readies herself to disengage her stake, but doesn't know what she will do afterward. If she flees, she will end up flying from the surface, helpless and ready to be collected by the Inorganic. If she waits, she will die a few seconds sooner.

The Inorganic fires its thrusters and shoots away in pursuit of the shuttle. She can't tell if it is closing the distance or if Jalindo is pulling away.

"Stacy," says Prabhakhar. "Focus."

Stacy looks away from the shuttle. Prabhakhar is right: This mission needs to be successful. The worst scenario would be Jalindo dying in vain.

"Take your stims," says Prabhakhar.

Stacy turns her head to the left and takes two sips from that side's tube. She swallows the bitter liquid, not relishing the increased heartbeat to come. Around her, the others shift position as they drink their own stims.

"Mirror check," says Prabhakhar.

Stacy unfolds the mirror from her chest plate, which reflects the displays on the front of her suit. Oxygen level, electrical system, temperature, water level, all nominal. She pushes her mirror back in place, flat against the suit chest.

"Alright," says Prabhakhar. "The target was last seen five hundred thirty meters from here at sixty degrees from north. Let's go."

Stacy's traveling partner is Prabhakhar. As commander, Prabhakhar's suit has a single red stripe length-wise on each arm and leg. Stacy approaches him, and, as rehearsed on Collins, hooks her line into his belt. He does the same with her belt. Contreras, in brown stripes, and Anderson, in blue, pair with each other.

With the almost nonexistent gravity, one thousand times lighter than Earth's, it would take little effort to fly from the surface. An accidental kick, a push with slightly more force than intended, and that would be it. Using the buddy system will reduce the likelihood of such accidents. Each person has a jet backpack, but the limited fuel means the packs should only be used for emergencies.

Prabhakhar unhooks himself from the surface first. As Stacy stays in place as the anchor, he glides centimeters over the surface until the slack in his line almost disappears, then grabs a rock and drives his stake into the ground.

Stacy clicks the button on her own stake, withdraws it from the ground, and pushes herself toward Prabhakhar. She passes him and continues until her line nears the end, then scrapes her fingers along the ground to slow her pace before planting her stake.

They continue in that manner, leapfrogging each other as they travel in the direction of the target Inorganic. The Solar System's first starship is still almost ten kilometers ahead, though they can't yet see it over the short horizon.

"Major." Anderson's voice is calm. "Another Inorganic unit is approaching at our ten."

Stacy turns to face the mentioned direction. A spindly figure approaches, just past the horizon. A transporter unit. From its smooth motion, Stacy can't tell if it is carrying a full load or not, but it is definitely coming their direction.

Transporter units have no weapons in a technical sense, but like other Inorganics, their metallic appendages could kill them without trouble.

Prabhakhar has already traveled farther ahead than the others, near the end of the line he and Stacy share. He looks so exposed out in the open, like a rabbit in a flat field. He plants his stake, then turns to face them. "Hide."

A small crater, the diameter of an outdoor swimming pool with the shallowness of a bathtub, is less than two meters to her right. It is the closest thing to a hiding place Stacy can see. She retracts her stake and drags herself along the surface toward the crater. Her fingers wrap around the crater's short rim, giving her the first solid grip she's had on the ground since leaving the shuttle, and she maneuvers herself into the wide area. She ducks below the rim, worried the Inorganic has already seen her. If it has, it will follow her in here and dismantle her suit as she watches. It might break her limbs in the process, or maybe she will just suffocate with the loss of suit integrity.

Stacy plants her stake beside her and holds onto it. Her breathing has stilled. An ominous silence fills her helmet.

A figure settles, chest-down, beside her. The suit's blue stripes indicate Anderson. The lieutenant's face shows through her faceplate, staring down with intense concentration. Contreras army-crawls into the crater on the other side of Anderson.

Seconds tick by. Stacy wants to peer over the crater's edge, but the Inorganic would see her. If it hasn't already. It shouldn't be taking Prabhakhar this long to reach the crater.

"Major," says Contreras. "You coming?"

No answer comes. Stacy exchanges a glance with Anderson. Did the Inorganic attack Prabhakhar? But no, Stacy would have felt it in her line.

"Sorry," says Prabhakhar. "Stuck. You all, stay put."

"Stuck?" Did his boot get wedged into a hole or has his tether snagged a rock? Did the Inorganic see him? "Are you okay?"

"Fine. No cover out here, though."

"Prabhakhar…" Stacy considers leaving the crater to help him, but that would do nothing except draw the Inorganic's attention to herself and the others.

"It's okay," says Prabhakhar. "I hope you're still recording. Maybe this will convince Ayaan I'm cool."

"This isn't the way to do it, Prabhakhar."

"Maybe it is. Tell him and Vanessa I love them."

"Major…" Anderson, beside Stacy, seems to stop herself from launching over the crater.

Stacy wants to cry. She can't see Prabhakhar, doesn't know how close the Inorganic is, but she knows it will be only moments before the attack comes.

Prabhakhar's line jerks, and a grunt comes over the radio. The line jerks again, straining at Stacy's belt. Her waist is dragged forward through the dirt for several centimeters until her legs bob up from the surface. If the line is pulled hard enough, it will haul her out of the crater behind Prabhakhar.

Stacy has to do something. She checks that her stake is solidly planted, then grabs the line with one hand and tugs.

The line doesn't budge. She tries pulling again, with the same result. Then it yanks, hard, with inhuman force, tearing Stacy's waist to the side and almost breaking her grip on her stake.

Contreras shifts his boots under himself as though to leap. "We need to save him."

"No." Prabhakhar sounds angry. "I ordered you to stay put."

His last word ends in a muffled cry of pain.

"Cut the line." Prabhakhar's voice hints at the threat of tears. "Cut it."

"But—" says Stacy.

Anderson's hand grabs Stacy's belt. Her other hand holds a serrated knife. For just a moment, Stacy has the bizarre thought that Anderson has snapped.

The lieutenant places the knife under Prabhakhar's line, serrated edge up, and begins sawing. Threads fray. Anderson's face through her helmet looks grim, full of self-loathing. With each movement of the knife, she winces as though she has been struck.

"Stop," says Stacy. "He'll die."

"I know." Anderson's voice is brittle.

"It's too late to stop it," says Prabhakhar. "When the unit leaves the area, you need to keep going. Finish the mission."

He sounds so calm. Resigned. As though he has expected this moment, or one like it.

The line snaps as the knife cuts through the final threads. Stacy holds onto the line, but the next yank from Prabhakhar's end jerks it from her grasp. It sails in an arc overhead, in slow motion in the low gravity, over the crater rim and out of sight.

Then nothing but the sound of her heartbeat and her breathing. For moments, no one speaks, and Stacy feels isolated in her miniature world. Prabhakhar says nothing, but she also hasn't heard a scream. She again considers peeking over the crater's lip, but doesn't know if the Inorganic has left yet.

A thump sounds, and a surprised cry crackles over the radio, and then silence.

THIRTY-TWO

STILLNESS. NO WIND. No movement in the sky. No air, no pressure, no water, nothing to keep her alive. Hundreds of millions of kilometers from Earth. And out there, somewhere, are the Inorganics.

Stacy turns to Anderson, who turns to her. Is Prabhakhar dead? The question shows in Anderson's face, and Stacy is certain Anderson can see it in hers.

Contreras mumbles something incomprehensible, then speaks more loudly. "That just happened. That really happened. I thought we'd all go at once, not one by one. Maybe in an explosion or torn apart, but all at once. Thought we'd take some of them with us, too."

Stacy doesn't know if it is safe to peek over the rim of their crater. The Inorganic might still be there.

After what seems like hours, Anderson shifts position again. "We don't have enough air to keep waiting. I'll check."

The lieutenant raises her head several centimeters, then ducks back down. "It's gone."

"Prabhakhar?" asks Stacy.

"He's…still there."

Contreras grunts. "We should have gone after that Innie. We just cowered here and let it kill Major Prabhakhar."

"We were under orders," says Anderson.

"Screw those orders."

"Sergeant." Anderson's voice has steel in it that Stacy has never heard before. "We're going to check on the major. Ms. Sterling, connect yourself to Sergeant Contreras."

Stacy unclips the spare line from her backpack and ties it to her belt clip, then hands the other end to Contreras. He ties her line into his belt. Now she depends on him for her life.

Anderson pushes herself forward, skimming the surface. Contreras and Stacy follow.

No more Inorganics appear while the three cross the short distance to Prabhakhar. The major floats several meters from the surface like a balloon, anchored by his stake. No gas leaks from his suit. Either it is already empty, or it remains intact.

Stacy and the others anchor themselves in place in a semicircle around Prabhakhar's stake. Anderson grabs Prabhakhar's line and pulls him down. No twitches in reaction. Stacy and Contreras share a worried look.

"Hey!" Anderson has Prabhakhar's body at chest level. She points at the major's chest pack. Digital displays show the life-support system's status. "It's still working. He might be…"

Behind the major's faceplate, his eyelids flicker open. His face squeezes in pain.

"Prabhakhar!" says Stacy.

"Yeah." He grunts.

"You're alive!"

He smiles for an instant before sucking in his breath. "Mostly. Inorganic broke a couple things."

There is nowhere to treat any serious injury, even if they had the time. If Prabhakhar has broken limbs or ribs…

"I know," he bites out. "End of the road for me."

"No." Anderson shakes her head.

"Yes." The major gestures to his backpack. "You're in charge now, Lieutenant. Explosives are back there. I'll call Jalindo. See if they can get me. If not…"

Contreras reaches for Prabhakhar's backpack and pulls out the explosives package. He passes it to Anderson, who shakes her head and indicates Stacy.

"Really?" Contreras turns to Stacy. "Are you sure we can trust her?"

Stacy waves the package away. "I'm here to observe. This mission isn't mine. I'm already more a part of the story than I want to be."

"I know," says Anderson. "But we need you, and this mission is important. I'm not asking you to set up the explosives or send the signal. But if you could carry this, it would be a huge help."

Stacy has already resigned herself to being part of the story, but this…

She doesn't want to destroy the starship. She knows Anderson doesn't, either. But maybe it is necessary. And she won't be setting the explosives herself. She will only be carrying them.

"Okay. I'll do it." Stacy clips the package to her backpack.

A hand grips her shoulder. Anderson.

"We should start." Anderson sounds defeated.

Stacy feels sorry for the lieutenant. Anderson has felt uncertain about herself the entire time Stacy has been at the station, and now command has been thrust upon her.

Stacy puts a hand on Prabhakhar's shoulder. "Are you sure you're going to be okay?"

"No." Prabhakhar waves her away. "But you need to go."

Anderson releases Prabhakhar's line a few centimeters at a time, letting him return to his position several meters above the ground. Stacy hates leaving him there.

There are now only three people left on a long-shot mission that already began with a minimal team.

"Ayaan would be proud of you, Prabhakhar," says Stacy.

"He shouldn't be." Prabhakhar coughs, then grunts in pain. "If I survive, I'm staying with the SDF. It's a good cause. It really is. We need people to make these sacrifices. But I'm sacrificing time with my family. So Ayaan shouldn't be proud of me."

"Go on." Prabhakhar waves them onward. "You have your mission, Lieutenant."

Anderson kicks off to resume their climb toward the target unit. While Stacy waits for her own turn to move, she stares into the sky. Did Jalindo escape their pursuer? If not, if they were killed, it means the rest will die on Juno, too, by suffocation if not something more violent.

They move as before, with Anderson planting her stake after reaching the end of her line. Contreras and Stacy move next. No one speaks as they cross the dusty plain.

Stacy doesn't know how long they have traveled when she sees a pair of Inorganics in the distance. One unit remains motionless as the other approaches it.

She is standing in an open field. If one of the units turns her direction, it will see her. She drops flat to the ground, planting her stake and holding onto its base, to lower her profile. She can't think of anything better to do. Contreras and Anderson do the same a few meters from her.

The Inorganics now stand close to each other. One of them extends its arms toward its companion.

Stacy zooms in with her oculars. The Inorganic with extended arms seems to be plucking an appendage from the motionless Inorganic. It places the appendage inside itself, then reaches for the other Inorganic again. This time, it twists off an antenna from the top of the Inorganic's body.

Stacy turns to Anderson and Contreras, but the others keep staring straight ahead.

Nothing else moves on the landscape ahead of her. How does it look to the Inorganics? They probably see outside the visual spectrum. Would she and her companions stand out or blend in?

As the trading continues, Stacy realizes the Inorganic isn't just taking select pieces from its comrade. It is dismantling the other unit completely.

Maybe the unit has malfunctioned or been damaged. Maybe it is obsolete now, or its tasks have been completed. Either way, there is a serial-killer quality to the proceedings, a cold-blooded snuffing out of a life. The eeriest part is how the dismantled Inorganic is just standing there, patient and docile.

A life. As though the unit is a living being. When did she start thinking about them that way?

Despite the grimness of the dismantling, Stacy doesn't want it to end, worried about which direction the Inorganic will go afterward. If it spots them, they will probably be killed. Prabhakhar survived somehow, either because he is good at playing dead or because the Inorganic was more interested in incapacitating him than killing him.

Minutes later, nothing remains of the other unit. It has been disassembled and placed in the surviving Inorganic's storage. The Inorganic strides from the scene in the opposite direction from Stacy and the others, disappearing over the horizon.

Stacy and the others keep still for several more minutes, waiting to make sure no Inorganics appear.

Anderson breaks the stillness. In complete silence, the lieutenant retrieves her stake and continues forward again.

After an interminable time, Stacy sees a chasm in the ground ahead of them. Ragged cliffs mark each side, with an unknown distance and an unknown drop between them. The cliffs stretch as far to the left and right as she can see.

"Hm," says Anderson.

Stacy wonders what formed the split. Juno didn't have tectonic activity, so it couldn't be geological in origin. Maybe a smaller asteroid plowed the split during a shallow impact, or maybe a larger ancient collision fractured the surface. Now that collision, a minor event in the Solar System's formation, will play an active role in the history of life here, a deciding factor in how humanity confronts its largest threat.

Stacy is the first to reach the rift's edge. She plants her stake a meter from the cliff and gazes to the opposite side. Even in Juno's weak gravity, no leap could clear that distance. The gap has to be as wide as a soccer field is long. And down…

Stacy peers into the depths. The dim sunlight, scarcely brighter than twilight, does not reach the bottom. There is no danger of falling quickly enough to die, not in the near free-fall conditions, but they could find themselves at the bottom and have to climb all the way out. That climb would probably deplete their oxygen. Or, if they used their jetpacks to extricate themselves, that fuel would be unavailable for future emergencies.

Anderson and Contreras stop on either side of her, planting their own stakes. They look at each other's dark faceplates.

Stacy gestures. "How are we going to cross that?"

Contreras gestures to the left. "Can we go around?"

"We don't know how far it goes," says Anderson. "We might not find a better place to cross. We'll do it here."

Stacy sips from her water tube. She meant to take one sip, but finds herself taking several long gulps. Maybe a last meal of sorts.

"I doubt this chasm can be too long," says Contreras. It's on an asteroid, so how big can it be? I still vote we keep looking for a place where it gets slimmer."

Stacy turns to him as though he has stepped on a landmine.

When Anderson speaks, her voice borders on cold. "Sergeant Contreras, I am in charge. We will cross here. I welcome any suggestions on how to do that, but that is what we are doing."

"Understood, Lieutenant." Contreras must realize how this moment will sound during the debriefing. Assuming there ever will be a debriefing.

"We have two options," says Anderson. "Use our jetpacks or jump and hope the gravity is low enough for us to make it."

"I can do the jumping." Contreras's tone is softened, as though in apology. "I'll use my jetpack if I need it. Once I get to the other side, I'll plant my stake so you all can either jump or use the rope to pull yourselves over."

Stacy imagines that leap. It would feel like jumping across the Grand Canyon.

"Sounds like our best option," says Anderson. "If you don't make it across for some reason, we'll still be able to pull you back with the rope."

Contreras retrieves his stake and bounces several steps back, letting himself settle to the ground. He lowers the arms of his jetpack. Stacy grabs her line in case she needs to haul him to safety.

"You ready?" asks Anderson.

"Always." Contreras takes one leap, descending in a long, slow arc, plants his foot on the edge of the chasm, and jumps.

Stacy holds her breath. Contreras progresses in slow motion in a shallow upward arc, arms at his side and legs behind as though being fired from a cannon. The moments stretch, seconds ticking past with only minuscule movement. His rate of ascent begins to slow as he soars over the chasm.

He peaks less than halfway across. Uncorrected, he will drop below the surface and hit several meters below the top. From the way his fingers twitch, he must have realized he will land short, too.

The scenery begins to waver. Not just the ground beneath Stacy's feet or the cliff across the chasm, but the stars, Contreras's suit, even Stacy's hands and legs. Stacy kneels, reaching for her stake with one hand to steady herself, but it doesn't help. The stake rattles, the surface rattles, even her body rattles, as though an earthquake has struck. But she feels no vibration, nothing beyond queasiness.

Did Jalindo and the shuttle impact the surface?

No, she realizes. A grav-engine has been activated.

She worried about this possibility before the mission, but she only thought of it occurring during the shuttle flight. Jalindo will now be in their own predicament, handling the shuttle and facing the disorientation of the disruption of the local gravity field while Inorganics are chasing them. And here, Contreras has been thrown off.

Stacy turns to Anderson, stomach twisting with the disconnect between vision and motion. Anderson, grasping her own stake, gazes at Contreras.

He still descends. His hand reaches for the jetpack's thruster controls on his suit arm, but Stacy doesn't know how he'll line up in the correct direction with distorted vision.

Stacy knows the shaking is a phenomenon of the grav-engine, but she still braces herself as though standing on a rocking platform. She releases her stake and grabs the rope with both hands, ready to haul Contreras to safety if he doesn't reach the other side.

A puff fires from Contreras's jetpack. With the shaking, Stacy can't tell if he aimed himself in the right direction. He accelerates and holds his arms wide, as if to embrace the rock face.

Contreras slams into the cliffside, several meters below the top. Stacy winces. The impact will have scraped the suit, maybe torn a leak.

The wavering stops. Stacy wobbles, holding one arm straight out to the side to regain her balance.

Contreras's limbs go limp as he slides down the rock. Stacy squeezes the rope, though it will do no good. She silently urges him to pull himself up.

His backpack strap snags a protruding rock, the strap straining as it supports his weight. Contreras is motionless; the strap stretches. Stacy plants her boots and braces her arms to pull.

"I'll get him," says Anderson.

Stacy holds up the line connecting her to Contreras. "I'm directly connected to him. Should I go?"

Anderson pauses. "Okay. Be careful. Be fast. He might have a leak."

Now that it is Stacy's turn, the distance looks impossibly far. "What if they turn on the grav-engines again?"

"Contreras and I are both connected to you," says Anderson. "I'll keep you from falling."

Directly across from her, about two meters from the top and to the right of Contreras, a thin ledge juts from the rock. She can use it as a grip and place her feet on the tiny protrusions below it. Then, after climbing to the other side, she can pull up Contreras.

"Okay." Stacy releases her stake, clutches it to her chest with one arm, and takes several steps back as Contreras did. She takes a breath. She is really going to do this.

She takes one large step and floats toward the edge of the cliff. Her feet plant and her knees bend into a squat. With her eyes locked on the thin ledge thirty meters away, she pushes as hard as she can and launches herself.

Within seconds, the extent of her body is fully above the chasm. Her arms shake. She could never do this on Earth. It is like flying without a plane. It is like a dream.

Her course dips more than she intended. She won't hit the ledge. A small burst from the jetpack might put her on course, but she can find another handhold instead of wasting the fuel. The slow flight gives her time to look for one.

What will Trevor think when he watches this video in twenty-something minutes?

The wall comes closer. Details sharpen. Sharp rocks jut from the wall. Puncture hazards. And there hangs Contreras, dangling from his stretching strap.

As the distance closes to a handful of meters, she reaches out and grips a tiny pocket in the rock with two fingers, then pulls herself up to the ledge. As she ascends, she arches her back so the chest of her suit doesn't tear on the sharper rocks. Her boots tap against the wall, then skid downward. She tries again, seeking the protrusions she spotted earlier. Finding them, her boots come to a rest. She reaches up for the next handhold and climbs.

Once her hand reaches the lip of the cliff edge, she gives herself a hard pull. She flies upward, hovering above the surface at the peak of her parabola, then settles to the dust.

"Great!" Anderson waves from the other side. "How is Contreras?"

Contreras hangs meters below her, unmoving, bent double with his face downward. His strap is on the verge of snapping.

"I can't tell." Stacy grabs the cliff's lip and pulls herself to her stomach, gazing down into the chasm. So deep.

Contreras is out of reach, but she can drop down to the next ledge and pull him up. Stacy slides her feet over the edge and lets herself fall. A moment later, her boots hit the ledge.

Before she can grab Contreras's arm, his backpack strap shears away. The backpack swings to the other side, wrenching Contreras with it. His body slams into the cliff face.

Then his arms and legs scrabble, and his head jerks up. With his free hand, he reaches up and grabs a jutting rock. He hangs, still, against the wall.

"Contreras." Stacy holds her hand out to him.

Contreras grabs it and uses her anchoring position to climb to her ledge. "Thanks."

In another moment, they reach the top and set their stakes in place. Contreras raises a fist in triumph. "Perfect! Just like I planned!"

Stacy forces a laugh, then studies his suit. "Contreras, your faceplate."

His gloved hand taps at the glass where a small crack has formed. "Yeah. Noticed that. The gravity changed on me at the end there. Got really heavy, so I smashed into the cliff pretty hard."

"Systems check." Anderson is still waiting on the other side of the chasm.

Contreras pops out his chest mirror and glances down, fiddling with buttons on his chest panel. Then he checks the backpack and his belt and starts planting patches on the largest tears. "Strap's busted. Small crack in my faceplate. Minor tears in my suit, but I can patch them pretty quickly. Looks like I banged myself up worse than I thought."

"Okay," says Anderson. "I'm coming."

The lieutenant crosses without incident, contacting the rock face near Stacy's impact point. Stacy and Contreras each grab a hand and pull her to the top.

After regaining her footing, Anderson performs a walkaround of Contreras's suit. Stacy follows the lieutenant, documenting it for the public and the SDF. The jetpack lies on the ground beside Contreras. Patches cover a spot on his chest, one on the underside of his arm, and one on his leg. The hairline crack in the middle of his faceplate means the faceplate's structural integrity has been weakened.

"We ready?" asks Contreras.

Stacy already knows the answer Anderson will give. She braces herself.

"Your suit is too damaged," says the lieutenant. "You'll stay here while we continue."

Contreras sounds unsurprised at her order. "Lieutenant, I understand the risk. I can keep going."

"You'll slow us down."

"Don't let me. Go full speed. I'll keep up."

"You'll stay behind, Sergeant. That's an order."

"Damn it, Lieutenant!" Contreras looks as though he wants to stomp the ground. "These things killed my cousin! I *need* to do this. I know the risks, and I am prepared to take them, and you need me."

"Contreras," says Stacy.

"I don't need to hear it!" he says. "I have waited for this moment for years! I have fought for it! I don't care if I die. We need to show the Innies they can't push us around anymore! They can't get away with killing us!"

The words hang there for several moments. Stacy wishes she could give Contreras a hug and let him know he isn't alone.

"Sergeant." Anderson's voice sounds strained, tired. "We're not here to be heroes. We have a mission, and I am in charge of making certain we achieve it. You will remain behind. That's an order."

"And what? Wait for Jalindo to maybe pick me up *if* they survive? Instead of doing something useful and making sure my death isn't in vain?"

"Yes," says Anderson.

"Well, that's stupid!" says Contreras.

Anderson doesn't waver as she faces him. "Would you be questioning the general or Prabhakhar if they were here?"

"What?" says Contreras. "I…"

"Then don't question me. I'm the authority here."

"Contreras." Stacy gives him a sympathetic look before realizing he can't see it. "Your suit is damaged, so you'll slow us down, and dying won't bring your cousin back. The Inorganics aren't worth your death. They're just machines."

Stacy wants revenge on the Inorganics, too. But even if she somehow achieved that revenge, the Inorganics would kill her and continue with their programming. Maybe they are conscious and maybe they aren't, but they will never care about her petty act of revenge.

"Fuck." Contreras unties his line from Stacy's and Anderson's belts. "I fucking hate this. You really think you'll be able to do this all by yourself, Lieutenant?"

"No." Anderson glances down at her suit and wipes dust from her chest panel. She turns to Stacy. "I know you came as an observer, but can you help me?"

"Help…" Stacy freezes. "You mean help plant the explosives."

"Yes."

Journalists observe. They do not become part of the story. Because becoming the story means people ignore the real story, and if Stacy becomes part of the story, she will be capitalizing on her father's death.

But the only way she has achieved results out here is by becoming part of the story.

Stacy releases her breath. "Okay."

THIRTY-THREE

STACY ACCEPTS THE communications package from Contreras. He shoves the book-sized box into her hands.

"I can't believe I'm being replaced by her." Contreras turns to Anderson. "This is the most important mission in the history of our species, and you're trusting it to someone who betrayed us?"

"Given the circumstances," says Anderson, "Stacy is the best choice."

Stacy ignores the lukewarm praise. Since she already has an explosives package strapped to her backpack, she ties the comm package to her chest. It makes her top-heavy and threatens to pitch her onto her face, but the low gravity helps her remain upright.

Contreras unties his line from Anderson's. "You don't have to do this, Lieutenant. Stacy betrayed us. And that was after you and I saved her ass. What makes you think she won't do it again?"

Anderson turns away from him again. "The discussion is over, Sergeant." Stacy can hear the doubt in her voice.

"Fine," says Contreras. "But I know how you two feel about this mission. Especially you, Lieutenant. If it were your choice, you'd let the Innies do whatever they want. We have this one shot now. I don't care what you believe, but you'd better not blow it."

"Thank you for your thoughts, Sergeant." Anderson leans down to grab her stake.

Stacy takes hold of her own stake and prepares to pull it from the ground. She checks her implant, which calculates the distance from the Inorganic that acts like Jason. Two hundred and twenty meters away, past the hill at the edge of Stacy's vision, if it stayed at its last known coordinates. The longer they wait, the less likely it is to be in the same location.

It should take them less than an hour to reach their target. Despite Stacy's initial misgivings, she finds herself hoping they will succeed and that their work will become a testament to the ingenuity of humans.

Contreras sets both his hands atop his stake and speaks in a low, reluctant voice. "Good luck."

"Call Jalindo," says Anderson. "Hopefully we'll see you back on the shuttle."

"Yeah." Contreras sounds unconvinced.

"Be safe," says Stacy. "We'll see you soon."

Maybe Contreras has the hardest job of the three of them. Waiting here, unable to do anything other than hope. It will be agonizing. Stacy hopes they don't let him down.

Anderson salutes, then retracts her stake and kicks off toward the hill. Once Anderson plants her stake at the end of her line, Stacy uproots her own stake, waves to Contreras, and pushes off toward the lieutenant.

When Stacy reaches Anderson, the lieutenant stares into the distance.

"It's kind of ironic," says Anderson.

Stacy turns to her. "What is?"

"It's the most important mission humanity has ever gone on, and the two people carrying it out both think it's the wrong course of action."

"Yeah," says Stacy. "That is ironic."

"But that's the military. Ready?"

"Ready."

As they get closer to the hill, the scene seems to shift. A small shift in shade or color. The stars remain constant, but the patches of gray move, forming new patterns every few seconds. It doesn't waver like a grav-engine test. This movement is something different.

The sands shift. "Do you see that?" Stacy asks.

"I see it."

Stacy zooms in with her oculars. The dust itself isn't moving, some of it in the same place it has been for thousands or millions of years. But dozens of tiny machines, no larger than fingers, skitter across the surface. They seem to be heading to the hill.

"Inorganics," says Stacy.

"Really?" asks Anderson. "I knew there were small ones. I just didn't know they were here, on Juno. I guess our sensors were always too far away to detect them."

The tiny Inorganics' presence here makes little sense. They can't carry as much raw material as the larger digger units can. Perhaps they perform intricate modifications to the starship's hull, but Stacy cannot think of a single reason for them to be *here*, so far from the starship.

"Should we follow them?" Stacy asks.

"We have a limited amount of time," says Anderson.

"But they're going the same direction we are."

Anderson glances up at the hill. "We can follow them as long as we're going the same way."

The Inorganics' destination soon becomes obvious. In the side of the hill is a small tunnel, an arched hole. The insect-like machines skitter inside.

The tunnel is dark, and Stacy can't see more than two meters past the entrance. The entrance is much larger than the small Inorganics, maybe even large enough for a human to enter, but it might not remain that size.

"I…" Anderson sighs. "We really shouldn't go in. We don't know what's in there, and it's not our mission."

Stacy smiles. She knows what the lieutenant will say next.

"But we should at least look," says Anderson. "It might be a shortcut."

"Yeah," says Stacy. "And we don't know if we'll ever come

back here again, so it would be nice to do a quick check, if nothing else."

By the time Stacy and Anderson reach the tunnel, the Inorganics have disappeared inside. The entrance only reaches Stacy's shoulders, but she can fit inside if she crouches. Its edges are smooth, which means it must have been drilled or carved by the Inorganics.

"What do you think is in there?" asks Stacy.

"It could be anything. A shortcut. A storage area. A place to process material at a safe distance from the starship."

Anderson activates her headlamp, which illuminates the first couple meters of the tunnel. Nothing but smooth rock walls and darkness beyond them.

Now that Stacy has reached the tunnel, she isn't sure she still wants to explore it.

Anderson crouches, retracts her stake, and enters. Stacy has no choice, then, not with the buddy system. She activates her own headlamp.

Once she has taken two steps, a warning pings in her head. "I lost signal."

"I know," says Anderson. "We'll turn back if we see anything dangerous."

Stacy wants to say the entire situation is dangerous, but she refrains and takes tentative steps forward. Her recorded data will be stored and then transmitted when she has a signal again. *If* she gets a signal again. If not, if she and Anderson never emerge from this cave, no one back home will ever know their fate.

There is no sound on this airless asteroid, and Stacy's suit quarantines her from the outside world, so she can't rely on touch or hearing to gain clues about what lies ahead. Even running her gloves along the wall tells her little except that she has contact with a solid surface.

She crawls forward, the top of her backpack occasionally scraping against the ceiling.

The tunnel twists once, twice. The walls remain featureless.

"Oh!" Anderson halts.

Stacy locks her hands onto the ground so she doesn't collide with the lieutenant. "What is it?"

"Look." Anderson moves to the side, allowing Stacy a view past her.

A small opening is ahead of them. Thousands of tiny Inorganics are packed into a space the size of a large chair, as though in a seance or orgy. Around them are blocks of metal connected with wires. The Inorganic units clamber over the blocks.

"What are they doing?" asks Stacy.

"No idea. I've never seen this before. No one has."

For several minutes, Stacy and Anderson watch the machines perform their arcane tasks. A trail of Inorganics comes from behind Stacy, crawling along the wall in single file. She reaches out and strokes the back of one.

Instantly, that Inorganic freezes, as do all the others in the line and those clambering on the blocks. Stacy takes a step back.

She prepares to turn and bolt, but the tight corridor would prevent her from turning quickly. The Inorganics would overwhelm Anderson and her before she even faces the right direction.

Then the Inorganics resume their previous activities. Stacy releases her breath. She shouldn't have interfered with them. She could have gotten them both killed and ruined the mission. Anderson kindly says nothing.

The view ahead begins to waver. Another grav-engine test has begun. She braces herself against the walls

As the walls, floor, and ceiling waver, the Inorganics levitate off the ground, spreading out into intricate swirling patterns. They form strings, which break apart and reform with other strings, over and over. After the fourth or fifth iteration, Stacy realizes the patterns match the oscillations in the scenery. These tiny Inorganics must be following the local gravity field.

The Inorganics don't make art, but it feels like art. Like a ballet or like wind chimes. Despite themselves, the Inorganics have made something beautiful.

The wavering stops, and the Inorganics drift to the ground. They depart from the metal blocks and swarm farther down the tunnel.

"I don't even know what that was, but it was beautiful," says Anderson.

"And we're going to destroy it." Stacy gazes down the tunnel in the direction the Inorganics went. "It seems wrong."

"I know. But those are our orders."

"Why would you follow orders that are wrong?" Stacy wishes she could see Anderson's face.

"Wrong orders are better than chaos."

"Do you really think that's true? Or is it just what the SDF told you?"

"It doesn't matter." Anderson steps toward the spot the Inorganics vacated. "It seemed like it had something to do with the gravity test."

Stacy crawls forward and peers at one of the abandoned blocks. The shell betrays nothing of what is inside, although it must contain some electronics because of the protruding wires.

She picks one up. It feels heavy, dense. "Should we take one with us?"

"It's not part of our mission." Anderson creeps to another block and picks it up. "And it's heavy. It could slow us down or throw off our balance."

"We're already off-mission."

"Yeah." Anderson's shoulders slump. "That's true. We'll take one, but if it impedes us in any way, we leave it."

Stacy turns so Anderson can place the block in Stacy's backpack. Will the Inorganics notice the blocks have moved?

After Anderson secures the block in one of the pockets in Stacy's pack, the lieutenant resumes the lead, crawling around the blocks before continuing down the tunnel. Stacy follows.

At each bend, she expects to see the tiny Inorganics again, but there's no trace of them. When Stacy and Anderson round the fourth bend, though, Anderson stops and gasps.

"What is it?" Stacy tries to peer over the lieutenant's shoulder, but can see nothing but the rock wall.

"Antennas." Anderson moves to the side, letting Stacy enter another small chamber.

Three antennas, small and with wires twisted throughout their structure, sit spaced equidistantly along the chamber's perimeter and all point in the same direction. They change their orientations in minute steps, but they always match targets.

"What are they pointing at?" asks Stacy.

"I'm not sure. Maybe one of the Inorganic units?"

Stacy has a hunch. She has her implant do quick calculations.

"They're pointing at Proxima Centauri."

"What?" asks Anderson. "Those antennas are?"

"Yes. That's why they keep moving. This asteroid is going in its orbit, and it's rotating, too. The antennas are compensating for the motion."

"Okay," says Anderson. "Why?"

"I don't know."

What do these antennas see in the Proxima system? Do they detect something new, something that can be detected even through the solid rock of this hill?

"We should go." Anderson's voice sounds dim. "This is…We could spend years studying this and maybe never understand it. But it's not our job. We have a mission."

And they can never return. The Inorganics will be more watchful in the future and will prevent future incursions. But maybe it's better this way. A mystery, an answer she will never learn, but which she will think about for the rest of her life.

"You're right," says Stacy.

Anderson leads the way. After a few more twists and turns, the cave walls begin to lighten. Before long, they can see the light from outside.

"Was this a shortcut?" Stacy asks.

"I don't know," says Anderson. "But we didn't have to climb over the hill, so I count it as a plus."

Anderson stops at the cave exit, stepping to the side. Stacy stops next to her and peers out.

They have arrived. There, in the craggy plain outside the tunnel, the target Inorganic drills into the ground below it, sending tiny rocks on shallow outward arcs. The same repetitive motions Stacy watched Jason perform so often on the computer screen in the Machining Room.

It looks sinister.

The Inorganic stands at the edge of a basin where a large swath of ground has already been dug. On the upraised portion, where the unit hasn't yet dug, a short wall encircles a deep crater. Darkness obscures all but the top few meters of the crater's sides.

Lighter-colored dust extends in an arc past the Inorganic's working area beyond the range of the digging tools. A shadow covers a large portion of the area. Stacy follows the shadow to its source.

There, beside the crater, rests the pod from Collins Station.

The exact pod Jason used to escape. No lights, no signs of activity. Motionless, but malevolent. Stacy remembers its door shutting as she tried to escape. How Jason trapped her inside, unconcerned that she and Young would die, just as the Martian Inorganic had been unconcerned about killing Stacy's father.

Jason is in that pod, and Stacy has no idea what it means to do here.

"Do you see it?" asks Stacy.

"I see it."

The target Inorganic continues working nearby, as though oblivious to the presence of the vehicle. Scoop after scoop of rock is deposited into the unit's storage cavity.

"Wasn't expecting that," says Anderson in a low voice. "Our plan is way off-nominal now."

"Why do you think it's here? On Juno? On this specific spot?"

"I have lots of guesses," says Anderson. "I don't have any answers. Maybe it was curious? Or maybe just out of fuel. Or maybe it recognized the unit's motions."

"Do you think it's talking to the Inorganics?"

"I don't know. Probably. There's probably a reason they haven't attacked it."

Jason adds an unexpected complication. How will it react when she and Anderson set down their explosives? How will it react when she sends the commands to the target Inorganic? "What do we do now?"

"Continue with the original plan." Anderson points to a spot to their left along the hill wall, behind a knee-height rock, closer to the unit and the pod than Stacy would like. "We'll put the explosives there, come back here, and send the signal."

The moment Stacy steps from the tunnel, a ping sounds in her head. She jumps, swiveling her body toward the Inorganic, worried it triggered an alarm.

Then she remembers: Her implant is telling her she regained signal. The stored video of her time in the tunnel will be transmitted, along with the real-time video. In a few seconds or minutes, the data from the grav-engine test will be stored aboard Collins and forwarded on its way to Earth.

Anderson bounces forward in front of Stacy, keeping close to the hill's wall. Stacy follows, glancing to her right every few steps to see if the Inorganic or Jason have noticed them.

She and Anderson are being so blatant with their movement, not bothering to hide. If the Inorganic even glances in their direction, it will detect them. Maybe it has already detected their presence and doesn't care. Humans aren't threats.

Maybe, after today, that assessment will change.

Anderson waits at the rock. Stacy stops beside her. The rock will hide the explosives packages in case other Inorganics somehow happen across them before their target does.

Stacy detaches the two explosives packages strapped to Anderson's backpack and sets them in the dust. She then turns so Anderson can remove Stacy's explosives package and the comm box.

While Anderson works, Stacy watches their opponents. The target Inorganic continues digging. The pod sits still and silent beside the crater.

"Do we need to do anything else?" Stacy asks.

"Just activate the explosives." Anderson kneels, twisting a knob on each explosives package. "Then we'll head back."

Anderson rises, then jumps past Stacy. Stacy waits until Anderson plants her stake inside the tunnel, then bounds to join her. Her signal disappears again once she steps inside.

Anderson pulls out the comm box and extends the antenna. "I really wish we didn't have to do this. I would love to see it launch. I want them to make it to the stars. I feel like we're the villains here."

"Well." At home, on Earth, people will see this scene in a few minutes. "I guess it's time."

Anderson aims the antenna at the target unit and pushes the button on the box. A light switches from blank to green. Stacy looks to the Inorganic unit, which should have received the signal. Will it leap to obey the order or attack Stacy and Anderson for trying to give it a command?

Moments pass, and nothing happens. Jason sits there, and the Inorganic continues digging.

"Is the box broken?" asks Stacy.

Anderson examines the digital display on the side. "Everything looks normal. It sent the signal. It just…didn't work. I'll try again."

The Inorganic continues digging.

"Maybe…" says Anderson. "Maybe it has some kind of anti-virus protection? Or something to protect against unde-sired bit flips, so their programming isn't corrupted? It would make sense for them to develop something like that."

"What now?" asks Stacy.

"Now…the backup plan is to retrieve the explosives and try to deliver them ourselves."

"Oh. Yeah." They will never make it. The Inorganics won't let them through. It is the worst sort of suicide mission, the one done only so people can feel better about having tried to do *something*.

Anderson turns to Stacy. "There *is* a chance. There's always a chance."

Anderson returns to the explosives, and Stacy follows. When she reaches Anderson, the lieutenant gestures for her to turn around so Anderson can attach the packages to her backpack. As Stacy complies, she notices movement nearby.

A troop of Inorganics, at least five of them. Diggers, transporters, and a processor. Whether these units were sent to intercept Stacy and Anderson because their activities have been noticed or because they stole the block, or if the Inorganics just stumbled across the humans, the mission is over.

"They've seen us," says Stacy.

"Really? The target? Jason? They're paying attention to us now?"

"Not *them*. New Inorganics are coming."

Anderson pauses. "Oh."

"We should have a few minutes."

"Right." Anderson tightens a last strap. "My turn."

Stacy turns and ties the remaining two packages to Anderson's backpack. "What now?"

"Head back to the tunnel and try to make it before they get here. Maybe we'll be safe in there. Maybe not. We should…" Anderson unclips herself from Stacy. "In case we need to use our jetpacks. Or…if something else happens."

It is all too easy to visualize one of them being caught, and the other being swung around by the line connecting them, anchored and unable to escape.

Anderson gives a bitter laugh. "I always wanted to be in charge of an important mission. Be careful what you wish for." She takes a light step, only rising a centimeter before coming down several meters away.

Stacy drops to her knees and pulls herself along the surface by grabbing hold of rocks and crevices. Like horizontal mountain climbing. She can't risk drifting from the surface now that she has lost her anchor.

"I'm sorry," says Anderson as they continue toward the tunnel.

"I thought *I* was the one who always apologized. What do you mean?"

The Inorganic troop will arrive in just over a minute. Stacy wants to run, but knows she would float from the surface if she tried.

"This mission's a failure, and I'm the one in charge. I should have done something differently. But we left Contreras, and our plan didn't work, and we're about to be… killed."

"What?" Stacy shakes her head. "We did everything we were supposed to do. We reached the target. We put the explosives nearby. We sent the command. It just didn't work. But that has nothing to do with your leadership skills. You got us here. Whatever else happens, happens."

"I guess…Space travel seemed so glamorous. Now it seems like it's mostly just grit."

Stacy concentrates on keeping her steps light, just the slightest of taps against the surface, so she doesn't propel herself helplessly above the ground. She chances a look behind her.

The Inorganics cover ground at a surprising speed, leaving a plume of dust behind them. Their legs move in blurs.

Moments later, it's clear their vectors won't take them directly to Stacy and Anderson. So what brought them?

"Oh."

"What is it?" asks Anderson.

"They're not here for us. They're here for Jason."

Anderson says nothing for a moment as her arc returns her to the ground, probably analyzing the Inorganics' movement as Stacy did. "I think you're right."

Stacy grabs a pair of rocks to halt her motion. Ahead, Anderson does the same.

The new Inorganic arrivals surround the pod, staying at least three meters away on all sides. For several minutes, they do nothing visible. Maybe they are communicating between themselves or with Jason.

Then the two diggers approach and tap the hull. In response, the hatch opens. One of the diggers enters.

"They're communicating," says Stacy. "What do you think they're talking about?"

"I don't know," says Anderson. "Let's keep moving and get to the tunnel while they're distracted."

The two of them start toward the tunnel.

From Stacy's peripheral vision, antennas swivel in her direction. The Inorganics have noticed them.

Inorganics don't attack unless provoked. Everyone says that phrase as though it is a protective mantra. But Collins Station has provoked them several times now, and Stacy and Anderson are deep within the Inorganics' borders, and Stacy stole one of those strange blocks.

The closest unit, the processor, approaches. It looks like a metallic crab, walking on six spindly legs that never seem to leave the ground. Two gripping claws extend from its main body. A gaping maw, used to smelt ore into a moldable form and large enough to swallow a full-grown human, constitutes its entire front side.

Stacy keeps still, hoping lack of motion will convince the Inorganic she isn't a threat. Anderson steps next to her. They say nothing. It feels like waiting in the woods for a bear to continue on its way.

The Inorganic comes within arm's reach of them, mouth open wide enough to scoop them inside. It is only a few centimeters taller than Stacy, but massive. Each of its arms probably weighs as much as she does. Its antennas focus on her.

One of its claws moves forward.

"No!" Anderson's yell sends throbbing pain through Stacy's ears. The lieutenant throws herself forward, wrapping her arms around the claw. With an effortless motion, the claw flings her to the side.

On Earth, Anderson would have flown until she slammed into the dirt. Here, she clutches her stomach as she soars through a slow arc taking her into the crater.

Stacy jumps to the side, as though juking around a defender in soccer, and bounds toward the crater. When she comes close enough, she leaps into the air and plucks Anderson from her arc. They lands at the crater's edge, Anderson in Stacy's arms.

"Thanks." Anderson lets herself drop to the ground.

"It's only fair," says Stacy. "You saved me first."

"Behind you!"

Before Stacy can turn, something slams into the back of her helmet, and she feels herself falling backward.

She doesn't stop falling.

THIRTY-FOUR

IN JUNO'S LIGHT gravity, Stacy falls for a long time. Above, she can see a narrow ring of sky. The Inorganic must have knocked her into the crater. As she falls deeper, the crater's narrow ring grows even narrower. Her arm hits the side wall, a soft pressure she barely feels through her suit but that sends her into a slow spin.

Wall, then darkness, then sky, then wall again, over and over. After several turns, the light from above disappears. Has Juno already entered night? She thought they had hours of sunlight left.

It feels like forever before she hits the ground, backpack-first. The impact presses her back upward, curving her spine. She bounces, turning in mid-air and landing on her chest. Her faceplate impacts something hard.

She reaches for the faceplate, feeling for a hole. With her gloves, she can't tell if the faceplate has hairline fractures or if it has no visible damage, but she didn't hear a pop signaling depressurization. Her suit retains its integrity.

Her arm feels bruised and tender. It doesn't feel broken, at least. And her head throbs, a dull pain making it harder to focus.

Pulling herself to her knees, she activates her headlamp. The beam illuminates curving rock walls, worn smooth and extending higher above her than her lamp can reach, surrounding her on all sides. Above, a distant number of meters away, is the starry sky. It is faint and circumscribed by darkness on all sides.

Stacy wonders what the Inorganic would have done to her had she not fallen.

She remembers Anderson. "Lieutenant."

No response.

Stacy scrambles to her feet, bounding upward in the low gravity and settling down at an uncomfortably slow pace. She turns, one step at a time, until she completes a full circle, but sees no figures in the illuminated area.

"Lieutenant?"

The lieutenant must still be on the surface. Did the Inorganics dismember her? Carry her off? Or is she lying on the ground, unconscious? Or dead?

Stacy checks the chronometer on her chest. It shows her EVA has lasted six hours and thirty-four minutes so far. Almost three hours of air left in the suit, then. If Anderson is still alive, they have that much time to return to the station.

Stacy steps toward one of the walls. As the floor curves upward, the sand slips beneath her foot. She leans forward to retain her balance.

Three more tentative steps, and she reaches the edge of the crater. Her light illuminates a sheer cliff wall. She places a hand against it. Unnaturally smooth, without purchase. She won't be able to climb it.

She jumps, reaching almost two meters, and kicks off from the wall. The kick propels her upward, and she reaches. Her fingers slide down the wall, scraping, clawing, as she floats to the ground. Her boots settle into the dust.

Stacy stares up. She still can't tell how far away the top is, but it doesn't matter. She can't climb the wall.

Maybe the jetpack will work, or at least take her higher to search for handholds farther up.

She pulls down the jetpack's arms from their upright position and activates the pack. On the station, when she activated the pack in training, it vibrated as it warmed up, and a ready light turned green. Now, there is no vibration and no light. She pushes the button again with the same result.

She swings the jetpack from her back. A crack runs along the side. Inside the exposed area, she sees two frayed wires.

She sinks to the ground, sitting, feet out. It is over.

It feels like her time in confinement aboard Collins, but worse. At least it is probably better than the fate she could expect if she were extradited to Uruguay.

No one will know what happened to her. If she can't transmit to Anderson, her transmissions aren't making it to Earth, either. The last thing her viewers experienced was her being hit and falling backward into the crater. They probably think she is dead.

Trevor must think she is dead. In three hours, he will be right.

A tear comes to her eye. She will never see him again, not even to tell him goodbye.

Years or centuries from now, when the Inorganics abandon this asteroid, maybe other people will find her corpse here and would wonder what happened. Maybe they'll even be able to identify her body. Or maybe the Inorganics will collect her and incorporate her suit into the starship somehow. She doesn't know what they will do with her body. What do Inorganics do with organic material?

At the top of the crater, a figure peeks over the edge. Stacy stands. "Anderson?"

A pair of antennas appear, and a pair of gripping claws. Sunlight glints off the metal. An Inorganic. It came to watch, to study how she dies. Always so patient and uncaring, with no more emotion than an ant tearing apart a leaf. Stacy is just another data point to it. She turns her back to it.

What are the other Inorganics doing up there? Harvesting Anderson's equipment? Carrying Anderson away?

And what is Jason doing? Did it leave, or is it talking to the Inorganics? Will it be incorporated, too, its identity subsumed by its spiritual descendants?

She remembers Jason on the screen at Collins, performing its programmed motions. The motions that led to this failed mission.

She straightens. In the initial planning stages for this mission, they considered sending the commands to Jason and only abandoned the idea because they couldn't guarantee the team would be in line of sight of the pod. But it is here, just beyond the crater wall above her. If Jason shares some of the same source code as the target Inorganic, it will be susceptible to the same commands as the target.

The signal didn't work with the target Inorganic, but Jason isn't a real Inorganic. It might not have the same safeguards as the real ones. If she can send the signal to it, it may attempt to retrieve the explosives. She has the explosives with her, so it might take her with the package.

But she isn't in line of sight with Jason. Once again, she can do nothing.

She has a mirror on her suit, though. She unfolds it from her chest panel. If she banks the signal off the mirror, she could possibly aim it at Jason, assuming it hasn't moved. She doesn't know which side of the crater it is on relative to her, but…Jalindo mentioned how lidar uses a rotating mirror to change the direction of the laser beam. Stacy could use her own mirror in the same way to send the signal in all directions.

Her fingers tremble, but her excitement makes her work quickly, and she needs all the speed she can get.

After placing the comm box in the dirt, she activates it and changes the settings so it transmits continuously. Then she twists the mirror free from her suit. She places the mirror in front of the comm box, rotating the mirror to bank the signal over the crater's edge. Once around, then twice, then again and again for several minutes.

Dust blows over the crater's edge and falls in a slow rain. Juno has no wind, which means something must have pushed the dust. Thrusters?

Before the raining particles pelt her suit, the pod appears above. It blots out most of the visible sky. The pod descends, passing down the walls in slow motion, like a leaf wafting its way to the ground.

Stacy backs away to the farthest edge of the crater. The pod comes lower, now just above the level of her head, and she can see through its windows. Lights blink on and off on the screens and panels, flashing along the crater walls.

Then it settles onto the crater floor, firing a brief burst from its thrusters to cushion its landing. Stacy shields her faceplate from the displaced dust. When the dust no longer patters against her helmet, she turns to face the pod.

The pod's hatch opens.

Last time she was this close to Jason, it almost killed her. She has no choice, though. With the lightest tap of her boot against the ground, she bounds forward and enters the pod.

It looks the same as when she and Young were trapped aboard. The consoles have gone dark, but the seats are in the same positions. Nothing has been damaged.

The hatch closes behind her, locking her in. If necessary, she can escape the same way she did before, by jumping out the hatch. She has her suit this time, and over two hours of air.

Thrusters fire. The acceleration feels unnatural. Stacy grabs the back of the nearest chair as the pod rises. In the front window, the crater walls drop away to reveal the surface as she leaves behind her tomb. A dusty field of rocks and craters stretches before her. Her implant pings to let her know her backlog of video is being transmitted.

She pulls herself past the three rows of chairs and stands at the window, hands against the wall to brace herself. The window gives a limited view of outside and shows nothing of the Inorganics. It shows nothing of Anderson. Maybe she is behind them, on the other side of the crater, watching the pod fly.

The pod starts forward, a few meters above the ground, coasting in the direction Stacy and Anderson were headed. Toward the starship.

Stacy is going to see it up close. Maybe even touch it. Jason has been commanded to drop off the explosives near the engines. Since it is like the Inorganics, at least a proto version of them, they might consider it one of them. It will be like a

Trojan horse. Or the Inorganics might realize exactly what the pod is and destroy it.

Her suit radio crackles. "Stacy? Is that you?"

"Anderson?" Stacy can still see no figures below out the window.

"It's me!" Anderson sounds stressed, but not in pain. She is okay. Stacy smiles.

"Where are you?"

"In the tunnel. I thought I saw you get knocked into the crater, but they knocked me out. I woke up a few meters away. I was trying to figure out how to pull you out without the Inorganics seeing me, and then I saw the pod go down there."

"I got Jason to pick me up," says Stacy.

"Oh! You sent it the command! That's brilliant! You can complete the mission!"

"I can."

"Ms. Sterling." General Young's voice sounds scratchy and distant. "I'm impressed at your resourcefulness. We're all counting on you. Not just those of us at Collins, but the entire human race."

Stacy starts. During the pre-briefing, General Young explained she would not interfere with how the mission was conducted and would trust them to carry it out to the best of their abilities. When Prabhakhar was taken, when Contreras was left behind, when Jason and the target were spotted, Young said nothing. What does it mean that she speaks now?

Stacy's breath catches. The starship peeks above the horizon. The roofs of the engines appear first. The rest comes in a slow reveal. High, square walls like a fort. Its collection of cylinders within those walls looks like distant towers. Scaffolding holds it up to the sky. It is, in its own way, beautiful.

So close. Walking distance. Humans will never get so close to it again.

It is like a magical object. This set of metal and wires was going to travel to another star system.

Except it won't, not if Stacy completes her task. She will be destroying this first ambassador from the Solar System, this marvel of technology and engineering. And for what? To allow humans to be complacent for a few more years before the Inorganics try again?

As the pod flies over Juno's dusty surface, it strikes her that back home, millions of people could be watching. They can see the seats of the pod, the washed-out landscape below, the curving horizon ahead, and the starship.

What do they think of this moment? Is she a potential savior, a way to give humans an opportunity to become competitive again? Or just today's entertainment?

If she manages to destroy the starship, if the Inorganics don't stop her or defuse the explosives, it will be a sensation. A big show. But then the real problem will continue: human complacency.

Stacy blinks to access her implant menu. Her fingers tremble as she navigates through subsections to reach the recording settings. Once there, for the first time in her career, she removes the emotion block.

Now, viewers are getting her unadulterated emotions: fear, anger, guilt, even pride. And this is the way it has to be, the way it has always needed to be to show people what the Inorganics are like. General Young was right the entire time. Stacy doesn't know why it took her so long to see it.

"Okay," she says. "I am the story."

She lets herself feel everything. Her hatred of the Inorganics for killing her father. She feels for Contreras, whose cousin's death shaped his life, and whose goal of revenge was denied him.

She thinks of Anderson's admiration for the Inorganics.

And she thinks of how, when her news stories began to achieve success, Instant USA tried to steal them. And how Lopez and the others released lies about her, trying to pull her down. And how they wanted to imprison her, silence her voice.

The starship comes closer. The most important creation of the millennium, or maybe history. So understated in its construction, nestled in a landscape even more drab and desolate than that of Mars.

She wishes she could stay, that she could walk among the trusses and engines of the starship. For a moment, she wishes, like Anderson, that she could accompany it on its journey.

And she feels guilt. So much guilt.

Stacy grabs the pod's door handle, yanks it downward, and leaps out the door.

The surface approaches. Despite knowing the low gravity will prevent her from slamming into the ground, some part of her primitive hindbrain screams that she will break every bone in her body and that this was a stupid decision.

When she hits the ground, she rolls to dissipate the impact. After several bounces with long, slow arcs, she comes to a stop and stands.

Ahead, the pod slows. It turns in a slow curve and then aims toward her, like a drone on a strafing run. Jason is coming back for her.

Stacy pulls off the backpack with explosives. No one told her how to deactivate them.

The radio crackles. "How close are you?" asks Anderson.

"I jumped out." Stacy opens the backpack. "How do you deactivate the explosives?"

"Wait, what? You jumped out?"

"Ms. Sterling." Young's voice sounds disappointed, but there's a hint of something else. Approval? "You may have cost the human race its future."

"I don't think so. Destroying the starship wouldn't have changed our future. We're not going to get anywhere by holding others back. We just need to start doing things ourselves. So how do you deactivate these?"

"Stacy…" Anderson sounds regretful. "I'm not going to tell you. We have our orders. Please deliver the explosives."

The pod slows as it nears. Maybe Jason won't try to kill her, or at least not yet. As it descends, it turns so the front points away from her. Once it settles to the ground, its thrusters kicking dust into plumes above the surface, its back hatch opens as it did in the crater. Maybe it is her imagination, but Jason seems more insistent than last time.

Stacy isn't stupid enough to try deactivating the explosives on her own. She pulls them from the backpack, takes four bounds toward Jason, and tosses the empty pack into the pod.

Jason doesn't move. The pack must not have been enough. Can Jason differentiate between the bag and the explosives? Will it attack her to take them from her?

The hatch closes.

Stacy releases her breath as the thrusters fire. The pod lifts from the surface, and Jason departs without her. It continues on its previous trajectory as though nothing has happened.

So that is it. The starship will survive. Stacy wonders if she will.

She braces herself. "Lieutenant?"

Anderson's voice is eager, desperate. "I'm here. What is your status?"

"Jason left. I still have the explosives."

"Okay." Anderson is silent for several moments. "What's your position?"

Stacy sighs. "I can't tell you that until you tell me how to deactivate the explosives."

"You'll die if we don't pick you up."

"If I give you my coordinates, you'll take the explosives and try again."

The starship's engines rise above the horizon like a distant city. The pod has almost reached its target. It descends. If nothing else comes from this entire mission, at least Stacy has given the public this view.

"Lieutenant." The general's voice crackles over the radio again. "If you give Ms. Sterling those instructions, you will be facing a court-martial. We have our orders."

Stacy opens her mouth to tell Anderson not to give her the instructions. But she stops. Anderson has her own choice to make.

"It's wrong." Anderson's voice sounds weary, as though the Universe has crushed her beneath it. "So many things on this mission have been wrong."

Stacy can imagine what the lieutenant is thinking. The sabotage of the IMS, hiding the Ratti Report, ignoring the danger of Jason, and now attempting to destroy someone else's achievement.

"Sorry, General," says Lieutenant Anderson. "I'm allowed to disobey orders that are unethical. And it is unethical to let Ms. Sterling die for no reason."

Anderson guides Stacy through the process of disarming the explosives. Stacy places the packages on the ground and follows the instructions with the precision of someone who realizes any slight mistake would result in her instantaneous death. When the lieutenant finishes, Stacy fulfills her own part of the bargain and reads her coordinates from her chest monitor.

"We're on the way," says Anderson.

Stacy's breath catches. "'We?'"

"Jalindo picked me up. We've got Contreras and even Major Prabhakhar with us. We're coming toward you now."

"You got Contreras and Prabhakhar! That's great!"

"Ms. Sterling."

Stacy's smile disappears. "General."

On the horizon, figures appear. Inorganics coming toward her. Maybe they know she attempted to destroy their ship, or they detected her just now. Their motivation doesn't matter.

"We will never have this opportunity again," says the general. "You have wasted all our efforts."

"No." Stacy watches the figures coming closer. "We made a deliberate decision about what we won't do. Now we need to make decisions about what we will do."

For the first time, Stacy has a clear idea of what she will do if she returns to Earth.

In the sky, a bright dot grows larger. Jalindo. It looks like the shuttle is going to make it to Stacy before the Inorganics do.

THIRTY-FIVE

SENSORS DETECTED A change in motion on the asteroid, alerting the station to the likelihood of the starship's imminent launch. Everyone on the Collins crew, on-duty or not, has gathered in the zenith observation cupola, fifteen people crowded into a space meant for five.

Young floats by herself at the back of the room, feet hooked into holds and arms folded across her chest. Always alone.

Stacy records it all without her nanocams and with her emotions unblocked. When the moment comes, she will approach the window for a closer view. For now, though, she wants to capture the atmosphere of this moment and what it means for the crew, and she wants the public to experience the moment from her point of view.

When Stacy returned from Juno, she expected General Young to confine her to quarters again for refusing to destroy the starship. Apparently, though, Inorganics dismantled Jason and the pod after their arrival at the starship. If Stacy had continued with the mission, she would have been killed. Young must have felt it wasn't necessary to punish Stacy for refusing to complete a mission doomed to failure. Besides, Stacy suspects the general agreed with her decision. It probably helped that Stacy brought back the block from the tunnel that was used in the grav-engine test, which might offer insights on physics to scientists and engineers on Earth.

Stacy wishes she could have saved Jason somehow. Jason had almost killed her during its escape, but without it, Stacy would have waited at the bottom of that crater until her air ran out. And after it had rescued her, the Inorganics destroyed it.

Or, they dismantled it, so maybe they kept its software and data, which includes the records from Collins. Maybe those records will accompany the Inorganics on their trip to the Proxima system.

"Stacy!" Anderson glides toward her from above.

Stacy smiles. "Lieutenant. You seem to be enjoying the occasion."

Anderson grabs the railing beside Stacy and swings herself to a stop with an ease Stacy will never have the time to achieve. "Well, yeah. It's exciting!"

"It is. And I heard there isn't going to be a court-martial."

"Oh, yeah." Anderson's grin gets bigger. "They decided I disobeyed an unethical order, which isn't a court-martial defense. General Young also said it was unlikely we could have readied the explosives in time to deliver them to the starship, and that my main failure was inadequately explaining my reasoning in the moment."

"Is that true?" asks Stacy. "Would we not have had time to deliver the explosives?"

"I don't know," says Anderson. "But the general advised me not to spend too much time thinking about it."

Stacy glances at the general, who is still floating alone. Young must notice the gaze, because she turns to Stacy and gives her a faint smile.

Stacy waves to indicate the station. "Do you think you'll come back here? Now that it's going to be kept open?"

"I hope so. I'm still serving the second half of my deployment out here. But I hope to rotate back again in a few years. Maybe I'll even be the one in charge someday."

"I think you will."

"Do you think the Inorganics will stay here after the starship launches?"

"That's a good question," Stacy says. "They might build another starship. It seems likely. Do you think we'll ever build one?"

Anderson frowns. "I'd like to think so. We don't have the technology now. Or the ambition. But maybe we will someday."

"I hope so. You and I brought back that block."

Anderson smiles. "We did. I can't wait to find out what's in it."

They stare out the window in silence. The Inorganics are likely completing last-minute preparations. Maybe checking electrical systems, engines, structural integrity. No one knows for certain what procedures the Inorganics follow, but Stacy has heard a lot of guesses over the last few days.

From whispered conversations in the background, Stacy can hear that Collins's sensors have detected a build-up in gravitational fluctuations in the vicinity of the starship. She glances toward the window.

Anderson points to indicate Halabi and Ko. "I'm going to get back. It was good talking."

"Lieutenant?"

Anderson pauses before kicking off from the wall. "Yeah?"

"It was good serving with you down there. You're a good leader."

Anderson beams. "Thank you! You went above and beyond." She punches Stacy in the shoulder. "Maybe obey orders a little better next time, though, right?"

They laugh. Anderson pushes off from the wall and returns to her previous conversation.

Stacy pulls herself toward Contreras and Harrison at the window. They squeeze together to make room for her.

"Hey!" says Stacy.

"Hi." Harrison doesn't face her. "You're overly cheerful for the occasion."

"She would be." Contreras flicks the window. "She surrendered everything to them."

Contreras hasn't spoken to her since the expedition. He will probably never speak to her again.

Stacy looks him in the eyes. "Destroying the starship wasn't right."

"It wasn't your choice to make."

"It was." Stacy's hands tighten on the rail. "I was the one there."

"Well, then." Contreras grunts. "You really botched it."

No one around them has noticed the heated conversation, all caught up in their own excitement. Harrison shifts position, then scrambles to keep from drifting away. A novice mistake, one Harrison shouldn't make at this point in her career.

"Contreras, I really am sorry." Stacy sighs. "I wasn't trying to hurt you, I—"

"Doesn't matter what you wanted." Contreras turns back to the window.

Stacy stares out the window a few moments, focusing on nothing. She glances over her shoulder and sees Thor gesticulating at Prabhakhar and Gulati.

"I should make my rounds," says Stacy.

Harrison nods. Contreras makes no acknowledgment.

Thor stops waving his arms when Stacy squeezes past Harrison to join the new group. Prabhakhar and Gulati smile in greeting, but Thor makes a face and ducks away. Stacy is surprised it hurts as much as it does.

"Hi," she says to the other two. "I'm sorry. I didn't mean to run anyone off."

"It's okay," says Gulati. "He was trying to convince us the Panamanian rebels were working with the Inorganics."

"Oh, is that what he was saying?" Prabhakhar clutches his side and grimaces. "I was having a hard time following."

Stacy laughs. "Sounds…interesting."

"So," says Gulati, "how are you enjoying the festivities?"

"This is what I came for. Prabhakhar, what did your family think of your part?"

Prabhakhar grins. "Ayaan is telling all his friends about it. Says I'm an action hero. I could get used to it."

"You might have to remind him when he's a teenager," says Gulati. "They're liable to forget the good stuff about their parents."

Prabhakhar waves away her concern. "I've got years before I have to worry about that. Besides, I'll probably be retired and Earthbound by then, so I'll be around all the time. He won't have a chance to forget how awesome I am."

Stacy and Gulati share a look, then laugh. Stacy wonders if Prabhakhar will ever retire.

"And congratulations," says Gulati. "On your extradition being refused."

Stacy nods. Something about her report has made her popular among the public. The current administration must have calculated that it would be political suicide to punish her.

"And," says Gulati, "I hear you accomplished your primary goal here."

"I did?" Stacy asks.

Gulati gestures to Jalindo. "Jalindo has their own fan club now."

Stacy laughs. "I hadn't heard. That's great. They earned it." She glanced over her shoulder. "Well, I should keep going. I want to talk to everyone before the big moment."

They wave their goodbyes, and Stacy guides herself between the other groups to reach Young. The general still floats by herself, as much as she can in the crowded room, watching the proceedings with a pensive expression.

"It's a nice party." Stacy comes to a crisp stop beside the general. "Good atmosphere, and a great view. But I was expecting hors d'oeuvres."

Young gives her a quiet smile. "You're always good at lightening the mood."

"Does it need lightening?"

"It's a somber moment." Young gestures to the crew. "But everyone is treating it like a party."

Stacy's face grows hot. "Sorry."

"Don't be. But it shows what we're fighting against. Not the Inorganics. Our own attitudes." The general gestures for Stacy to stop recording.

Stacy obliges, confused. "Something off the record?"

"This is why I sabotaged the IMS," says Young.

Stacy's jaw drops. "You're admitting it?"

"I am."

"I mean, I knew you did it. I'm just surprised you admitted it. And I understand your reasons, but it's still…not what I would have expected."

"I'm glad I can still surprise people."

"But…" Stacy frowns. "That's all you wanted to say? But you knew I already knew that. Was there some reason you said it now?"

Young points to Thor, who glides away from them with an expression of vindication. "He'll spread the rumor. The best way of getting a story discredited is having it labeled as a conspiracy theory."

Stacy makes a face. "I don't know…" She starts recording again, feeling like a puppet.

They say nothing for several moments. Young seems to study the crew as though recording in her own mind exactly what this experience is like. It will be the most historic occasion anyone here ever witnesses.

"I heard," says Stacy, "that you're returning to Earth."

"Yes." Young's face has more lines than when Stacy arrived almost four months ago. "Only half the crew are people I would have chosen. The other half doesn't share my views on the Inorganics. That kind of heterogeneity of opinion wouldn't have happened when I had influence at Command."

"But you're staying in the SDF, right?"

"I plan to." Young's gaze turns wistful. "For so long, I thought I could build the dream by living it. I thought this distance gave me a greater lever to move the world, but it didn't work that way. I should have realized my loss of influence sooner. So I'll return, and I'll claw my way back to the top, and I'll lead the SDF in the right direction. I'll keep us from abandoning space."

Stacy suppresses a smile. Young is going to run the entire SDF the way she ran Collins Station. Maybe, though, she is the right person for the job. "You did manage to keep the station open."

"Yes, I did." Young smiles. "I convinced the SDF we should continue monitoring this area of space. See what they can learn from the remnants of the Inorganic base here. This station's work isn't done."

"It's a good idea. We still don't know enough about them." The question of their intelligence level is still open, though Stacy suspects Jason's departure gave people things to consider. And there is that tunnel on the surface with its mysterious boxes.

"What about you?" asks Young. "Your agency has gotten some notoriety from this assignment."

"Well." Stacy shrugs. "We're going to focus more on the Inorganics now."

Young raises an eyebrow. "Not the answer I expected to hear."

"I hid from the topic for so long. I'll still cover other topics, too, because people in terrible situations still need to be heard, but this topic is the most important one we need to face. How we react to the Inorganics will determine the future of our species. Maybe we can actually push people out of their apathy."

"Maybe we'll work together again, then."

Stacy shrugs. "Maybe." Though likely not, after Young repeatedly threatened Stacy and then imprisoned her.

Someone points to the window, and the cacophony quiets. It must be starting. A sudden sense of the moment's enormity strikes.

"This," says Young in a whisper, "must be how the Russians felt when Neil Armstrong walked on the Moon."

Stacy turns to the general. "I'm on."

She kicks off toward the window and takes her designated place at the center. Grabbing a handhold below the center of the cupola, she steadies herself and stares outward toward Juno. Although she feels guilty about the arrangement, taking the prime position instead of the people who worked multiple tours at Collins, it makes sense. She makes certain to give the others plenty of room to see around her.

She zooms in with her oculars until the starship comes into view.

The odd, unaesthetic vehicle hangs like a flower bulb over the asteroid, its four scaffolds serving as a stem. In slow motion, the stem's intricate trusses fold upon themselves beam-by-beam as they peel from the ship. Tiny sections melt together, condensing downward in controlled motion until the scaffolds repose on Juno's surface.

The starship hangs in place, an object suspended as if at the apex of an upward arc, unmoving and full of potential. Then it wavers, presumably from the gravitational manipulators, its appearance warping like the air above a hot road in summer. The window, the walls, Stacy's own hands waver, too.

The ship drifts free, glinting in the dim sunlight, a leaf on water departing the shore. Tiny blue flares appear on the thrusters at each node. They fire for a moment, briefly outshining the stars, then soften to nothing.

Someone claps. Slow, steady, solemn. Then another person joins, then another. Then the rest of the room joins. It isn't joyous applause, but a concession of victory.

This round, at least. Stacy will make sure there are future rounds.

The starship fades from view.

Stacy continues recording.

ACKNOWLEDGMENTS

OVER THE YEARS this novel has been under development (it started as a short story), many people have critiqued it and pushed it in better directions. Thank you to Amanda Fox and the people at critters.org for helping with this novel and with everything I've written.

Thanks also to my amazing wife, Julie, my awesome sister Amanda, and my patient mom for all the encouragement, and to Emmett Smith for always supporting my creative stuff and for the Star Wars toys back in the day. To Rohini Coorg and Brett Coombs for talking me up to people, and to everyone else who has supported me.

Thanks to my editor, Maddy Leary, who had the daunting task of hacking through the jungle of fluff and streamlining this book into its present form. And thanks to Rob Carroll and the Dark Matter INK team for supporting an unknown author.

—Robert E. Harpold

ABOUT THE AUTHOR

ROBERT E. HARPOLD has been writing stories since he was seven years old, and most of those stories will be shown to no one. In previous jobs, he traveled to Greenland and Antarctica and operated spacecraft. Now he designs spacecraft trajectories. His dream job is the same as everyone else's: astronaut. He is married to the most amazing wife, and together they have a wonderful daughter and son.